THE MOON ROGUE

Arc of the Sky Trilogy, Book 1

L. M. R. Clarke

The Moon Rogue © 2019 by L.M.R. Clarke. All Rights Reserved.

All rights reserved. No part of this book may be reproduced in any form or by any electronic or mechanical means including information storage and retrieval systems, without permission in writing from the author. The only exception is by a reviewer, who may quote short excerpts in a review.

Cover designed by The Gilded Quill
www.thegildedquill.co.uk

This book is a work of fiction. Names, characters, places, and incidents either are products of the author's imagination or are used fictitiously. Any resemblance to actual persons, living or dead, events, or locales is entirely coincidental.

Castrum Press
Visit the publisher's website at www.castrumpress.com

Printed in the United Kingdom

First Printing: March 2019
Castrum Press

Print Edition
ISBN-13 978-1-9123274-5-4

TABLE OF CONTENTS

THE MOON ROGUE 1
TABLE OF CONTENTS 1
CHAPTER ONE 3
CHAPTER TWO 13
CHAPTER THREE 18
CHAPTER FOUR 23
CHAPTER FIVE 28
CHAPTER SIX 37
CHAPTER SEVEN 43
CHAPTER EIGHT 49
CHAPTER NINE 52
CHAPTER TEN 56
CHAPTER ELEVEN 64
CHAPTER TWELVE 70
CHAPTER THIRTEEN 78
CHAPTER FOURTEEN 84
CHAPTER FIFTEEN 90
CHAPTER SIXTEEN 95
CHAPTER SEVENTEEN 100
CHAPTER EIGHTEEN 105
CHAPTER NINETEEN 111
CHAPTER TWENTY 117
CHAPTER TWENTY-ONE 123
CHAPTER TWENTY-TWO 130
CHAPTER TWENTY-THREE 138
CHAPTER TWENTY-FOUR 144
CHAPTER TWENTY-FIVE 149
CHAPTER TWENTY-SIX 157
CHAPTER TWENTY-SEVEN 162

CHAPTER TWENTY-EIGHT 168
CHAPTER TWENTY-NINE 176
CHAPTER THIRTY 181
CHAPTER THIRTY-ONE 187
CHAPTER THIRTY-TWO 193
CHAPTER THIRTY-THREE...199
CHAPTER THIRTY-FOUR 204
CHAPTER THIRTY-FIVE.. 209
CHAPTER THIRTY-SIX... 215
CHAPTER THIRTY-SEVEN 222
CHAPTER THIRTY-EIGHT 227
CHAPTER THIRTY-NINE 232
CHAPTER FORTY...238
CHAPTER FORTY-ONE 245
CHAPTER FORTY-TWO 250
CHAPTER FORTY-THREE...254
ABOUT THE AUTHOR 259
CONNECT WITH THE AUTHOR.. 260
BOOKS BY THE AUTHOR 261
   NOVELS 261
      ARC OF THE SKY (3 BOOK SERIES).. 261

"To Barry, my unwavering Heart."

CHAPTER ONE

Mantos

Mantos Tiboli, Imperial Prince of the Masvam Empire, was heir to the throne by a hairline crack. Two eggs had rested in two divots on two identical stone pillars. Identical wrought-iron branches curved around them, rising into tall spikes surrounding the leathery spheres. Everything the same, everything equal, both eggs cared for the same way in the same warm air. It was a miracle, something unheard of, even in the annals of time. Never before had two eggs been brought into the world together—not since the time of the gods themselves.

Armed guards and males of the household watched over them. They stared, eyes never leaving the leathery shells, waiting for the blessed moment when the future emperor would hatch. But which one would it be? The larger egg, black dappled with gold? Or the smaller one, silver and smooth and glinting in the candlelight? It was rumored that courtiers and potwashes alike took bets, though it would mean their heads if any were caught. To bet on the future emperor was shameful, but the glint of coin was too great a temptation.

Mantos emerged from his silver egg first, all razor claws and stubby tail, golden eyes glimmering. His first sight was a joyful smile, and the first sound he heard a whoop of joy.

After the briefest of moments, brother Bandim escaped from his black and gold shell, too young to see and hear that the joy was less for the second hatchling. The spare.

It was only by virtue of that brief moment that Mantos found himself standing at the edge of his father's bed, twenty-one cycles later, on the cusp of becoming emperor.

Bandim lingered further away, cloaked by shadow. He stared at their dying father, unblinking. "Is he awake?" he asked.

Slowly, Mantos shook his head. "I don't think so."

"Will he wake again?"

Mantos paused before he answered. The truth stilled his tongue, until duty bade him answer his brother. "I don't know."

For the longest time the brothers stood in the lavish bedchamber, watching the erratic rise and fall of their father's chest, listening to the rattle of his breath and the spluttering of the candles. This was the same bedchamber they had been hatched in. It was the bedchamber that would become Mantos' upon his father's death.

And what then? Mantos thought as he fingered the fine embroidery of the bedspread. His claws passed over the scenes picked out in golden thread: conquests, killings, triumphs. His stomach lurched. *Soon the crown will fall upon my head, as will leadership of the largest empire in the land. An empire that swallows everything in its path. An empire that I want nothing to do with.* His eyes flicked to Bandim. *But an empire I must command. The alternative is unthinkable.*

Until losing his speech three days before, their father, Emperor Braslen, had still commanded his advisors, poring over crinkled maps that servants brought to his bedside. He was still talking strategy, showing Mantos the next steps in his grand plan.

"We will break the Metakalans once and for all," Braslen had said. Despite the wheeze in his voice and the tremble in his hand, fire blazed in his eyes. "Too long have they held out against us. Now that the Selamans have been crushed, we can focus our attention on Metakala—but don't forget, we must leave enough military might in Selama to quell any rebellion. We will roll our borders into Metakalan lands, and then we will strike against the Althemerians. Metakala is nothing more than a stepping stone to our true quarry. The Althemerian queen disrespected me twice: once when she denied my marriage offer, and again when she would not marry her daughters to my sons." The fury in Braslen's eyes made Mantos want to step back, but he held firm. Braslen snarled. "We will *crush* them."

Dutifully, the prince listened and nodded at the right times. He knew the Selamans had been crushed. He'd been there. He'd planted the Masvam flag in their capital. He'd torched the banner that once hung in their ornate long hall. He'd slit the throat of the queen beneath its flaming remains. *Crushed* wasn't even the right word. *Decimated* was closer to the mark. Crops and shipyards set alight in white-hot flame, cities brought to ash and ruin, females and younglings trampled to death on the streets... *And for what?* Mantos thought. *Land? Power?* He suppressed a snort. *More like rebellion. More like death.*

As always, he dared not share those thoughts. Once, he'd had a confidant, but... Mantos shuddered. *Fonbir and I dare not communicate about these matters any longer,* he thought. *Princes on opposing sides of an impending war... It isn't prudent, as much as my heart aches for him.*

An obedient son, Mantos always played his part. He was a scholar, a diplomat, and most importantly, a warrior. It was expected. As the heir to the Masvam throne, he could be nothing else. No matter what the Metakalans or the Althemerians or the

Linvarrans might believe, he thought, the Masvams saw their males as soldiers, protectors, while other cultures denigrated theirs. Males were nothing more than simpering pets to them, those lands with queens and empresses. That was why they resisted Masvam rule with blood and steel. They saw Masvam ideals as dangerous, against the natural way. But how could that be? The Masvams followed the Light and did as the goddess commanded. *We inhabit the holy words, where the male is power and strength*, Mantos thought. *They live a lie, where females are leaders and warriors. It's against the natural way. Our way is the natural way.*

Mantos sighed and dropped the hem of his father's bedspread. Bandim came a little closer, his face lit by the fine white candles their father favored.

Like Mantos, Bandim had a fine figure. They were tall and wiry, strength without bulk, and favored their mother's coloring. Their skin was a deep brown, and their armor—thick scales running in patterns across the body—was burnished gold, with straw-like head fronds straight and black as night. In the light, Bandim's eyes were opalescent yellow, just like Mantos'. Both princes were adorned with jewelry: rings, bracelets, and fine gold chains that wound around their curving horn crests, dripping with colored gemstones. They wore identical pendants around their necks: two crossed Tiboli lightning strikes with a round shield between them. Their jewels were bright but their robes were black, a sign of respect for their dying father.

Soon they would wear white. White to help Braslen's spirit find its way to the temple, then to the Light.

But not yet.

Bandim fell in beside Mantos and clasped his sharp claws, polished to fine black points, against his flat stomach. His horned tail shifted, the thick bulk lying against the fine muscles of his legs.

"He doesn't have much time left. His life's thread is ready to snap," Bandim said. There was a pause, and his tone shifted. "You will continue with Father's plans, won't you?"

It was phrased as a question, but said as a command. *You don't care that he's passing into the Light*, Mantos thought. *All you care about is the opportunity it brings for you, brother. You've never hidden your disdain. Don't try to, even now that he's dying.*

Mantos drew himself to his full height, the scales of his neck unfurling. They widened like a golden ruff, licking at the periphery of his vision. He stared at his brother. Hard.

"I have given my word," he said.

Bandim twitched his tail and raised himself to meet Mantos' eyes. His own neck pulsed, the scales unfurling in a mirror image of Mantos'.

"Words are words," he said, speaking with the wise and confident tone that had fooled many housemasters and teachers. One quality Bandim had in abundance was intelligence, even at the cost of kindness and compassion. "You can speak them and still not believe them. I know you've given him your word." He drew his scaled brows low, raised a claw, and pressed on Mantos' scaly chest plate. "But the question is, have you given him your *heart*?"

Mantos' nose slits widened. He narrowed his eyes. "Do not presume to touch me, brother."

Bandim chuckled, though it was a mirthless sound. "Don't presume to act as if you're already the emperor."

With deliberate slowness, he withdrew his claw. When he smiled, his sharp teeth glinted. His face, so like Mantos' own, was patterned with scaled armor, his eyes deep-set and golden. His brows were fine, his mouth lined at the corners. It was like looking in a cracked mirror, the features similar, yet in some way distorted. Mantos wished they were more different than alike. He despised how similar they looked, being such opposites. *I am of the Light*, Mantos thought, *and he dwells in the Dark.*

His neck scales didn't retract until his brother stepped away.

"Leave," Mantos said, turning back to their father. "I want to be alone with him."

Bandim lingered for a moment, then gave a shallow bow. He turned, robes whirling, and was gone.

Alone, Mantos listened to his father's shuddering breaths. He brushed a translucent frond from Braslen's forehead.

"I fear my brother won't obey me when you're gone," Mantos whispered. "What shall I do then? How can I command an empire if I cannot keep my own house in order?"

His father didn't reply.

Mantos huffed a quick breath and shook his head. *Even if you were awake, you wouldn't answer*, he thought. *You'd push it back on me.* "What will you do to get your house in order? How will you force your brother to obey?" *But those are your ways, Father, not mine. I'm not like you, and I'm not like Bandim. I wish...* Tears welled, but Mantos pushed them away. *I wish that just once, we'd seen eye-to-eye. That just once we could have been father and son, not emperor and emperor-in-waiting.*

Wishing was, as his father always said, for fools. Exhaling long and hard, Mantos remained at the bedside, waiting, trying not to wish.

The Vigil was a long-held Masvam tradition. Offspring stayed with their waning parent, waiting for the flesh to die, the thread to finally snap. Mantos' first duty as emperor would be to share word of his father's demise. There would be no herald. There would be no grand ceremony. Clad in white, he would walk onto the balcony of the speaker's bowl. It was an ancient thing, built by emperors of long ago, allowing their voices to carry to the hundreds in the assembled crowd. Mantos would stand at the ornate balcony rail and wait to be seen. There would be courtiers stationed below, their eyes ready to catch a glimpse of the imperial prince. As soon as one saw Mantos, their wail would fill the courtyard.

"The emperor is dead!"

A wave of white would spread across the empire: white clothes, white flags, white banners. Mantos would stand on the balcony as the bells tolled, staring across the stone city to the temple. He would remain in place until the beacon blazed in the cloak of night, starting his father's journey to the Light.

I never truly thought I would be here, he thought. *I imagined Father would live forever.* Braslen of House Tiboli had reigned for thirty-five cycles. More advanced in age than their mother, he was on the cusp of old age when he took the crown.

Mantos clenched his teeth. *Mother. Someone should tell her.*

Phen of House Yru had been a beauty in her youth, so Mantos was told. For as long as he remembered, she'd been a sickly female, whose wits had long deserted her. Not long after his hatching, his mother had dropped him. Clattering down a flight of stairs, his tiny body had been broken. The details changed depending on who told the tale, but each telling ended the same way. On seeing the youngling, broken and dead, Mantos' mother had screamed her grief. From the depths of the palace, a temple novice appeared, whisking the dead body away.

Something had happened. Something magic. Something *Dark*. And Mantos had returned from the dead.

But instead of rejoicing, his mother had blamed herself for the folly, and was never the same again.

Mantos placed a claw on top of his father's papery palm. Braslen didn't stir.

"Would things have been different if the accident hadn't happened?" he asked. "If mother hadn't lost her wits?" Flashes of Bandim's fury flickered in his mind. "Would my brother hate me less? Might he even love me?"

No response. Mantos lifted his father's claw. He rubbed circles on the leathery armor of the back of his hand.

Prince Mantos was good at many things. He was skilled with a sword and bow, and his mind was as deadly as any weapon. Not one book in the ornate palace library had escaped his greedy eyes. Yet there was one thing he couldn't master: deciphering his brother. *How can we look so alike and yet be so different?* It was a puzzle he couldn't solve, no matter how many books and scrolls he read.

The solution had eluded their father, too.

"Your brother is a strange sort," was his standard response. "He concerns himself too much with lore and with...unsavory beliefs."

Unsavory beliefs, Mantos thought. *That's a meek turn of phrase for the worship of a demon.* Rumors lurked in every corner of the palace and down every dank alleyway of the city. Prince Bandim was in league with a Moon Rogue and the false goddess Dorai—what a joy it was that Mantos was to be emperor, and not such spawn of the Dark.

Of course, Bandim never showed his true face to his father. To Braslen, the rumors were folly, nothing more than jealous slander propagated by opposing houses. It didn't matter what they said. What mattered was that his second son was as pure as the first. Even Mantos knew it was a lie, and he sometimes wondered if a shadow of truth lingered in his father's gaze as he looked on the younger brother. But it didn't last long. As always, the emperor concentrated on Mantos.

"You must lead the empire to new glories," Braslen said, grasping his startled son's hand in his shaking talons for Mantos had thought him unconscious. "Finish my work and spread the reign of House Tiboli from sea to sea. Continue what my father started, and plant the seeds of glory for your younglings and your youngling's younglings..."

There was a rattle, and a slow wheeze. Braslen's grip slackened. Those were the last words Emperor Braslen of House Tiboli spoke to his son before he slipped truly into unconsciousness.

As it turned out, they were the last words he spoke at all.

♦ ♦ ♦

BANDIM

Bandim didn't draw his hood over his horned head. His face was clear for all to see. *Why bother? It's no great mystery where I'm going. And who could move against me?*

His cloak swept behind him in a sable wave as he made his way to the outskirts of the city. The buildings, fine stonework that glimmered in the setting sun and arched windows to accept the Light, gave way to darker coils of decrepit towers. *What they see above shows the foolishness of the Light*, Bandim thought. *The Dark is pure and shows more truth than their Light ever will.*

Nestled in an ancient stone dwelling, the Temple of Dorai's location was an open secret. It was an unremarkable building in a narrow street of broken cobbles; only those invited were welcome to cross the threshold.

Few city folk craved such an invitation. Bandim snorted and rounded the final corner on his journey. The Light was dying, and so was his father. If this sunset was to be Braslen's last, Bandim needed to be ready to act.

Outside, the temple was unimpressive. Inside was different, all thanks to Bandim's devotion. Since finding the love of the Goddess Dorai through high priestess Johrann Maa many cycles before, Bandim had funneled gold into the hands of Dorai's priestesses. Instead of the derelict monstrosity it had once been, the inner chambers were lined with black stone, smooth and perfect. What once had been dilapidated catacombs from a civilization long gone was now an underground palace fit for an emperor. The floor sloped into the embrace of darkness, what the followers of the Light called *evil*.

Fools, Bandim thought as he thrust open the doors, startling a young attendant. The believers in Nunako looked to the Arc of the Sky. They trusted in her, thinking the Light would consume the Dark. Accepting an offered mask and taper, Bandim descended into the temple proper. Little did they know, it was the Dark that swallowed their brightness. The Dark would always prevail.

The meager light flickered, sending shadows dancing across the smooth walls. Today would bring the reckoning for Bandim and his beloved Johrann. His wondrous priestess would harness her powers. *With Father soon breathing his last, the stage is set for her—for me. My moment has finally come.*

Masked figures, male and female alike, drew back as he approached, bowing in deference. Face covered or not, they knew who he was. They didn't question him as he swept through the underground caverns and into the altar room.

He fell to his knees before the five-armed effigy of the Goddess—three arms on the left, only two on the right.

The statue stood proud and condemning. In four of the god's hands were the tenants of belief in Dorai: a spade for work, a book for knowledge, a shield for defense, and a sword for battle. The final arm was outstretched, one long claw pointing at the onlooker. The sixth arm was gone, wrenched from its socket by the goddess herself, sacrificed to protect the True Believers.

As soon as Bandim's knees hit the stone, a voice bade him rise again.

"An emperor does not fall on his knees," it said. Out of the shadows stepped Johrann Maa, high priestess of the Dark. "You are part of her. You are the Goddess' Hand."

She was a strange creature with unusual coloring: armor of purple and skin of blue, and unusually tall, as tall as himself. *No one in the world is like my Johrann*, Bandim thought. She was entirely unique. Her eyes, grey and flecked, pierced through him. Though she was many cycles older than him, she didn't look it. Bandim's mouth went dry every time he saw her.

He rose again and climbed the few steps to the altar. This time, Johrann went to her knees. The tips of her horn crest tapped the floor. Her fronds were tightly bound, not a single one out of place.

"Rise, dear Heart," Bandim said, reaching for her. "I'm not emperor yet."

Johrann rose, silent as a shadow, keeping her hand in his. Even in the darkness of the altar room, her eyes glimmered as they met his.

"You're at the foot of your throne, my prince," she said. "It won't take long to ascend the last few steps."

Bandim kissed the backs of her armored knuckles. "Not until my father dies."

Johrann inclined her head.

"As you wish," she said. "Your brother's life has been in my grasp since he was a hatchling and your mother asked me to save him." She lifted her chin and stared, her eyes hard as stone. "Once I cut your brother's thread, your mother will regain her senses. With life returned to her body and gone from his, she will live anew. There is no way around this, Your Grace. They are bound together, a life for a life. That is the way."

Bandim held her look, his yellow gaze steadfast.

"I understand," he said. "My mother is a nuisance, and undeserving of a place in my empire."

Memories of her absence crashed into him like waves, and Bandim winced. It had never been fair, being left without a mother. His cousins had mothers. The younglings of other kingdoms and queendoms had mothers. He didn't even have the luxury of a dead mother to be mourned and comforted over.

All Bandim had was an absent father, and a brother who looked the same. He didn't even have his individuality. He was just Bandim, the younger. Bandim, the spare. Bandim, always lesser than Mantos.

But then he found Dorai, her comforting words, and her sixth arm wrapped around him. And he found Johrann Maa. She gave him comfort too, and for the first time, Bandim heard what he had always wanted to hear. She said he was special.

"You have been chosen, my sweet," she had crooned in his ears. "Dorai will make you her vessel. One day, all her power will be yours, and you will show the world that you are the rightful emperor."

That was what they worked towards. That was the reason Bandim lavished the temple with gold. That was why the converts to Dorai grew in number, their good news spreading in shadows, until there were more of them than the fools of the Light could comprehend. The One True Goddess would return to the world, and Bandim was the vessel who would save them all.

Of course, it hadn't always been that way. When at first Johrann had revealed it was she who'd saved Mantos and taken his mother away, Bandim's blood had boiled. He had been ready to cleave off her head.

"I'll kill you!" he'd said, an adolescent newly gendered—the same as his brother, not even striking out in difference as a female.

But she had held him to her, cooing and shushing, until his rage turned to tears.

"It was an error," she said, "something I did when the arrogance of youth was still upon me. And I'm sorry, my dearest Bandim. It's my fault you were denied your throne. Now I'll do everything to make sure you get it back, and the power of Dorai, too. Isn't it written in the Book of Divine Tears that 'the servant will err once but will bring greatness to the vessel? The One of Two, pushed aside, will rise like flame, and the goddess will inhabit him'? I am the servant, and you are the vessel. I have erred my once. I will not err again."

Returned from the rush of memory, Bandim leaned into Johrann's touch as she brushed her claws against his masked cheek.

A set of feet clattered along the hall outside. The steps grew closer and louder until they skidded to a halt outside the chamber. After a moment, there was a steady knock.

Johrann blinked, her gaze shifting from the door to Bandim. "I must change to my Masvam colors."

Bandim inclined his head. No one knew of Johrann's truth except him. Her colors, blue and purple, still struck as strange. Sometimes, she said, the folk could only take so much oddness. It was better to feed them morsel by morsel, until they listened even when the hand that fed them was empty.

Johrann closed her eyes. There was a whirl of warm wind, and he watched the slow sap of blue and purple from her body, to be replaced by the Masvam norm of brown and gold. She looked like any other female now, though taller. *My Johrann*, Bandim thought. *My magical Johrann.*

She brushed down her dark robes and permitted entrance.

A temple novice stumbled in, clad too in dark robes. Her head, covered in deference to the goddess, was bowed.

"My prince, my priestess," she said, breathless. "News from the palace. The emperor... He's dead."

At once, Bandim and Johrann's eyes met. She said nothing. For a moment, Bandim stayed still, allowing the words to ebb and flow in his mind. *He's dead.* A slow smile crept across his face. *He's finally dead!*

Then he schooled his expression and turned to the novice. "Get out."

The female scurried away, leaving them alone once more. Bandim grasped Johrann's hands, holding them in a vice grip.

"It's time," he said. "Today the Light's demise begins, and the Dark will paint a sable sky above all nations." He pressed the backs of her talons to his lips, savoring the moment. "Do it, my love. Start my journey. First an emperor, and then a goddess. Bring it to me as you have promised."

"I will, Your Grace," she said, squeezing his hands in return. "For you, and for the truth of Dorai."

Releasing him, Johrann turned to the five-armed effigy of Dorai and closed her eyes. Remaining silent, she lifted her hands.

There was no great fanfare. There were no swirling lights. There was simply the warm wind. Bandim thought, *The Dark is silent. The Dark is pure.* His breath came in shallow waves as he watched and waited. At last, his life's desire would be fulfilled. *Mantos dead for once and for all, and me in the seat of power, ready to bring the truth of Dorai to all the folk of the world!*

Johrann turned to him again.

His breath hitched. Her eyes glowed red. Her lips stretched with a leer. Her voice came as a delighted whisper.

"It is done."

♦ ♦ ♦

MANTOS

On the balcony, Mantos stood in abject silence. Newly clad in white, he waited as the sun slipped below the horizon. Only a few moments before, the thread of Braslen Tiboli's life had finally worn through. The death was silent, a simple stilling of the heart and a final exhalation. Mantos had gripped his father's hand as he slipped away. It was peaceful, but it brought Mantos nothing but torment.

He's gone. Now rule falls upon me, not as a crown, but as a chain to bind me. Father, I wish you could have lived forever and spared me from this torment.

Wishing is for fools, Mantos.

His father's words echoed in the depths of his mind. Mantos' heart ached, not just for his father's absence, but for everything that was to come. *I don't want to walk this path...but I have no choice.*

As the sun set and the moons shone bright, the stationed courtiers looked up. As their eyes fell on the prince clad in white, the first shout rose.

"The emperor is dead!"

Despite the grief that threatened to topple him, Mantos remained steady, silent. The first wail was joined by another, then another. Below, the courtyard brightened with candles, lanterns blossoming like vines. Through it all, Mantos stood. The dark cloak of night fell upon the city. Sounds of mourning drifted from below. After a time, when the sky was black, the Temple of Light flared orange and red. *Our colors*, Mantos thought. *The colors of duty. Of a power that's now mine.* Flaming tongues sang the emperor's demise. They rose to the Arc of the Sky. To the Light.

Mantos' eyes brimmed, but he dared not shed a tear. He didn't have that privilege any longer. On gaining the crown, he lost much. As emperor, he must do what the empire expected him to do. He must be their leader, their everything...

There was a sudden tightness at his throat, like an invisible hand grasping his neck. Tears spilled unbidden as his chest heaved, unable to bring in air. He stumbled, fell on one knee, grasped at the balcony rail with scrabbling claws. His eyes blinked and swam, and something deep within him stretched. Tightened. Something was ready to snap.

Father? Is this death?

Without fanfare or swirling lights, Mantos crumpled.

His thread was cut.

CHAPTER TWO

Emmy

Closing her eyes, Emmy counted to three as a familiar and unwelcome figure entered Madame Krodge's Apothecary. Before she opened her eyes again, Emmy began a silent chant. *Still your tongue. Don't say anything.* It should have been easy, but it wasn't.

Mr. Amra Bose strode straight to the counter, other customers stepping aside to let him pass. He was middle-aged, perpetually puffed by his own self-importance, wearing clothes typical of the husband class. He wore colorful fabrics, draped from the shoulder and kept in place by brooches of colored glass. The hem of his cloak was pinned by enamelwork, raising it from the common filth of the streets. His horns were polished and his scales shone: the picture of a perfect husband.

Bose laid his elaborate hat on the counter and peeled off his gloves, one claw at a time. His two companions, other husbands that trailed on his spiked tail, hovered at his shoulders with their chins stuck high in the air as Bose unsheathed his final claw and slid the gloves aside.

Bose drummed his talons on the counter. "Well?"

The sight of his smug face made Emmy want to retch. Regardless, she stretched her lips into a thin smile. "How may I be of service today?" she asked. The words threatened to break her teeth.

"Madame Bose is returning from Linvarra tomorrow, providing all is well," Bose said. He turned to appreciate his companions' sympathetic nods and added, "The goddess be blessed. You know what it's like. Home from fighting in King Eron's service, bravely protecting us from the Masvam threat. She deserves to be looked after."

Mr. Bose's eyes widened, and he brought one hand to his thin lips. He glanced over his shoulder before returning his watery gaze to Emmy.

"Oh, I *misspoke*," he said. "You don't know what that's like, do you?" He chuckled. "Despite coming of age, you've still never entered the service. Krodge paid the

Coward's Tax for you, so you've never risked your life to keep the wicked Masvams out." Bose grinned, showing two lines of sharp teeth. "Well, I suppose not all females can be as good and brave as my beauteous wife. There are always...exceptions."

He looked Emmy up and down, mouth curling in disgust.

Emmy tried to let her mind escape her body, to flee from the pulsing thoughts that invaded like knives. The effort was futile. All she could think of was pulling Bose over the counter by his nose slits and... *Best not think about it.* Heart pounding, she balled her claws into fists. "What is it that you need from me?"

"If there's no one else available to assist me," Bose said, glancing over her shoulder into the rooms behind, "I suppose I can put up with you."

Emmy clenched her jaws. There wasn't anyone else, and Bose knew it. Emmy was the only one who worked in the apothecary—apart from the mistress upstairs, of course. It had been that way for all of Emmy's sixteen cycles.

"I hoped you'd have some powdered garba root," Bose continued, "but I'm sure that, as usual, you don't." He turned to his companions again and rolled his eyes. "One does appreciate the great power of a healing paste mixed with such a rare commodity, but..."

"Actually," Emmy said, "I ordered some just for you, as you're always telling me how useful it is. It's fifteen bickles per measure."

She kept her face as straight as possible, but on the inside she was grinning. Bose's mouth opened and closed several times as he contemplated the information, knowing other customers were staring at the back of his head.

"Well... I..."

Emmy's face twitched. Bose cleared his throat, trying to regain composure.

"Madame Bose, of course, didn't mention any wounds. She writes to me *so* often. I would know immediately if there was something wrong, even if she didn't say so outright. Thus, I shan't need your overpriced goods."

His companions shook their heads and tutted as other customers murmured. In truth, fifteen bickles was an agreeable price for a valuable commodity.

"I would be pleased if you would, instead," Bose continued, "provide me with five measures of sicklestem juice." He simpered. "I add it to Madame Bose's tea for its relaxing properties."

Before she could respond, Emmy forced her tongue into her mouth and clamped down with her teeth. Sicklestem juice was hardly just relaxing. It made a powerful sleeping draught. It could kill. There should have been a law to control the sale of it, but there wasn't.

Without speaking, she spun around. She couldn't say anything. Emmy the Moon Rogue was enough of a villain in the town of Bellim already. Taking a deep breath, she looked for the sicklestem juice.

Behind the counter stood Emmy's pride and joy. Stretching across the length of the shop was a set of glass-fronted cupboards that cost the moon. Each vertical sweep was organized into categories. There were sections for medicines and remedies, of course. Others were for cooking, or for cleaning. The most colorful shelf was devoted to buttons, thread, and beads.

Krodge's provided everything a husband needed to make a comfortable home for his wife. Roots, juices, sap, dried insects, live insects, fungi, herbs, animal bones... The list went on. Everything was locked in an ordered prison, behind glass doors more valuable than most of the contents. Krodge coveted extravagance. To the old crone, nothing was more important. Emmy suppressed a shudder. She herself was at the bottom of Krodge's list of things to covet.

Emmy lifted a thick-bottomed decanter from its perch and turned back to Bose. "Has sir brought his own phial?"

Mr. Bose smirked and reached into his bag. His claws moved with ease at first, but soon began to scrabble. His face twisted with frustration, then darkened with embarrassment. "In my haste to prepare for Madame Bose's return, I have neglected to bring one."

Emmy smirked. "Very well," she said, "you may buy a phial for one bickle, or you may borrow one for three cren, to be returned tomorrow."

Mr. Bose's eyes bulged. "Scandalous prices."

His compatriots nodded in agreement. However, when Bose looked away, they cast anxious glances at Emmy.

This was too rich. She held the decanter aloft, swirling the amber liquid, and raised an eyeridge. Bose glared at her before he huffed his answer. "Fine. I shall rent one."

As she had expected—the little miser. Emmy fetched a thin phial. She measured the sweet-smelling nectar, corked it, and placed it on the counter. "That will be one bickle and a cren."

Glowering, Bose reached for his purse. He tossed two coins—the bickle large and thick, the cren thin and pierced with a hole—across the counter. "There."

Emmy, with painful slowness, set each on her money scale in turn. She stopped short of testing them with her teeth. Bose's face was in a satisfactory blaze of fury. Satisfied, Emmy bowed. "Thank you for your custom."

Bose deposited the phial into his bag, then snatched up his hat and gloves. "Good day," he spat.

He turned. As he did, his friends marched to the door. Bose swept off, but stopped on the threshold. He half-turned. "I detest being served by such a half-breed," he hissed.

The following silence hung like lead.

Emmy said nothing as Bose chuckled. When he left, she stayed at her post. Her job. Her existence. She closed her eyes, took a breath, and sighed. It was going to be a long day.

When the sun finally painted the sky orange and sent the customers home, Emmy locked the door. She surveyed the shop, her shoulders drooping. Grime glimmered in the fading light. One of her eyes twitched at the sight of her prized bitterberry plant lying on its side. Soil spilled in clumsy waves. She grumbled as she righted it. *No one has any respect*, she thought. *And they call* me *a beast...*

Afterward, she fetched a broom and began to sweep. As the shop returned to its tidy state, Emmy's insides fell into order. Maintaining cleanliness was an endless task. In moments of madness, she wanted to leave the place to its filthy demise. Emmy shuddered. *No*, she thought. She couldn't live with it—and if the mistress ever came downstairs again, she'd beat Emmy halfway to the Dark and back.

The mistress was Madame Krodge, proprietor of the only apothecary in the port of Bellim. Emmy's earliest memories were of watching the broad female dole out powders and liquids with an expert flick of the wrist, but the memories weren't gilded ones. While other younglings frolicked, Emmy was forced to work. And she was beaten. And it had always been that way.

Emmy shook off the memory and wound her way to the back yard. The air was salty. Wisps of light from the three moons slipped out from behind dark clouds. They were Nunako's three faces, the Goddess' eyes watching over the world as inky night spread towards the horizon.

Emmy had lived with Madame Krodge all her sixteen cycles, though she was not her mother. *Tormentor* was closer to the mark.

Emena, get in here! Emena, you beastly Moon Rogue! Emena, come closer and receive your punishment!

Krodge was always right, and Emmy was always wrong. No matter what Emmy did or said, Krodge always had a correction or a criticism. And from Emmy's youngest cycle to more recently, when Krodge was confined to her bed, there were her painful daily lessons.

When the shop was closed, cleaned, and ready for the next day, and Emmy had prepared the mistress' supper, she would kneel at the end of the table. She placed her hands on the top, palms upright. Krodge would reach for her switch.

The lessons always went the same way. "What are you?" Krodge would ask.

Emmy would obediently reply, her eyes cast down. "I am a Moon Rogue."

Krodge clucked her tongue. "And?"

"I am an inconvenience."

"And?"

"I am truly grateful for all you have given me, Madame."

Krodge would bring the switch down hard, once on each palm. "Don't forget it."

Then she would eat her meal, and Emmy dutifully stayed on her knees until the crone was finished.

"It's for your own good, you know," Krodge would sometimes say, but there was never any compassion in her tone.

Many of the stories of Emmy's life were just the same. The earliest such story was one Krodge delighted in telling. She said that at first, she thought the little bundle on her doorstep was a free meal. To her unending disappointment, instead, she found a youngling—a deformed youngling. A Moon Rogue.

No one in Bellim looked like Emmy. It felt like no one in the world was like her. Emmy had the same long body; the same long, triple-jointed legs; the tall crest of horns; the pointed ears; and the long tail, complete with spikes. Granted, she was half a head taller than most, but this was hardly a detail to scorn her over. There was one inescapable difference between Emmy and the others that they did scorn.

The folk of Bellim were typical Metakalans, with brown skin and red armor—thick scales that ran across the skin in patterns. Their fronds, a mane of thinner, longer scales atop the head, were colored anything from palest moons' light to darkest wood. But Emmy wasn't like that.

Setting the broom aside, she raised her arm. Even in the darkness, the difference was clear. Her skin was sickly blue, her armor deep purple. Her fronds were straight and sable. These were differences that no one could, or would, ignore. Folk stared. They whispered. A demon. A Moon Rogue. Emmy was something different, and entirely unwelcome.

Emmy pulled herself from the murk of thought again. *There's no point in dwelling on something you can't change*, she thought. *I wish things were different, but they aren't. So I just need to get on with my life.* Shaking her head, she finished cleaning and went to the kitchen.

After stoking the fire that blazed in the pit, Emmy filled a heavy kettle with water and hung it on an iron hook. Its thick bottom hovered over the smoldering wood. Krodge would want tea, and it had to be on time. Every night was the same.

Too young to strike out alone, too strange to be accepted anywhere else, Emmy stayed with her mistress even though it was torture. What choice did she have?

As the water boiled, Emmy sat on the stool by the fire and folded her arms. She closed her eyes. *Another day over...*

Sudden hammering sent her heart into spasm. Emmy leapt up and loped to the shop, keys jangling. A dark hand cupped against one of the gleaming window panes. A red eye peered underneath. When it spied her, the familiar face erupted with relief. "Emmy!"

She rushed forward, fumbling for her keys. When the door swung open, her only friend was there.

Zecha. And he was cradling a body.

A dead body.

CHAPTER THREE

Emmy

"Emmy, I need your help. Please!" Zecha cried.

He pushed his way into the shop. He laid the body on the ground. She was Linvarran by her colors, green armor and yellow skin. Her blood was red, like anyone's, and pooled on the clean floor.

Emmy shook her head. "What have you *done*?"

The pool of blood crept outward in a crimson arc. Emmy clenched her fists. *I've told Zecha a thousand times not to include me in his disasters!*

She glared at him, but it didn't matter now. He grabbed her forearms, his claws like vices.

"Emmy, please," he said. "I found her in the Wailing Woods. She's been stabbed, but I think she's still alive. Please, help!"

Emmy stared at the body of the young female. Her age could have been anything from twelve and newly gendered, to forty cycles or even more. Her limbs were well-muscled, the sort of muscles servants got from scrubbing pots and hauling rocks. But the female was short, which gave her a stocky appearance. Her face was crisscrossed with enough scars to speak the unspeakable, of torment and a life not worth living.

Emmy shook herself from Zecha's grasp. His expression fell. "Emmy, please!"

Her eyes met his. She stared into the red pools. She sighed. *I can't escape from this one...* "All right."

Her heart could never turn Zecha away.

Emmy dropped to her knees. Blood soaked her tunic as she held the palm of her hand to the female's mouth. She was still breathing, just. Fear closed Emmy's throat. Regardless, she exposed the wound: the female had been stabbed between the ribs, right near her heart.

The female's yellow skin was covered with uncountable bright scars. Blood wept unendingly from the deep gash. It had the almost-diamond shape of a knife. Emmy schooled her breathing and dug deep in her memory, trying to remember all Krodge had taught her about wounds near the heart. Krodge had knowledge others didn't, of the placement of the organs in the body. She had travelled the world, learning everything she could from different folk, imbibing their medical ways. Krodge even said she'd cut into the chests of dead folk, but Emmy wasn't sure if that was a gruesome truth, or a wicked lie to frighten her.

"All right, Zecha," Emmy said slowly, pulling off her apron, "take this. Hold it against the wound."

Zecha's eyes widened and he shook his head, but Emmy thrust the cloth into his hands and pressed it to the slice. The female didn't flinch.

"Don't take it off until I tell you."

Emmy slipped under the counter, keys jangling. She unlocked several cabinets, claws flying across the shelves. She crushed the ingredients—bindlewart, juice of the arra fruit, a cornucopia of herbs—to concoct a well-rehearsed healing paste, and tried not to consider the futility of it all. *She should be left in peace to die*, Emmy thought. *But Zecha has no sense, so here we are.*

She fell to her knees at the female's side again. Gesturing for Zecha to withdraw the sodden apron, she thrust the concoction into his hands. "Cover it."

Giving him no time to argue, Emmy ducked off to retrieve her stitching box.

By the time she returned, the bleeding had lessened. Emmy motioned for Zecha to slide back. From the box, she withdrew a glimmering knife, a thick fish-bone needle, and a roll of thinly-pulled animal guts. Sixteen she may have been, but she had the skill of someone twice her age, or more. *It's the only gift Krodge ever gave me.*

She threaded the needle and, with the greatest care, used the knife to cut away the ragged edges of the wound. Then she set to work, passing the fish bone and hair through the skin in a practiced cadence. Her hands tingled with a strange coldness, the same as they always did when she was healing. She'd never spoken of it to Krodge, but it was always there, a secret, knowledge for her alone. If she asked and found that all apothecaries and healers felt this same odd sensation, it wouldn't be anything special. For Emmy, it being special gave her something Krodge never could. It gave her a thin sliver of self-satisfaction, of pride.

The wound stitched tight, Emmy tied the gut-thread and sat back. Her hands warmed. Her work was likely all for nothing, she thought. The female might already be dead. Even so, she leaned to check her breathing, surprised when warmth ghosted her palm. Emmy pressed her tongue into her cheek and raised an eyeridge. *Well, there you have it. She's alive—for now.*

"Will she live?" Zecha asked, his brown skin pallid.

"I don't know," Emmy answered. When Zecha's face fell, she relented. "You got her here in time, so it's possible."

"Good."

Zecha exhaled, and cycles fell away from him. He had a thin face, a short horn crest, and muscular arms most males didn't possess. His armor played against the darkness of his skin, shimmering like a coat of amber jewels. Zecha railed against what males were supposed to do. He always had. He balked at cookery and sewing. He hunted, and in fact was the best shot with an arrow Emmy had ever met. As a youngling, Emmy had struggled to make friends, but had gravitated to Zecha's strangeness. Similar in age, neither accepted, they became outcasts together.

"Well," Emmy said, placing her tools on the counter, "alive or dead, I can't leave her here. Help me carry her to my room."

"My hands are filthy," Zecha said.

"Mine too," Emmy said, one corner of her mouth rising. "It doesn't matter."

Emmy took the female's torso. Zecha took her legs. Together, they edged their way to Emmy's bed.

When they placed her on top of the mattress, Emmy tutted. The creature stank. "I'll have to wash her."

Zecha ran a hand through his thick fronds. Their straw paleness grew streaked with healing paste.

"And I should go," he said. "The sun's down, and I'm not supposed to be on the street."

"Why were you out so late, anyway?" Emmy asked. "You know it's not safe."

Zecha looked at the scuffed toes of his boots.

Fury rose in Emmy's throat. "You were hunting again, weren't you?" she asked. Bashful, Zecha nodded. Emmy crossed her arms. "One of these days you'll get caught with that bow, and you'll be tossed into a cell—or even killed!"

"I know," Zecha said, his words soft. "It's just..." He raised his head, eyes ablaze. "I can't understand why they won't let me join the service. Just because I'm male doesn't mean I can't fight." His indignation faltered. "I keep thinking that if I practice hard enough, become good enough, they might change their minds."

His knife-edge sorrow made Emmy's heart ache. He dropped his gaze again. Emmy laid a hand on his shoulder.

"It isn't fair, I know," she said. "You're as good with a bow as anyone I've ever seen, maybe even the best. But that doesn't matter to them. When they look at you, all they see is a male, and males don't fight." She gave a soft laugh. "Just like when they look at me, they see a demon."

Zecha placed a hand on hers. His claws were callused from his bow. "You're not a demon," he said. "You're my best friend."

Emmy found herself enveloped in a sudden embrace. She stiffened for a moment. Zecha was tactile, and Emmy wasn't. She never had been. It was hard to embrace others when the only touch she was used to was the strike of an open palm. However, she relented and returned the squeeze. Zecha wasn't like Krodge or Bose or any of the cruel others. He was kind, and a true friend.

Emmy drew an arm's length away and tipped her head towards the kitchen. "Use the rear door," she said. "You won't be seen."

Sorrow expelled, Zecha flashed a bright smile. "You really are my best friend, you know."

Emmy planted her hands on her hips. Her lips quirked.

"It's not hard to be the best when I'm your only friend. Now, shoo. Be safe. And don't trample my herb garden!"

Grinning, Zecha waved and slipped away like a wisp.

Returning to the shop, locking the door, Emmy stared at the new mess that shone in the moons' light. A heavy thud grabbed her attention, and she closed her eyes. *How long has Krodge been calling? She won't be pleased...*

"Emena!" the old female screeched. "Where is my tea?"

Each word was punctuated with a strike of her walking stick. Dust fell from the roof beams.

"Coming, Madame!" Emmy called, hurrying to the kitchen.

A haze of steam hung in the air. Emmy prepared the tea. An expensive import from Mellul, a country far across the sea, it smelled of smoldering parchment. Emmy sliced hunks of bread and slabs of white cheese to accompany it, then journeyed up the creaking stairs.

She listened at Krodge's door for a moment before she knocked.

"Get in here!"

Emmy acquiesced.

Krodge's tawny eyes were on her straight away. Her thin lips curled with venom.

"What in the name of Nunako, Lady of Light, is going on?" she snapped. For someone allegedly dying, her voice was powerful. "I've been listening to a commotion in my own home, wondering if I'll be murdered in my bed. And where have you been? Ignoring the poor wretch who brought you up when others cast you aside! Come here!"

A scowl framed Krodge's eyes, and her face was haloed by a tangle of fronds.

Though she knew what was coming, Emmy did as she was told. She always did. Setting the meager meal by Krodge's bedside, she approached, knelt, and waited for the blow.

It soon came. Krodge brought her stick down on Emmy's head with speed and strength that defied her age.

Stars danced behind her eyelids. Emmy's knees buckled and her claws dug into her scalp. She didn't make a sound. The pain ran in rivulets down her skull.

"Inconsiderate little Moon Rogue!" Krodge cried. "I've given you a home. I've given you a profession that will keep you for the rest of your life. You're to inherit this place when I'm dead. And considering what insufficient morsels you bring to me, my death is close at hand!" She jabbed a finger at the tray, though stopped short of toppling it.

"You don't understand just how much you need me! Once I'm dead, there'll be no one left to protect you!"

Emmy clutched her head, suppressing a groan as her sight returned. Through tears and blood, she stared at the creature in the bed. No one left to protect her? When had Krodge ever protected her?

Krodge never admonished the bullies who called Emmy names. She encouraged the insults, joining in with glee. *Moon Rogue, Moon Rogue! Go back to your hole and die!* Emmy's chest tightened. Her head burned.

She pictured herself snatching the stick from Krodge's gnarled claws and driving its point straight through her dark heart. Shame and frustration filled her. She swayed on her knees, sucking in a hard breath.

Krodge glowered. "Get out!"

At that, Emmy fled. Lurching to the kitchen, she leaned on the door frame. She clutched her head, her talons freshly red.

Then her ears twitched. Her brow furrowed. *What's that noise?* Someone was knocking. This time, it was on the rear door. Still pressing her head, she crossed the kitchen. She lifted the latch.

It was Zecha. "Emmy?" he asked. "What happened?"

His tone was soft, almost loving. Emmy lifted her hands from her head, staring at the blood.

"She hit you again, didn't she?" Zecha asked. His lips were pursed into a thin line. "This is why we need to leave this place."

The pain in her head muddled her thinking. Emmy tried to speak, but only a groan escaped. Her claws went back to her head. More warm moistness greeted her.

"Come on," Zecha said. "Let's get you cleaned up."

CHAPTER FOUR

Bandim

How tragic. How dreadful. How *convenient*. Bandim's lips curled in a vicious smile. His father was dead. His brother was dead.

Bandim had never been happier.

For the past day, he'd played the grieving brother and son. He'd donned the white of grief, pretended to enjoy the comfort and succor of others' tears and condolences. Yes, it was a shock. Yes, it was a tragedy. News of the emperor's death was expected, for Braslen had been ill for some time. But Mantos' sudden passing had cut the population to its core. It was the subject of talk at every meal and on every street corner.

To the outside world, Bandim wore a mask of pain. But to his military advisors, he wore a face of determination. Already his plans were in motion, ships sailing for the weakest links in Metakalan defenses: the unfortified port towns on the southern coast. There had been some protest against the practice. It wasn't the Masvam way. Masvams had only fought armies for hundreds of cycles, said the wizened advisors. Masvams didn't build their empire on dishonor and the targeting of innocents.

Those advisors had been quickly dispatched, replaced by those loyal to Bandim and Dorai. It was a practice Bandim spread through his whole court, even down to the servants. Lovers of the Light, out. True believers in the Dark, in.

Everything is coming together, Bandim thought, *just as Johrann said.*

There was one problem, however.

His mother.

Bandim's soft-soled shoes were silent on the steps as he ascended Grieving Tower. It was so called because the consorts of emperors, upon the deaths of their husbands, locked themselves in its midst, shrouded in grief. Such was the tradition. One had flung herself from the topmost window, but it wouldn't happen again. That empress had loved her husband. Love matches were uncommon. Marriages to empresses or emperor consorts were decided long before the younglings gendered. Love didn't drive alliances and expand borders.

Snorting, Bandim continued the long climb, two hundred and fifty steps, spiraling up and up and up. As far as anyone knew—including his brother, including his father—Empress Phen had lost her wits, addled by the guilt of nearly killing her hatchling. Saved only by the intervention of a mysterious temple novice, Mantos had lived, and Phen's spirit had died. At least, that was the story.

That novice had been Johrann Maa. The magic used was Dark, and the cost was dear. Phen had sacrificed herself for her son, but now, her work was for nothing. *I will have what is mine*, Bandim thought. *I will have my right.*

Climbing the last round of the staircase, Bandim's thoughts grew bitter. Of course, his mother did what she felt she had to do. Mantos was the first hatched. Mantos was the heir. And what of Bandim? Cast aside, not good enough. Never good enough. Every muscle in his body tightened. She could have let nature take its course. She could have let Mantos die. She could have let Bandim's fate unfurl as it was meant to: to fulfill his purpose, to become the emperor.

But she hadn't. Since Bandim discovered the truth from Johrann, many cycles before, all affection for his mother had ceased. But he knew something Johrann did not. Truth burned within him. Not only would Johrann deliver him the empire, but she would deliver him the power of the goddess, too. He would be the goddess incarnate, and it wouldn't matter that his mother didn't love him as much as his brother. Everyone would love him as their goddess, the one who would save them all.

When he reached the final twist, Bandim stopped. He faced a window. Warm night air drifted through, and the three moons hung low. This was the topmost window; the window one empress had thrown herself from. Bandim's lips curled. Perhaps, today, there would be a second.

With that, Bandim continued his journey.

Now that Johrann's spell was finally broken, twenty-one cycles since it was cast, Mantos' life was no longer saved. At last, he was dead. His body lay in state beside their father's, ready for ritual burning on the temple pyre. Once again, Bandim snorted. They should have been burned already, their ashes scattered to the wind. But as beloved as both were, the ceremony was postponed to allow for sufficient grief. The emperor and his heir were to be given up in flames to Nunako, the Goddess of Light, on Midsummer's Eve.

Midsummer's Eve was never a normal day for the fools of the Light. But this cycle, something more brought a snarl to Bandim's face. He reached for the brass latch on his mother's chamber door—locked from the outside, not from within. He wrenched back the bolt. This cycle, Midsummer's Eve was also the Lunar Awakening, a supposed gift from the goddess Nunako. All three moons would fall into line, one behind the other, and all prayers would be answered.

Moons and wishes and prayers, a conduit to a false god... Ha! That wasn't the true nature of the so-called awakening. As soon as he was on the throne, Bandim would purge the blasphemy, and return the world to the truth of Dorai. Dorai would live within him, *be* him, and he would be her, just as it was written.

Bandim thrust open the chamber door. The smash dissipated. In its place was rustling—skirts on crisp rushes. A pair of golden eyes flashed in the gloom. Bandim smirked. "Hello, Mother."

Phen crept from the shadows like a cautious animal. Her arms were tight against her flat chest, her dress hanging in rags from her bony frame. Glinting in the scant candlelight, her eyes languished in dark circles. They were the same bright yellow as his own, undiminished even after twenty-one cycles in solitude.

"Bandim." The word rattled from her throat as her bony claws reached to him. "Is that you?"

"Yes, Mother."

His tone should have been warm. It should have been welcoming, supportive, a mother and son reunited after many cycles apart. But it wasn't. It was cold as a Vhaun wind, and bit at the exposed skin of Phen's throat.

"I...I don't understand. How can this be?" She grasped the front of Bandim's robes. "You were a hatchling when I last saw you. How is it possible that you're so...grown?"

At the sight of his mother's gnarled hands, Bandim's face twisted with disgust. He shoved her off. Phen slipped on the ancient rushes and toppled with a shriek. Her unkempt fronds spilled around her like a grey pool. When she looked at him again, her eyes were bright with fear.

"You cannot be my son," she whispered. "My son wouldn't treat me this way. Who are you?"

Bandim chuckled. Phen's wretched frame tried to clamber upright. As she dragged herself towards the bedstead, every fiber of muscle flexed under her dark skin.

"Oh, I *am* your son," Bandim said. "But perhaps not the son you wanted."

"What?" Phen asked as she struggled to stand. "I wanted you both, sons or daughters. It didn't matter. I wanted you *both*." She stilled, eyes darting. "Mantos," she breathed. "Where is Mantos?"

"You see!" Bandim spat. "You call for Mantos because I'm not what you want. I've never been what you wanted!"

Phen leaned on the bedpost and jerked her head from side to side.

"No!" she cried. "I loved you both. I *love* you both. Exactly the same!" Realization spread across her face, memories of so long ago filling the lines in her skin. "Where is Mantos?"

Bandim's laugh was eerily light. "Dear Mother," he said, reveling in the news, "has no one told you?"

"Told me what?" Phen asked, throwing herself against Bandim's chest. She grabbed fistfuls of his robes. "Told me *what*?"

Bandim's laugh dissipated, but his lips lifted in a barbarous smirk.

"I'm so glad I can give you this news myself," he said. "It might be the sweetest part of it all. Dearest Mother..." He paused, letting the weight of the moment crush her. "Your beloved son is dead."

There was a beat of absolute silence. Phen's eyes flickered, searching for a glint of truth. When she found it, she screamed. "No! It can't be. I made a deal, my life for his!"

Bandim snatched her hands, clenching them so hard she keened with pain.

"I know the deal you made, Mother," Bandim growled. "I know what you did for *him*." He spat the final word like a curse. The bones of Phen's wrists ground in his grip. "I know what you did for him," he repeated, each word more ragged than the last. "You sacrificed your life to save him. And yet, you didn't need to—because you had *me*."

Phen's eyes widened. "Bandim, I—"

He cut his mother off with a slap to the face. She spun across the floor. Bandim stalked towards her, nose slits flaring as enmity consumed him.

"No!" he cried, clamping his hands on her withered arms. "Don't defend your actions! You had me. You didn't need to save him. He was dead. He lost his life in the natural order of things, yet you chose to interfere. And not only that, you took yourself away from me! You left me with Father, who gave all his attention to Mantos—and I was left with nothing! No mother, no father, an endless string of nurses and housemasters and teachers—but no one who cared for me."

Phen's breath fluttered. "Bandim, I would have done the same for you! I did what I had to do to save my youngling. If it had been you who fell from the nest, I would still have sacrificed myself."

"Lies!" Spittle foamed at the corner of Bandim's lips. "You showed how little you cared for me when you gave your life for him. I could have been the emperor. I was *meant* to be the emperor! Fate kept me back at first, but set itself to rights when that runt fell from the nest. But you destroyed my chances, all because you loved him more!"

His chest heaved. The scales and plates of his neck and shoulders pulsed and rose. Phen cowered like a wounded animal, her body trembling under his rage.

Tears tracked her cheeks, though they elicited no sympathy. Bandim kept his grip strong.

"You're wrong," Phen whispered. "You're so wrong. My son, my son—"

She reached for his face, but Bandim thrust her away, fury bubbling anew. "Do not presume to touch me, *Mother*," he spat, the words echoing his last with exchange with Mantos. "I am the emperor now."

Something changed within Phen at those words. Her yellow eyes strengthened, and she regained her balance. She straightened her crooked back and drew herself to her full height, eye to eye with Bandim. Her tail twitched from side to side, the muscles flexing after an eternity of stillness.

"And I am Empress Phen of House Yru, wife of Emperor Braslen of House Tiboli. And more importantly, I am your mother."

Bandim's cold chuckle echoed off the chamber walls. Phen's courage flickered in the darkness. He would snuff her insolence out soon enough.

"My mother you may be," he said, taking a few slow steps towards her, "and you *were* wife of the emperor. You *were* the empress. But Father is dead. You're a widow. No empress has reigned supreme on the throne. You have no choice. I own you now, and I'll do with you as I please."

Defiance blazed in Phen's eyes, though there was a new waver in her voice. "And what will you do with me?" she asked. "Keep me locked up to rot in this prison?"

"Dear, dear Mother," Bandim said gently. Then, without warning, his hand shot out, gripping her chin. "Why would I keep you here? You're the dowager empress, after all."

A fleeting moment of relief spread across Phen's face. At that, Bandim locked his jaws on his prey.

"I won't leave you here to die." He brought his mouth to her ear. "I'm going to kill you."

CHAPTER FIVE

Emmy

Sunlight crept through the cracks in the shutters. Emmy buried further into the pile of blankets on the hard floor, shivering against the cold. Then she realized: hard floor? Cold?

This wasn't her bed.

Emmy jerked upright, fronds cascading over her shoulders. She blinked, taking in her surroundings. It was dark. Her sandals were by the door, parallel with the wall as always.

The scarred female was still in her bed.

Pressing a hand to her head, Emmy frowned. Material—a bandage. How?

Memory flooded back. Zecha.

The cloth came away in a stiff clump of dried blood and frayed edges. *A bad job*, Emmy thought, lips pulling in a soft smile, *but at least he tried.* She struggled to her feet, winding the bandage around her hand. She turned to the bed.

The creature nestling between her sheets was pallid, the rise and fall of her armored chest shallow. *At least she didn't die in the night. That would have been hard to explain.*

The acrid stench of the female's unwashed body caught in the back of Emmy's throat. She reached across, throwing open the shutters. The salty tang of sea air flooded in with morning light. Emmy took a few deep breaths, willing the stink to leave. "Now," she said, "let's see how your wound is healing."

She exposed the female's gash. Already it looked better. It was red, now ringed with bruises that stood in sharp relief against her yellow skin, but the stitches held firm. *Considering the depth of the puncture, she'll have a deep scar.* Emmy gave a gentle snort. *I don't think she'll mind.*

She traced the white web of scars that covered every part of the female's skin like cobwebs. They even crossed the top of her plucked head. *What did she do to deserve such torment?* Emmy wondered. A flash of the hag upstairs and her walking stick made

Emmy shudder. *Perhaps not a lot...*

She pulled the covers up, then threaded her talons through the female's chipped horn crest. Her skin was warm, but not alight with fever. Emmy clucked her tongue. *A good sign.*

Trying to ignore the thump in her head, she dressed and went to the shop. The memory of dirt and blood curdled in her throat. She had a lot to do before she could open the apothecary. She had to open every day except templeday, and that only came once a week.

But as it turned out, she didn't have a lot to do at all.

Emmy noticed two things. Firstly, the floor sparkled. Secondly, Zecha was propped against the shop door, his head bowed in sleep. A dagger rested on his lap.

"Zecha?" Emmy asked.

He didn't stir. Emmy repeated herself, loud enough to send Krodge into a fury.

Zecha jumped, dagger poised to strike. As he found his bearings, his eyes went from wide with fear to crinkled with sheepishness. "Oh."

He looked from the weapon to Emmy and back again, then sheathed it with a blush. "Good morning," he said, as if the circumstances were entirely ordinary. "Did you sleep?"

"I did." Emmy shook her head. "You didn't need to stay."

"I couldn't leave," Zecha said. "I couldn't rouse you. And after I cleaned, I couldn't find your keys. If I'd left, anyone could have walked in."

Emmy folded her arms, but a smile pulled at her mouth. "Well, thank you," she said. "That was very kind."

"It's okay," Zecha replied with a lopsided grin.

Emmy raised an eyeridge. "Why did you come back?" she asked. "I remember the knocking at the kitchen door, then I saw you, and then..." She shrugged. "I woke up this morning."

Zecha stretched his arms wide, their muscles flexing. "I had a feeling the old crone wouldn't be happy," he said. His face twisted. "I came back to make sure you were all right—and I'm glad I did."

wouldn't

Something shifted in Zecha's face. There was a new fire in his eyes. Emmy shook her head, turning away. They'd danced this dance many times. "No, Zecha," she said. "I'm not leaving. Not yet, anyway."

Pouting, Zecha folded his arms. "We could go anywhere," he said. "We could hop on a boat and just leave. Althemer, Mellul, Haelog, Linvarra..." He threw up his hands. "Anywhere would be better than this place."

"It's not that simple," Emmy said. "I can't leave Krodge. Without me, she would die." This was true, but also a lie. Emmy would happily let the crone rot in her bed. But Bellim, as unwelcome as it made her, was an ironic safe haven. At least here, the folk knew enough not to kill her, since she had the apothecary's knowledge. That was her only saving grace. "And anyway," she continued, pushing that thought aside, "who knows what we could sail into? You know the Masvams prowl the seas, not to mention the danger from Valtat slave ships. We could leave our lives here and sail into something much worse."

Sensing defeat, Zecha let his arms hang loose. "I know. I just... I wish things were better."

Emmy patted his shoulder. "Maybe one day we can be who we are. For now, we put up with what we have."

Zecha's grin returned, though its sparkle had dulled. "You're right," he said. "You're always right."

Beckoning him to follow, Emmy led him to the rear door. "Stay safe today, Zecha," she said. "Try not to get into trouble."

"No promises," Zecha replied.

Before he left, he reached out an arm. Emmy offered her own. Zecha grasped her bicep and she did the same to his, squeezing each other in a traditional Metakalan goodbye.

Releasing her, Zecha slipped through the gate and disappeared. Emmy exhaled and closed the kitchen door. Inside, Krodge banged anew.

But a new noise diverted her attention. There was scratching at the back gate. A head of unruly brown fronds appeared, seen through the slats, and then disappeared again. Emmy touched a claw to her temple. Of course.

Curly-fronded Kain, the youngling with unruly brown fronds, skipped into the rear yard. Like all younglings, they were neither male nor female. Their father Leeve, a dark-skinned male with a permanent glower, followed behind. He trailed his cart into the yard. It was laden with wood, chopped by his wife the day before.

"Morning greetings, Leeve," Emmy said.

Saying nothing, Leeve piled the wood in a small lean-to as Emmy fetched the weekly payment.

When she returned, Leeve was watching as Kain kicked a row of her precious plants. As she saw leaves fly from her bindlewart bush, Emmy's nostrils flared. Her neck scales rose. "Stop that!"

Kain blanched and ran to Leeve's side, clutching the hem of his coarse over-tunic. With narrowed eyes and tight lips, Leeve reached for his payment.

Emmy passed him the coins, five bickles, and an extra cren for Kain, the payment she had given every week since Leeve had first come around, peddling his wife's wood.

Leeve accepted the payment, but plucked up the red cren and turned it over in his hand. He looked at her from under his drawn brows, and Emmy swallowed. There was something in his eyes that spoke of anger, of disgust. It was a look Emmy was used to, since she was a Moon Rogue, and therefore not worthy of courtesy.

In a swift movement, Leeve launched the cren at Emmy.

The coin bounced off her armor and clattered to the ground with a dim clink. Leeve glared anew through his tangled fronds, then lifted Kain onto the wagon.

Emmy wrenched the discarded coin from the ground. She turned it over in her own hand. She brushed the pad of her talon over the hole in its center. *I've given Kain a cren every week for as long as I remember*, she thought. *Why not accept it now? Because I spoke sharply?*

As Leeve pulled the cart away, Kain stared at Emmy with tearful eyes. Emmy pursed her lips. It was too early to tell, but she suspected Kain would manifest as male when they came of age. That was unfortunate. Gendering was difficult, but at least life gave more possibilities when you became female. Except for Emmy, of course, but she was used to being the exception to every rule.

The father and youngling's words carried over the wall as they moved to the next shop.

"The Moon Rogue shouted at me, Poi," Kain whined.

"Yes, she did," Leeve said. "Stay away from her. She's poison, Kain. Poison. We won't accept any more charity from her."

Emmy's back stiffened. Her tail grew rigid. *Moon Rogue*. That was what they all said.

"*Run away, it's the Moon Rogue!*"

"*Tainted! Tainted!*"

"*She'll never make it to the Light!*"

Emmy stormed into the kitchen and slammed a pot on the table. It was a lie, designed to frighten younglings into doing what they were told. Emmy cast handfuls of grain into the pot and fetched water. As far as she could see, she was no different from anyone else, except for her colors. But her difference painted her as an outsider, something to be tolerated because there was no other apothecary in Bellim, and folk needed their medicine.

They even held her at arm's length when they called her to visit the sick. She would tend to the cases of eyepox in younglings, trying her best to preserve their sight, and they would still keep away. They didn't hesitate to call her when the wasting disease, Breathstealer's Plague, came upon one of their elderly, or when the Lurking Death brought a whole household to its knees. But equally, they wouldn't grasp her arm in greeting. They would allow her to cross their threshold, but not as a friend. They would pay her in coin, but never in thanks.

No. Underneath the knowledge Krodge had given her, Emmy was still a Moon Rogue. She wasn't welcome in the temple of Nunako. She wasn't welcome in the Central Circle when pageants were performed, or to watch the bright explosions of fireworks lighting up the night sky.

Moon Rogues were evil. They were tainted, forgotten by the goddess. That was why Emmy looked so strange, purple and blue like a bruise. If it wasn't for Krodge, the town would have nailed her to a stake and let the gargons pluck out her eyes. It was also why Krodge had taught her "lessons" every day for so many cycles.

Emmy slammed down the water jug and snorted.

Some days, she wished she *was* a Moon Rogue. If she was, she could punish them all by sucking out their spirits, or whatever it was Moon Rogues were supposed to do. She could have her revenge on Krodge, finally give her what she deserved.

Emmy mixed the grain and water so hard it slopped over the sides. She stared for a moment, biting her lower lip. She didn't need to be a Moon Rogue to have her revenge on the crone. She could add a little sicklestem juice to her food, each meal another dose, and finish her off...

No. Emmy shook her head hard enough to make her thoughts spin. She couldn't do that. No matter what Krodge said, no matter what any of them said, Emmy was good and kind. She wouldn't do harm, not even to those who had harmed her.

She hung the pot over the fire and stoked more life into the flames. Once they roared, she pulled her long fronds until it hurt. The pain in her scalp was easier to bear than the pain in her heart.

Moon Rogue, Moon Rogue! Go back to your hole and die!

◆ ◆ ◆

Several days passed before Bose showed his face again. "Is it true?" he asked. His hands were clasped over his heart as he stared.

Emmy kept her lips straight as she tipped creyhorn powder into a cloth bag. She was worn out from running to and fro from the shop to her wounded charge, for the injured female still hadn't woken up. She hadn't the time, nor the patience, for any of Bose's silly games.

"I don't know what you mean," she said.

Bose huffed. He turned and rolled his eyes at his companions. They did the same, adding unimpressed clucks with their tongues.

"Is it true," Bose said, intoning each syllable as if talking to a simpleton, "that you saved someone's life?"

Emmy passed him the bag and folded her arms. She needed to have a word with Zecha. Who else had he spun the story to?

Bose accepted the bag with a simper. Emmy was deadpan. "I don't know what you're talking about."

"By the goddess! It's been the talk of the town for days!" Bose pulled himself to his full height, which wasn't particularly impressive—he was at least a head shorter than most other Metakalans—and tried to look down on Emmy. "I hadn't been able to ask before, for my beloved Mrs. Bose returned to me."

Ignoring his preening, Emmy lifted a talon.

"It's true," Emmy said. "Now, please. A half-bickle."

Bose threw the coin into Emmy's hand and sneered. Payment accepted, she gestured to the door. "Now, if you don't mind, I'm busy."

Bose was silent. He flicked his red gaze over her with slow arrogance. "You may have saved a life," he said, "but you are still a *beast*."

Emmy stiffened. She bit back tears. "Leave."

With a victorious grin, Bose retreated in a whirl of skirts and robes.

The rest of the day passed with little conversation. Emmy couldn't speak around the lump in her throat.

After her chores were done and the mistress was sated, she collapsed on her blanket pile. Not her bed. She didn't even have the luxury of that. It had been given over to the scarred female, who showed no sign of being well enough to get up and finally be out of Emmy's fronds.

Staring at the ceiling, Emmy counted the cracks in the roof beams. Why did folk think they could treat her like an animal? It all came back to the same thing: because she was a Moon Rogue. Maybe Zecha was right. Maybe they should leave.

Her attention was caught by a thin moan. She sat up. The female in the bed stirred. Beyond caring for her wound, Emmy hadn't given much thought to what would happen when she woke up. Now that life returned to her, reality bit, cold and sharp. What could Emmy tell her?

She was spared the trouble as the female settled again. Undressing for bed, Emmy peeled off her tunic, leaving just her undershirt next to her skin. She was about to remove her hose when the female stirred again.

This time she turned, groaned, and opened her eyes. They were deep and dark in the failing light.

Emmy froze. The female sat up and winced, settling one hand on her chest, over her wound, and the other on her plucked head. She turned. Their eyes met.

Emmy offered an arm—and everything fell to pieces.

"Demon!"

The female sprang from the bed, leaping forward, grasping for Emmy's throat. She missed. She slammed into the wall, turned, and dove back, striking Emmy's jaw with an iron fist.

Pain erupting from the blow, Emmy stumbled, blankets coiled around her ankles. Shaking the blur from her eyes, she ducked as another punch came her way. "Please, calm yourself!" she cried.

"Moon Rogue! Tainted!"

White rage scalded Emmy like molten metal. No longer thinking, she struck out, landing a blow on her attacker's temple.

It felled her.

"I am not a Moon Rogue," Emmy screeched.

Banging erupted above them. Krodge. Emmy raised a hand to slap her victim, but the wretched creature scrabbled back, cowering.

"No! Please! Sorry, I am!"

Sense returning, Emmy dropped her hand. Her indignation was cooled by stark realization.

"No, *I'm* sorry," she spluttered. "I shouldn't have... Here."

She reached to help the female up. Instead of taking the offered arm, the female burst into tears.

Emmy's arm hung suspended as shame flowed through her. To make a female cry took something special, a cutting deeper than the knife that had plunged into this female's chest. The female buried her face in her hands. Emmy's throat tightened as she tried to think of something—anything—to say. Words eluded her.

"I'm sorry," Emmy repeated. "I am, really."

After several agonizing moments, the female revealed her puffy face. She kept her chin down.

Emmy held out her hand again. This time, the gesture was accepted. Emmy settled her on the bed and tried to smile. There was another moment of excruciating silence.

"May I check your wound?" Emmy asked eventually.

The female blinked, settling a hand on her chest. "O-okay," she said.

For the first time, her youth was apparent. Emmy placed her at around fourteen cycles, younger than herself. Emmy knelt before her and pulled down the neck of her tunic. While the gash was red and bulging around the stitches, none had torn. It was a miracle, really. Somehow, the blade had missed anything vital to life.

"You'll have a scar," Emmy said, "but the wound will heal."

The female did not respond. She smoothed out her tunic's neck and sat, stiff-backed.

Her youth swept Emmy's ire away. She stood, trying to smile. "Would you like something to eat?"

She received no reply except a blank stare, but the pools of shadow caught by the female's jutting bones said enough.

Fetching bread and weak beer, Emmy returned. The female hadn't moved, but her eyes brightened at the food and drink, and she drained the beer in one gulp. Emmy poured more. "What's your name?" she asked.

The female took another long drink, then shoveled a piece of bread into her mouth. Her first answer was incomprehensible. Swallowing, she tried again. "Charo," she said. "Charo, my name is."

Reaching out, Emmy grasped Charo's upper arm. "I'm Emmy," she replied.

Charo blinked and stared at the outstretched arm, before mirroring the gesture.

"*Not* a Moon Rogue?" she asked, prodding Emmy's skin and armor.

"No, I'm not," Emmy said, half-amused and half-exasperated. "I'm just...me."

Releasing her grip, Charo plucked up more bread, picking at the crust. "Where I am?"

"Bellim," Emmy replied, "in Metakala."

Charo's words were strange, not quite what Emmy was used to. They were similar enough to be understood, though the inflections and word order were odd. Charo sat forward and rubbed her eyes with the heel of one hand.

"Why here am I?" she asked. "Thought...thought me I was dead."

"You almost were," Emmy replied. "My friend found you in the Wailing Woods and brought you here."

Charo's eyes widened. "A healer, you are?"

Snorting softly, Emmy shook her head. "Not really," she said. "I'm just a lowly apothecary's apprentice."

"A healer you should be," Charo said, her strange words filled with innocent conviction. She sucked the crumbs from her talons. Then she looked at her abdomen again.

Emmy's smile faded at the sight of her many scars. "What happened to you?" she asked.

"Stabbed," Charo replied. The word was flat. "Fell in the mud, I did. Couldn't keep going. And...stabbed me, she did."

"Who did?" Emmy asked.

"My owner..." Charo's breath hitched. "Pulling her cart, I was, but me...tired. Travelled from Haetharro—far north, a country. Walking for weeks, pulling her along in that wheeled thing, I was. Slipped. Couldn't get up, and... Stabbed me, she did."

Charo let the tunic fall and drew her arms tight to her sides, bringing her knees together. Emmy was silent for a moment as she tried to muster words of comfort.

"You're fine now," she said, the words tentative. "And you're free. If your owner wanted you dead, she's not coming back." Emmy's eyes roved over the patchwork of scars and dents and slashes in Charo's mossy armor. "You can go home."

As soon as the word was out of her mouth, Emmy winced.

"Home?" Charo spat. "Home I do not have. Torn from home when just a youngling I was. And Haetharro? Never will I back there go." Her tone was venomous. "*Ever.*"

"You don't have to," Emmy said, her voice low with capitulation. "You're free."

Charo's already drawn face tightened. She broke into thick sobs. Emmy clenched her fists. Her guts wrenched. She didn't know what to do or what to say. Where was Zecha when she needed him? He was better at emotions.

Charo's sobs emanated from something that cut deeper than Emmy could stand. The female curled into a ball and rocked back and forth, her tears soaking the too-large hose Emmy had dressed her in.

Needing to escape, Emmy stood. "I'll make some tea," she said.

She hurried to the kitchen. She cleared the dishes, stoked the fire, and tried desperately to think of a story to spin for Krodge. The crone's banging had ceased, but that didn't mean Krodge had forgotten. Emmy sprinkled the tea leaves into the pot and sighed.

CHAPTER SIX

Emmy

Emmy straightened her back and breathed deeply. She balanced the tray of Krodge's evening victuals on one hand and knocked with the other. And she waited. Unfortunately, waiting gave her time to think.

In the days following Charo's consciousness, the two had exchanged few words, except when Zecha appeared. *He could get a reply from a tree*, Emmy thought. She, on the other claw, had no idea what to say. The more she thought about what happened, the tighter the knot grew in her stomach. Things weren't normal. Her precious order had been taken away. Life had never been pleasant, but at least it had been predictable.

Emmy chewed her lower lip. Why was she keeping Charo here? When Krodge found out, Emmy's life wouldn't be worth living. The crone would be furious, not just at the idea of a freeloading guest, but because Emmy had been keeping secrets from her. She should have told Krodge. She should have been truthful when the crone asked about the commotion. But in the moment, thinking of the female's desperation, she had lied. Now, it loomed over her like a knife held above her head by a threadbare string. Emmy needed things to go back to the way they were.

Eventually she was granted permission to enter.

Krodge watched as Emmy set the tray on the bedside table. Emmy's eyes sought the walking stick. She couldn't see it.

Waiting to be addressed, she stood with her hands clasped. Krodge faced her and raised a talon, beckoning Emmy closer. Emmy didn't hesitate, though her heart began to thunder. She approached and knelt as always.

"Emena," Krodge said, gesturing to one pointed ear, "is there something I need to hear?"

Emmy stilled, heart pounding even harder. "Well..." she began.

Clasping her hands on her rotund belly, Krodge narrowed her eyes. "Yes?"

Emmy's mouth worked, but all that came out was a dull croak. Something changed in Krodge, a dark glint to her eyes. She launched her hand out and clamped it around Emmy's throat, her claws digging into the soft skin. "Why is there a stranger in my house?"

Waves of breath pulsed against Emmy's face. She spluttered, trying to pry Krodge's fingers from her neck. Her eyes bulged, and her vision blurred at the edges.

"I hear everything!" Krodge bellowed. "I know there is someone here!"

Emmy's eyes rolled back. Krodge released her grip, only to bring her walking stick down like steel. Even as her back blazed with pain, Emmy refused to cry out. It would only lead to more pain.

Staying in her kneeling position, Emmy gasped for breath.

"I was waiting for you to tell the truth," Krodge said, "but now I see I shouldn't have had faith in you. What is going on?"

"Yes," Emmy cried, "there is someone else here! She was brought to me by some of the townsfolk. She was nearly dead. I did everything you taught me to try to save her." Her words stumbled over each other. She looked up, hoping they placated Krodge even a little. "Everyone in town knows about it. They know I was only able to save her because of how well *you* taught me."

Sitting upright in the bed, which creaked under her considerable weight, Krodge raised an eyeridge. "Get up."

Emmy did as she was told and resisted the urge to lean against the wall, though her knees were weak.

"How is this female now?" Krodge asked. "Will she live?"

"Yes, Madame," Emmy replied. "She's getting stronger every day."

Krodge tapped one thick talon on her chin and nodded. "I see. And folk are interested in her, are they?"

Emmy nodded. "Yes, Madame. Everyone who comes in asks about her."

"Good," Krodge said, settling back against her pillows. "In that case, once she's able, you will put her to work. She was saved by my knowledge and is being fed by my profits. I think she owes me a little servitude." At Emmy's look of disdain, Krodge waved a hand. "I have no interest in keeping her as a slave," she said. "But there's an Althemerian custom I'm quite fond of. It's about owing a debt to those who have helped you. This female, she's to work in the shop for no pay for three weeks. After that, if she satisfies me, you can pay her a pittance. A half-bickle a day should suffice. Or she can get out. I don't care. But make sure she knows that for the next three weeks, she doesn't have a choice."

Emmy nodded, saying nothing in the hope that Krodge would dismiss her.

"Get out," Krodge said, waving her hand again. "Go and relay my instructions."

Relief coursing through her, Emmy retreated, the burn at her neck abating. Straight away, she found Charo at the kitchen table.

"You're to work for my mistress for three weeks," she added as Charo's eyes widened. "She says you owe her a debt."

Charo remained silent for a moment. Then she stood. "All right," she said, inclining her head. "I will."

Eyes bulging, Emmy's mouth gaped.

"You've just been freed from servitude. Why don't you leave? You don't have to do what she says. You could go now, and I couldn't—*wouldn't*—stop you."

Charo shrugged, smiling.

"Different, this is," she said. "I have choice, for time first in my life. And," she added, her face coloring, "I like it here. And I don't know anywhere else."

Memories of Krodge's "lessons" flashed in Emmy's mind.

"You don't know what you're getting into," she said. "Krodge isn't pleasant."

"Stabbed you, ever?"

That question made Emmy stop. She flicked through her mind. Had Krodge ever tried to kill her outright? No, she hadn't. But what she had done had left scars. Where Charo's marks were easily seen, Emmy had an invisible web.

"No," Emmy replied, "but she's done other things. She's hurt me."

"Servants, all mistresses hurt them." Emmy bristled at the word, but said nothing. "Is expected. If she not try to kill me, is improvement on my last mistress."

In truth, Emmy wasn't so sure.

Over the next few days, Charo proved to be pleasant company. At first, it was strange for Emmy to share her living space with someone other than Krodge. But she got used to it, like breaking in a new pair of boots: unnoticeable at first, followed by an easy comfort that she could wear for days.

The young female's speech improved effortlessly. Charo was adept at many things, from trimming and mixing to measuring and crushing. She was charming with the customers, even Mr. Bose.

At the end of another long day, Charo set to sweeping the floor without being asked. Emmy attended the glass cabinets, making sure the labels were straight and forward-facing. So absorbed in her task, she jumped when Charo called her name.

"Emmy?"

There was a gentle tilt to Charo's lips that made Emmy flush. She turned and tried to smile back. "Sorry. What did you say?"

Leaning on the broom handle, Charo tipped her head to one side. "I asked what Middlemerish is. It's not something they have in the north, but I've heard lots of folk talk about. It's happening soon, but I don't know what it is."

Her mouth opening in an "o" of realization, Emmy folded her arms on the counter.

"The Middlemerish Festival is when worshippers of Nunako celebrate the goddess, the Lady of Light," she said. "It's all about being thankful and celebrating the goodness of Nunako. People come together to drink and feast and pray."

Charo nodded. "It sounds like the Haetharran Festival of Fee, the Northern god of light and growth. They have lots of gods up there."

Emmy smiled. "There's only one goddess here," she said. "Nunako, the Light and the Giver."

She quoted from the Gospel of Nunako, a book she'd only been able to read in secret, as Krodge forbade her access to it, as well as to the temple. Not that she would have been welcome in the temple of Light, as tainted as she was.

"In the midsun, Nunako would 'with steadfastness and determination bring into existence the workings of life.' We celebrate the Goddess' power and how she brought everything to life. Midsun is what we call Middlemerish—some places call it Midsummer's Eve. At Middlemerish, you write down your prayer for the rest of the cycle and tie it to one of the bows of the Great Tree in the Central Circle of the town," Emmy continued. "It's the tallest in the whole of Metakala, so lots of people come to Bellim to celebrate Middlemerish. The higher the bow you tie your prayer to, the more likely it is to be answered by the goddess. The festival's good for the apothecary. Many folks think their Middlemerish wish will be granted if they coat their offering in special concoctions—concoctions that can be bought in Krodge's Apothecary, for the right price." Emmy snorted. "Why go to the bother of making one when you can get one already mixed? I wouldn't be surprised if Krodge herself made up the practice. She'll do anything for a bickle."

Charo's eyes grew round. When she spoke, her voice was small.

"Do you believe prayers can be answered?" she asked.

"I don't believe in anything," Emmy said vehemently. The words that came out next surprised even herself. "Sticking a piece of dead leaf or parchment to a bit of an old tree isn't going to do anything. There's no point in wishing for anything. All there is in life is hard work. That's it. And no magical spells or enchantments, or divine intervention, is going to change that."

Nodding, Charo straightened. She began to sweep again, though the movement was lackluster. "And what's the Lunar Awakening?" she asked. "I've heard a lot of folk talk about that, too. About how special it is, and how it only happens once in a thousand cycles."

"Don't they know anything in the north?" Emmy asked, trying to deflect from her own outburst with levity. At Charo's scowl, she tamed her smile. "The Lunar Awakening is something that's been mentioned in holy books and folklore for a long time. It's said that the goddess Nunako's power comes from the moons as they cross the Arc of the Sky. They're known as her three faces: Dato, Rafa, and Akata. When they're stacked on top of each other, the faces talk, so their power is threefold. It's said to allow Nunako to walk among us again." Emmy shrugged. Recklessness loosened her tongue again, and she went on. "In truth," she said with a final pause, "I don't think any of it's real."

Charo looked up. She blinked. "I feel the same way." Her words were slow and quiet with subdued anguish. "I've been to lots of places, seen lots of temples to lots of gods, but...I've never believed in any of it."

For a moment Emmy and Charo looked at one another. Emmy felt a smile pull at her face. There was something about Charo that spoke to Emmy's core. The simmering pain beneath the surface was how Emmy felt herself. They may have been different in many ways, but some similarities bypassed colors. Charo wasn't just someone Emmy worked with anymore. Now, she was a friend.

Their moment of companionable quiet was shattered as Zecha burst through the door.

"Hello, Emmy," he said, dancing across the floor and ending with an elaborate bow. "And hello, Charo."

Charo smiled back, fiddling with the brush.

"Hello, Zecha," she said.

The two held one another's gaze for a few moments. Emmy shook her head. There was something about the way they looked at one another that she couldn't understand. She never understood how folk could get close to one another, even marry and have younglings. The spark of whatever made that happen simply wasn't there for Emmy. It never had been and, she suspected, it never would be. And she was perfectly content with that.

Not wanting to dwell on the issue any longer, Emmy planted her hands on her hips. "Soup, Zecha?"

Charo and Zecha laughed about something as they followed her to the kitchen, staying close to one another. Emmy prepared a tray for Krodge and set three bowls on the table. There was a large pot of soup bubbling over the fire. Charo attended it, still chattering with Zecha.

Emmy caught a glance of Charo's limbs in the glow of the fire, and she winced. The scars on Charo's arms, legs, and face were thrown into stark relief as the light of the flames illuminated her. Emmy shook her head. It had taken a lot of abuse to become as good at household chores as Charo. Shaking off her musing, Emmy shifted her attention to Zecha.

"How's business?" he asked, perching on one of the long wooden benches.

"Busy. Middlemerish is soon, after all."

"True," Zecha replied. He turned to Charo. "How are you finding working for such an *illustrious* apothecary?"

Emmy rolled her eyes. Charo chuckled.

"I'm enjoying it," she said, the skin of her face reddened by the fire. "I'm very grateful."

"You'll learn a lot from Emmy," Zecha said. "She's talented."

Emmy rolled her eyes again and shook her head. "Zecha, hush."

Nonplussed, Zecha shrugged. "I'm only telling the truth," he said.

Charo flushed and turned away. She lifted the pot from the fire. As her muscles stretched and flexed, Zecha was at her side to take the weight.

Emmy watched as Charo stepped back, her brows drawn together. She managed to chuckle.

"I'm so used to being the one who does all the fetching and carrying and making," Charo said as Zecha brought the pot to the table. "It doesn't feel right to have someone else do it for me, especially—"

Charo snapped her mouth shut to trap the words, but Zecha knew.

"Especially by a male?" he asked. He shook his head, his expression still amiable. "Don't worry, I understand. I'm used to it. And you'll learn to accept help, I think," Zecha said. "I can't imagine that it's easy to adjust to a free life. You are free here, aren't you?" he asked with one eyeridge raised, his gaze flicking to Emmy.

"Oh, yes!" Charo said. "I'm free. I could leave any time. I just..." She looked at Emmy. "I don't want to go. It's nice here. I get shelter and a bed, and a little money. Money!" Her face beamed with delight. "I've never had money in my life. Emmy even bought me these new clothes and sandals," she said, turning to show off her garments. "They're new. I've never had anything new before."

As the two prattled about their lives and Charo ladled soup into bowls, Emmy stood back and watched. Warmth permeated her abdomen, loosening the ever-present knot in her stomach.

Then she looked down at the tray. Krodge's tray. Her heart grew cold. *Perhaps one day, I'll be free*, she thought. She glanced at Charo, her plucked head now covered in harsh spikes of newly growing fronds.

Perhaps.

CHAPTER SEVEN

Phen

She'd been in the tower for three days. On each of those days, Midsummer's Eve and the moons drew ever closer. And on each of those days, her son's threats came closer to fruition.

Once more, Phen found herself sprawled on the floor. Bandim loomed over, face twisted in a leer.

"Bandim, please!" Phen cried, her talons scrabbling on the stone. "Who's put these thoughts in your head? I'm your mother! You shouldn't have turned out like this."

"Perhaps I wouldn't have if my mother had been with me!" Bandim roared, stalking towards her. "Perhaps I would have been filled with the joys and wonders of life if you'd been there to show me. But you weren't!"

"Bandim, *please*!"

Phen cowered, memories returning of the fateful day so long ago when the priestess had saved Mantos' life. Phen never even knew her name. There wasn't time to ask, and then...she had given her life for her first-hatched.

Backing her into a corner, she flinched as Bandim brought a hand up to strike her.

"You made a deal that took you away from me!" He delivered the slap. "And this is what you've received in return. You tried to circumvent the natural way and you've been punished for it. Now the path of fate is unfurling at my feet once more. One empress has thrown herself from the topmost window of this tower." He paused, his mouth twisting. "Why not another?"

Phen screeched. Bandim raised his hand again. Before he could arc it down to his mother's face, there was a cough. Phen stared at the doorway. A guard of indeterminate age, middling rank, and unusual height stood in the arch, bearing a long pike. The first of his horns was cracked. He bowed as he spoke.

"Your Grace," the guard said. "I'm sorry to intrude, but I have news." His eyes flicked to the huddled figure on the ground, then back to Bandim. "News that's best discussed in private."

Phen cried out when Bandim kicked the sole of her bare foot.

"There are no secrets in my family. Not anymore." He strode towards the guard. "What is it?"

The guard paled under his burnished helmet. He tried to speak, but no words came forth. Growing impatient as the silence stretched on, Bandim snarled."Your emperor has commanded you to speak!"

The guard swallowed and nodded.

"Your Grace," he said. "It's the priestess, Johrann Maa. She's taken ill, and she's asked for you. She said it was urgent, otherwise she wouldn't have called for you."

Phen watched as her son's face fell, for a moment showing a chink of fear. Whoever this priestess was, she was someone he cared for. At least that meant he was capable of some form of love.

"*What?*"

"Yes, Your Grace."

Bandim strode past the guard. "Make sure she doesn't leave," he said. "If she does, I'll gut you myself."

The guard gulped and nodded. "Yes, Your Grace."

With that, Bandim slammed the door. The sound of the key turning in the lock made Phen's heart sink. She was trapped. There was no escape.

The weight of her son's absence weighed so heavily on her that she couldn't stand. Instead, she lay where Bandim had left her. She stared at the guard. He stared back.

Then the male cast aside his long pike. Phen winced as it clattered to the floor.

He hurried to her. "Your Grace," he said, taking her hand.

"What's going on?" Phen asked as he pulled her upright. "Who are you?"

"A friend," the guard said, his tallow eyes sparkling with a mix of youth and age and intelligence that made him impossible to place. "That's all you need to know." He took the cloak from his shoulders and draped it around Phen's bony form. "I need you to come with me."

"Why?" Phen asked, drawing back from the stranger's touch.

Even as she asked the question, a voice in her head responded: *Does it matter? If you stay here, you'll die.* Another voice added, *What if this is a trap? What if Bandim's waiting outside, ready to pounce on you?* Uncertainty coiled around Phen's throat like black vines.

The guard crossed to the door and dug in his tunic pocket.

"Your Grace," he said. "Bandim will bring destruction to this empire and the entire world. I intend to stop that from happening, and I need your help to do it."

He fished a set of keys from his pocket. As they rattled, Phen's breath quickened. She didn't understand what the guard was saying. Destruction to the empire and the world? What she did understand was that this was a chance to flee from her son—and the sharp possibility of this being a hideous trap.

The guard gave a soft "Yes!" as he found the right key. He slipped it in. The lock clicked as the key turned. The door swung wide, revealing freedom.

The guard ushered her out. The first thing Phen did was glance in all directions, looking for Bandim's smug face. But she saw nothing but shadow.

At the threshold of the stairs, she couldn't help but stop. She stared at the window. The low moons were framed in it, nearly upon one another. This was the window an empress had thrown herself from, the same window Phen's sole surviving son had threatened to throw her from to a gruesome death on the cobbles below. Perhaps she was about to be thrown, the guard acting on Bandim's orders. Perhaps her son was in the courtyard below, waiting to watch her smash.

The guard took her arm, pulling her forward. His face looked strange, like a wisdom or a secret loomed behind his eyes.

"Your Grace, we must go to the temple," he said.

"The temple?" asked Phen. "Why?"

The guard took her hand and guided her down the spiraling stairs. "There are things that have happened over the course of the last thousand cycles you cannot understand. Folk have meddled with powers they have no knowledge of."

Phen startled at that. *Such as me.*

The guard went on, his words echoing off the curving stone walls.

"There are others who..." His voice softened and, for a moment, he looked vulnerable. "There are others who haven't done as they should. The world has rotted from the inside out. And if Bandim comes to the throne, it will be destroyed in fire. I need to get to the temple of Light so I can bring Mantos back."

"But he's dead," Phen said, her eyes filling. "He cannot come back."

The guard stopped and looked at her from a lower stair. There was something about his eyes that made her recoil. They were the eyes of the strange priestess from many cycles before, on the day she brought Mantos back from the dead. It was a look that spoke through centuries and said more than words ever could.

Phen swallowed. She had dealt in magic before, but it had made no difference. Mantos was dead. In the end, life turned full-circle.

"Trust me," the guard said, starting their downward journey again. "Please, trust me and come with me. We need to flee. The story of illness won't buy us much time."

"The story?" Phen asked.

The guard nodded. "A lie," he said. "A convenience. Bandim will find out soon enough, and if he catches us, we'll both be dead."

Phen's heart thundered as they slipped through the courtyard, away from the Grieving Tower, miraculously unseen. She scurried along, swaddled in the cloak of the unknown guard. She hadn't gathered the courage to ask who he was. Perhaps later. Perhaps when she was out of the long reach of her son's stranglehold—so long as the guard didn't kill her first.

Regardless of her fears, Phen followed in the wake of the guard, driven by desperation.

Shards of pain stabbed her as they turned a corner, away from the palace proper. They wound through the warren of servants' quarters and guards' barracks. Phen flinched at every shadow. How could Bandim do this to her? She loved him. She would have done the same for him, had it been he that tumbled from her arms. *They're my sons, equal to each other.*

That thought stopped her cold. The guard kept running, but Phen couldn't will her withered legs to move. They *were* her sons, she corrected herself. Now she had lost them both.

The guard turned and jerked to a stop. He sped back and took up Phen's arm, gentle enough for a commoner, but not gentle enough for the dowager empress. In spite of the situation, Phen wrenched herself free. "Don't touch me," she snapped.

The guard's eyes widened and he grabbed her again, this time with no fringe of delicacy. He pulled her close. "We don't have time to stand on ceremony."

In his sudden anger, his voice shifted. It sounded lighter, more like a female's. He took a deep breath to calm his ire and briefly closed his eyes.

Up close, Phen could see the fine details of the guard's face. He had thin planes, wide lips... She recoiled sharply, filled with shock. "You are *female*!"

The answer that came was simple: "Yes."

The female cast her guard's helm aside, the pretense of masculinity now gone. The stranger was transformed. She spoke with a clear voice, tinged with an accent Phen had never heard before. But strangest of all, before Phen's eyes, the female's skin and armor changed, now blue and purple, something Phen had never seen before.

"I am no palace guard," the female said, "but I can save your sons. Or at least, I can try. To do it, I need you." The female pulled Phen forward. "We need to get to the temple of Nunako."

The temple. Where Mantos was. Phen's lips started to form a question, but the female raised one sharp-clawed talon.

"Questions later," she said. "For now, we run."

This wasn't the first time Phen had trusted in a stranger. The priestess from long ago, muttering her spells, talking about a thread for a thread and a life for a life. Now there was this female, who'd already tricked her. How could she trust her? A phantom open-handed slap struck Phen, and Bandim's face loomed. No. She had to trust her. The only other option was death.

They escaped the compound of the palace over a high wall. Her body weakened from cycles of atrophy and already exhausted from their run, Phen despaired at the idea of scaling the sheer brick. She needn't have worried. The unknown female had both rope and grapple, and scaled the wall with Phen on her back as easily as taking an evening stroll. *Who are you?* Phen thought. *Why are you doing this?* She dared not voice her questions as they fled.

Sticking to back alleys, they hopped over stinking puddles of sewage and the bodies of paupers lying in the filth. As they crept towards the great mound upon which the temple sat, Phen's eyes brimmed. The shadows were her veil of mourning.

The grand spire of the temple was edged in the silver of the moons. Phen's throat closed. Mantos' body was lying within. Braslen's, too. *How can I go on?*

The strange female went to Phen's side. This time, the hand that tugged her along was gentle.

"Do not despair," she said. "I can bring your son back." At Phen's wide-eyed terror, she shook her head. "I am no Moon Rogue, but there is movement among the stars. Shadows are passing over us, and we need the Light. Please, trust me."

Ignoring the instinct to flee, Phen nodded. What would she return to? Death at her son's hands, or death on the streets as a beggar? There was no choice to make. She let the female lead her, ducking past the heavy presence of guards.

The temple echoed in its emptiness, but the cavernous interior was filled with light. Candles burned bright on every surface, lined on shelves, swirling in patterns on the floor. It was bright as day inside, and rightly so, for the Light guided souls home.

In the center, directly under the vaulting spiral of the roof, two bodies lay on pyres, awaiting their rebirth in flame. The roof would open, and their spirits would be released with the cleansing smoke.

Without thinking, Phen ran. Her tattered skirts billowed around her stick-thin legs, her strength returning at the sight of her family. Her clothes ripped as she clambered up the funeral pyre, exposed skin mauled by the kindling. When she reached the top, her limbs froze.

Her husband, now an old male she barely recognized, and her son, a mirror of his brother, both lay in state, preserved for viewing.

But dead. Cold.

Phen's body trembled, threatening to topple her from the pyre. She fell to her knees, sticks groaning under her weight. Splinters bit her legs, but she didn't care.

"Braslen... Mantos..."

The names were little more than squeaks. The other female mounted the pyre beside her, face set like carved marble. She crossed to Mantos' prone form. "I will carry your son."

"And...my husband?" Phen asked.

No change flickered over the female's face.

"I cannot bring him back," she said. "There was no sorcery in his death. The goddess has called him, and he must obey."

She stripped Mantos of his elaborate state dress and unwound the jewelry from his horns. Swiftly, she wrapped the body in a plain cloth.

"There's a ship waiting for us," she said. "It's a little way outside the city, but I can carry Mantos."

"A ship?" Phen asked. She couldn't take her eyes from her son's prone form. "A ship to where?"

"To a friend," the female said. "I can bring your son back, and perhaps even your other son. I need your help to do it, but it will all be for nothing if we don't leave now. We must go."

Phen's chest constricted with unasked questions. She clambered from the pyre and watched as the female hefted Mantos' body over her shoulders. Then she leapt to the floor with the grace of silk.

They slipped out of the temple of Light, into the waiting darkness.

CHAPTER EIGHT

Phen

When they reached the boat, Phen could cry no more. Instead her body was racked by dry sobs of desolation. Seeing her son's limp body slung over a pair of strange shoulders was enough to break her. What she did was for nothing. Phen gave up her life to save Mantos', and now he was dead anyway. *And I've lost Bandim, too.*

Her feet were sliced to ribbons. Her legs were caked with mud. Her chest was tight. Her heart ached. *My sons...*

Yet as they clambered onto a disused pier, towards a boat creaking and bobbing on the dark water, there was a drop of hope. The female with the cracked first horn said she could save Mantos, that she might save Bandim, too. Phen had to trust her. She had to take the chance.

But there was still lingering doubt. The last time Phen had trusted someone strange, it came at the cost of her life. The temple novice hadn't been a blue and purple stranger, but she was still strange, with her incantations and her eyes that spoke of centuries.

As she followed, slipping on slimy boards that threatened to give way beneath her, Phen's mind reeled. What if it was a trap? What if it was Bandim who awaited her, ready to slit her throat for her betrayal? Her hands trembled as she climbed into the rickety boat, but there was no one waiting in its dark embrace.

After laying Mantos along the length of the boat, the other female plucked up the oars. Phen fell to her knees, the craft bucking beneath her. She pulled her son's head into her lap, winding her claws through his elaborate death braids. Strangely, he wasn't stiff, and the rot of death hadn't permeated him. He felt cold but soft, as if he was simply sleeping.

But he was dead. This was what Phen had tried to stop before. Now she had to try to save him again.

Sticking close to the shadows that clung to the coast, the strange female rowed off.

Phen watched as the twinkling lights of the temple and palace dimmed. Then they rowed around a spur of land, and all that remained was rock and ruin.

Still stroking Mantos' cold head with one hand, her other atop his twined claws, still bedecked with rings, Phen swallowed back tears. She stared at the female. Now there was time for questions, and perhaps she would get answers. "Who are you? What is your name?"

The female gave a rare smile. Her long arms pumped back and forth, a steady cadence that propelled them deeper into the darkness.

"My name is Bomsoi," she said. "That is who I am. That is all I'll ever be."

Phen wound another of Mantos' braids around her talons. "What does that mean?" she asked.

The reply came with a thin laugh. "Nothing," Bomsoi said. "Nothing and nothing."

Phen's tongue burned with questions, but she kept her mouth shut. Did she mean her name *meant* nothing, or did it *mean* "nothing"? There was little point in asking for an explanation. The female was skillful in her evasiveness. So instead, Phen turned her eyes to the stars.

Some winked at her. Most were still. More impressive than any of the diamonds that hung on the dark blanket were the moons: three huge pearls, overlapping.

"The Lunar Awakening," she whispered. "By Nunako, I can't believe I've lived to see it."

Then the words swung back at her, a slap to the face. Tears budded again. She was alive and Mantos was not, she thought as she passed the back of her hand over her son's cold cheek.

"It is a time of great power," Bomsoi said. "It is a time that comes but once every thousand cycles. That is why I need you. That is why I need you *now*."

Terror and fury swirling within her, Phen snapped. "Where are we going? Why do you need me?"

Not flinching at the rage, Bomsoi jerked her head over her shoulder. "We're going there," she replied.

Before Phen could ask, she received the answer. Looming tall and proud above them, far enough from the shore that the darkness protected it, was a ship.

"Who—?"

"An old friend of Mantos'," Bomsoi said, "and of mine. He will protect us."

The sleek vessel was resplendent in cloth sails that rose like grey ghosts. Salt caught in Phen's throat. *By the goddess*, she thought. *I've never seen a ship so large.* One detail was familiar, though: the elaborate carving of a two-headed serpent on the prow, the gods Ethay and Apago, the joining of good and evil. That, combined with the beauty of the ship, meant only one thing.

"Althemerians!"

Bomsoi nodded as she brought them closer. The waves rippled and pulsed, as if the

Althemerian ship was the ocean's heart.

"Yes," Bomsoi said. "Althemer is one of the few lands untouched by Masvam hands. Your son was—is—or will be again—close to Prince Fonbir."

That name drew Phen back into her memories like a whiplash. Fonbir, Prince of the Island Queendom of Althemer. "The last time I saw Fonbir, he was just a youngling, only a few cycles older than Mantos and Bandim."

"He is no youngling now," Bomsoi replied.

She set the oars back in their notches as ropes rained from the deck above. Securing them to the hoops stem and stern of the little rowboat, she placed two claws in her mouth and whistled loud and clear into the night.

With that, they rose from the water.

Phen clutched the sides of the boat. Her stomach lurched more than it had on the waves. She watched as the silver-edged darkness below drew away. Soon enough, they were hoisted to the deck. A figure waited for them. Phen squinted through the darkness.

"Fonbir? Is...is that you?"

The young male cut a striking figure, gilded in the light of the moons. He stood with a straight back, short but commanding, with dark skin and armor black as night. He wore long embroidered robes, with a thick travelling cloak around his shoulders. Around his waist was a heavy chain, though he stood strong under its burden. His head fronds were red and clipped short. Like all high class and royal Althemerian males, he wore a veil over his face, just under the eyes, to protect him from the vision of others. Most striking of all his features were those eyes. Phen had never seen anything like them. They were deep-set and entirely white, apart from two pinprick pupils. The sight was exceptionally strange.

"Empress?" Fonbir asked, his voice low.

"Not anymore," Phen replied.

The prince clicked his talons, and an attendant stepped forward to help Phen onto the deck. The stillness shattered when Bomsoi stepped onto the ship, cradling Mantos' body. At the sight, Phen's legs turned to water. Only the attendant's grip stopped her from collapsing to the deck.

"Please, help me bring back my son," she breathed.

Nodding, Fonbir turned his attention to Mantos' prone form. Even in the darkness, pearls of tears glittered in his white eyes.

CHAPTER NINE

Bandim

By the time he reached Johrann Maa's chambers, Bandim's mind was in turmoil. If she'd sent for him, that meant she must be gravely ill. She knew better than to bother him with silly trifles. And if she was gravely ill, that meant she might die. And if she died, everything Bandim had worked for would fall apart.

He wrenched open the heavily-carved wooden doors of Johrann's chambers–those that had once belonged to his mother–and sped inside, only to stop short at the sight he beheld. Johrann was sitting at the dressing table that had been gifted to Empress Phen by King Eron of the Metakalans some cycles ago, carefully plaiting her long fronds. She started at his sudden appearance, and let her braids fall. "Your Grace?"

It took a moment for the significance of the scene to sink in. Clearly, there was no illness.

Bandim's rage erupted like a spurting flame. "Betrayal!"

Johrann sprang from her stool as if he had struck her with lightning.

"Your Grace?" she asked again.

Shoulders heaving as he seethed, Bandim strode forward, reaching out for her. His anger bloomed purple and his claws twitched, but a semblance of sense returned to him. He withdrew his hand as she recoiled. It wasn't her fault. It wasn't her scheme.

"I was told you were ill," Bandim said, clenching his teeth. "And here you are, fully well–and I look like a fool!"

Johrann tentatively leaned towards him. "Who said such a thing?"

"A guard in my mother's tower," he replied. As the words escaped him, a horrible possibility reared its head. His mouth went dry. What motivation could there be for such a lie, except..."I need to get back to the tower, *now*."

Johrann started to ask for clarification, but Bandim was in no mood to explain. He strode from her chambers, and she followed in his wake. He tried to keep as much decorum as he could as he crossed the palace. It wouldn't do for his subjects to see their emperor running back to his mother's tower in a frenzy. Yet inside, he indeed felt frenzied. Inside, he felt sick. How could it be possible? Who would want his mother, someone most undoubtedly thought was dead? Was it someone from inside the palace, or the family? Or was it a plot by his enemies to destabilize his rule right from the beginning? Possibilities raced through his mind like charging animals.

By the time he ascended the many steps to the top of the Widow's Tower, his hands were trembling so hard they could barely grip the thick carved banister bolted to the curving stone. When he reached the top, his worst fears were confirmed.

Johrann was right on his heels as he stopped at the threshold of the chamber that had been his mother's prison. Now it was empty save for the echoes of her presence, like the unmade bed and the meager scraps of uneaten food he had allowed her.

"She's gone," Bandim said. He balled his trembling hands into fists. "That guard, whoever he was, has done this. I want him found and brought to me. I'll slit his throat with my own claws!"

Johrann, who'd been hovering at his shoulder, slipped past him and entered the room. She crossed to the bed, tugged the edge of the covers to smooth the wrinkles, and turned back to him. Her expression made Bandim's blood boil. She was smiling.

His ire rose again like flames and he took one step forward, reaching out to strike the grin from her fine features. Instead of recoiling, she strode to him and grabbed the hand that sought to beat her. The lines around her eyes were tight with fear, but still she smiled. She clutched the hand in both of her own, squeezing tightly.

"Your Grace," she said, "please don't despair over this. Yes, your mother is gone. However, it's of no consequence."

The desire to strike her reared again, but Johrann still held onto Bandim's hand. He could have wrenched free from her grip, but something in her face made him stop and listen. It was the look of someone who was about to tell a truth. "Explain."

His single word evoked his power. Johrann briefly bowed her head and continued to smile.

"I know your mother was a cruel being," she said. "I know you wanted to give her what she deserved, after all these cycles. She deserves the fear. She deserves the pain. Most of all, you deserve the chance to exact these things upon her. I know you're angry that she's gone, and the idea that you've been betrayed by one of your own guards cuts deeply. You will find out who has done this, and you will punish them as you see fit. However, please don't despair beyond this personal loss. Your Grace, your mother was practically dead for many cycles. She is weakened and has no power. Whoever has taken her has simply given themselves the burden of a broken and useless female to bear."

Bandim thought on her words for a moment, but there was still doubt under the rage. "And what of how my enemies might take advantage of this situation?"

Johrann's laugh was light, and she reached for his other hand. She brought both to her lips, kissing the backs of his knuckles.

"Your Grace, in order for your mother's disappearance to have any value for those who seek to hurt and destroy you, she would have to have some value to you beyond the ability to take her life. Do you care for her?"

The stupidity of the question made Bandim's brows furrow. "Of course I don't."

Johrann smiled wider. "Would you go to great lengths to get her back?"

Bandim shook his head. As he answered, he followed Johrann's thoughts. His insides settled. "No."

"Do you love her?"

Bandim needed no time to think of his answer. "No. I never have."

"Then, Your Grace," Johrann continued, pressing the backs of her claws to her forehead, "what have your enemies achieved? What power have they gained over you? In truth, none. They can ransom her, or threaten to kill her, but will that mean anything to you?"

Squeezing her claws, Bandim brought her hands to his chest. "No."

Her truth calmed him and the love in her eyes soothed his ire.

"Then they cannot use this to hurt or undermine you," she said. "If they ask for a ransom, tell them they would have to pay you to take her back. If they threaten to kill her, thank them for saving you the burden of doing it yourself. I know you wanted to give her what she deserves, and to have that taken from you is intolerable. However, please don't fret, Your Grace. Your enemies can do nothing to you with this. She's of too little consequence."

"You're right," Bandim said. He grasped her chin and tipped her head up. He held her gaze. "What would I do without you, my Johrann? You're the voice of reason in my passion. You temper me and keep me even."

Unable to bow her head in humility, Johrann closed her eyes instead.

"I am but your servant, and the servant of Dorai," she said. She opened her eyes again. "And soon enough, you and Dorai will be one and the same. At the gathering of the pious in three days, I'll help you to finally fulfil the will of the goddess. Dorai will return, living in you."

Bandim released Johrann's chin and slid his hand to the side of her face. He caressed her armored cheeks with his thumbs, staring into the deep grey of her eyes.

That was his next step. First, he had sought to seize the crown. It was his hatchright, taken from him by his mother's wretched love for his brother. Taking the throne had been easy, thanks to Johrann. No one suspected his hand in Mantos' death. How could they? There was nothing to suspect. The young male had collapsed in his grief. That was what they all thought, because that was the story Johrann had seeded in them. Her cleverness knew no limits, Bandim thought. She primed a few servants, some merchants, and even a handful of nobles loyal to the Dark, with more details to spread. While it was tragic to lose the emperor and the heir so quickly in succession, had it actually revealed a weakness that was now gone? If Mantos could succumb to grief so easily, would he have made a good ruler? He'd been known for his bravery in the battles of his father, but had his toils in war spread cracks through his strength? Had it drained his resilience?

The answer Johrann provided for those mouths to spread was yes, he was weak. No, he wouldn't have made a good ruler, and wasn't it better that this weakness was exposed before he ever took the crown? While Bandim may have believed in things most folk found difficult to accept, wasn't it for the best that a strong and true ruler was to wear the crown? Those few mouths spread her words through their circles, and soon enough, the entire court, city, and country were agreed in the idea that Mantos would never have been a good emperor. It was much better that Bandim, the true heir, was plucking up the mantle of rule. It wouldn't be long until he was crowned. By the time he was, Bandim fully expected Mantos to be a distant memory.

That was only the first part of their plan. The second part was the most important, and the part that would allow Bandim to achieve everything that he'd always dreamed of. Within days, Johrann promised to fulfil that which was promised in the Book of Divine Tears: *The One of Two, pushed aside, will rise like flames, and the goddess will inhabit him.*

"I am the One of Two," he said.

Johrann laid her palms flat on his hands, still pressed to the side of her face.

"And I am the True Believer," she replied. "I will ask for the return of the goddess, and it will be granted. Now is a time of destiny and triumph. Dorai will return to this world and live within you. You will become her, and you will know no bounds."

Bandim leaned forward to kiss her. Johrann's lips felt as they always did; soft and welcoming, yet cold. At their touch, the memory of his mother's disappearance seemed like an ancient tale.

"We will succeed," he said, kissing her again. "You'll bring me everything that I want."

"I live but to serve you," Johrann said. "I will deliver you power and glory. I will crown you with Dorai's power, and once I have, no one will be able to stand in your way. They can steal your mother, but they cannot stop you from spreading the truth of Dorai across the world."

"I'll make them all see," Bandim said. "And I promise you, I'll be the ultimate winner. And I will have my mother back, and I will kill her."

Johrann grinned. "Nothing can stop you."

Bandim grinned back. "Nothing can stop me."

CHAPTER TEN

Phen

The journey to Kubodinnu, the Althemerian capital, took many days. At all times, Phen stayed with her son's body. Strangely, it didn't grow foul and mangled like unburned corpses did. It remained cold, as if frozen.

Fonbir stayed with Mantos too, grief etched into his young face. He and Phen sat on either side, eyes fixed on Mantos' prone form. They stayed silent in their grief for some time.

When Fonbir broke the silence, he spoke his own language. "We were in love."

Phen could understand him well. She knew many languages, for it was part of her training. House Yru had betrothed her to Braslen Tiboli from the moment she'd hatched, and Phen spent her whole life working towards that goal. When she gendered, it didn't matter if she was male or female. Either way, she was to marry the future emperor. That was the way of the Masvam empire. Male-female unions were more desirable, for they made having younglings easier. But there were always ways around these things, and once an emperor decreed than an egg was his, that was all that mattered.

A wan smile crossed Fonbir's lips, muted behind his veil.

"We visited one another, and shared letters, and we knew we had to be together." His smile faded. "That was before the great schism between our countries. Your husband wanted to marry my mother," he said, casting her a sidelong glance. "But Mother knew that you weren't dead. No matter what Braslen told her, Mother had an insider. She knew you were still alive, if incapacitated.

"When she said no to his request, your husband suggested a different union. He wanted my sisters to marry your sons. Again, Mother would have none of it. She wouldn't let her queendom fall to Masvam rule."

Phen gave a brief nod. Listening to Fonbir transported her back to her youngling days, spending hours in lessons, being lectured on great histories and empires. Before she had slipped away from the world, Althemer had been an ally of the Masvams, despite their differences. Now it seemed everything had changed.

"Mother severed all ties with the Masvam Empire, and forbade me from seeing Mantos," Fonbir went on. "I wasn't even allowed to send letters." His face softened, and he touched Mantos' shoulder. "It didn't stop us. We made a codex, exchanged secrets, told lies so we could kindle our flame. And we did, and I think we grew deeper in love because of it."

Phen grew bold and placed her hand atop Fonbir's.

"I wouldn't expect any less from my young," she said. "I would have done the same."

The idea that her son was in love with another male wasn't a shock to Phen. Those great histories she had learned of were full of all kinds of unions. Two males, two females, a male and a female, and the complicated weave of consorts when partners were joined in union by marriage bonds, but not by passion. Such was the way when younglings were betrothed to one another before they gendered.

"I'm sorry that our countries are now enemies," Phen said. "I knew your mother, briefly, many cycles ago."

Fonbir nodded. "It's a great shame, but it's reality."

For the remainder of the journey, the two huddled in the cabin with Mantos. The coast of Althemer eventually appeared through the murk of darkness and fog. Fonbir slipped off, his belt-chain clinking, leaving Phen alone with her son and her weariness. Eventually, they docked.

Bomsoi returned, a clatter of Althemerians with her. There was something long and dark draped across her hands. Phen stilled, narrowing her eyes.

"Your Grace," Bomsoi said. "It's time to leave. However, neither you nor your son can be seen. No one is to know you are here." She held her hands out, letting the length of dark fabric drop. "Wear this so no one will see you."

Phen accepted the garment—a heavy cloak with a deep hood—and turned to Mantos. "What of my son?" she asked.

Bomsoi gestured for the Althemerians behind her to come forward. They approached the body and worked their claws underneath it. Together, they lifted him. Phen reached for her son, but they carried him away.

"He will be brought into the palace within a crate," Bomsoi said. "He will be safe, I assure you."

"I don't want to be parted from him."

Phen went to follow her son's prone form, but Bomsoi stepped between them. She placed her strong hands on Phen's shoulders.

"He will be safe," she repeated. She drew the hood over Phen's horn crest, arranging the fabric so it shrouded her in shadow. Then she reached into her pocket and withdrew a veil, attaching it across Phen's face. "For now, you must come with me. It's dark, and there are few folks about. Still, keep your head down and say nothing."

Phen remembered little of the journey from boat to palace. She was bundled into a carriage and, despite her fears, the rocking of the journey made her sleep. She dreamed of Mantos and Bandim, the younglings she never knew, playing and fighting.

She awoke with a jolt. The carriage door was opened, and Bomsoi reached out a hand to help Phen down. Light was spreading from the horizon.

There was no pomp, no ceremony for the arrival of a foreign empress. *Of course not*, Phen thought. She was no empress. Not anymore. So much had changed, and nothing for the better. She followed Bomsoi and Fonbir from the carriage, through winding streets she didn't know, eventually passing through a narrow gate in the palace walls. It was an ancient thing, half-hidden by gnarled vines, yet the gate didn't creak when it opened. It was silent, and its silence spoke of how often it was used. Things weren't so different at the bones of life, Phen thought. All kings and queens, emperors and empresses, had their secrets, their hidden ways.

Phen was such a secret now, hidden in the twisting lower vaults of the Althemerian palace.

She didn't remember falling into bed. What she did remember was the glorious feeling of a feather mattress, then nothing.

When she woke, it was night again. There was a rolled parchment on the table, lying in a pool of yellow candlelight. It was sealed with blue wax, the sigil of the Althemerian empress: a twisted two-headed serpent, a crown above each head.

The floor rushes crunched beneath Phen's feet. The wax broke in whitening shards. The parchment scuffed as she unrolled it. It was a summons to meet Queen Valentia. Phen held the scroll for a moment, glancing around. A secret she may have been, but she still needed to be presentable for an audience with the queen.

Fresh clothing had been hung over a screen, and within moments of her rising, an attendant entered with hot water in an ewer. He kept his eyes averted like a servant should, and left without a word. However, he stopped at the threshold and turned. This time he looked her straight in the eye; then he spat on the floor and left. In the world of her own empire, she would have had him struck for such impudence and sentenced to three weeks in a cell. But this wasn't her world. She was a Masvam, and the enemy here. Even the water couldn't take the edge from that chill.

Having washed, Phen dressed in the strange clothing. Instead of the elaborately wrapped and tied Masvam garments she was used to, she wore a fitted tunic over a finely woven shirt. The tunic was blue leather, stamped with the twin serpent motif. Her legs, so used to being free under her long robes, were trapped in fabric hose. In the empire, only commoners and soldiers wore hose. The empress would never have been permitted to wear such a thing.

As she pulled on the tall leather boots that had been left for her, Phen shook her head. She was looking at someone else. This wasn't her at all. She turned to the long, polished plate, surveying the stranger inside it. It would have been easier if they'd given her clothes like Fonbir's, long robes that covered the body from neck to ankles. At least that would have been similar in some way. But that clearly wasn't the fashion on Althemer.

Turning from the plate, Phen breathed deeply and knocked on the door. It opened. She was flanked on both sides by guards, one male and one female.

Unable to help herself, Phen scanned their clothing. It was identical from the tunic to the hose, from the helmets to the dagger scabbards on their left hips. Phen corrected her earlier thought on clothing: it wasn't the fashion for *royals* on Althemer. Her lessons came back to her again. On this island nation, the common folk and the military were mixed, male and female alike. For the royals and other high-status individuals, things were different. Males wore veils to protect their virtue, and chains around their waists to show deference to their mothers or wives. They were placed on pedestals by their families, required to be pure and perfect. They had to be. Males were the ones who were sent from their homes to other countries, to marry into royal families far from home. The females stayed behind, required to protect and preserve the queendom.

The female guard cleared her throat, pulling Phen from her thoughts.

"We are to bring you to Her Highness," she said, eyes glinting beneath her helmet.

"Of course," Phen said. "Lead the way."

The female stepped in front of her, and the male stepped behind. Together the three wound their way through a warren of dark corridors.

The passages narrowed as they walked, and there were no windows. The darkness was lit only by the torch the female plucked from the wall outside Phen's room. Phen's heart quickened as they continued deeper into the palace. They met no one else on their journey—apt, Phen thought, for keeping her a secret. She knew she wasn't going to meet the queen in a public space, or even somewhere in the palace proper. The darkness made it seem like she was deep underground, hidden from prying eyes.

Reaching a heavy wooden door, the female guard struck it twice, then stood back.

"Enter," a voice said.

The guard twisted the metal handle and opened the door. Phen followed her into a small room, the male guard behind them.

Light from torches danced on the stone walls, and against the wide wooden shutters that lined one wall. *Shutters*, Phen thought. That meant they were above ground after all.

The room was sparsely furnished, with a simple table decorated with dripping candles in stout metal holders. Around the table were six leather-padded chairs. Queen Valentia sat at the head. Around her shoulders was a thick and winding serpent. It slithered around her neck, but never tightened. It nuzzled its hooded head into the queen's pointed ear.

On her left sat Prince Fonbir. He gave Phen a brief smile, while another female regarded her with cold eyes. She was younger than Fonbir, but alike enough to him that Phen knew they were siblings. Fylica, that was her name. It struck Phen as well that there was another princess—an older one—who wasn't present: Valaria, heir to the Althemerian throne.

Queen Valentia was older than Phen, but likely younger than she looked. Kingship, queenship, the mantle of an emperor—all these things led to the same conclusion: premature demise. For some it was death in battle. For others it was the slow crush of power and responsibility. Valentia's red fronds were fading, growing translucent with age. Her arms bore the outline of once-strong muscles, now weakening. Her brown skin was tight on her knuckles.

Dismissing the guards, Valentia bade Phen to take the free chair. Bowing, Phen did as she was told.

"My son tells me your son is dead," the queen said, her voice level as she passed one talon down her serpent's long body. "I also know that your husband is dead, and that your other son, Bandim, is on the throne." She shook her head, her expression softening. "For all of these things, I am sorry." She sat back, her horn jewelry tinkling as it moved. "In truth, I thought you were dead as well. I hadn't heard anything of you in many cycles, since my spies were all ousted by your husband."

Phen clasped her claws on her lap. "I suppose I was dead, in a way," she said. "Now I don't know what I am."

Fylica leaned forward. She was the image of her queen, an echo of the past

"You are still responsible for your son's actions," she snapped. "Even before his father's death rights, Bandim must have been planning his military campaign. He's rolled his armies over Metakala, gaining more territory for your wretched empire. Even now, my sister is risking her life to save those countries your people would destroy, and—"

"Fylica," Fonbir snapped.

The younger female tutted and shook her head. "Your love for the Masvams is well known, brother."

Fonbir went to react, but the queen slammed her hand on the table, commanding silence and obedience in one movement. Phen jerked back.

"Enough of this folly," the queen said. Her serpent stiffened and hissed. Valentia glared at one offspring and then the other. "You shame me with your actions."

The prince and the princess sat back, the former more cowed than the latter. Fylica glowered. Fonbir looked away.

Queen Valentia leaned back and her serpent relaxed. She laid her claws on the table and drummed them. The torchlight glinted on her rings, which held jewels the same bright blue as her serpent's eyes.

"It was not my choice to bring you here," she said to Phen. "It's best if no one knows who you are. Your late husband drove a deep wedge between our countries. Masvams aren't welcome in our land." Her eyes gleamed, grey and cold; then they warmed. "However, I trust my son and I trust my advisor."

Phen narrowed her eyes. *Advisor?*

The queen called out, and a figure entered the room, tall and imposing with a cracked first horn, dressed in an embroidered black tunic. Phen turned.

"Bomsoi," she said. "Of course."

With a shallow bow, Bomsoi stood off to the side. Queen Valentia gestured to her.

"The Stranger—Bomsoi—has been in my service for many cycles," she said. "She's been sent to us from the gods. There are things she knows and does that I will never understand. But I trust that she has come from beyond the veil of death to help us, as is written in scripture. The Stranger asked if she could retrieve Mantos' body as a holy work, and she told me you weren't dead. And she tells me that Bandim, on the Masvam throne, will bring about our destruction. And therefore, you are here—as is your son's body."

Valentia leaned back and surveyed Phen for what felt like an age. Phen felt a sting of panic. "What are you going to do with me?" she asked.

The queen looked to Bomsoi, who stepped forward.

"I need to resurrect your son," Bomsoi said. "The gods have commanded it. He shouldn't be dead."

Phen's eyes bulged. "*What?*"

Valentia ignored her and continued. Her serpent wound slowly around her neck. "We cannot permit Bandim to continue on the throne. His father is barely dead, and he's already cutting a path to us through forest and flesh. The sovereignty of the Queendom of Althemer will not bow to Bandim Tiboli, or to any other Masvam. If we help return Mantos to life and to the throne, he will owe us a great debt. He will stop the destruction and leave us in peace."

Ears ringing, Phen gripped the edge of the table.

"But what are you going to do with me?" she asked again. "Why did you bring me here, along with my son's body?"

Bomsoi clasped her talons behind her back. All eyes were on Phen, though only Fonbir's and Bomsoi's were friendly.

"This isn't the first time Mantos has died, is it?" Bomsoi asked.

The question cut at Phen's throat, and her mouth fell open. "How do you know that?"

"It's common knowledge," Fylica said. Her look of disgust made Phen recoil. "The empress meddled with evil magic, and it cost her life."

"It wasn't evil," Phen said, her voice wavering. "There was a novice, in the temple of Nunako. It wasn't magic, it was prayer. It was the will of the goddess. She...she said she could save Mantos—and she did. Yes, at the cost of my life, for she used my thread to bring back Mantos' own. But it wasn't evil magic." With each word, her tone grew more desperate. She looked to Bomsoi, the stranger in purple and blue. "Was it?"

Bomsoi nodded, a slow and deliberate movement. "It was magic," she said. "It was an evil power."

Phen buried her face in her talons, trying to suppress her sobs. Of course it was magic. It couldn't have been anything else, and deep down, she'd always known it. But magic was wrong. Magic was evil. Dabbling in it damned you to eternal punishment. It meant you were tainted, far from the loving embrace of Nunako and her Light.

"What have I done?" she asked.

Queen Valentia's voice rang through the torch-lit chamber.

"You have sinned," she said, "but Ethay and Apago teach us that sin can be forgiven. An evil deed can be outweighed by a good deed." She gestured to Bomsoi. Her serpent followed her point. "The Stranger walks among us so we can all atone for our sins. If you submit to her, you will be forgiven—by the gods, at least."

Phen looked up again. Valentia's eyes were cold and unyielding. But Bomsoi's were bright, shining with a vehemence that gave her a sliver of hope.

"I can save Mantos," Bomsoi said, "and I may be able to save Bandim. For the sake of all you believe in, and all those you love, allow me to do what must be done."

The world weighed on Phen's shoulders. The maw of the afterlife opened before her. Phen's throat tightened. What should she do? What *could* she do? If she didn't do as the Althemerians asked, they'd kill her. Even if she did what they wanted, what would they do with her afterward? Once she'd been used, in whatever way, to bring Mantos back to life, what further use would she be? Phen had hung between life and death for so long that she knew nothing of the Masvam way. Once upon a moon, she would have known all Braslen's strategies. He told her everything in the confines of their chamber, his head in her lap, speaking of his hopes and dreams and victories.

She had no such knowledge now. Any of her intelligence was twenty cycles out of date, belonging to the wrong emperor. Why bother to keep a secret when it was no longer needed? They could do away with her in silence, a quick slit of the throat in the darkness.

Memories of Mantos, dead as a youngling, then dead again on his funeral pyre, returned to her. What did it matter if she died? All that mattered was her sons and their lives. Resolve steeling, Phen looked from Bomsoi to the queen. She clasped her hands on her lap. She nodded.

"I'll do it," she said.

Queen Valentia inclined her head, but she did not smile. She spoke to Bomsoi, but kept her eyes on Phen. "Tonight, Stranger?"

"Tonight, Your Highness," Bomsoi replied.

Phen swallowed. She should have asked questions. What was tonight? What would she have to do? But her throat was dry, and the words wouldn't come.

CHAPTER ELEVEN

Emmy

Shaking her head, Emmy huffed. "No, that's wrong."

Charo glanced up, bewildered. The ties of her mella, a Metakalan garment that wrapped around the waist and between the legs, hung like limp straw. She shrugged. "I don't know what I'm doing!"

"That's clear," Emmy replied.

Laughing, Charo thrust the ties into Emmy's claws. "You do it!"

Emmy gladly acquiesced.

Her chamber was a mess of colored fabric. Clothing was strewn over the bed frame and pooled on the floor, an eruption of memories from a dusty trunk. *I haven't seen most of this in cycles*, Emmy thought. *I've rarely had anything to celebrate.*

But this Middlemerish festival was different. It meant something, and Emmy's determination burned. *I'll make it special. I have to.*

Charo wasn't as impressed by the scenario. "I don't like these," she said, plucking at the mella. "They're not a northern thing."

Emmy tutted. "Does the north know anything?" she asked, mirth swirling in her eyes. "It sounds like a different world."

"In a lot of ways, it was," Charo replied.

Tying elaborate knots to secure the mella, Emmy chuckled. Mella twisted tightly around the waist and left the lower legs exposed, a deliberate design to showcase the intricate ribbons of Metakalan footwear.

"I'm surprised I can remember how to do this," Emmy said as she worked, pulling the mella's ties round and round, winding them in looping knots. Done, she picked a bulky package from the bed and pressed it into Charo's hands. "Here. You'll need these."

Unwrapping the cloth, Charo's jaw fell. "New shoes!" she said. "Just like yours!"

A warm wave of pleasure flowed through Emmy at her friend's elation. Charo's arrival had been unexpected, but now was not unwelcome. Since coming to the apothecary, Charo had taken the brunt of Krodge's vitriol. To her, it meant nothing. To Emmy, it meant everything. To get through the day without the crone screeching in her ear, or hitting her, or belittling her... She ducked her head to hide her smile. It meant more than Charo could know.

Charo set the wooden sandals on the floor and stepped into them. "How do you wear the ribbons?" she asked, eyeing them warily.

"I'll show you," Emmy replied. Gathering the red ties, she arranged them in a graceful crisscross. Satisfied, she stood. "There. You're done."

Charo took in the outfit, wiggling her clawed toes. "It looks beautiful."

Emmy fetched a polished plate and held it up, giving Charo a better look. "It looks beautiful on *you*."

The younger female stepped forward, placing tentative claws on the shining brass. "Is that me?"

Emmy nodded. "It is. You look wonderful."

Charo's skin had gained a lustrous hue, and her fronds sprouted red and thick. The shine of her green armor made her scars fade away.

"I can't believe that's me," Charo said. "Thank you."

In the plate, her eyes found Emmy's. Waving off the thanks, Emmy set it aside. "I'm not done," she said, "so don't thank me yet."

Reaching for a smaller package, a smaller wrapping of soft cloth, Emmy smiled. "I hope you like it."

Charo accepted the bundle, blinking. She waited, her talons poised.

"Open it," Emmy said.

Needing no further encouragement, Charo undid the wrapping. The cloth unfurled like a soft flower, revealing the precious surprise inside.

"Oh my," Charo breathed.

In her hands rested a headdress wrought of spun silver. Its loops and coils were strung with red and yellow stones, polished to a high sparkle. Charo looked up, struggling for words. "Emmy, this is... It's..."

Saying nothing, Emmy placed the headdress on Charo's horns, arranging the stones in a gentle flow. She stepped back, surveying her work with a wide smile.

"You can't go out on Middlemerish without a headdress," she said, "so there you are."

She could have said more, but she didn't. Instead, she slotted her own headdress over her horns, peering in the plate to arrange it.

"I've never worn this," she said. "I bought it a few cycles ago, thinking I'd get the chance to go out once I'd gendered." Her laugh was cold. "How wrong I was. But now I get to wear it at last." She turned to Charo. "I'm glad."

"I am, too," Charo replied, her claws endlessly plucking at her clothes. "I always wanted to go to a celebration."

"Today will be a good day," Emmy declared. "It'll make up for all those cycles of nothing." Emmy raised an eyeridge and smirked. "Zecha wants to give you a wonderful first Middlemerish. He has a good heart, if not always a clear head." *Not to mention he's grown quite fond of you.* "Do you remember what to do when we arrive?"

Nodding fervently, Charo grinned. "Yes," she said. "I have to give the traditional greeting. I remember it."

"Good, good. Now let's go," Emmy said in a tone that brooked no argument. "We don't want to be late."

Not sparing Krodge a farewell, they strode into the intense sun.

The Central Circle, a long circular street on which the apothecary sat, was a hive, full of colorful revelry. Every patch of grass and cobble was covered. There were food and drink stalls, jugglers, bards, and even a few rolling stages, from which companies of travelling actors plied their trade.

Vaemar, huge feline creatures used as mounts or to pull carts, languished in the sunshine, suffering under their heavy coats. Krodge had owned a vaemar once upon a moon, but Emmy tried not to think about Zesi. His loss was still too painful, though he'd died and been burned cycles before. Apart from Zecha, he'd been her only friend. She'd spent many nights in the rear yard, curled into his long fur. A gentle thing, his dark eyes only ever looked at her with love.

Pushing away the thoughts to stop tears welling, Emmy shaded her eyes and glanced up at the clear blue sky. Now wasn't the time to focus on loss, but was a time of celebration. She was determined it would be, for once, a good day.

Flocks of gargons flew overhead, leathery creatures that carried messages of celebration to and fro across the town, and from even further afield. They hooted out hoarse cries, the sound mingling with the cacophony of music and merrymaking.

However, all the noise and color and action of the Central Circle still wasn't enough to camouflage the strangeness of Emmy and Charo. Passersby stopped to stare as they passed.

Emmy kept her chin up and her back straight, trying to let the words wash over her. Still, anxiety at being among the townsfolk gnawed in the pit of her stomach. She could feel their gazes biting into her. Their words were loud and cruel.

"It's the Moon Rogue."

"And she's with that slave."

"Filthy, the both of them."

"They're tainted for certain."

Truthfully, Emmy would gladly have spent Middlemerish inside, as she always did, for this very reason. Folk were worse than cruel. But Charo had lit with excitement the moment Zecha suggested a celebration, and Emmy had no intention of taking that joy away from her.

As they strode forward, they passed through the sea of scowling faces. Charo glanced around, nervous, a little behind Emmy but close to her shoulder. Many of the looks were directed at her. Infamous enough in the town as the stranger who almost died, her status as a former slave turned nearly as many heads as Emmy did.

"Don't worry about them," Emmy muttered, even though worry flowed through her. "They're not worth your notice."

Charo nodded, but the fear on her face didn't abate. For good reason, Emmy thought. A mob of revelers could turn violent at the click of a talon.

They passed the tree without attaching a prayer. Even so, Emmy found herself making a wish.

Please let us have a free life, she thought. *Me, Charo, and Zecha. Let us be free.*

It seemed a foolish thing, wishing when she knew it wouldn't be granted. Regardless, she'd done it, and she supposed it couldn't do any harm.

The walk to Zecha's rented rooms was short and, thankfully, apart from stares and comments, uneventful. The house was a lopsided wooden structure that looked like it was held together by prayer alone. Zecha waited for them at the ramshackle gate, an easy smile on his face. Beside him was a smaller male, who Emmy recognized as Zecha's landlord Mr. Charber. He looked at Zecha with indulgent eyes. Zecha beckoned them towards the house and gripped their forearms in turn. Charber did the same.

"Welcome, welcome!" Zecha said, as if the house was his own.

Emmy accepted their embraces. Charber was pleasant enough: had never insulted her, was quiet, and kept to himself, so his touch was tolerable.

There was a pause as they waited. Emmy tapped Charo's shoulder.

"Oh, yes!" Charo said. She composed herself to recite the traditional greeting. "Thank you for inviting us to your home on this most joyous occasion."

Emmy patted her arm. "Well done," she whispered.

Zecha grinned all the wider. "The pleasure of your company makes this day great," he replied.

His eyes lingered longer on Charo than on Emmy. It didn't go unnoticed, and Charo grinned. Emmy watched the interplay, the flirtation as strange to her as the feel of the headdress on her horns. She didn't understand physical attraction, and had no desire to puzzle it out.

With the formalities over, Charber ushered them to a long grassy area at the rear of the house, which was well-cultivated with vegetables and bustling with folk celebrating. The smell of roasting meat floated through the air long before they saw the fire pit in the middle of the yard. A thin male shimmered through the smoke, turning a glistening animal on a spit. With a splutter, Mr. Charber scuttled to him, lecturing about the appropriate speed for handle-turning. The male didn't seem concerned.

Zecha led Emmy and Charo to an area away from the crackling fire. Several plump cushions were spread on the ground, nestling in the shade of a thick-trunked Daxo tree. Some folk sat there already, other tenants and neighbors. Though Emmy settled apart from them, a few still threw her filthy looks. Younglings of mixed ages stopped their game of chase to stare, slack-jawed, as the Moon Rogue sat among them. Emmy kept her gaze on her friends, trying her best to ignore their ignorance.

The smell of meat drifted on the warm breeze. Emmy wiped sweat from her brow. The Merish day was stifling, and the fire didn't help. Even the meager shade from the Daxo tree did little to comfort them. Emmy watched as the cook labored in the heat, using a rusty hook to fish a large pot from a nook in the flames.

Glancing upwards, she peered through her claws at the blueness beyond the leaves. At the gargons as they passed, free as the wind. At the wisps of clouds floating slowly overhead. Emmy was often jealous of clouds and gargons and anything that had its autonomy. If only she could have the same. If only.

Zecha appeared with three cups of sweet wine, breaking her musing. "When was the last time you went to a Middlemerish Festival?" he asked Emmy as he passed them around. "You've never come to one of mine before."

He fell onto a cushion, arranging his legs and tail underneath him.

"I don't know if I ever went to one," Emmy replied. She swirled the wine. Sunlight edged the ripples. "If I ever did, it was with Krodge when I was no older than a hatchling." She drank. "Anyway, I didn't much want to go to festivals, considering how folk treated me," she added, casting a sidelong glance at the other guests. "I knew I'd be stared at more than the actors and clowns."

Zecha's face puckered with anger and sorrow. "That's the past," he said, loud enough for everyone to hear. He raised his cup to the small gathering. "To peace in our time, to friendship, and to keeping the Masvams at bay."

The toast was meekly met, though Charo and Emmy joined in with pleasure.

A tinkling bell sounded, declaring the feast ready. Zecha was up and back with three servings before Emmy could blink. He gave each of them a thin wooden plate, heaped high with carved slices of meat, vegetables, bread, cheese—everything that made a feast great.

Zecha gladly explained this, and the traditions of Middlemerish and the moons, to Charo when she asked.

"At the beginning of everything, Nunako claimed the moons in the Arc of the Sky," he said. His smile was one of pleasure, though Emmy suspected it had more to do with Charo's proximity than the lore of the moons. "When they come together on the Lunar Awakening, Nunako, the Lady of Light, walks among us again, like she did so many cycles ago. Each of the moons has a different meaning," he went on. "Dato is the yellow moon, which Nunako placed closest. The smallest and slowest, it reminds us that in times of trouble, you don't need to be the largest or strongest to survive. You just need to be brave. Dato isn't as swift in the sky as the others, but it never fails to rise and fall.

"Rafa, the Middlemoon," he continued, "is the Heart. The heart is in the middle, because everything we do should come from love. It's fast, because sometimes we act by our hearts without consulting our heads.

"So the last moon is fastest of all. Akata is behind the others because it's the seat of wisdom, and it's the fastest because we need to be reminded to use our heads. It encircles everything, as all actions should be taken not just with heart, but with knowledge."

Good food and good drink flowed freely, and as the sun sank below the horizon, the little group turned their attention to the skies. Nunako's three faces were upon one another, and it was time to spread the Light and welcome the Lady of Light back to the world.

As was tradition, Metakalans bought fireworks from the Belfoni for an elaborate Middlemerish display. The brighter the celebrations were, the happier the Goddess' faces would be. The more they talked to one another, the stronger their power, and the more likely they would answer the folks' prayers.

Soon enough, the first deep boom resounded beneath their chest-plates. The wine-loosened crowd cheered in anticipation. But there was no brightly colored eruption.

Emmy sat up, listening. "What's going—?"

The rest of her sentence was lost under another deafening boom—then another. Emmy shared a sharp glance with Charo and Zecha before the three leapt to their feet and tore out to the street. Another explosion split their ears. The air sizzled.

"What's happening?" Zecha asked.

Emmy's throat was empty, her mouth dry. Faces appeared in windows, and coils of females churned in confusion. Then fast and heavy footfalls tore towards them. A burly female reached them, waving her arms.

"In the name of the goddess," she cried, breathless, "we're being attacked!"

With those words the bottom fell out of Emmy's world.

CHAPTER TWELVE

Johrann Maa

Johrann Maa, alone and resplendent in her blue and purple, kissed the floor in front of the Great Shrine. The black marble sparkled in the scant torchlight. *Now is the time*, she thought. *The Lunar Awakening is upon us. We must do what must be done.* With that thought, she prayed.

"Great Goddess of the Dark, Unparalleled Dorai, please bestow upon me your grace and mercy as I humbly supplicate myself before your Divine Presence. Help me as I carry out your bidding and put your great plan into motion, so that we may destroy those who defame your magnificence."

Johrann kissed the floor again, then sat back on her bare heels. Her robe fanned out and her black fronds pooled around her as she leaned forward. Lighting another stick of incense, she placed it in a holder amongst the others. Her eyes slid upward to the glittering effigy of Dorai before her.

Beneath the figure's bare feet was the dead body of the False Goddess Nunako, elaborately finished with red jeweled blood that trickled into a pool at the foot of the statue.

Dorai's polished eyes stared, unwavering. Johrann held her powerful gaze. The goddess had always been her true companion, the only friend Johrann had through cycle upon cycle of degradation, of being cast out by others for being a Moon Rogue. She barked out a laugh. None of the heathens of the world knew what a Moon Rogue really was. They cast the term about in slander, throwing it onto anything they did not understand. To be a Moon Rogue was to be a True Believer in Dorai and her wonders. It was the purest vocation in the world.

Johrann stood, her robes falling like tongues of flame, and pressed a kiss to the tips of her talons. She placed it at Dorai's feet as a slow smile spread across her lips. The Lunar Awakening was upon them. Soon Bandim would fulfil Dorai's truth, would bring the goddess back to the world, and all followers of Nunako and the so-called Light would supplicate themselves to the rule of the True God.

They might steal Mantos' body. They might free his mother. But they wouldn't succeed in their folly. The word of Dorai, as written in the Book of Divine Tears, would be done. Johrann had erred once and would not err again. That was what was written.

She slipped into her false Masvam colors and out of the high-ceilinged chamber, tall and imposing, into the depths of the underground temple. The disappearance of Mantos Tiboli's body was unfortunate, but was of little consequence. She couldn't feel his presence, as he was dead, and the dead couldn't interfere in their affairs. As for his mother? Johrann chuckled aloud, the noise echoing through the cavernous and pillared corridor. Phen could do nothing. She was a waste, a fool.

Johrann strode on silent feet through the empty corridors. The believers had been summoned and had dutifully assembled in the great underground amphitheater. The only light was a scant shimmer from a wall torch or candelabra, but Johrann needed none. *I do not need light to obscure my vision*, she thought. *The Darkness is clear, if only your eyes are open to it. They are all blind to the truth. They cling to desperation. It's folly.*

The polished gemstones of her horn jewelry cast colorful streaks along the smooth walls. She sped towards the sunken central hall. Two temple novices wrenched the door open, bowing as she passed into her realm. Johrann was met by her priestesses, all dressed in black. They were females who'd dedicated their lives to serving within the temple and worshipping Dorai. They formed a guard around her, silent and pious.

As soon as Johrann crossed the threshold, the central hall grew silent. All eyes were on her behind their black masks. Every seat in the hall was taken, and poorer believers lined the back walls and the walkways. They leapt from Johrann's path, not daring to touch the High Priestess.

There were believers from all walks of life in the amphitheater. There were common weavers and potwashes. There were soldiers, military leaders, and all those loyal worshippers of the True Goddess who'd infiltrated the Masvam government, paving the way for Bandim and Dorai. There were those Johrann had known for many cycles, the earliest of her converts. There were also newer believers, still bright and flaming in the power of their conversion.

All her life, Johrann had worked to build this world. Yes, it was for Dorai, and yes, it was to put Bandim in his rightful place on the Masvam throne as the goddess incarnate in this world. But more than that, it was to fill the gaping wound in Johrann's heart.

As a hatchling she had been abandoned. As a youngling she had been rejected. As her anger grew, a strange heat had invaded her, as if there was fire at her fingertips. It was a welcome power. Young Johrann could heal wounds with her hands, or tear gashes through flesh with no need of a knife. She could save, or she could condemn. But the folk feared her, no matter how hard she tried to do good.

"That thing is tainted!" they said.

"Evil!"

"Moon Rogue! Kill it!"

Johrann had fled their burning torches and their sharpened knives. She ran over high mountains, she crossed wide seas, she passed through burning deserts, but no one would show her compassion.

On what she thought would be her last day, she lay face-down in the sand, slowly baking in the blistering heat. But something happened. A miracle.

Dorai came to her.

"Johrann Maa," the goddess had said.

Lips cracked and eyes encrusted with sand, Johrann couldn't answer. But the voice didn't leave her.

"Johrann Maa," it said again. "I am the One True Goddess, Dorai. You are a strange creature in this world, but you have untold power within you. You are rejected, but it does not need to be so. If you promise to obey me and bring me back into this world, I will save you. I will make all folk respect you. I will raise you above all others, and you shall be my Heart. Seek out the Book of Divine Tears in the Masvam Empire and worship me. Seek the underground, the One of Two, and worship me. Build a temple and a throne for me. And above all, worship me."

Johrann, just sixteen, had wrenched her head from the scorching sand and found her voice. "I will worship you," she rasped.

The Goddess' voice stayed with her, soothing and protecting, until a caravan of travelers came upon her. She was saved, just like the goddess said.

Thus, in her second cycle, Johrann went into the Masvam Empire and honed her power. She learned to change her colors, to manipulate minds, and to interfere with life and death. She read the Book of Divine Tears, learning the truth of Dorai.

She erred in bringing Mantos Tiboli back from the dead. But that was written, and was before she realized how important Bandim was to Dorai's cause. It was before she realized he was the vessel, the One of Two, in whom Dorai would live anew.

Striding straight-backed down the rows of the amphitheater, Johrann raised her arms high above her head. It was time to show the worshippers of Dorai who she really was. It was time for them to see she wasn't just the High Priestess, but the Heart of the goddess. Only Bandim had ever seen her true colors. Now it was time to show them all.

As she walked she closed her eyes, kindling the great flame of power within her. Her skin burned, smoke rising, and she changed.

Gasps echoed from the circles of masked worshippers. No longer did she wear a false shroud of Masvam colors. Instead Johrann stood proud, showing her blue and purple to them all. *This is who I am*, she thought. *I am not afraid.*

The believers rose from their seats, pounded their fists on their chests, and roared their approval. This was the start of what they'd worked for. This was the time of reckoning.

"By the One True Goddess!"

"Johrann Maa, praise be!"

"Bring the goddess back to us! Please!"

Johrann schooled her face with demure respect, willing the worshippers to calm. They were from all ranks of society, but all their eyes shone with fervor for the True God.

With a queen's poise, Johrann stood at their center. The round altar bore another statue of Dorai. Beside it was an elaborate throne, hewn from a solid block of black marble. Johrann didn't sit. The throne wasn't for her, nor was it really for Bandim. It was for the goddess when she walked among them, and that time was now. Johrann stood to the side of the throne, awaiting the herald.

"Emperor Bandim Tiboli!"

Cocooned by guards, the emperor strode forth. Resplendent in his orange and red state robes, Bandim descended. His subjects bowed as he passed. The mask on his face was darkest black, his red and white makeup shining bright underneath. The Tiboli lightning bolts were drawn upon his cheeks.

Johrann fell to her knees as he approached. She bowed, her horns scraping the floor. "Your Grace," she said. "We are humbled by your presence."

Bandim's response echoed in the silence. "Rise," he said. "You are the True Believer. You do not bow to me."

Johrann tilted her head upwards, but remained on her knees. "No, Your Grace," she said. "You are the vessel. You are the Hand. I am merely the Heart."

Chuckling, Bandim held out an arm. His yellow eyes glinted. "And what is a Hand without a Heart to guide it?" he asked. "What is a Hand without a Heart to keep it alive?"

Accepting the offered claws, Johrann rose, meeting him eye-to-eye. "You honor me," she said. "I am but your humble servant."

"Humble you may be," Bandim said, touching her cheek, "but you are most important to me." He looked to the gathered crowd. "To all of us."

He released her and gestured to the rows upon rows of waiting faces.

"Today is a great day in our empire—indeed, in our history," he said. His voice carried easily in the amphitheater. "In spite of what the followers of the wretched Light have done, in spite of how far they degrade themselves in a false attempt to stir their cause by stealing my brother's body, we will prevail."

The deep rumble of fists pounding chests sounded their approval. Bandim raised his hands for silence.

"Today I will not be crowned with paltry gems and so-called precious metal. Today, High Priestess Johrann Maa will crown me with the greatest glory: the One True Goddess herself! You bear witness to a moment that will change our world forever. No longer will we be persecuted. No longer will we be vilified. Now we will show the fools of the Light what true power is!"

The crowd erupted in cacophonous cheers, chanting for their emperor. The sound heralded the conclusion of Johrann's life's work. She bowed as Bandim sat on his throne in the shadow of Dorai, revelling in the elation.

Then she turned to the congregation. She closed her eyes. Breathed in. Breathed out. She waited for silence. When she opened her eyes again, she began, a player on her self-made stage.

"My pious companions," she called, "the time has come for us to excise the poison of the false goddess Nunako and all those who refuse to acknowledge the One True God, Dorai." There was a rumble of agreement. "We are here for a great moment. For many cycles I have studied our scriptures, and watched the movements of the stars and moons as they cross the Arc of the Sky. The cursed moons nestle together, their voices distracted by each other. The power of the Light is diminished, and now is the time to act. Now is the time to end this madness and return the Great Goddess to us!"

The room erupted with elation, ringing from all positions, front and rear. After a moment, Johrann held up her claws.

"My brothers and sisters, I implore you for your help. We must ask our beloved Dorai for that which was promised to us. For does it not say in the holy scripture, 'when the moons lie equal and the sun is at its closest, if the True Believer asks for my return, it will be granted'? We must ask the Great One to crown our emperor, the One of Two, with her true glory!"

The jubilation of before was replaced by a roar of elation.

Then it was cut short by one word.

"*Blasphemy!*"

Every set of eyes swung from Johrann to a gnarled figure. He stood near the front of the amphitheater, one talon pointing at Johrann. She didn't know who he was, and that spoke volumes. She had hundreds of true worshippers, and she knew the devout by face and name. But those who didn't come to the temple of Dorai as often as they should, those who lived on the periphery of belief, Johrann didn't know them. There were always dissenters, she had found. There were always those who said they believed, but didn't follow words with action. Finding them was like looking for a white pebble in a mountain of teeth, but now, this one had shown himself to her. It was time to excise the rot.

Unfazed, Johrann walked towards him with deliberate slowness, pursing her lips. The old male's arm trembled, but he kept his chin high.

"Do you not know the dangers of summoning the goddess?" he asked, his voice wavering. "Do you not know that conjuring the Great Spirit in her true and pure form is impossible? It has been tried, and it has never worked. It will only bring great pain. You seek to kill us all!"

Johrann stopped before him and stared with level eyes. She let the silence that followed his words draw on. She looked to Bandim. He nodded.

Thrusting an arm out like a whiplash, Johrann seized the male's throat. The room stayed silent as stone as she clamped her hand tight, dragging him to the circular altar and its statue of Dorai. The male clawed at his neck. Johrann tightened her grip. Bandim, seated on his throne, watched it all.

"Oh, my dear," Johrann purred, "how foolish you are." She thrust the male to the floor and bore down on him until their flat faces nearly touched. The silence was broken, filled with harried whispers. Johrann's nose slits flared as she spoke through gritted teeth.

"How dare you speak to me of blasphemy? *Me*? I have spoken to Dorai herself! How dare you have such little respect!"

Johrann pulled back. Then, with no warning, she stamped her heel onto the male's throat. He squeaked and spluttered and clawed at his neck, his face growing purple. Saliva burst from his lips. Johrann didn't relent.

His dark eyes rolled back. Blood trickled from the corners of his mouth. Johrann lifted her foot and jammed her toes under his shoulder, sending the body thudding down the stone steps. It landed in a mangled heap. Once it was still, Johrann tilted her chin and glowered at the gathering of masked faces. "Does anyone else wish to cry *blasphemy*?"

Silence reigned. Johrann smiled. "Good. Let that fool's impudence be a lesson to you all."

She looked to Bandim, who nodded his blessing, caressing the arm of the elaborate throne. Johrann continued to the congregation.

"Blasphemy?" she asked. "How is it blasphemy to fulfil the duty that has been handed down by the word of the goddess? The only blasphemy that has been spoken in this chamber has been the words of this traitor." She motioned to the crumpled body at the foot of the altar. "My words come directly from Dorai and must not be questioned. Anyone who thinks that is blasphemy will share his fate."

Washing herself of the stink of death, Johrann turned her attention to the altar and the effigy of Dorai. "Brothers and sisters, it is time to bring about our destiny."

Every set of eyes focused on the five-armed statue that loomed tall among them. It was a chilling tableau of triumph over the false believers, and every jewel glimmered in the darkness. Johrann's body tingled as power flowed through her. The unwavering obedience of the followers of the Dark made her heart sing. It was all she deserved.

She had always known she was bound for greatness. Cast aside, unwanted, she found solace in the Dark love of Dorai. *Now, everyone who mocked me and tormented me will regret the day they were hatched!*

Johrann once more bowed low to Bandim. "Your Grace," she said, "I am honored that you have come to be with us on this blessed day, even as your armies decimate the Metakalans."

"It is I who am honored," Bandim said. As he spoke, he stood. Then, sending ripples of shock through the congregation, he bowed to Johrann. "My armies march against the bodies, but your actions today will be the final blow against the heathens and will guarantee victory for our empire."

All around her, the followers bowed like a great unfurling flower. Johrann tried to suppress the smile that bloomed on her face. The burn of self-justification burst with renewed brightness.

As the emperor sat, Johrann climbed atop the altar. Pacing on its shimmering surface, she raised her hands.

"My friends," she said, "the most glorious day has finally arrived. Today we welcome our beloved goddess Dorai back to us. Today marks the reckoning for the blasphemous followers of Nunako and their Light."

The room pulsed with anticipation. Johrann's words echoed against the walls and in their hearts. She grinned. It was so *easy*.

"Already our beloved emperor sends righteous soldiers to cleanse the heathens so that the vanquishing may begin. Here, today, we will bring our hearts together to strike a blow against those who deny our truth. We will return the glory of Dorai to our world and annihilate the unbelievers forever!"

The gathered crowd burst into a frenzy, jumping in elation. Arms and tails swung with fervor. Johrann pumped her fist aloft, leading the shrieks.

"Get to your feet, friends!" she called. "Lend me your thoughts and your hearts, and we shall bring the Beloved back to our world!"

Every arm lifted, outstretched claws blooming. Even Bandim rose, raising his hands.

Johrann's heart pounded. Sweat poured from her brow. It was time.

"Great Goddess Dorai, the Unparalleled, the Beloved, the Great Spirit," she said, incanting all Dorai's names, "I give myself to you as the True Believer, on this day when the moons lie equal and the sun is at its closest. In full view of your faithful, I give my body as a sacrifice for your Great Works. I offer myself to you as a conduit, the servant of the vessel and the One of Two, Bandim Tiboli. Please return your beauteous countenance to this world through his body and mine, and finally rid us of the Great Evil as you have promised!" She took a deep breath. "Rise!"

Johrann's words dissipated, and then there was silence. No one dared to breathe.

A deep *clunk* emanated from everywhere and nowhere. Lighted torches were snuffed by a sudden whirlwind of heat. The temple shook, showers of dust raining down. The vaulted roof groaned and howled.

Then Johrann screamed.

Knife-sharp pain pierced her skull. Blackness consumed her. She shrieked into the abyss as she rose from her feet, scorching wind twisting like a tornado. This had been written. This was known. Consumed by pain, Johrann screeched but held true. *This is the will of the goddess. I will worship her and obey!*

Blood wept from her eyes and ears, flowing from the corners of her mouth, dripping from her claws. Thousands of voices echoed, drowning out her thoughts until she could feel nothing but the discordance of terror. Johrann gave one final, forceful yelp, and the chamber plunged into impossible darkness.

Despite it, one figure was clear: Bandim. He stood in the beautiful night, holding her gaze.

Johrann knew what she had to do.

She placed her claws on the emperor's face. The heat that coursed within her pooled at her fingertips.

In that moment the miracle happened. Something moved from one to the other. The essence, the spirit, the *truth* of Dorai flowed through Johrann's talons and deep into Bandim. He jerked back, body racked with apoplexy, but his face was fused to her claws. His skin sizzled. He screamed.

"Do not fear," Johrann whispered. "All will be well."

She pressed her mouth to his. His eyes snapped open. He returned the fervent embrace.

And that was it. The deed was done.

Dorai was back in the world.

CHAPTER THIRTEEN

Phen

Once more, Phen found herself flanked by guards, both female this time, winding through the Althemerian palace. This time the journey was more fraught. Before, Phen had known what awaited her: an audience with the cold ire of the queen. Now, as she gripped the hem of her soft leather tunic, she bit her lower lip. She had no idea what awaited her. All she knew was that Bomsoi needed her to return her son to life. It could have meant anything, and that thought stole the breath from Phen's chest. Once before, she had sacrificed herself for her son. What was to say it wouldn't happen again?

Eventually they reached the receiving chamber she'd seen the queen in before. The first guard struck the door twice, then stepped away, waiting for permission. Phen gripped her tunic tighter.

"Enter," a voice said.

The guard opened the door, and Phen walked in her wake. The chamber was much like before, with a wooden table in its center. But the chairs were gone, and no candles stood on its wide surface. The shutters were still tightly closed, keeping out the moons' light. Phen had spied the moons earlier that evening, neatly stacked atop one another. The Lunar Awakening. The single day Nunako, Lady of Light, would walk among her folk once more.

There was little light in the chamber. Phen stopped herself from snorting. It was fitting. There was no love in the chamber, either, and the darkness fit that. Queen Valentia stood at the head of the table, her talons stretched against its surface. Once more her offspring stood beside her, Fylica on the right and Fonbir on the left. Bomsoi stood to the side, dressed again in black, her hands clasped in front of her.

Valentia held Phen's gaze, the intensity of the stare boring into Phen's skull. She twisted her hem more, but held the queen's eyes.

"Phen of the Masvams," Valentia said. Her voice echoed into every stone corner.

"Will you do as you are asked? Will you help to save my folk and this world from destruction?"

Valentia's face was as stern and commanding as a stormy sea. Phen licked her lips, then nodded. "Yes."

Valentia clicked two of her talons together, and immediately an attendant opened the door and stood in its arch, ready for her orders.

"Bring the body in," Valentia said.

Hands shaking, Phen kept her eyes on the door. Within a moment, the attendant and a partner entered the chamber, carrying Mantos' body in a shroud.

Phen's head spun. It wasn't like the last time, when the temple novice had pulled the tiny Mantos into her arms. His body had been flaccid, head lolling against the novice's arm. Blood had still trickled from his nostrils, warm and sticky.

Now Mantos was grown, a tall and imposing figure. Or so Phen chose to believe, for she hadn't seen him upright. Now she couldn't even see his face, but she could imagine the cold planes beneath the undyed fabric. The coarseness of his fronds still lingered on her hands. The shine of his eyes was still unseen, for they lingered beneath his papery lids.

The attendants laid the body on the table. They opened the shutters to let in the light, then left without a word. They took the torches with them, but the room was afforded light from the moons. Phen stared at the three moons, settled over each another like stacking cups. The Lunar Awakening, Phen thought. It was finally here.

Her gaze returned to the body on the table. The edges of the shroud were picked out in silver. Underneath was her son, her beloved youngling, for whom she had sacrificed her life once before. Even as they stood in the chamber, wrapped in a coldness that went beyond the chill from the stone walls, Phen didn't know what they wanted from her. In some way she was needed, but Bomsoi had kept her in the dark. Perhaps, she thought, bunching her talons into fists, it was because of what would happen to her. She'd been robbed of her wits once to save her son. A life for a life, the novice had said. Phen had assumed it meant death, but it was not so. This time, it might be.

I will die for you, Mantos, she thought. *You deserve life more than I.*

Bomsoi approached the table. Her hands stilled over the body, and her eyes flicked up to Phen. Then she uncovered Mantos' face.

He looked peaceful, as if simply asleep. Phen's knees threatened to buckle, but she stayed strong. Whatever magic Bomsoi wielded, it had already kept her son's body from putrefaction. The next step was bringing him back to the living world.

Bomsoi unlaced the front of the shroud, revealing the body beneath. Mantos was clothed in a simple gown made of the same undyed material. It was simple, humble. It didn't speak of a male who was to be emperor. But then, Phen knew, in death all were equal. The poorest or the grandest: everyone had to stand in the presence of the Lady of Light and answer the single question: *who are you?*

Approaching the body, Phen laid a trembling hand on his cool forehead, lacing her talons around his horns. Had Mantos already stood before the goddess and pleaded his case? Was he already enjoying eternal succor at her table? If so, what right did they have to take him away from that? Phen smoothed down his fronds, still wrapped in tight death braids, and shook her head. They had no right to wrench him from the Light, yet Bomsoi, the Stranger, said it must be so. Phen flicked her gaze to her, the creature who'd spirited her away from certain death. Bomsoi gave the tiniest of nods. Phen did the same in reply. It was time.

Thus, they were gathered in a stone chamber, with the light of the moons streaming in. Phen looked around, from Bomsoi to Valentia to her offspring. Princess Fylica's face was hewn in an eternal scowl. Prince Fonbir, behind his veil, inclined his head. His white eyes, so strange, shone brightly. There was hope there, the hope of a lover seeking his special one. Phen returned her gaze to Mantos, lying prone, bathed in light.

"Are we ready, Stranger?" Queen Valentia asked.

"We are ready," Bomsoi replied. "I wait only for your consent."

At the queen's nod, Bomsoi stepped forward.

"Today we do the work of the gods," she said. "Today we right a terrible wrong and put into motion events that will change the world."

From inside her tunic she drew out a small knife. She looked to Phen and nodded.

Phen swallowed. Hard. This was it.

A life for a life.

"Give me your hand," Bomsoi said, reaching for her. "His life was bound to yours for many cycles. You wove a bond with the underworld that cannot be undone. His life was sustained by yours, kept from death by you. Now, with the help of the moons, it is time for your life to bring him back again."

Phen swallowed again. She blinked. A thousand unanswered questions swirled in her mind. Yet when she looked at her son's pallid face, the need for answers fell away. She stepped forward. She held Bomsoi's gaze.

"I will do what I must," she said, placing her hand in Bomsoi's, "even if it kills me."

Bomsoi squeezed her talons, then brought them to her mouth. She kissed the backs of Phen's claws. "The will of the gods be done," she said. "But if the gods are kind, they will not levy the heaviest of penalties."

Phen licked her lips, closing her eyes for a moment.

"I am ready," she said. "A life for a life; that was the price last time. I am willing to pay it again. He is my son. I would tear myself limb from limb if that would save his life."

In the corner of her eye, she saw Queen Valentia incline her head, and press two of her foreclaws to her lips. It was a sign, something Phen had learned long ago when studying their culture.

It was a gesture of respect.

They were enemies, and Phen was in her custody, but something in her words must have struck a chord within the Althemerian queen. *We are both mothers, and that binds us,* Phen thought. *Were our positions reversed, I believe she would do the same as me.*

Bomsoi gave Phen's hand a final squeeze, then turned it over to expose the fleshy palm. "If we are lucky, the gods will not demand your life. But I do need your blood," she said, raising the knife.

"More magic," Phen said, the words catching in her throat. Then reality bit, and she barked a laugh. "I'm already damned for using magic once. Why not again?"

Bomsoi shook her head and reached to take Phen's hand in her own. "This is not dark magic. This is the will of the gods." Her face became deadly stern. "I need your blood, or your son will never live again."

Fear exploded in Phen's mind, and in that moment she wanted to turn tail and flee. Her heart pounded. Her mouth went dry. She closed her hand tight, the talons digging into her soft palm. Bomsoi wanted blood, but that might not be enough. Reality bit and her stomach lurched. *I'm going to die.*

But when she looked beyond Bomsoi, to the figure lying prone on the table, she closed her eyes. If her life was demanded, then so be it. Even if it wasn't wanted by the gods Bomsoi spoke of, there was still the threat of death at the hands of the Althemerians. But none of it mattered. All that was important was her son's life. It was all she'd ever worked to protect.

"I only ever wanted him to live," she whispered.

"Let him live now," Bomsoi replied. "Open your palm to me."

Phen trembled. The moment stretched into a lifetime. Every memory she had of Mantos came back. The moment she was called to the blessed moment: the eggs were hatching! She remembered kicking off her shoes and bolting into the bedchamber, so unbecoming of an empress, but she hadn't cared.

She remembered watching as the tiny hatchling poked through the silver leather of his shell, fighting with all his might to join the world.

She remembered her whoop of joy as her first-hatched was placed in her arms. His claws were so sharp and his rumble of hunger so sweet.

She remembered Bandim, escaping not long after, joining his sibling in her arms. She remembered the sweet joy of having two hatchlings, the first time such a thing had occurred since the time when the Goddess Nunako walked among the believers.

Most of all, she remembered the sudden absence of her hatching in her arms. She remembered the sight of him, broken and bloody, all because of her. She remembered the keenness of utter pain and the spark of hope the temple novice gave her.

She remembered the moment her life was bound to his, and then she remembered no more. Not until she woke in a chamber with no windows, haggard and pained, a stranger in the world.

Phen looked to Valentia once more, who returned her gaze with shadowed eyes. Phen looked at Bomsoi, who inclined her head.

"Open your palm to me."

Slowly, Phen unfurled her talons, exposing the flesh of her palm.

"The will of the gods be done," Bomsoi said.

Phen's heart pounded anew. Her whole body trembled as Bomsoi brought the knife down and slid it over Phen's exposed skin. Blood wept from the straight cut, but Phen withheld her whimper. She gritted her teeth and watched the hot red liquid pool in the cup of her hand and threaten to trickle between her talons.

Bringing her to the body, Bomsoi placed the bleeding palm on Mantos' forehead, just under his first horn. Then she slid it to each of his cheeks and wiped blood over his lips. Phen's breath was shallow and her head was light. She pressed her bleeding palm into the fabric of her hose. The pain was nothing at all. All she could feel was the knife-edge of grief, blunted by an ever-growing bud of hope.

Mantos, come back to me.

His face was painted with her blood. Bomsoi reached over his body with both hands, breathed deeply, and started to chant.

Phen stepped back, rapt as the Stranger set to work. Her language was strange and archaic, like nothing Phen had heard before. It was a language of the beforetime, the words twisting and twining around each other. The more Bomsoi spoke, the faster the words came. Her eyes were clenched shut. Her brow shone with sweat. The air cooled, and her breath ghosted.

Phen kept her palm pressed to her thigh. The warm bloodstain spread. Her heart still pumped, her breathing coming in shallow gasps that puffed into the air. The room grew colder and colder, and Phen looked to the queen and her children. Each kept their eyes on Bomsoi and the body. Fonbir's beaded with tears.

There was a searing *crack*, and Phen jumped. The whole room shifted as ice penetrated the walls, cracking the stone, climbing in sparkling tendrils. It crawled the length of Mantos' body, winding like the vines of Bomsoi's language. The entire room trembled with power. Phen trembled too.

The Stranger drew in a deep breath and finally opened her eyes.

"Rise!" she cried.

Phen scrabbled backwards until her claws met freezing stone. Bomsoi's eyes, once grey, now glowed bright and blue, shining as if the power of the moons was channeled through them. Phen's breath stopped and her throat closed as the presence of such power washed over her.

Bomsoi's chanting grew to fever-pitch, and she raised her hands over the body. Blue light played on Mantos' face, painting the blood purple. Phen's blood. The blood that would make him rise from the dead.

Phen prayed, her chest burning from lack of breath. *Please, Lady of Light! Bring him back to me!*

There was a deep *clunk* from everywhere and nowhere. Phen's eyes darted to and fro, looking for the source. Bomsoi was silent now, her gaze fixed on Mantos' body.

Then it happened.

Phen's son, her *dead* son, sat up on the table. His crossed Tiboli lightning strikes glinted at his neck.

"Mantos," Phen whispered, her breath now coming in ragged gasps. "Mantos!"

He looked at her and, for the first time since he was a hatchling, their gazes met.

His eyes glowed blue.

CHAPTER FOURTEEN

Emmy

The air filled with harrowed screams, some of them Emmy's own. The screeches were punctuated with booming explosions. The stinging taste of panic tainted the air like sulfur as folk clattered along the streets, desperate to escape. The ships vomited wave upon wave of soldiers. Fighting was futile. Running was the only option. Even battle-hardened former Metakalan fighters were gathering their younglings to them and throwing the vital objects of their lives into bags.

Zecha disappeared into Charber's house and reappeared with a sweeping bow and a quiver of arrows on his waist. Emmy headed towards the surging crowd on the street.

"I need to get to the apothecary," she said. "Krodge is still there. I...I can't leave her for the Masvams to kill."

A voice that rang with justice sounded in her mind. *Why not? Perhaps you could finally teach* her *a lesson.* Emmy batted it back. *No. I must be better than that.*

Charo jerked an elbow at the swirling maw outside. "Emmy," she said, "we could be killed trying to make our way through the crowd. Who knows how many enemies are out there, whoever they are."

"We know who they are, Charo," Emmy said. "It can only be the Masvams. They've come at last, and there's nothing we can do to stop them."

Charo had no reply.

"Let's go," Zecha said. "We're definitely dead if we stay here. We might survive if we can get out."

"We can go to the apothecary, gather supplies, and get Krodge," Emmy said. "Then we'll run."

The streets pulsed with panic and fear as the trio wound through the swirling crowds. As they reached the end of Charber's street, the vista opened into the large space of the Circle, and Emmy's chest tightened. From there they could see right down to the port. Clear as glass, there were the three towering Masvam ships. Their tall masts stretched upwards like dead trees. They bled soldiers, their curved scimitar blades glinting in the moons' light.

Emmy jerked back, covering her pointed ears as another explosion ripped through the air. She stared, wide-eyed. The ships sent burning masses through the sky, a grim imitation of the fireworks they'd expected. Emmy cringed as a missile passed overhead and dealt a killing blow to buildings on the other side of the Circle.

With giant sailed vessels sending balls of fire through the air, the friends struggled to break their fascination with the macabre display. Eventually, Emmy shook her mind clear and grabbed Charo's wrist. "Come on!"

They bolted the rest of the distance to the apothecary. At the door, Emmy fumbled for her keys. Taming her hands, she thrust the door open and pushed the others inside. She slammed the door shut and fell against it, breathing hard.

From upstairs, Krodge screamed. "Emena! What's going on?"

"I'm coming Madame!" Emmy called. She turned to her friends. "Gather what you can. Blankets, food, extra clothes. Forget everything else."

Charo nodded and dashed to the kitchen. Zecha stayed in the shop front, his bow taut and ready in his claws. Krodge was still screaming.

"I'll be there in a moment, Madame!"

Emmy stumbled on the words. It would be so easy to leave Krodge to her fate. It might even be a kind of justice. The thought kept returning. *Teach her a lesson.* Emmy's throat tightened as she pulled a woven satchel from under the shop counter. Krodge wasn't her mother, after all. Krodge was her keeper, the one who shackled her to the apothecary with cruel words and terror. If the situation was reversed, Emmy told herself, Krodge wouldn't risk a talon to save her. This could be Emmy's chance to escape once and for all.

Unwilling to face the choice, Emmy turned to her glass cabinets, fumbled for her keys once more, and jammed one in the lock.

It wouldn't turn.

Emmy pulled and jerked at the key, but it wouldn't twist in the lock. Krodge kept screaming. Emmy's heart hammered in her chest. *Why did I come back? I should have just left her!*

"Argh!" Emmy wrenched the key out and shook her head. She looked from the cabinets to the keys and grimaced. There wasn't time for niceties. It had to happen.

She plucked up her measuring scales and cast them forward. The glass shattered into countless glimmering pieces, taking many of the jars and phials with it. There was renewed screeching from Krodge. Emmy closed her eyes, berating herself for her tears. Crying over cupboards when their lives were at risk was foolish, yet she still felt sharp sorrow. Her precious order was gone.

Shaking herself, Emmy filled her satchel with what she thought she needed and what hadn't been destroyed. She shook her head. It wasn't enough, but she didn't have much choice.

A crash came from outside. She shared a harried glance with Zecha. His face was drawn. Families streamed past, females wielding weapons from glinting blades to kitchen ladles and table-top shields. Younglings hung from their fathers' arms. Emmy spared Zecha another glance before running to her chamber.

She threw on a pair of heavy boots and ripped the headdress from her horns. The metal bent and torqued. Grabbing another bag, Emmy stopped. She bit her lip and made another decision.

She wrenched her bed aside, revealing a trapdoor. Snatching her keys, she released the heavy latch.

Inside the hidden chamber were thousands of bickles, half-bickles, cren, crom, and pip. The light of the moons' rise made the slumbering coins sparkle. This was the money she'd earned, *her* money, something that had once been Krodge's but wasn't any longer. Emmy's coin, a well of gold, something that gave her hope on her darkest days.

But not this day. No amount of coin could save her from the Masvams. Grabbing fistfuls of wealth, she stuffed some of her savings into the bag.

There was a thunderous smash. Zecha screamed. "They're here!"

Emmy shoved the trapdoor closed, hefted her bags, and tore from the room. The usurpers bellowed. Krodge screeched.

"I'm coming, Madame!"

Charo appeared in the doorway, armed with two knives. "It's all I could find," she said.

Emmy grabbed her wrist and propelled her into the kitchen, bags swinging around them. "Krodge always kept weapons under the kitchen table."

She threw her bags on the floor and upturned the table. It smashed on its side but revealed glinting knives—*fighting* knives—attached underneath by leather straps.

Crashing and smashing invaded. Zecha still screamed, but Emmy couldn't make out his words. Krodge screeched and screeched. Blood roared in Emmy's ears as she unbuckled the knives from the table, keeping one and giving Charo the other.

"We have to get to Zecha and Krodge," Emmy said. "Then we need to get out of here. Come on!"

She hefted her bags and flew from the kitchen, ready to take the stairs two at a time and pull Krodge from her bed—but she smashed against a hulking body that stank of sweat and seawater and blood. She bounced backwards, skidding on the rushes.

"Well, well, well," the Masvam soldier said, grasping her tunic. His eyes narrowed in first realization that she wasn't like other Metakalans. "What this is? A demon, yes?"

Thick fingers snatched at her but Emmy twisted from his grasp and drew her arm up, ready to attack. She launched forward, striking out, but the knife connected with a sudden shield. It bore a sigil, a lightning bolt as strange as the Masvams' words. The blade quivered, then clattered to the ground. Emmy drew back as Charo leapt forward. The Masvams slipped aside, sending Charo headlong into the wall. She crumpled.

One Masvam grabbed Emmy while another lifted Charo by the throat. Emmy did the only thing she could think of. She screamed. "*Zecha!*"

She was silenced when strong talons coiled around her neck.

"You play nice," the Masvam whispered, his breath hot on the side of her face. His words were strange, just like Charo's when she first arrived. They spoke another language, but it was similar enough for Emmy to understand parts. "Don't try your magic or I'll dispatch you right quick. I would arrange that gladly."

Emmy writhed in his grasp, staring at Charo. Charo's eyes pleaded as she stared back. Emmy sucked in a sharp breath. Her head swam from the choke-hold, white moons dancing in her vision. Her ears filled with the blows of her own heartbeat and the screeches from upstairs.

Three more Masvams tore in. One of them headed straight up the stairway.

"Krodge, " Emmy choked.

The hand grew tighter around her throat.

"What keeps you?" the oldest of the new arrivals asked. He had a hatchet face and a snarl on his lips. "Have you them yet or not?"

"We got nasties, Ysmas Mamusan," Emmy's captor said. "Tried to slash with knives. But not now. They subdued."

Both Emmy and Charo were released from death grasps. Air raced into Emmy's chest, sweet despite the stench of unwashed soldier. Charo tried to slip the Masvam's grip entirely, but he was on her again. He grabbed her from behind, shoving her to the wall.

"Tie them," the oldest Masvam, Mamusan, barked. He glared at Emmy and crossed his hands in front of his face, some kind of ward against evil. "Double knots on this," he said. "Tainted."

A soldier wrenched Emmy's arms back. Rope bit her wrists. Charo received the same treatment. Trussed like game, they were deposited in the shop. Emmy struggled to right herself, writhing against her bindings. Question upon question came at her. Why were the Masvams tying them up? What was their goal? Masvams were famous for killing their victims. But they were also famous for their battles against other armies, soldier upon soldier. It had never been their way to attack the common folk. That was why towns like Bellim had no army, no protection. They weren't supposed to need it. But now... Emmy shook off the questions, bringing her mind back to the present.

The apothecary was in ruins. Shelves had been torn from the walls. Soil and blood littered the floor like a gory carpet. The grand front window was in pieces, sparkling like a thousand tears. But that paled in comparison to the pitiful lump on the floor.

"*Zecha!*"

Their friend was tied like a hunted carcass, bleeding from his mouth. His head lolled. His eyes were glazed. Emmy's heart lurched and she tried to wriggle from her bindings, willing the goddess—*any* goddess—to help her. But it was in vain. She was bound tight.

For a moment there was silence. Emmy's breath stuttered. *Silence*—nothing from upstairs. *Krodge?* Emmy thought. *Is she...?* Her stomach dropped. Bile rose in her throat. Yet at the same time, the little voice was back. *Justice.*

"Right, petals," said the older male, "let see us what you've in your bags."

He tipped out the contents. Money spilled like a golden wave.

"Look to this," he said. "Much coin."

The gathered soldiers bayed.

"Is good," the leader said. Then he turned to one of his wiry companions. "Kelom, what have you?"

"Food and rags, Mamusan," the one named Kelom replied. "That all."

Another Masvam appeared. His front was soaked with fresh blood. He grinned.

"No things of worth up there," he said, wiping his dagger on his leg. "Just an old pchak with big mouth. To us no use. Finished her off, I did."

The Masvam's words rolled in Emmy's head. *Finished her off, I did.* She looked at him. She looked at the blood. Krodge's blood. Her stomach pitched. *She's dead...* Her mistress' words from so long ago came back to her.

Once I'm dead, there'll be no one left to protect you!

In a strange way, the old crone had been right.

Emmy was filled with despair, yet it was tinged with something else. It was a kind of macabre relief. Krodge was finally gone. Unfortunately, Emmy couldn't enjoy it.

"Right," Mamusan said, brushing off death as he brushed off his hands, "take these to the boat. Search for more coin. Then burn it."

Kelom bowed and turned his attention to the prisoners. Emmy screeched and writhed as he hefted her over his shoulder. She got a clout to the face as a reward.

"Shut up," he grunted. "Demon thing."

Battered as she was, Emmy still wanted to spit at him. Beyond the blows and the choke-holds, there was something that consumed her last strength.

Finished her off, I did.

Those words reverberated in her mind as the Masvams moved off with their newfound riches.

The dark streets were filled with the clash and wail of battle. Mamusan and the others joined a stream of Masvams bearing bodies or herding cowering Metakalans to their ships. Many were still caught in the heat of blood lust. Corpses littered the ground.

Even as she was hefted through the streets, listening to Charo bite and kick against her captor, fearing for Zecha, so limp over a Masvam's shoulder, hearing the blasts of bombs and the snick of metal through skin, those words kept playing in Emmy's mind.

Finished her off, I did.

When they passed a mangled corpse with its throat cut, her eyes widened. Blood pumped from the wound, spilling down the male's neck, but the expression etched on his face in death was worst of all. It was harrowing.

It was one of *betrayal*.

It wasn't just the gore or the expression that caught her eye. It wasn't just the loll of the head. It was the face: unmistakably Amra Bose. The words changed in her head.

Finished him off, I did.

Looking away, Emmy jerked upwards. Her gaze latched on the shop. Her home. Now gone.

The building was dark.

Then a Masvam threw a lighted torch through the broken window.

Her work. Her world. Everything she had ever known. Her memories. Her *life*.

Then there was fire.

Flames burst onto the street, enveloping the building in red destruction.

"Madame!"

She cried despite knowing Krodge was dead. She cried despite the cycles of pain and torture she'd endured. She cried because, though things had been bad, she'd wanted it to end this way.

"NO!"

For her outburst, she received another blow to the head. Everything went dark.

Finished her off, I did...

CHAPTER FIFTEEN

Bandim

The only sound in Bandim's chambers was the rhythmic in and out of his breathing. The emperor sat in an opulent chair by the empty fireplace. The cold ashes within were as grey as his mood. The shutters were closed tightly against the midday brightness and his servants had long since been banished. Bandim sat, alone and silent, staring at his reflection in his gilt-silver handplate.

As he moved it from side to side, his image warped, growing thinner or fatter depending on the angle at which he held it. *Fitting*, he thought. *Warped is exactly how I feel.*

It had been days since Dorai had given him her presence, yet all was not as Bandim had anticipated, or how Johrann had prophesied. He felt the goddess within him, but there was no symbiosis. Johrann had claimed he would become the goddess herself, and that all her might and power would flow through him.

Johrann was wrong.

Worse still, his brother's dead body had disappeared. No matter what Johrann said, it still worried him. He wouldn't settle fully until his brother's body was burned.

Bandim shook his head but kept his eyes fixed on his reflection. Since Johrann had channeled Dorai into the world and into him, all Bandim had felt was himself as always, but with a vacant pocket somewhere within that hadn't been there before. It was as if Dorai had invaded his body but was hiding in the dark recesses of his mind, constantly out of reach. He leaned forward and brought the handplate closer to his face. His careful examination of his features continued, yet he could still find no trace of the goddess there.

"You'll see her in yourself," Johrann had said. "She'll give you a sign to show you she's there, ready to share all she has."

Bandim stared deeply into the reflection of his own face, searching for something. Anything. But he saw nothing that hadn't been there before. He had the same flat face, the same yellow eyes blinking back at him.

There was nothing.

Frustration built in his chest like the swelled banks of a river in flood. Bandim grunted and cast the handplate from his grasp. It skidded across the stone floor, clearing a path through the fresh rushes. The situation was intolerable. Johrann had lied. He wasn't the goddess. He was still just a male.

Not known for his patience, Bandim had quickly tired of his advisor's vapid assurances that all would be well. Instead of his constant companion, Johrann was now seldom a guest in his presence, despite her pleading. With or without the goddess, Bandim was still emperor, and his word was law.

"Your Grace," Johrann had said, her eyes brimming, "if you don't let me work with you to unleash your inner power, the goddess will never grant you her gifts. Don't send me away. Let me help you."

Working for Dorai's power wasn't part of Johrann's promises before. She had felt her failure through the harsh flats of his hands.

The handplate discarded, Bandim instead stared into the dim grate of the fireplace. He didn't know for how long, but eventually his attention was diverted by a deferent knock at the door.

"Enter," he said, not turning.

Soft footsteps entered. The door was closed gently. His guest waited in obedient silence until Bandim deigned to grant them his attention. As soon as he saw who it was, his face drew tight with anger.

It was Johrann.

"I told you not to return," Bandim said, rising slowly from his chair.

Johrann kept her eyes averted from his gaze and clasped her hands in front of her waist.

"I know, Your Grace," she said. "However, I've come to appeal to you to let me try once more to help you."

He could have simply turned her away. Told her to get out, even shouted it had he wanted. But even that seemed too easy. Bandim was an emperor, and emperors must be obeyed. It was time to reinforce that issue with Johrann.

His soft slippers made little noise as he crossed the room to her. She kept her eyes on the floor as he walked, just as she should.

Bandim grasped her throat with his claws and pinned her to the wall before she knew what was happening. White-hot anger coursed through him, boiling his blood. The edges of his vision blurred as fury consumed him. Bandim bared his teeth and growled.

"You need to learn your place," he snarled. "You may live in the empress' chambers, but that doesn't make you the empress. You have played me a merry tune, promising me the sun, the moons, and the stars, and what have you delivered for me?"

He tightened his grip around the thin slip of her neck. "Nothing!"

His temper burned brighter and his whole body flashed hot, as if he was engulfed in flame. He clamped his jaws together as ire consumed him. His nose slits flared.

Johrann squeezed her eyes shut as she tried to extricate herself from the tight clamp of his claws. That only urged Bandim's temper to flame.

"My word is law!" he said. "I told you not to return here, yet you have. Not only do you lie, but you disobey as well. You have promised me much and delivered me nothing. And now you have the audacity to enter my presence again, your arrogance leading you to think I'll take you back into my favor. No!"

Something flared within him with that word. A well of power rose within him, and his claws squeezed tighter.

He smelled the charred flesh before he saw the smoke.

Under his fingertips, Johrann's skin smoldered. She shrieked in agony, writhing to escape from his grasp. Bandim's eyes widened at the sight, shock keeping his grasp tight around her neck. Then thought dawned like a tawny sun and he released her.

Bandim stumbled backwards, staring at his hands. A bright red glow formed in his palms and snaked to the tips of his claws. Inside, fire as hot as a funeral pyre coursed through him. But fear began to dampen it, and he stuttered.

"What...what is this?" he asked. "What is this power?"

Johrann's neck still smoldered, but it was as if she couldn't feel the pain. Instead of tending to her wounds, she stared at him, jaw slack with awe.

"Your Grace," Johrann whispered, "it's happened at last. Look at your hands." Her shaking claws rose to touch her neck. "Look at what they've done. Look at the power, how it glows upon you. And your eyes, they glowed red too!"

She threw herself forward and fell at his feet. "Hand of Dorai," she said, her voice thick with emotion, "your powers are awakening. Your true spirit is returning!"

Fear gave way to abject joy. Johrann's words made Bandim's heart sing. He couldn't take his eyes from his hands. They glowed and pulsed as Dorai danced within him. At last, it had happened. At last, he could feel Dorai's presence. She inhabited his every corner, no longer invisible but flaring and glowing with fire.

Johrann had been *right*.

"This is...tremendous," he said. "I feel more powerful than I've ever felt before."

"You're not just *more* powerful," Johrann said, clutching at the hem of his robes. "You are all-powerful."

Ignoring her attempts to rise, Bandim clicked his talons. "Get me my handplate."

Immediately, Johrann scrabbled across the floor and found the plate, unscathed from its crash. She shuffled forward on her knees. Bowing her head, she held it up. Bandim snatched it from her talons and brought it to his face.

His breath caught. His eyes did glow red.

"It's true," he said. "My eyes... Now I have the power of the goddess within me."

He delved back in his thoughts, tracing the journey that had awakened his powers. "It was fury," he said. "My anger woke the goddess."

Johrann spoke, her mouth stumbling with the speed of her words. "Of course," she said. "'And when Dorai struck down the unbelievers with righteous anger, her eyes shone as bright as the midsun.' It is written! Your anger is Dorai's anger, righteous and terrifying!"

Bandim kept his gaze in the handplate. His claws tightened on the carved wooden handle. Anger. That was the key. His lips widened in a macabre smile. He had enough of that for three goddesses.

He flicked his eyes to Johrann, still prostrate on the floor. His smile faded.

Bandim pulled her to her feet by her collar. Residual heat pulsed through him.

"The goddess lives within you, awake at last!" Johrann said.

She reached for his hands, but Bandim snatched them away, still grasping his handplate. His anger reared again as a plan formed in his mind. "No thanks to you," he snarled.

Johrann recoiled as if struck. "Y-your Grace..."

Right she may have been, Bandim thought, but that didn't mean he needed to give her the satisfaction of his acknowledgement. He didn't need to be thankful to her, especially not now that he was truly more than just an ordinary male.

"Johrann Maa," he said, his voice low and dangerous. "You have proved yourself an unreliable advisor."

Her face fell and she shrank back. "I live only for you," she said. "I have never, ever sought to deceive you."

Bandim drew his eyeridges low and shook his head. "You have failed me," he said. "It should have been you that discovered the catalyst for my powers. I should not have had to find out for myself."

Johrann cast herself at his feet once more, and he allowed her to lavish kisses upon them. *Suffer*, he thought. *You deserve it.*

After a moment he stepped away, eyes back on his reflection. He glanced at her through the handplate. "However, you can redeem yourself," he continued.

"Anything, Your Grace," Johrann replied. "I'll do anything for you."

Bandim allowed himself a self-indulgent grin at her scrabbling before he schooled his expression into a solemn frown. As much as he wished to punish her, he couldn't push her away. Regardless of anything else, she was the only one of her colors he knew of, and the only one with any knowledge of the secrets of the goddess. While he didn't want to, he knew it was true. While he tried to deny it, he knew the reality. He needed her, for she was the one who'd opened the world up to Dorai. But his need didn't make them equals, and the more in her debt she felt, the more influence he'd have upon her.

"You will help me unlock my true potential," Bandim continued. "You know more of this power than anyone, unworthy as you are. If you prove yourself worthy by helping me harness Dorai's greatness, you will be welcomed back into my counsel. Until then you are nothing but a servant to me, and you will be treated as such."

Johrann smiled, an expression of complete devotion. "Yes, Your Grace," she said. "I'll do it. I'll prove to you that I am loyal."

Bandim shook his head, still staring at himself in the polished plate. His red eyes shimmered and shone. "It's not your loyalty that is at fault," he said, "but rather your arrogance."

Johrann's expression crumpled as if she had been stung. But she nodded and licked her lips, bringing her hands together. "Yes," she said. "I've been arrogant, and I've failed you. But I'll prove you can trust me. I will be nothing but a humble servant for your means."

"Good," Bandim said, staring at her through the plate. "The Althemerians won't be able to stand up to my powers once the goddess is strong within me. I will decimate them, just as my father wanted. I will prove to him, as he watches from the afterlife, that I was the true heir. It should have been me. I will raze the entire world, be the greatest emperor that ever lived, to show him that he and Mother were wrong!" Bandim's heart sang, his flesh tingled, and victory burned through him. "I will be all-powerful. I will crush the world. Nothing will stand in my way."

His mouth was a savage slash as he delivered his next words.

"I am the goddess incarnate."

CHAPTER SIXTEEN

Emmy

Why am I rocking?

Emmy turned and tried to cuddle her blanket, but there was no blanket. The soft flesh of her unarmored cheek scraped against rough wood. A sudden reek of stale bodies and detritus invaded. Bile rose in her throat as realization flooded in.

She jerked up, only to be toppled by the pitch of a wave. Gulping and retching, Emmy blinked in the gloom. Where was she? Surrounded on all sides by metal bars, her throat tightened. *We're on a Masvam ship!*

All around her were Metakalans in cages. Faces blinked in the gloom. Her old neighbors, those who had tormented her. They were all the same now, she thought, locked up like animals. She snorted, wondering if they still felt superior.

The sea dipped, eliciting a mournful chorus. It was followed by splashing and an unbearable stink. Emmy's memory came back in flashes. The terror of the explosions. The mania of the streets. The capture, the apothecary, the destruction...

Krodge and Bose. *Dead.*

And Zecha! Emmy jerked forward, scanning the cages through the darkness. He had to be all right. Tears beaded. He just *had* to be all right.

"Emmy, are you awake now? Emmy! Emmy!"

Emmy turned in the tiny space, cursing her thick tail, and pressed her face to the front bars. They were locked tight. Many sets of eyes blinked through the darkness, but none belonged to the voice she sought.

"Down here!"

Emmy squinted, her head swimming. A familiar face shone in the darkness. "Charo!" she cried. "Are you all right?"

But their conversation was cut short, for their words uncorked terror.

"We've been captured!" someone wailed.

"We're going to die!" said another.

Emmy gulped against another wave.

Charo stared from a low cage. The details of her face were obscured by shadow, but fear shone bright in her eyes.

"Where's Zecha?" Emmy asked.

Before Charo could answer, another familiar voice sounded through the blackness. "I'm here," said Zecha.

Unsure where the voice came from, Emmy's ears fought for the sound. He was close. "Zecha?" she called.

"Yes, it's me," came the weak reply.

"Where are you?"

"Right below you, I think. Can you feel this?"

A claw poked through a crack in her cell floor. Emmy snatched it. "Yes, I can," she said, the twist in her gut abating.

Their touch lingered for a moment. The moment of joy was torn by a terrified wail.

"We're doomed," one of the voices from before said. "Nunako is punishing us. We're doomed!"

The comfort of Zecha's touch disappeared. "How long have we been in here?" he asked.

"About a day, I think," Charo replied. "It's hard to tell when there's no sun or moons to guide you."

"We need to do something," Zecha said. "We can't just sit here."

He grunted and twisted, pressing his eye to the crack in the floor.

"These must be slave ships," Emmy replied. "Why else would there be cages? But the Masvams don't take slaves."

Charo grunted. When she spoke, her tone was bitter. "Not until now."

"Maybe they got the ships from the Valtat," Zecha offered. "The slavers wouldn't sell their ships, but the Masvams would certainly take them."

"However they got them," Emmy continued, "there must be locks on the doors. But there might be rust, or weak patches, or something might come loose."

"Are there guards down here?" Zecha asked.

"Not that I've seen," Charo replied. "No one's come in or out since we were shoved in here."

Emmy leaned forward and edged her claws through the gaps in the bars. The hinges were cool under the pads of her talons, but they felt strong. She moved on to the lock, pulling and twisting it, but to no avail. She sat back, shaking her head. "I'm locked in tight," she said.

"Me too," Charo replied.

Zecha's voice was hopeful when he spoke. "My lock is rusty. If I keep working at it, who knows? It might come loose."

Emmy smiled and poked her talon through the crack in the floor. That was Zecha, always hopeful. "If anyone can do it, you can," she said.

Zecha touched her claw, wrapping one of his around it. "I hope so," he replied.

Time passed. From below her came the *tap tap tap* of Zecha working at his lock. There were times when it stopped, and he was asleep. But more often than not, he kept working at it.

Darkness swirled like inky tendrils. It closed around Emmy's throat like claws. She rubbed her skin, a meager fight against the gathering cold. Glancing at the other cages, she swallowed. Metakalans lay bloodied and beaten and unconscious. She knew them all. Charber was there, as was Leeve.

Kain wasn't.

Emmy shuddered. Kain was probably dead. She couldn't see any younglings on the boat.

That thought spurred her into working at her lock again. She knew it was futile, but she had to do *something* to help.

There was little conversation as another day passed. The only sounds were of despair and hopelessness, the bitter crashing of the wind, and the battering of waves against the ship's dark hold. Emmy flexed her legs in a feeble attempt to soothe the agonizing cramps brought on by her hours of working at the lock. But the action brought little comfort, in the same way that poking and prodding the lock brought little joy.

The ship dipped and rose on tumultuous waves, bringing fresh nausea to the cargo. The stench caked Emmy's mouth and lined her nostrils. Charo swore as the ship leaned to and fro, filling her low enclosure with a flood of rottenness.

Emmy put her face in her filthy hands. She wished it was a dream, but it wasn't. It was worse than any nightmare. It was as if the goddess had heard her Middlemerish prayer and warped it. She'd asked for freedom, but received capture instead. Emmy would have given anything to go back to the way things were, even with Krodge and Bose. At least in Bellim there was the possibility of freedom. At least there, had she gathered the courage and determination, she could have left. But the hard reality of the stench and the screams kept gnawing at her.

Fear steered her claws back to the lock. Then there was a new sound, metallic and moaning, right below her.

Emmy stared down as a miracle from the goddess unfolded.

One leg stretched from the cell beneath her, then another. Zecha stumbled to his feet, limbs and tail flailing. His delight lit the darkness. "I'm out!" he said, patting his front. "I'm actually out!"

Emmy's grin was so wide it hurt her cheeks. "How did you do it?"

Zecha pressed his face to her bars for a moment, his smile matching hers. "The lock was rusted," he said. "I knew if I kept working at it, eventually it would pop."

The sight of a Metakalan standing outside the bars spread hope like wildfire.

"Oh, Nunako be praised!" said a voice. "Someone's out!"

"Free us! Free us!"

The hold filled with a cacophony of elation.

"Oh, I knew the goddess would save us!"

"We can be free again!"

"Hush!" Zecha cried. "They can't know one of us is free!"

His voice struggled to rise above the clamor. Emmy threaded her claws through the bars.

"Shut up!" she hissed. "He's right!"

The noise only grew louder, rising in a harried crescendo. Why weren't they listening? Another thought fought back. *They're not listening because they don't respect you. Why should they? You're just a Moon Rogue.* Anger swirled within Emmy and she clenched her claws around the bars until they bit into her skin. That was her old life. That was when she was crushed underneath Krodge's boot heel. That was when she was stuck in the apothecary, too scared to leave, too scared of what might happen to her.

Things were different now. She'd had been taken from that life. Krodge would never crush her again. And under the rule of the Masvams, they'd all be the same. None of them would have freedom or respect. Emmy's whole body trembled, and she bit her lower lip, squeezing her eyes shut. What did she have to lose?

Her voice struck like lightning. "*QUIET!*"

The power of the sound stunned her. Never before had she yelled so loudly. There had never been the opportunity, except alone in the woods. Even then, Emmy had been too scared to scream in case she drew attention from a hidden hunter, who would tell the story, which would get back to Krodge, and then Emmy would receive a beating. Now the sense of strange liberation outweighed even the fear of her shout summoning a Masvam.

There was absolute silence in the hold. Zecha froze in front of her, half-poised to attack, half-ready to run. "Emmy," he said, a slow smile creeping onto his face. "I didn't know you could yell so loud."

"Neither did I," she replied.

"Wow," Charo said, grinning up from her lower cage.

Emmy grinned back, but the elation of finding her voice ebbed away. They were still in the ship's hold. Only one of them was free. It wasn't enough. There needed to be a next step. Her friends seemed to follow her unspoken train of thought as their faces fell too.

"What do we do now?" Zecha asked.

He clung to the cage bars, desperately keeping balance on the pitching deck.

"We need to keep the noise as normal," Emmy said. "They can't suspect. They haven't been down yet, but that doesn't mean they won't—"

A rolling wave interrupted her. Zecha was saved from a face-first introduction to the deck only by the tight winding of his claws in the bars.

Once the ship was stable again, Emmy continued.

"Zecha, try and free some of us first," she said. "Any rusty lock is easy game. Once a few of us are out, we'll get everyone freed, and—"

Something scraped against the hold door. Keys jangled. Zecha paled.

With a crash, light and fresh air flooded in, blinding them. Emmy's gaze flicked between Zecha and the gaping hole—and the thick silhouettes standing in it.

"What happens here, filth?" a Masvam yelled. "You make noise and—"

At the sight of Zecha, the sailor stilled. His eyes narrowed and his tail twitched.

Horror descended on Zecha's face.

The Masvam walked forward, teeth glinting. "You to die, filth," he snarled.

Then he bolted towards Zecha, blade drawn.

CHAPTER SEVENTEEN

Emmy

Zecha screeched and took a long slash to the head, then found himself pinned against the cages.

"No!" Emmy cried.

Blood poured from a fresh wound, rivulets of red running down Zecha's face. The Masvam pressed his forearm to his victim's neck, allowing only a sliver of air to pass through Zecha's throat.

"Think you that you escape?" he snarled. "Think you that you save your friends can?" He laughed again. The sound sent an icy shudder down Emmy's spine, right to the tip of her tail. "Pshala," he spat. "Metakalan make me laugh. Could I snap your neck now and—"

"Yamor, *cease*."

As Yamor released his throat, Zecha breathed in sweet life. Still pinned, he couldn't double over to scrabble for breath. Emmy silenced her sigh of relief and pressed herself tight against the bars.

Three more Masvams strode up the deck, trailing the tang of salt and beer. Two of them, Emmy knew. Mamusan and Kelom. The other, three torques of gold on his upper arm, was unknown.

"But Ysmas Pesmam," Yamor said, his words petulant, "he deserves die."

"By not your word or hand," Pesmam snapped.

Pesmam shoved Yamor aside. Freed at last, Zecha gasped for breath.

"Your name, what is?" Pesmam asked. His orange eyes glinted.

Zecha gulped more air and shook his head. Pesmam grabbed his chin, jerking his head up, crumpling his face.

"Your name, what is?" Pesmam said again.

Still Zecha didn't reply. Pesmam wrenched him up by his half-crushed throat.

"I let not Yamor your life take," he snarled, "but will I if—"

"Zecha!" a voice cried. "His name is Zecha!"

Emmy's eyes snapped to Charo, whose face was lined with despair. Pesmam dropped Zecha and clicked his tongue.

"You, *Zecha*," he said, his tongue stumbling on the unknown name, "is fool. Need you punishment."

"Throw him to the sea!" Kelom said, rubbing his claws in glee.

"Shut up," Pesmam snapped. Kelom recoiled. "Too easy."

Pesmam cupped Zecha's chin in one hand. Zecha tried to look anywhere except at the Masvam, but found himself forced to stare into his eyes.

"Far too easy, it would," he purred. He rubbed a gentle circle on Zecha's cheek. Zecha stiffened and tried to jerk away. "Need I to make example of *Zecha*."

He released Zecha's head and turned towards the rows of cages. Yamor pinned Zecha's arms.

"A lesson, this is," Pesmam said in a grand voice. Despite the oddness of his language, the meaning was clear. "Prisoners of Masvam Empire, all you. Escape you, or try, will you to afterlife hastened—lingering and painful it be."

He turned to Zecha and stared, chin held high. His orange eyes flickered. "First, you be."

Pesmam jolted forward. There was a dull sucking sound and it took a long moment for understanding to dawn. Time stilled. Zecha stared at Pesmam. Then he looked down—at the dagger jutting from his abdomen.

Emmy couldn't even scream. All she could smell was blood.

Pesmam yanked the dagger out with a twist and Zecha finally howled, clutching at his stomach and falling to his knees, tail between his legs, his talons turning red.

The captain stepped back and wiped the dagger on his salt-stiffened trousers. His lips curled and he took a long look at the sets of eyes that stared at him from the darkness of the cages. He pointed to the prone form.

"Watch him die," Pesmam said. "Decide you to follow him, know you what awaits."

At that, Emmy found her voice again. "Zecha, no!" she cried.

Pesmam grunted, lips twisted in a mordant grin.

"Come," Pesmam said. "These *pchak*, no food." When the Metakalans' fear rose, it fed Pesmam's satisfaction. He spat on Zecha's head. "Thank you, your dying friend."

With that the three Masvams strode off. They sealed the hold behind them. The slam rattled Emmy's teeth. Once more they were left in grim darkness. The sweetness of the sea air was gone.

Emmy didn't care about that. "Zecha!" she cried.

The only response was a sudden thump, followed by a whimper just audible above the creaking ship.

"Zecha, can you hear me?" Emmy continued, her voice rising. "Zecha, please!"

"Zecha, answer her!"

Charo's voice was a sharp strike. Zecha moaned again and struggled to rise. He slammed, facedown, onto the filthy deck. Detritus lapped around him. Blood coursed from his wound.

No matter how hard they tried, they could elicit no further response.

"Zecha, no," Emmy whispered. "Don't leave me. I need you."

In the darkness, truth shone. It wasn't until those words were uttered that Emmy realized how true they were. For the longest time, Zecha was the only one who never judged her appearance, never called her a Moon Rogue, never cast her aside. Until Charo, he was the only one she called a friend. He was always there with kindness in his eyes and joy in his heart, despite his longing to be something he couldn't be.

And now? Emmy's gaze slid sideways to Charo. She was slumped against the bars, one claw stretching for Zecha's hand. For the sweetest of moments, Emmy had had two friends. Now, it seemed, she would be left with one again.

No.

Determination rose. She wouldn't lose Zecha, not if it took everything she had. Not if it killed her. Drawing in a deep breath, Emmy reached for her lock again.

She rattled it, wrenched it, planted her feet on the cage front, yanked as hard as she could. Emmy grunted, growing more desperate with every minute. Zecha was below her, and he needed her. She could save him, she just knew it. Somehow, she knew she could. Her mind was reeling, but she knew if she got to him, was able to lay her hands on him, somehow she could save him.

Everything else fell away. The sounds and smells of the hold, the sharp taint of others' desperation. All that mattered to Emmy was saving her friend.

"Zecha," she said over and over like a mantra. "Zecha, Zecha, Zecha..."

Fatigue pressed upon her, but Emmy kept going, until her mantra turned into a series of sobs.

Her despair was interrupted. "Emmy, don't torture yourself."

Blinking, Emmy looked to the source of the voice. In the darkness, Charo's eyes were lost in black shadows.

"You need to stop," Charo said. Her words were leaden. "It's pointless. You'll never open it."

Emmy shook her head, desperate claws aching as they kept working at the lock. "What choice do I have?" she asked. "Zecha's going to die. I need to help him."

Her gaze slid to Zecha. He still hadn't moved. Her heart clung to the hope she could get out, or that they might be rescued, that they could get Zecha help...

"Maybe..." Charo started. She trailed off, as if the words she was to speak cut her tongue. "Maybe Zecha's better off dead."

Her voice hitched as the name passed her lips.

No.

There was a frantic scrabble as Emmy yanked at her cage again. Her shoulders rose and fell. Her fists clenched and unclenched to the rhythm of a sudden, silent battle-chant. "I won't accept that. I won't accept that!"

"Emmy..." Charo began.

Ignoring her, Emmy kept working at the lock. The tips of her talons bled into the metal.

"Emmy!"

This time it was Charo's voice that struck like lightning. Emmy stilled.

"Listen to me," Charo continued. "I don't want to be a slave again. I'd rather die. And I mean that. I'd sooner cut my own throat."

Her voice hitched. Tears tracked down her face, cutting a sharp line through the grime. Her hands and shoulders pulsed as she stared at Zecha's prone form.

"But working and working at something," Charo went on, "that will never come to anything is pointless. It's madness. So stop. Just...stop."

The sting of Charo's words sobered her, and Emmy reluctantly released the lock. "Charo, I..."

Emmy knew Charo needed words of encouragement. She knew, as a friend, that it was her job to keep trying, in spite of everything. That was what was supposed to happen. That was why she'd pulled and pulled at the lock until blood coursed down her claws and her hands. But the naked honesty of Charo's words took her own words away.

Charo filled the silence between them.

"Maybe Zecha is better off dead," she repeated. Her voice was flat. "I say that because I know what our future holds. It'll be filled with humiliation, servitude, and an eventual lonely death when we're no longer of any use. I've been there. I've lived as a slave, and it's no life at all. You're not considered a living thing. You're passed through families like a possession. You're bought and sold in the same way as livestock."

"Charo..." Emmy said, but nothing further came.

Charo kept talking, the words monotone.

"I was taken into slavery when I was six," she said. "It was the Valtat. They got me. The Masvams let them through their borders, into Linvarra, where I was hatched. I don't know if I had a moi or a poi, or siblings, or any family at all. I was chained by the neck and pulled onto a podium, and they were shouting things in languages I didn't understand. Then I was bought. My first job was as a potwash in a scullery, where I was chained to the wall for nearly all the day. I've been bought and sold five times—five times from six to fourteen. And then I found you." Her voice changed, suddenly thick with tears. "And I found Zecha, and everything was all right—until the Masvams came. But that's why I say Zecha is better off dead, and we might as well be, too."

Tears flowed down her grime-encrusted face again.

Emmy swallowed against her own tears. It was the first time Charo had spoken of her life before the apothecary, apart from the mention of the mistress who stabbed her.

"I understand all that," Emmy said, "but I have to try and save him. He's my friend. He's—"

Emmy's words died as a muffled boom sounded in the distance. Cries of fear gave way to the numbness of shock. Then the Metakalans burst into whispers.

There was another blast. Charo's anguish broke. She stared with a twist of confusion that mirrored Emmy's own.

Cocking her head to the side, Emmy listened hard. "Something's wrong," she said. "They're shouting."

Sure enough, the crew's cries rose with further blasts. The hold erupted with a barrage of shouts. Above, the explosions drew closer.

"What's happening?" someone cried.

"Is this it? Is this the end of us?"

Emmy ignored them and gritted her teeth. She didn't care about the others and their fears. She didn't care about what was happening outside. She had eyes for only one.

Zecha's prone form slid on the deck, covered in filth. *If this is the end, so be it*, she thought. *If we must die, I'd rather we died together.*

At least in death, perhaps they would be free.

CHAPTER EIGHTEEN

Emmy

Screams and cannon blasts sounded overhead, muffled by the thick wood of the hull. Tremors shook the beams above and rattled in tune with the captives' terror. The Masvam ship rocked like a cork in the great sea. Emmy clung to her cage as fear took hold. Those who hadn't grabbed their bars were bucked and tossed inside their tiny prisons. Emmy kept her eyes on Zecha and tried to keep her tears at bay. His body rolled with the waves.

As the ship lurched, he tumbled across the length of the hold, landing in a crumpled heap at Charo's cage. She pushed her hands through the bars and wound her talons into his filthy shirt to stop him rolling again.

The ship jerked again. Surrounded by shrieking and screeching, Emmy felt like a character in one of Krodge's bedtime tales of Moon Rogues and demons. Metakalans pounded on bars and rattled doors with desperate claws. Some even came loose. The momentary bubble of joy didn't last long. They were trapped below the deck of a beleaguered ship. There was little elation in that.

Above them there were more blasts. Emmy's breath came faster and faster. What was happening? Who was attacking? Could they be friends, or would they be more enemies? There was no way to know, and that made Emmy's heart hammer. She scrabbled forward and clawed at her lock again. If some of the other cage doors came loose, surely hers could, too...

An ominous creaking came from above, followed by what sounded like a tree being felled. Whatever it was hit the deck above, sending deadly tremors through the hold. Emmy stopped her work and listened. The hold was silent, every ear listening.

There were more vibrations.

Then came screams, thundering footsteps, and the clash of sword on sword. The ship was being boarded. That was the only explanation Emmy's spinning brain could find.

The fighting above seemed to last for eternity. Emmy's fight with her lock continued. She was about to give up when there was a flash of cold and *clack*—something happened, and the lock dropped to the deck.

"I did it!"

She shoved the cage open with freezing claws and untangled herself. Straight away she went to Zecha, pulling him from Charo's grasp, laying his head on her lap.

"Help him," Charo said, her words thin with despair.

Emmy was forced to lay Zecha's head in the filth to allow her claws to reach his wound. The stab was deep, the edges ragged. Emmy's breathing hitched as her medical knowledge laid out the likely outcome before her. It was like Krodge was speaking in her head.

A deep wound, through the stomach. Excess bleeding with filth penetrating from the outside. From the inside, filth from the bowels seeping into the wound. It needed to be cleaned. Even then, the likelihood of survival was low. It was easy to sew the outer wounds closed, but the inner damage was a different story.

Emmy couldn't breathe. With Charo it had been easy. There had been no damage to the fleshy inside of the body. But Zecha's stomach... It was different. She was sure of it. It would be difficult.

But it is not impossible, came Krodge's voice.

In an instant Emmy was back in the kitchen of the apothecary, with a dead body stretched out on the table—an entirely illegal practice, but Krodge felt herself above such archaic laws. She had opened the female, exposing the myriad of organs within. Emmy had only been ten, but she'd watched with fascination, not disgust.

"Study the insides," Krodge said. "Sometimes you need to get your claws into the inner workings of the body to save it."

The crone had taken Emmy on a tour of this inside world, smiling in conspiracy, knowing Emmy was so under her control that she'd never tell of these journeys into the unknown. And if Emmy had spoken? No one would have believed the Moon Rogue.

Emmy blinked and stared at the wound with new eyes, scanning it with every measure of expertise and memory she had.

It was deep, but she could save him. She just knew it. If only she had the equipment, a knife, pulled-gut thread.

You don't need that, a strange voice said.

Emmy stilled, gripping Zecha hard. The voice wasn't her own, nor was it Krodge's. It was unknown yet strangely familiar, as if she'd heard it many cycles before.

Lay your hands on him, the voice continued. *You've done it before. Stop the bleeding. Save him.*

Emmy swallowed. She shut her eyes. This was it. She'd lost her mind. A voice in her head, a voice that sounded familiar? It wasn't real.

Even so, the strange coldness tingled anew in her talons, and she opened her eyes once more. Zecha lay prone, filthy, dying. She might have lost her mind, but she could help save his life.

Trembling, she placed her hands on the wound.

The coldness came in waves, pulsing from somewhere deep inside. It was all for nothing. It was her imagination. It was a fever dream, unreal, foolish. But then, she thought, her eyes never leaving Zecha's pallid face, what did she have to lose?

She kept her hands on Zecha for some time. Beside her, Charo reached out. The tips of her talons brushed the edge of Emmy's shoulder. The three stayed like that as confusion and fear swirled around them, hundreds of Metakalan voices crying out their fear. Above them, the sounds of combat continued. Emmy's coldness abated, replaced by the warmth of love and the hope she had somehow saved him.

After a time, the metallic slice of sword on sword ceased. With it came silence in the hold, a silence that was only broken by the jangle of keys, the slide of a barrel into a mechanism, and the smooth turn of a lock.

Light and sweet air spilled into the hold, and Emmy had to shield her eyes against the brightness. Her eyes focused, and she saw two figures silhouetted against the sky.

"By Ethay and Apago," a strangely accented voice said. "It stinks in here."

"What are they carrying?" the second odd voice asked. "Livestock?"

The figures stepped forward. Emmy couldn't breathe. These were the folk who'd attacked the ship. They had dark skin and dark armor, and bright eyes that shone like jewels. Emmy had seen many of their kind before, coming into Bellim's port on ships with a two-headed serpent on the prow.

"Althemerians," she whispered. Her grip on Zecha grew tighter.

"By the gods," the first Althemerian said, her voice low. She kissed her fist, then laid it on her chest. Her arms jingled; they were covered with many bracelets. "They weren't transporting livestock."

Those Metakalans who'd been freed from their cages lunged forward, grabbing for the strangers.

"Thank you!"

"By the goddess, you've saved us!"

Beside her, Charo rattled against her cage and grinned. "They've come to free us," she said.

Emmy tried to smile in return, but something Krodge had said not long before came back to her.

There's an Althemerian custom I'm quite fond of. It's about owing a debt to those who have helped you.

She glanced at the rising tide of Metakalans, now being held back by more and more Althemerians. Eventually they let the captives scramble onto the deck. Emmy clutched Zecha's body to her, shielding him from the stampede. With those already freed out of the way, Althemerians—both male and female—came along the length of the hold, striking off the locks of those still enclosed. Not all the cages bore living survivors. That thought spurred Emmy's tongue into action. "Help!" she cried.

A wiry Althemerian male approached her, wearing a weatherbeaten blue tunic and the heaviness of a life of battle on his face. Two twined serpents were picked out in thread on the chest of his uniform.

"My friend," Emmy said. "He's been stabbed. He needs help."

"Easy," the Althemerian said, his many bracelets jangling. "Easy now. I'll get a healer."

He disappeared from the hold, returning with two others. One was male and wore the same uniform as the first Althemerian. The other was female, a different symbol on a black tunic. It was a strange thing, colored red, a heart within an eye. Many bags hung from her belt, heavy with their contents. She knelt at Zecha's side and pried his eyelids open, checking for signs of life. She used her left arm, which bore many more bracelets than her right.

"He isn't dead," Emmy said. "I know he's not. Help him!"

The female—a healer—nodded and gestured for the males to lift Zecha between them. He was slung from their hands, prone but no longer bleeding.

"He isn't dead," the healer confirmed. "I'll see what I can do."

The three disappeared up the deck with Zecha, and Emmy went to follow, but a cry from Charo stopped her. Another Althemerian struck the lock from her cage and Charo extricated herself. Straight away she threw herself into Emmy's arms, wrapping her own around Emmy's tall, thin body.

"We're saved," Charo whispered, "and Zecha will be okay."

Unable to speak in return, to say everything would be fine, Emmy pulled away and took Charo's hand. Together they slipped into the flow of freedom, their limbs cracking and loosening after so long in captivity.

Emmy took in heavy swallows of freshness, trying to quiet her hammering heart. The unsullied air caught in the back of her throat. If their saviors had been anyone but Althemerians, she might have had more joy. Unfortunately, that was not to be.

Alongside the captured Masvam ship was a long Althemerian rig, complete with flags streaming in the sea breeze. They bore the entwined serpents of the Althemerian gods. It was the same sigil found on the chests of their "liberators." Emmy had seen it long before, struck onto the backs of foreign coins. Remembering Krodge's words, the image didn't fill her heart with joy.

Neither did the sight that greeted her when she looked at the deck.

Hewn bodies littered it, a garden of murder. Kelom was there, his insides spilling out, death's scream on his face. Yamor's head was at arm's length from his body. Another commotion came from up the deck. Emmy and Charo followed the noise, pushing their way through the crowd.

It was Pesmam, struggling in the grip of his Althemerian captors.

He was brought before a striking female with dark skin and armor and sparkling green eyes. Her uniform was richly embroidered with serpents in greens and blues and silver. There was something about her that commanded attention. Charo and Emmy couldn't look away. She wielded a heavy sword, and her arms were bedecked with hundreds of sparkling bracelets.

"As captain of this slave ship," the Althemerian female said, her voice regal, "you have committed a grave crime. I, Princess Valaria of Althemer, condemn you to death for your wickedness, on the authority of my mother Queen Valentia and the balance of Ethay and Apago."

Emmy and Charo looked at one another, sharing the same thought. *A princess?*

Pesmam's struggle grew stronger as he was forced to his knees, but he was no match for his captors. The Althemerian princess, Valaria, raised her sword.

Pesmam was held in place. He had no final words. His last gesture was to spit at the princess' feet.

The blade was sharp and swift. Pesmam's body slumped to the deck of his ship, while his head was held aloft by the princess.

"So is the justice of the Twin Gods, and of the Queen of Althemer!" said Valaria. Then, all grandness gone, she handed her sword and Pesmam's decapitated head off to an attendant. "Put that somewhere. I'll need it later."

"Yes, Princess."

Pesmam's headless corpse was tossed into the sea. The princess turned and disappeared. The atmosphere was one of unabated elation. Althemerian sailors brought supplies from their rig, taking charge of the Masvam ship. The injured were transported to the other vessel, the Althemerian sailors' feet light on the planks slung between the ships. *They have to take care of Zecha*, Emmy thought. No matter what Charo said before, surely it was better to be a captive and alive than dead and free.

Regardless, she was certain he wouldn't die.

Emmy thought of the coldness in her hands and the voice in her head. It was madness, but she couldn't help but hope that she'd helped him somehow.

Despite her assurances that life was better than death, a niggling doubt was at the back of Emmy's thoughts. Charo's earlier words echoed back.

I've lived as a slave, and it's no life at all.

Charo's current words were tinged with the half-delirium that swept across the deck of the ship. "We're free now. Once Zecha's better, we can make our way back to Bellim, or what's left of it. Or we could go somewhere else. Or—"

Emmy grabbed Charo and pulled her aside. She kept her hand clamped on Charo's shoulder.

"What's wrong?" Charo asked, her eyes searching Emmy's face.

"I wouldn't be so hasty."

Emmy's expression bore no joy, and Charo's grew pained. "What do you mean?"

she asked. "We're free from the Masvams."

"We're free from one slaver," Emmy said, gesturing at the flag of two twined serpents flapping in the breeze, "but we've been saved by the hand of another."

Charo's eyes went wide and glassy, and she shook Emmy's hand from her shoulder. "No," she said. "They've saved us. They're not slavers, not like the Valtat..."

Emmy chuckled, but the sound was dry.

"Don't they know anything in the north?" she asked. "The Althemerians have saved us, but by their laws, we now owe them a debt. They'll keep us until they decree that debt is repaid." She choked out another laugh. "Don't you see? We haven't been given our freedom at all."

CHAPTER NINETEEN

Mantos

He tugged the hem of the bed shirt over his head and smoothed out its creases. For a moment, Mantos of House Tiboli stood in the middle of the strange chamber, listening to unfamiliar sounds. Far-off bells tolled in high towers. Ethereal chanting rose from the temple of Ethay and Apago, just like it had every other day since he'd awoken in this strange place. He clenched his fists, the skin tightening, growing pale. The rings he still wore were like jaws around his talons.

Mantos Tiboli had returned from the dead.

The last thing he remembered was standing in his mourning whites on the grand balcony, listening to the sound of anguished cries from below.

"*The Emperor is dead!*"

Candles blossomed in the courtyard. Long tendrils of light spilled out, winding around the city he called home.

Then he couldn't breathe. He had fallen on one knee and felt the thread of his life grow tight.

Then there was nothing.

Now Mantos wore a stranger's clothes, stood in an unknown chamber, and didn't know if he was alive or dead or somewhere in-between.

He brought one hand up to the divot at the base of his throat, talons closing around the crossed lightning strikes and shield that were the symbol of his house. His name. His family.

He scoffed, pressing the pad of his thumb into the gold. The pendant was a symbol of what he used to have, and what his brother had sought to take from him. He should have wrenched the chain from his neck and cast the pendant into the fire. But he didn't.

For some time, he remained on the woven carpet with his claws around the pendant, waiting.

For what?

Eventually, he released the chain and flexed his claws, rolled his shoulders, swept his tail back and forth. He felt the roughness of the weave beneath his feet and the coolness of the linen on his chest. He felt the breeze wafting in from the open window, bringing with it otherworldly chanting.

He had returned from the *dead*.

I wish I could remember something, he thought, drumming his toes on the ground. Every sensation was strange, as if he'd been encased in ice for a thousand cycles. The world felt off—a perception beyond being in a new place and wearing clothes that weren't his own.

He was on Althemer. Fonbir was here, his beloved of so many cycles. Finally they stood on the same land, breathed the same sweet air. And when Fonbir snuck into Mantos' chamber, his trusted guards standing watch at the door, they could be together. It was like a dream had come half-true.

Mantos rubbed his hands along the length of his arms. Only a half-truth because while they were together, it wasn't what Mantos had dreamed of. It was strange, like an image in a warped plate. His ability to touch his beloved Nabi, the nickname reserved for Fonbir alone, shocked him like lightning. They could lie in each other's arms, simply exist in one another's company, but there was something else, something strange, that dwelt in Mantos' chest, even as he stared into his lover's strange white eyes.

It was a thought that made his blood run cold.

He had returned from the *dead*.

Mantos curled his toes into the rough mat and closed his eyes. Nothing made sense. No matter how he tried to wrap his mind around the thoughts that plagued him, he couldn't shape them into any sense. He'd been dead, and was now alive. He'd been in the Masvam Empire, and was now on Althemer. He'd lost his life, but he couldn't remember what came after. He couldn't remember the Light.

Perhaps there is no Light, he thought. *Perhaps there's nothing after death.*

That thought frightened him to his bones.

Mantos walked to the window, pulled open the shutters, and stared into the courtyard. A great fountain rose from its center, and the sound of temple chanting drifted on the breeze. Althemer, the island of serpents with their two-headed god, maintained constant devotion with chants hour after hour, day after day. Everything in their architecture was a tribute to Ethay and Apago, with winding lines like a serpent's body and twin symmetry everywhere. Mantos cast his gaze into every nook of the courtyard and shuddered. Being here didn't feel real, yet it was. He rubbed his arms once more.

Another strange occurrence stunned Mantos, something he never thought possible. Especially not on Althemer, so far from home.

His *mother* was here.

The moment he met her eyes, Mantos' heart had stopped. For his whole life, Phen of House Yru had been enclosed in a tower. He'd never seen her eyes so clear, her face so full of life—and terror. She was alive and well, dressed in strange clothing, *talking* to him. Touching him. Crying over him. Mantos shuddered. Nothing made sense.

He leaned out of the window, pressing his palms to the wide sill, and stared at the long drop below. So far he hadn't been allowed to leave this chamber. Phen and Fonbir visited him, both always flanked by guards. There were more guards at his door, standing watch to ensure the Masvam prisoner did not escape. Mantos knew they didn't know who he really was. It wasn't the sort of information a wise leader shared with those who didn't need to know. To them he was a prisoner: high-ranking, no doubt, but there was nothing to indicate he was a prince. *An emperor*, Mantos corrected himself.

Even servants were denied access to him. They left food at the door and didn't enter for his slops.

"Queen's orders," the surly guards had said.

Those were the only words they spoke to him. And rightly so, Mantos thought. The guard shouldn't consort with the prisoner. It was dangerous and foolhardy. Conversation slipped so easily, and information could be gleaned that the speaker never meant to share. A clever prisoner knew this. A clever prisoner would do anything to find a foothold to help spring his escape.

Mantos knew this well, and so did the guards. Thus they remained silent, not even looking him in the eye.

The only stranger to grace his presence was the creature of strange colors. *The Stranger*, they called her. Bomsoi. A magician. A life-giver. Blue and purple, what Mantos would call a Moon Rogue. When she visited him, she asked how he was, how he felt, was he well? Mantos responded in monotone. He was fine. He felt fine. Everything was fine.

It wasn't, though. His waking moments were filled with contemplation. He thought of his death and the lack of Light. The lack of anything. Distressed, he tried to bury his musings by concentrating on *feeling*: the texture of the rug, his clothing, the gentle pass of his hands over his soft skin and the roughness of his armor scales.

The days were easier than the nights. In the darkness it was difficult to banish the brooding wonder of whether there was life after death, or whether the Light was real or not. Worst of all, his sleep was poisoned, filled with strange figures and faces—and white-hot agony.

When he dreamed, his body was torn in two. Fissures opened, pulling and stretching skin and muscle and bone until he was ripped apart. Nothing stopped it. The torture came night after night.

A reluctant weariness overcame him, and Mantos forced his body back to the bed's soft embrace. He tucked an arm under his pillow and lay on his side, curling his tail between his legs. He breathed slowly, willing his mind to grant him a semblance of peace. He tried to think of anything but the terrible splitting, the tearing in two, the invasion of his body by *something*...

Then he was watching himself from afar: tiny, isolated, adrift on a sea of loneliness. Clanking surrounded him and unseen chains bound him, all undercut by a whine that rang in his chest. Then the figure spoke, and he knew it was not himself.

"Mantos! Mantos!" The creature turned in circles, calling out, whirling into nothingness. "Mantos!"

No matter how he tried, he couldn't move forward. His arms and legs were leaden as he struggled and flailed.

There was no warning for what happened next.

A howl erupted from his throat as Mantos split from head to tail. It was like a hot knife slipped through him. All he knew was pain. Reality swirled as he screamed, desperately trying to put his body back together. The figure that wasn't himself shuddered towards him. This time, it wasn't crying out. It was *grinning*.

"Mantos, Mantos..."

Bandim!

And yet, it wasn't. Something was strange, as if the creature was a reflection of his brother in an unpolished plate.

"Dear brother," Bandim whispered. "I will find you..."

In a whirl of heat and dust the voice distorted, whining and stretching until Mantos could bear no more. He pressed his hands to his ears, chanting in vain protection.

"Stop! Stop!" he cried. "Leave me be! Leave me be!"

Uncountable hands were on his body, touching and grabbing and pulling him apart, and—

"Mantos, *Mantos!*"

He jerked upright, bed covers tumbling from his soaked skin. His eyes roved, trying to find the owner of the hands. When he caught Phen's gaze and felt the softness of her skin, tears flowed. "Mother..."

Phen took him in her arms.

Mantos fell into the embrace. Before, his mother had been a pitiable figure, caged in the prison of her mind. She was someone his father never spoke of. She was the wretched waif in the Grieving Tower, someone he was forbidden to visit, though that never stopped him. But he never expected to look into her eyes and see recognition there.

Now she was here. Now she held him in her arms. She was real.

"Shh, shh," Phen cooed. "It's all right, my sweet. It was another dream. Another terrible dream."

Memories of sleepless nights came back to him, a youngling wishing for his mother's embrace, receiving nothing but cold air and silence. He had needed her. *Needed* her. But now she was with him, truly alive and well. And she held him as long as he needed.

He'd come back from the *dead*.

It was all too much.

When his tears abated at last, thunder rolled in the distance. Phen touched his face, brushing stray droplets with the tip of her thumb. She traced his armor.

"My son," she whispered. "I can't believe you've come back to me."

Swallowing against his tight throat, Mantos mirrored her gesture. "I can't believe *you've* come back to *me*," he said. "All those cycles of secret visits... I never thought I would hear your voice."

Phen kept her hand on his face. Thunder rolled again, growing closer.

"I'm here," she said, her voice strained. "I wouldn't have left you if I hadn't been forced. But it was my life or yours. There was no choice to make. I had to keep you safe."

There was a flash in the darkness, but Mantos didn't flinch. His focus was entirely on his mother. His *mother*, who for his entire life had been a husk lingering on life's periphery. Someone with two dead eyes and no voice.

Phen smoothed fronds from his face. "Tell me about your nightmares," she said, her voice soft as silk. "Please, tell me."

The words had a pleading edge. Mantos closed his eyes. The air grew heavy, as if the weight of absence fell with the coming storm. Where had she been for every other nightmare? Where were her words of comfort then? The moment of anger passed like a shadow. She'd been in a tower, half-dead to keep him alive.

"It was Bandim," Mantos said, opening his eyes again. "He was taunting me. Threatening me. And he was...different. Changed. It was him, yet there was something more. Something dangerous and powerful."

Phen clasped his claws. "He's not who I expected him to be," she said. "I never thought my younglings would try to harm me, yet he did."

As the words slipped out, Mantos' eyeridges drew downward. "What did he do?"

He could see his mother curse her loose tongue. Regardless, she answered.

"He told me he would kill me," she said. "For days, he visited me. Every time, he said he would throw me from the tower. He would say I flung myself out in grief for your father—and for you." She gulped against Bandim's bitterness. "I think he would have relished my death."

A crack of lightning split the sky, bisecting the open window. Phen began to weep. The first drops of rain fell. Mantos brushed a talon under his mother's eyes.

"My brother cannot understand the world beyond the reach of his own claws," he said. "Bandim resented me from the day he understood why you were gone."

Phen leaned into Mantos' touch.

"I just wanted to save you," she whispered. "I didn't want to push him away. But I haven't given up on him." Hope shone in her eyes. "He's sick in his mind, but surely he can be cured. He's dabbled with the Dark, but surely he'll return to the Light. Bomsoi brought you back to me, and you were dead. If she can do that, she can do anything."

The memory of the nightmare and the darkness in his brother's eyes cut like a knife. Unable to stop himself, Mantos shuddered. It was more than a mere dream. The feelings were visceral. Real.

"But at what cost?" he asked. "This strange power Bomsoi wields, and the power of the novice from cycles ago, it comes at a cost. First, it was your mind. This time, it's my sleep."

Phen squeezed his hands. "They're just nightmares," she said. "The feelings will pass."

Mantos shook his head—a deliberate movement, left to right. "No, Mother," he said. "They're more than that."

Phen loosened her grip and tilted her head to the side. "What do you mean?"

Mantos extricated one hand and rubbed his eyes with the heel of his palm.

"There's pain, Mother," he said. "So much pain. When I dream, it's as if I'm being ripped limb from limb. I can feel everything, every ripping muscle and cracking bone. My body is torn apart and Bandim taunts me." His voice grew thick, but he beat back the tears. "These aren't ordinary nightmares. Somehow it feels like the strange magic has bound me to Bandim. I'm not dreaming of him. He's there in my mind."

Outside, rain pounded. The sky was so murky it looked like Merish had passed and was gone forever. Phen pressed a kiss to her son's temple and wound her claws into his unbound fronds.

"I will speak to Bomsoi," she said. "Perhaps there's something she can do."

Mantos shook his head and lifted a hand to lay atop his mother's. "I don't hold out much hope," he said. "I'm alive again, but I think this is the penalty wielded for it."

Phen drew him into a tight embrace. "Oh, Mantos," she breathed.

Mantos sank into his mother's arms, but the words of his dream still swirled forth, haunting him. Always there, always biting.

Mantos, Mantos... Dear brother, I will find you...

CHAPTER TWENTY

Bandim

His attendants unpeeled his state robes, and cleaned the make-up from his face. Bandim allowed himself a small sigh. It had been a long day. The bright orange and red silk, colors of House Tiboli, fell in waves and were swiftly whisked away to be cleaned and pressed. The soft cloth on his face wiped the red and white paint from his face and smudged the Tiboli lightning bolts until they were gone. Perhaps they were gone forever this time. They were symbols of his father and his brother, but not Bandim himself. *I should replace them with the five arms of Dorai,* he thought, *not only on my face, but on my banners and soldiers as well.* He added that thought to the list he held in his head of changes that needed to come.

Stripped of the trappings of his office, Bandim was wrapped in a soft shirt and a felted kilt, with a silken robe draped around his shoulders. His dressers retreated, and his cup-bearer Yameteth came forward with sweet wine and food before she disappeared into the background again. Bandim settled in the chair by roaring fire, dipping hard biscuit into a goblet polished to an impossible gloss.

Expanding an empire was just as difficult as expected. Of course, he was well prepared for the task of empire-building. *This is why I was meant to be the emperor,* Bandim thought. *I'm the rightful ruler. I know what I'm doing.* In the first weeks of his reign, he'd kept many of his father's advisors, courtiers, and servants. Bandim tapped the softened morsel of biscuit on the rim of the cup. But as time passed, he knew he had to plant his own folk in all roles, from the humblest to the highest—just like ridding the empire of the Tiboli lightning bolts. It was time for a great change.

Strip the walls of dissent, and line them with a tapestry of support.

That was one of Emperor Braslen's frequent shards of wisdom on recounting the tale of his ascension.

Bandim sank his teeth into the biscuit. Those words were never meant for him. Always they were for the moonson, Mantos. Regardless, Bandim intended to use every piece of his father's knowledge to his advantage.

It was necessary, for there were rumblings of dissent now that the truth of Dorai came to the fore. But the folk would know the real truth, and would see what was right. And those who refused to believe and bend? *I will crush any who try to move against me.*

From the corner came a little flash of fear. It was as if young cup-bearer Yameteth read his mind, and he was able to feel her emotions. She lingered in the flickering light, hardly daring to breathe. Bandim remained facing the fire, but clicked his talons and pointed to his side. "Come here."

Like the obedient young thing she was, Yameteth came forward. She was recently gendered, a disconnected cousin from the outskirts of House Tiboli. Many Tibolis from the edge of the family had been welcomed back into the fold. Those who had once hidden behind masks in the sunken temple were now above ground and strewn through the court: including, to Bandim's delight, his cousin Tesselica. A handsome male, a son of his father's long-dead brother, Tesselica had been one of Bandim's few friends when they were younglings—until his uncle dragged Tesselica away.

He says I'm not to play with you any longer. Words of a letter written long-ago were still burned into Bandim's mind. *He says you're dangerous. He says you're of the Dark. But I know you're all right. I'll keep writing when I can.*

Letters had been sparse, and eventually stopped when both younglings gendered and went about their lives—Bandim as the spare, and Tesselica training under his father. Their eyes had met again in the temple and as soon as he was able, Bandim brought his cousin back into his confidence. *He's like me. He understands.*

Yameteth's story was different. Her parents were dead, and even when alive, they'd been no one. Her guardianship had been handed over to the crown many cycles ago. She was young, innocent—and perfect for Bandim's needs.

As she reached his side, Yameteth kept her eyes downcast. "Yes, Your Grace?" she asked.

"Tell me," Bandim said, dipping biscuit in wine again, "what do the palace servants think of Dorai?"

The flash of fear became a stench of terror. It tasted of smoke and flame. Bandim swirled the taste in his mind. It really was as if he could feel her emotions.

"Your Grace?" Yameteth's voice wavered.

Bandim took a sip of his drink, savoring it as much as her fear. "You heard what I said, Yameteth. Tell your cousin Bandim what the simple folk feel about his plans. And don't dare lie to me. I will know."

Yameteth's entire body trembled. "Your Grace," she said, her voice wavering. "I…"

Bandim set his cup aside and turned to her. He beckoned her forward to stand in front of the fire. "Your emperor has asked you a question," he said. She took her place in front of him, with her back to the flames. "You must answer."

Her throat bobbed, her eyes continually blinking. Tears spilled and she fell to her knees, her tail wrapping around her buckled legs. "Your Grace, some of the folk are scared. Some of them fear that we're straying so far from the Light that we'll never be safe again."

Her truth was bittersweet, harsh yet expected. Bandim leaned forward and placed a hand under her chin. "May I show you something, Yameteth?" he asked.

She could do nothing but agree. Bandim clamped his talons hard, passing into the soft flesh of her cheeks, and he pushed forward. His knees hit the fur rug, and he held her whole weight by her face. Her head hovered ever-more dangerously above the flames.

"Do you feel the fire?" he asked.

"Yes!" Yameteth cried.

"Do you see its light on my face? Dancing, painting me?"

"Y-yes!"

Her fear intensified. Sweat broke on her brow.

"And do you see the shadows?"

"Yes!"

"The Light cannot be trusted!" Bandim said. "Light changes. It comes and goes, it builds and it fades. But the Darkness is always there. It always waits, trustworthy when the wretched Light flees!"

He pushed her back until the ends of her fronds singed.

"Tell your fellows, the ones who say that we stray from the Light, that it is wretched, and we don't need it to be safe. The Light lies! The Darkness is the only thing that we can trust."

"Yes, Your Grace! Yes! Please!"

Her fear was sharp now, and burning. Where it ended and the flame began, Bandim couldn't tell.

He wrenched her forward again, safe from the fire. He released her face and grabbed her by the shoulders. "Tell them for me," he whispered, bringing his face close to hers. "Do it for your cousin."

Her face flooded with tears. "Yes, I will. I will!"

He pulled her in for an embrace, winding his arms around her bony frame. "Good," he said. "You are loyal and obedient." He drew back. "Now, do as you are told."

Yameteth scrambled to her feet and fled, her fear overwhelming her training to never turn her back to the emperor.

Bandim didn't care. As his cup-bearer withdrew, taking the stench of fear with her, he returned to his chair by the fire. For many hours, his eyes stayed focused on the flames.

It was much later in the evening when Johrann Maa came to his chamber. He left her waiting long after her knock. When she eventually entered, he didn't beckon her forward for some time. Even when he did, he didn't look at her. The whole time he kept her waiting in silence. Her lesson in humility and obedience was far from over.

At length, Bandim turned his gaze to her. She was garbed in simple temple robes, without even the horn jewelry she wore as high priestess.

"Your Grace," she said, bowing.

Bandim responded with silence, flicking his eyes up and down her tall, thin form. Gone were her silk slippers with fine embroidery, and the jewels were removed from her fingers. Some of the rings she wore had belonged to Bandim's mother. His father had kept Empress Phen's things locked in the empress' chambers, across the palace from his own. Those had been Johrann's chambers, though with her failure, Bandim had removed that privilege. She wouldn't have the honor again until she delivered her promise to fulfil his power. So far, she was no closer to achieving that.

Bandim's eyes were drawn as always to the four circular scars on her cheek. The imprint of his fingertips was always on her. All she had unlocked so far was his anger, the burning power that branded her, and a few paltry tricks. He could make small candle flames flare brighter and stoke embers back into fire, but there was nothing befitting a goddess. Where was the great power Johrann had promised?

Even though he knew why she was here, he asked the question with disdain. "What do you want?"

Johrann kept her eyes on the floor. "May I be permitted to administer Your Grace's next lesson?"

Slowly he spread one hand, gesturing for her to assume her usual position, kneeling before him.

"Pray that you achieve something this evening," he said. "My patience and kindness wears thin."

Nodding in silence, Johrann knelt on the rug. She took his hands in hers and massaged his pale palms.

"The spirit of Dorai moves within you," she said. "Every day you gain more control over this power."

Bandim's face darkened. "Dorai does not move within me," he said. "I *am* Dorai."

She stilled in fear before nodding vehemently. "Yes, Your Grace. Of course. I misspoke. You are Dorai, and every day you learn how to grasp your powers once again. Every day, more of our followers believe in you. And every day, we learn together."

She dared not say she taught him. He didn't need to taste her panic to understand why.

They went through all he'd learned. Harnessing the beating power within, he conjured greater flames from the fireplace. He made the fire in the hearth dwindle into nothing but a dim ember, only to bring it roaring back to life.

"Spread your influence, Your Grace," Johrann said. "Close your eyes and look for the fire. Where does it dwell?"

As darkness enveloped him, Bandim's mouth went dry. His mind probed beyond the room, feeling every fire in every grate, and the fine ladies who gathered to them. The blazes in the kitchens far below, with sweat-soaked boiler boys keeping the ovens aflame.

And Bandim could taste them all. Their sweet hopes. Their candied dreams. The smoky twist of fear that nothing good would come to pass.

"I feel it all," he whispered.

"Touch it," Johrann said. "Manipulate it."

Bandim breathed hard, squeezing her hands. *Do as I wish*, he thought. *Obey!*

Every flame did.

Their own fire spluttered and burst across the hearthstone, landing upon them, lighting their clothes. Bandim felt nothing but power. The flames spun around them as every fire in the palace whipped into a frenzy. He couldn't hear the screams, but he could feel them. Skin scorched. Blood boiled. Feet fled. Bandim grinned and opened his eyes to the joy of the flames that surrounded them.

"It is mine," he said. "It all belongs to me."

"Remember this feeling," Johrann said. "Remember the power of the flame. With that memory, you'll be able to conjure fire from air. Your powers awaken and you begin to truly manifest as Dorai."

"I feel the power," Bandim whispered. "Everything. I feel it all. The flames. I can manipulate them. I can create them."

Johrann turned Bandim's hands over, holding his palms upwards.

"Then do it," she said. "If you feel that you can, do it now. Make flame from nothing. Once you can do that, you can do anything."

Breath sucked away as if suffocated, Bandim's brow broke out in a sheen of sweat. His palms were clammy, but he closed his eyes. He concentrated. *Do as I command. Flames, appear! Do it now!*

It started as a little spark in the pool of his hand, but it grew and grew until eventually a raging red flame burned there, hot enough to scorch their faces. Johrann drew back, but Bandim did not. He lifted his other hand to touch the flame, passing his hands through it as if it was colored air.

"Your Grace," Johrann whispered, her cheeks blackened with smoke. "You've done it. You've made flame. You are truly Dorai!"

Bandim stood, spreading the flame across his hands. Both alight, he lifted them high above his head, dangerously close to the wall hangings above the fireplace.

"I am the goddess," he said. He tossed the flames from one hand to the other. "I am Dorai. With this power, I can conquer anything—the rest of the Metakalans, the Althemerians at long last." His face was dark in the shadow cast by his flames. "I'll show Queen Valentia what pain truly means. I'll burn her entire country and make her watch. Then I'll cut her head from her neck."

Johrann remained at a distance. Her eyes were ablaze. "Yes, Your Grace," she said.

"Do it. Do it all."

Clicking his fingers, the flames were gone. His hands were cold, bereft, yet Bandim still smiled. He pulled Johrann into an embrace, walking backwards to the bed. Finally she had redeemed herself. Finally she had delivered his power.

"My Heart," he said, falling backwards. She fell on top of him. "I could do none of this without you."

"And I am nothing without you," she replied.

They embraced. Together, they flamed.

CHAPTER TWENTY-ONE

Emmy

As the ship glided into the giant harbor, Emmy's mouth gaped. The Althemerian port of Athomur was majestic, nestled between two huge spurs of land. The water glimmered like gemstones as sunlight sparkled on the waves. The twisting buildings glittered too, made of sandy stone that caught the light.

"It's so beautiful," Charo breathed.

Emmy nodded. Countless vessels cut the water: from the smallest of galleys, manned by females with faces eroded by cycles of salt air, to ships with impossibly tall masts, built in the new fashion. Their gigantic sails caught the wind, propelling them for hundreds of miles.

The liberated Masvam boat approached the shore through a floating forest. The ships split into distinct sections. To the right were the merchant vessels, their colored sails furled, unloading wares into shallow shore boats. To the left the ships were darker, with sleek lines and rows of cannon. Their decks swarmed with blue-garbed Althemerians.

"I've never seen ships so huge," said Charo.

"The Masvams want the title, but the true masters of the sea are the Althemerians," Emmy said. She shifted, casting her eyes away. "Now they're our masters too."

Charo made no reply.

When they reached the city, they were swallowed whole. Enormous walls soared upwards, their tops patrolled by marching soldiers. There were towers at intervals along its length, a cannon in each belly.

The princess disembarked first, attendants trailing on her heels. Pesmam's head newly dangled from her belt. When she reached the gangplank, she thrust it aloft and let out a fearful battle cry.

"Long live the queen!"

Every face on the dock snapped towards her. A chorus of elation followed, all those on the shore crying their allegiance. The princess threw the head at a soldier she passed.

"Mount that somewhere," she said.

Then she was gone, swept off on a wave of royal attendants and cheers.

There was no time to gape at the spectacle. Emmy and the others were herded ashore by new guards.

"All right," one yelled, "follow me! And be quick about it!"

Emmy and Charo jolted as the crowd surged. Mounted Althemerians on huge feline vaemar formed columns beside them. Soon they marched through a thick archway, into the city proper.

They snaked between tall stone buildings covered in carved serpents, and along cobbled pathways. Filthy younglings pulled faces and screeched at them. The more well-to-do shied away. The scents of foreign food, foreign air, foreign skin, were pervasive.

"Where's Zecha?" Charo asked, pressing into Emmy's side. "I can't see him."

Emmy scanned the jostling crowd, her height giving her clear sight above others' heads. She could see no trace of Zecha. *Let him be safe*, she thought. *I don't know what I—what* we *would do without him...*

She shook her head, winding her talons around Charo's. "I don't know," she said. "We can only hope he's getting help."

As their journey continued, the stark reality of capture bit like a knife. There was no welcome for them. City folk jeered at the snake of slaves.

"We own you!"

"Your lives are ours now!"

"You're nothing but life-debtors!"

Emmy jerked as a rain of pebbles and nutshells fell on them. As they wound on, the taunts grew louder, the missiles heavier, and it wasn't until the mounted guards stepped in that it ceased.

"Get out of the way of the queen's possessions!" one of them bellowed. "If you don't step back, Sharptooth here will sort you out."

As if on command, the huge vaemar bared its fangs and growled, the sound coming from deep within its cavernous chest. No one dared defy it. For Emmy, Sharptooth wasn't the frightening part. It was the soldier's words. *Possessions*. That was all the Metakalans were. *They don't care about our lives. Just our use to them.*

Charo grabbed Emmy's filthy arm and twisted her by the shoulder. "Emmy, look!" she cried.

She pointed to something a little way off. A cart bumped along, carrying bodies on stretchers. It was pulled by a stout and shaggy vaemar, much less impressive than Sharptooth.

"It's Zecha! *Zecha!*"

Their friend lay entirely still. Charo's elation faltered. "Is he...?"

The question hung unfinished. Emmy shook her head. "No, he's alive," she said, her heart quickening. "Look at who's leading the vaemar. That's one of the Althemerians from the boat!"

It was the healer who'd tended Zecha on the boat, in her black tunic with the red heart-in-eye symbol. Bags and satchels still hung from her belt like ripened fruit, heavy with what must have been medicine.

"She wouldn't be with him if he was dead," Emmy said, her grin blooming. "They must be able to help him."

A voice cracked through her happiness. "Move along!"

The mounted soldier atop Sharptooth glowered at them, digging her heels into the beast's sides. The infamous teeth were immediately bared. Immediately, Charo and Emmy fell in step with the other Metakalans again, their hearts racing.

"Not that I wish they did things differently," Charo said, "but I don't understand. Why are they tending the wounded?"

Emmy shrugged as they kept walking. "Perhaps they don't want to be like the Masvams, or the Valtat," she said. "If they make a habit of looking after their slaves, even if they don't need to, they look more compassionate."

Charo shook her head, her lips pressed into a thin line. "A slave is a slave, no matter how you say it," she said. She lifted her arms, baring her scars. "It doesn't matter if they say they're kind. They're not."

Emmy's head was filled with memories of Krodge, now dead.

She shook off the thought as the healer slapped the vaemar's rump. It growled, but picked up its pace. Soon the cart and Zecha were out of sight. The procession of Metakalans was left behind, weaving through unwelcome streets.

The walls of stone were less oppressive than the walls of jeers. They passed through gate after city gate, winding through different parts of the city. They passed through a wide square filled with market stalls, surrounded by grand buildings. The Althemerians who entered and exited through the grand carved doors were dressed in luxurious clothing. The males, curiously, were veiled, and wore decorative chains around their waists. It seemed the richer the male, the heavier the chain.

Eventually they passed through the final archway into a wide expanse of green. As they tracked the coast, the Althemerian countryside swept outward. To their left, smooth hills gave way to forests of the tallest trees Emmy had seen. To their right, the sea stretched out blue and silver. Some of Emmy's tension uncoiled. Freed from taunts, the quiet of the land outside the city was sweet. She gulped in the scenery, curiosity overwhelming fear for a blissful moment. Emmy's trained eyes roamed over the flora and fauna. *Arraplant, valkern, twistwart, skella*, she thought.

They walked south for half the day and, as the sun rose high into the clear sky, many of the captives wilted. Regardless, they were forced to march on. It wasn't until dusk began to encroach that they arrived at their destination.

Tendrils of smoke curled against the starlight, rising from somewhere in a dip. Hidden by the swell of a yellow hill, not far from the sea, a strange settlement appeared, its boundaries marked by wooden walls lit with bright torches. Emmy glanced around, trying to take in every detail. The ground was of packed earth, and the structures within the walls looked cobbled together from whatever could be found. It was like a miniature city, complete with a smithy and row upon row of barracks. Its population was made of folk of many colors. They weren't all Althemerians, but they all wore the blue, with the twin serpents on their chests.

The Metakalans were shepherded to the middle of the wooden city. Emmy and Charo were jolted and pushed, finally coming to rest in the middle of the crowd. There was a smell of greenery from the forest that stood to the side of the camp. There was another smell, too: a danker, more insidious stench. *Fear*, Emmy thought. *It's fear.*

In front of the crowd, three figures stood on a large podium. A female and a male stood at military attention, flanking a second female who had her arms crossed. She had dark skin and armor, and her blue eyes shone with unveiled contempt. The evening breeze wasn't strong enough to pluck the red braids that licked her back like flames.

"Pathetic," she said. "You are all pathetic."

There was no sound from the captives. Emmy's mouth was dry. The female was dressed in the same blue tunic, but wore a padded leather surcoat over it. She showed her rank by the silver bars at her neck, and the thick buckle at her waist. Many bracelets shimmered on her arms, more on the right than the left. Her braids swung as she spoke.

"I am Commander Pama, and this is the Hutukeshu Encampment. You have been liberated by the Hand of the Queen." Her voice carried across the flatness of the camp. "Consider yourselves lucky that you weren't killed alongside our other enemies. You have been saved from certain death under the boots of the Masvams, who would no doubt have subjected you to torture, maiming, and even death."

Her words fell on Emmy like lead.

"This favor comes with a price," the female continued. "Each of you now owes Queen Valentia a debt. You will stay in her service for a cycle. Once your debt has been paid, you will be free to stay here or return to your own country, or what remains of it, for your service makes you non-blood citizens of Althemer."

"We won't stand for this!" someone shouted.

Emmy couldn't place the voice without the face. She turned, squinting through the crowd.

The female on the podium clicked her claws. Two soldiers rushed in and seized the speaker, dragging her to the front. It was one of the butcher's apprentices from Bellim, a female renowned for having a loose tongue and an empty head. Shoved to her knees in the dust, the glint of a knife appeared at her throat.

"Your words mean nothing here," braided Commander Pama said. "What is decreed by the Queen is law, and you must obey that law, or die." She laughed and leaned forward. "Tell me, what is your name?"

"Drenna Haldra," the female said, "of Bellim."

"And what is your profession?"

Drenna's throat pulsed under the threat of the knife. Even so, she tried to answer with confidence. "I am a butcher."

"A butcher, providing food and doing dirty work that most seek to avoid," the commander said. "Well, Drenna Haldra of Bellim, you will now butcher only Masvam meat."

She straightened and signaled for Drenna's release. The butcher clutched at her grazed throat and stumbled back into the crowd. Lips curling, Commander Pama continued.

"In this camp, you belong to the queen, but you answer to me. Each of you will be asked your name and your profession, just like your companion Drenna. If you have a purpose that we deem useful, you may well retain it. If you serve us faithfully outside combat for a cycle, your debt will be repaid. Most of you, however," she continued, "will join our military might." She narrowed her eyes and dropped her voice. "Be warned. You should be honest when asked your profession, for liars will be sent to the front lines of our armies."

A shiver rattled from the tip of Emmy's tail to her neck. She glanced at Charo, who shook her head and mouthed, *What am I going to say?* Emmy said nothing, but planted a comforting hand on Charo's shoulder.

Commander Pama went on.

"Even if you have a profession, you may choose to fight, for it is the quicker path to freedom. We require only five cycles of loyal service in our army." She chuckled, but the sound was cold. "However, it is also the quicker path to death. You will train to fight in the Queen's Army and if we require you for battle, you will go. If you die, then you will go to your goddess as heroes. If you live and serve your five cycles, your debt will be repaid and you will be free." Pama drew herself upward, her last words spoken with an air of finality. "Remember: your debt must be repaid. Those without honor, who try to escape, will be killed."

With that, she strode from the platform, disappearing in a whirl of blue tunic and red braids.

She left a bustle of activity in her wake. Althemerians brought tables and chairs onto the podium. The air trembled.

"I'm going to be sent to the front," Charo said, looking up to Emmy. "What profession do I have?"

Emmy squeezed the hand on Charo's shoulder.

"You've got a lot of skill, Charo," she said, "whether it's a profession or not. Tell them about your past, and they might assign you to someone as a maid." Charo pulled a sour face at that. "Or," Emmy offered, "you could say you're my apprentice. That way we might go somewhere together."

"And what happens when they find out I lied?" Charo asked. She gave a rueful smile. "I only know how to sweep the floors."

Emmy shook her head. "You know more than that," she said.

Charo didn't reply.

Around them the crowd began to move again, urged on by Althemerian soldiers. Emmy slid her hand from Charo's shoulder to her talons, grasping them firmly. "We should try and stick together, Charo."

Charo interlocked her claws with Emmy's and stared through the crowd. "What about Zecha?" she asked. "What will happen to him?"

Emmy's words died in her throat. She shook her head. There was only one place for Zecha if he lived. The army. It was his only choice.

The crowd was herded forward, this time to the platform. Althemerians peered down, armed with scrolls, quills, and ink, poised to rewrite the course of the Metakalans' lives.

Charo grunted as she was shoved up the stairway, stumbling onto the plinth. Emmy followed, pressed on from behind. For a moment, everything stilled. There was no wind. The flames didn't flicker. Faces didn't move. Bodies were frozen. Emmy watched, taking it all in. How had it come to this? In the noiseless camp, there was no response.

Charo was beckoned forward first, too far from Emmy for her words to be heard. Emmy gnawed her bottom lip. *Don't send her to the army*, she thought. *Let her be safe.*

"Next."

That single word pulled Emmy forward. She stopped in front of the male—a Linvarran, with green and yellow colors like Charo—who glanced up from his parchment. He regarded her with indifferent orange eyes for a moment. Then, as realization unfolded and he saw that Emmy wasn't a usual Metakalan, he leaned forward, quill poised. "You're not like the others."

Emmy suppressed a grunt. Even here, being processed by the Althemerians, she was still an outsider, a stranger. "I'm Metakalan," she said. "I just look different."

One of the other scribes leaned into the first and whispered, his eyes focused on Emmy. The first scribe nodded and returned his attention to his charge. "Name?"

"Emmy."

She watched as he scratched her name on the parchment, never taking his eyes from her. "Profession?"

"Apothecary."

The scribe raised an eyeridge as he scratched the word into the column beside her name. "I see," he said. "Very interesting."

Emmy, not caring whether the scribe thought she was interesting or not, looked up the length of the podium. Charo was already being led away. She glanced over her shoulder, catching Emmy's eyes for a moment, before she disappeared down the wooden stairs. Emmy cast her eyes upward, mouthing a prayer. *Please let Charo be safe.* It was a vain attempt to pray to the Lady of Light, a deity in whom Emmy didn't really believe.

The scribe set down his quill and stood. Emmy, her attention back on him, blinked and furrowed her brow. None of the other scribes had risen.

"You'll have to come with me," he said.

"Why?" Emmy asked.

The scribe showed a flash of irritation as he stepped from behind his table. He was a short male, with close-cropped brown fronds and an officious demeanor. "Just do as you're told," he said, "and follow me."

Sweat began to seep from Emmy's palms as the scribe led her across the plinth and down the same stairs Charo had descended. Dust whirled from the parched ground with every step they took. She glanced around, seeking any glimpse of her friend. She paused, her feet heavy with fear.

Darkness fell on Emmy's shoulders. Charo was nowhere to be seen.

The scribe looked over his shoulder and tutted at her slow pace.

"Come along," he said. "You need to report to your new post."

CHAPTER TWENTY-TWO

Emmy

They crossed the flat compound, dodging small clumps of other processed Metakalans, until they reached a low wooden structure. It had a wide door, on which the heart-in-eye symbol was drawn in red paint.

The scribe pushed the door and held it open for Emmy. The small gesture struck her as strangely respectful, a feeling she'd rarely felt before.

Inside were row upon row of beds. Emmy brought a hand up to her nostrils and mouth. There was sickness here, and she knew the smell well. Those in the beds were ill, not injured. The air was filled with the sound of their moans. Emmy glanced around and dropped her hand, puzzled. There were scant few folks in black tunics to tend the sick. Emmy could only see two, both female.

As they entered, one of the female healers glanced up at them, away from the female she tended. Her green armor and pinkish skin painted her as Belfoni, not Althemerian, and her chest was emblazoned with the red heart-in-eye. However, she was no ordinary healer. Her authority spoke through the bars at her neck—like Commander Pama's, but wooden rather than silver.

The scribe ushered Emmy towards her, and Emmy's throat grew tight.

"I have something for you, medicine-rel," he said. "This is Emmy. She...says she's an apothecary, so I've brought her, as you asked."

The Belfoni healer rose from her place at the sick Althemerian's bedside. She was a striking creature. Unusually tall, a similar height to Emmy, she wore many bracelets on her arms—again, more on the right than on the left. She had an easy smile.

"Thank you, Nila," she said, walking towards them and wiping her hands on a scrap of cloth. "We need more *tsimi*, and an apothecary is a good place to start."

Tsimi? Emmy's eyes narrowed at the word. She'd never heard it before.

"I must return to my post," Nila said.

There was something in the way his eyes darted from the Belfoni healer to the rows of the sick that Emmy had seen before. It was the same look that neighbors cast at houses struck by pestilence.

"Of course, Nila," the medicine-rel said. "Thank you."

The scribe gave a shallow bow, then turned tail and left as quickly as he could.

The medicine-rel planted a hand on Emmy's shoulder, and Emmy glanced up. The healer's grip was firm but, strangely, there was a flash of coldness at her touch. For a moment, Emmy's mind jumped back to the boat.

"How did you escape the attack?" the medicine-rel asked. "I didn't," she said. "I was taken prisoner, just like all the other Metakalans."

Emmy pulled away from the healer's touch, her brow furrowing.

The Belfoni's face was impassive. "Not that attack. The attack on the Uloni."

Uloni? Emmy had never heard that word before. She shook her head, gritting her teeth in sudden fear. What did this mean?

The medicine-rel tilted her head to the side. Her eyes were green and piercing. "You don't remember, do you?"

Fear rising, Emmy balled her claws into fists. "I have no idea what you mean," she said. "I don't know what 'Uloni' is."

Something passed across the healer's face at that. "No matter," she said, but her tone belied the words. It sounded like it *did* matter. "Forgive me."

Emmy wanted to reach out, to ask, *what do you mean? What does* Uloni *mean?* But fear kept her hands and tongue in check. She didn't know this female. She could be cruel, or perhaps just mad. Emmy gritted her teeth so hard now her jaw ached.

The medicine-rel turned and gestured to the beds that surrounded them, the subject of an attack and Uloni now firmly closed.

"We don't have enough skilled healers to tend the sick," she said. "We've been struck by *shengi* for the third time in three months. Your job will be to help me."

"*Shengi?*" Emmy asked. Her brow furrowed. This creature spoke with many words she didn't know.

The medicine-rel waved a hand and seemed to prod the back of her mind for the correct word. "The Althemerians call it Lurking Death."

Emmy went still, and pressed her lips into a thin line. "Oh."

The Lurking Death. A sickness marked by vomiting, fever, shaking fits, and, if untreated, a slow and painful death. There was no true treatment, but those who received care were less likely to perish.

"It's not an easy thing to deal with," the medicine-rel said. "All we can do is give what aid we can and hope the ill recover. We've lost countless lives since *shengi* struck, partly because we have so few *tsimi* to attend them. That is why I need you."

Emmy ventured a nod, but her attention was on the folk stretched out on the beds.

The sick were from all parts, likely others for whom the Althemerians had decided they owed a life-debt. There were Selamans, Linvarrans, and Belfoni, all suffering from the Lurking Death in the same way. There were a handful of Metakalans as well, sick and exhausted from their long journey on the slavers' boat. *Death is color-blind*, Emmy thought. *It takes us all the same.*

She scanned the beds, looking at each Metakalan face. She recognized them, but she couldn't see the one face she wanted. Her chest grew tight and she balled her claws into fists. Never mind the talk of Uloni, whatever that was. There was a more important matter to attend to. Where was Zecha? Why wasn't he here?

"My friend," Emmy said, "he was injured on the boat and taken away on a cart by a healer. I need to find him. I need to know if he's all right."

Raising a hand, the medicine-rel smiled. "If he was ill or injured, he's in this camp," she said. "All shipbait comes here."

"Shipbait?" Emmy asked.

"Those brought here from other lands," the medicine-rel said. "The Althemerians take many folks from the seas. Their ships prowl the waters, attacking their enemies. Anyone they save, they bring back to their lands. Hutukeshu is the largest of the encampments, where those who owe life-debts are taken." She folded her arms. Her short sleeve pulled upward, revealing the edge of something strange on her upper arm. "You'll be treated well enough here," the medicine-rel continued. "The Althemerians are not cruel, but they enforce their laws strictly. You won't be beaten, but you will also not be allowed to leave."

Emmy's mouth was, once more, dry. The air felt close, and the stench of illness hung over her like a dark cloud. She couldn't move, feeling more like a statue than a living thing.

"Emmy," the medicine-rel said.

She placed a hand on Emmy's shoulder again. There was another flash of cold. Emmy snapped from her trance. The Belfoni healer smiled, though it was a smile of sympathy. "I know how you're feeling," she said. "I know what it's like to be taken by the Althemerians."

She pulled up the short sleeve of her tunic, revealing a wiry forearm. Part of her green armor was scarred with two entwined serpents and a number beneath. Emmy winced, and her breathing grew shallow.

It was a brand.

"They mark your flesh," she said, pointing at the scar. "The serpents, to show who owns you. The date below shows when you were taken. That's how they know how long you've served them and when they can let you go." The healer let her sleeve fall and looked at Emmy in half-apology. "I'm afraid I'll have to take you to be branded as well."

Emmy blanched, her hand leaping to her arm. The imaginary brand burned under her fingertips. Armored skin was tough, but intense heat could penetrate it easily.

"I'm sorry," the medicine-rel said. "I don't agree with the practice, but the

Althemerians say it must be so."

Emmy let her hand drop again and both her arms hung uselessly at her sides. She didn't know what do to or what to say. Her mind reeled, and her thoughts kept returning to her friends. Zecha was somewhere, his condition unknown. Would he live or would he die? Would Charo's words of warning be as true for life with the Althemerians as with the Masvams?

Maybe...Maybe Zecha's better off dead.

Emmy swallowed and shook her head, the movement slight. It wasn't just Zecha she was parted from. It was Charo, too. Her fate was entirely unknown. Was she taken as a maid for some wealthy Althemerian? Or was she taken into the army? Emmy suppressed a shudder. She wished for the former, for then Charo would be safe, or at least safer. How the Althemerians treated their servants, Emmy didn't know. But if Charo was taken as a soldier, there was a chance they might see each other again in the camp. The sharp tang of that selfish thought burned her. If Charo was taken as a soldier, there was more than a chance she would be killed.

The medicine-rel's voice pulled Emmy from her thoughts.

"Come," she said. "You need to wash, and then we must get to work. Medicine-yarim!"

At her call, one of two other black-tunics scurried towards them. The Linvarran female clasped her hands behind her back and nodded attentively. However, when she took in Emmy's appearance for the first time, her face crumpled with disgust. The female healer didn't need to say anything, for Emmy knew her thoughts. She'd seen that look on so many faces, so many times.

Moon Rogue!

The medicine-rel clicked her talons to get her subordinate's attention again. "Fetch warm water, a cloth, and a clean uniform," she said. "Finally, we have another *tsimi*."

The medicine-yarim nodded, but her attention flew from the medicine-rel and back to Emmy. She scowled, her dark eyes narrow. "Yes, Medicine-Rel."

She disappeared for a moment, returning with clothing slung over her arm and an ewer of water with a rag draped on its rim. Emmy accepted the items with a grateful nod, but the healer didn't nod back. She stepped away, still scowling.

"Back to work, Medicine-Yarim," the medicine-rel said.

Emmy blinked at that. Medicine-Yarim, Medicine-Rel... Realization dawned.

"Your name is Rel," she said. "The scribe, he didn't call you medicine-rel. He said Medicine-*Rel*."

Rel tilted her head to the side.

"Was that not clear?" she asked. "Your language is like the Althemerian tongue. I thought it was the same, in fact." She chuckled. "'Medicine' is what all healers are called—*tsimi*, in my language. You will be Medicine-Emmy."

"Oh," Emmy said, feeling foolish.

Rel placed a hand on the small of Emmy's back and urged her towards a set of screens, canvas stretched over wooden frames.

"You'll fall into the way of things, Medicine-Emmy," she said. "Now, wash and change, and then you can get to work."

Safely tucked behind the screens, away from prying eyes, Emmy did as she was told.

Her tattered garments fell on the ground in a pool. Emmy was glad to shed them for more than just their filth. The mella was a reminder of the happiness of Middlemerish, when she had friends at her side and was free from Krodge's heavy yoke for one blissful day. Emmy stopped. Her hands trembled. A twinge of guilt pulled at her as the Masvam sailor's words returned.

Finished her off, I did.

Trying not to think about that, or Zecha or Charo or Uloni, Emmy scrubbed herself with the cloth and lukewarm water. Why should she feel sorrow for someone who made her life a misery? Krodge wasn't worth grieving for. Neither was Bose. She was free from them for good.

Emmy stilled her hands. It would be a cycle before she was truly free. Unless she died, of course. She snorted. Some freedom.

As clean as she could get, Emmy pulled on the uniform. The black tunic was too large, and was made of soft leather that didn't pinch and constrict. The red heart-in-eye settled on her chest. She traced the outline with her talons. She was Medicine-Emmy now, an Althemerian healer. *How swiftly life changes*, she thought.

Wringing out the cloth, she gathered her belongings and slipped out from behind the screen. Rel was attending a patient again, as were Yarim and the other healer Emmy had not yet met. Emmy went to Rel's side.

Watching the Belfoni healer work was like watching herself. Her hands moved the way Emmy's would. The pouches at her belt were full of the same ingredients Emmy used—bindlewart, juice of the arra fruit, a cornucopia of herbs. Rel moved with compassion, pressing a comforting hand to the forehead of the ill or gently grasping their hands. Her rank may have been higher than that of the other healers, but she did the same work in the same way. Everything was painted with warmth and kindness.

Rel rose from her patient and beckoned for Emmy to follow. They crossed the room, winding through rows of the sick.

"You look the part now," Rel said, "but can you act it, too? How much does this apothecary know about healing?"

"I know enough," Emmy said, tugging on the hem of her tunic. "I've dealt with the Lurking Death before."

"Oh?" Rel asked. "What is the best treatment?"

Emmy licked her lips and shook her head. It was a silly question. "There is no treatment," she said. "All we can do is make the ill comfortable and try to ease their symptoms. But there's nothing I know of that will extract the poison."

"It's no poison," Rel said, "but you're right. That's what makes it so deadly. The sickness jumps from body to body, and we cannot stop it."

She reached for her belt, laden with bags of ingredients, and unbuckled it. She held it out to Emmy, who accepted it with reluctant claws.

"Use your knowledge, and we'll see what we can do," Rel said. "It may be that the Metakalans know more than the Althemerians when it comes to illness."

"Yes, Medicine-Rel," Emmy said, buckling the belt around her waist.

"If you need anything else, ask myself or Yarim—whom you met—or Asri, the male healer." For a moment, Rel's eyes grew dark. "Work well, Medicine-Emmy," she said. "The Althemerians aren't in the habit of feeding useless shipbait. If you do not perform your function, you will not retain it."

Emmy's whole body tightened. Her tongue grew bold. "What will happen then?" she asked.

"You'll have a life of hard labor building the queen's roads or toiling in the fields," Rel said. Her face darkened. "That is, if you're lucky. If you're unlucky you'll be sent to the military, whether you can fight or not." Rel placed a hand on Emmy's shoulder once more. Again, there was a flash of cold. "Work well, Medicine-Emmy," she said. "We need good *tsimi*."

With that she turned, wound her way back through the rows of beds, and disappeared into a side room, behind a canvas curtain.

Emmy stared down at her new belt. She plucked at the bags that hung there. When she did, her breathing settled and her chest didn't feel as tight. But a looming sadness fell upon her, dark as if the sun and the moons had withdrawn their light. This wasn't the life she'd wished for, in secret, on the day of Middlemerish. Her wish hadn't even been a huge one. She hadn't wished for wealth, or power, or glory. All she'd wished for was a free life with her friends at her side.

Now she had neither of those things.

She snorted and crossed to the first pallid face she saw, a Selaman lying prone on her bed.

Wishing was for fools. She knelt by her first patient's side and pressed her hand to the Selaman's forehead. Too hot, typical of the Lurking Death. Emmy opened the bags at her waist, running through the list of Krodge's palliative potions in her head, checking off what ingredients she had and what she needed.

The Selaman half-opened her eyes, then turned in her bed. Her head jerked over the side, and she vomited onto the rushes on the floor.

Wishing is for fools, Emmy thought as she brought her hand to the Selaman female's back, rubbing circles as she voided her stomach. *And if these last few days have taught me anything, it's that the gods aren't real.*

The Selaman slumped, exhausted, and Emmy gently laid her back onto the bed. She glanced around, saw a cloth and water by the bed, and began to clean her patient's face.

"There now," Emmy said. "Rest."

She wiped the last of the vomit from the female's mouth and sat back on her heels. No. The gods definitely weren't real.

For the rest of the day, Emmy worked her way through the jumble of patients. For hours, she cleaned vomit and wiped sweaty brows. She made what she could, concoctions to bring down fever and soothe upset stomachs. She held bodies as they convulsed, racked by the Death. Her black tunic was so splattered with detritus she dared not look at it. *Don't think about it*, she thought. *Just do your job.*

Several times, Emmy caught Rel looking at her. She was favored with a smile and a nod, but Emmy didn't smile back. There wasn't much to smile about.

That was, until she moved on from one patient to another. It took a moment for her to realize what she saw. The Metakalan colors she recognized straight away, but there was something more.

Something familiar.

Her heart stuttered. "*Zecha!*"

There he was, hiding amongst the ill and injured all this time. Emmy grasped one of his hands, pressed the talons of her other hand to his forehead, and laced them around his horn crest. "Zecha, you're alive!"

He didn't respond, lying silent and clammy on the bed. A lump formed in Emmy's throat. She pulled his blankets down and hitched his shift up, revealing the raw wound in his stomach. It was stitched—not as well as Emmy would have done it—and, while swollen, didn't appear putrid, as she'd imagined it would.

A thought invaded her mind and she jerked backwards, releasing him.

Lay your hands on him. You've done it before. Stop the bleeding. Save him.

The strange voice. She hadn't thought of those words since the boat.

She shook herself. It meant nothing. She hadn't helped save Zecha's life. It was whoever the healer was who'd cleaned and stitched his wound. Not Emmy, not with some kind of coldness from her fingertips.

"Have you found your friend?"

Emmy startled at Rel's voice. She looked up. Rel was smiling softly. She knelt and inspected the patient's wound.

"Yes," Emmy said. "This is Zecha."

"Zecha here has received a terrible wound," Rel said. She ghosted her talons over his stitches, but didn't touch them. "I'm very surprised to see he's alive." She glanced sidelong at Emmy. "Were you with him when it happened?"

Emmy nodded, the events on the ship playing back in her head. "I was," she said. "It was a Masvam. He stabbed Zecha in the stomach as a punishment, because Zecha managed to get free."

"Did you help him?" Rel asked.

Frowning, Emmy leaned back. What kind of question was that to ask? "I tried to," she said, her tone tinged with defense. "I was locked up. I tried to get free. Eventually I got free and went to him, but there was nothing I could do."

Except lay her hands on him and feel the cold power. But that wasn't real, just a figment.

Rel tugged Zecha's shift down and pulled the blankets back up to cover him.

"Keep a close watch on him," she said. "Wounds to the stomach are often deadly, though it seems young Zecha here has been unusually lucky. Most with a wound like that would already be dead."

Emmy nodded. Rel stood and rested her hand on Emmy's shoulder as she did so. Once more, there was a coldness to her touch.

Cold power from Emmy's hands. A coldness to Rel's touch...

Emmy shook her head hard. It was nothing. There was nothing happening. Instead of dwelling on it, she placed her hand on Zecha's chest and whispered, "Come back to me, Zecha. I need you."

Her friend didn't reply.

CHAPTER TWENTY-THREE

Mantos

The palace flooded with bad news. Flocks of leathery gargons swooped from all directions. Mantos sat on the window seat, stuck in his chamber in a dusty tower, watching the creatures arrive and depart. *I wonder what the letters say*, he thought. *Information about my brother and his schemes, no doubt.*

Mantos pressed his back to one of the cold stones wall of the deep window and set his feet on the other. He toyed with his lightning-strike pendant as he watched from his perch. He and his mother had been spirited to their respective towers, hidden from prying eyes. As the day waned, Mantos counted the stones in the courtyard below, listened to the idle splash of the grand fountain in its middle, and wondered why he was alive.

What use am I to Queen Valentia? he thought. *I know nothing of my brother's plans.* The thought plagued him as he stared at the folk crossing the courtyard. The Althemerians had no intention of bowing under the might of the Masvams. That was no secret, for they never had. Once, when Mantos was an ungendered youngling, the two nations had held an uneasy peace. Now they were enemies, the battle lines drawn in Queen Valentia's ink. She would never marry a Masvam, nor marry her offspring to Masvams. Braslen, furious, had spent the last cycle and a half of his life working towards Valentia's punishment: crushing the Althemerians under his boot heel.

Mantos turned from the window and closed his eyes, his brow furrowing. He knew of *Braslen's* plans. He knew the strengths of the army, how many soldiers and ships they had. He knew how Braslen's conquest was to unfold, for he'd been implicit in its planning. Mantos, the heir, at the heart of the fighting, pushing their borders forward. He had pressed through Selama and killed their queen. Next were Metakala and King Eron.

But, Mantos thought as his head lolled to the side, those were Braslen's plans. He opened his eyes again and focused on the window. He tracked the ripples in the glass.

Bandim was not Braslen, and there was no guarantee he'd do the same thing. What information Mantos had might not be of help to Queen Valentia, and she must have known that. Mantos thought back to all the things Braslen had said about Valentia. She was strong, intelligent, as good a ruler as a female could be. She was canny and brave, and commanded the respect of her folk.

Valentia was no fool, Mantos knew. So why bother to bring him back to life if he had no real use to her? Unless...

A thought struck him, hard as a hammer blow. Mantos let his legs drop, turned, and sat on the edge of the window seat.

The true emperor of the Masvams was in her debt. What better conquest was there than controlling the Masvam Empire?

None. That's why I'm alive.

The door opened. A set of light feet entered, but Mantos didn't look up. Instead, he stared at the rushes scattered on the floor. The feet approached, and a voice broke the silence.

"It will only be a matter of time before the queen calls you."

It was his mother.

Mantos still didn't look up. He began counting the rushes.

"Mantos," his mother said. "Please."

With a sigh, he finally looked up. "I know," he said.

Phen's footfalls were soft as she approached. Mantos took in the image of his mother, dressed in clothing more befitting of his father. Nothing was stranger than seeing her alive and well, though her face was pained.

"What will you tell her?" Phen asked.

Mantos shrugged one shoulder, a slow up-and-down movement. "It depends on what she asks me," he said petulantly.

Annoyance flitted across Phen's face. Mantos held up a placating hand.

"I shouldn't be so flippant, I know," he said. "The reality is that I'm in her debt. I know it's only my rank that keeps Queen Valentia from clapping irons around my wrists."

"*We* are in her debt," Phen corrected. "She saved my life as well."

Mantos gave a small nod and slid off the window seat. Phen touched his arm and tried to smile. "The Althemerians are our only allies now," she said. "We have no one else."

Mantos' voice was suddenly cold and sharp as steel. "Allies?" he asked. "They're not our allies. They're our captors."

Phen withdrew her touch. Mantos felt the absence of her warmth on his skin.

"Is that what you'd say to Fonbir?" his mother asked. "Would you call him a captor?"

Mantos' brow furrowed, and his mouth twisted with confusion. What did she know about Fonbir? And more importantly, how did she know it?

"Fonbir told me of your relationship," Phen said. For a moment, she smiled. "I told him I wasn't surprised that my youngling had carried on a forbidden love behind their father's back. It's what I would have done."

Reeling from the revelation, Mantos fell back onto the window seat. He scanned her face and found nothing but kindness, and a hint of pride. She didn't share her husband's ire for the Althemerians. Then again, he realized, she'd been out of her wits when Braslen had severed all relations with the Althemerians. Why would she hold any anger towards them? Mantos shook his head. *There must be much that's changed for her.*

"Unfortunately," he said, "Fonbir has no power here. The princesses are next in line for the throne, despite his greater age. Males don't reign here. It's not he who is the captor. It's his mother."

Phen nodded. She laid her claws on her son's shoulders.

"The queen will ask you for the empire's secrets," she said. "She'll want to know every detail you know. How many troops Bandim has, how many ships, where the weaknesses are in our borders, and what Bandim is likely to do next."

Mantos settled a hand on hers and nodded.

"I must hand over Masvam secrets and betray my brother," he said. "I must work to take back my crown, my empire. But..." He shook his head, letting his hand fall again. "The empire was never mine. Father was dead less than a day when I...I died. I didn't rule. I wasn't the emperor. I was never crowned."

Phen's eyes were bright, and she squeezed his shoulders. "That doesn't matter, my son," she said. "You're destined to rule. It's in your blood."

"I was *not* destined to rule," Mantos said slowly. "I received the throne by accident, by virtue of hatching a few minutes before my brother. I shouldn't have lived past my second hatchingday. It was only because of you that I did. The Althemerians talk as if Bandim is a usurper, as if he doesn't deserve the throne. But he does deserve it. He was supposed to reign. Fate has finally dealt him that which he was entitled to long ago." Mantos shook his head. "We're Masvams. We conquer, and we spread our borders. If that's what Bandim intends to do, who am I to stop him? The Althemerians might rail against it, but it's the Masvam way—much as I don't agree with it."

Phen's expression twisted. She withdrew her hands and bit her bottom lip, shaking her head. Mantos' flesh tingled with a sudden coldness. A secret sparkled in her eyes, and Mantos stood. "Mother? What is it?"

"Mantos, I..." Phen looked away. Her throat bobbed as she swallowed. "Bomsoi... She told me something. Something about *why* she could bring you back from the dead. It's something that concerns your brother."

She stared through the window, into the solemn afternoon. It was Mantos' turn to place a hand on her shoulders. He gently turned her around.

"Mother, what is it?" he asked. "I don't understand what happened to me. I don't know why I died, or why I was brought back. Whatever you know, I need to know."

When Phen looked up at him, there were tears in her eyes. Mantos tilted his head to one side. "Mother?"

"Your brother," Phen said, her voice thick. "He…"

Words failed her, and Mantos gave her the gentlest of shakes. "Mother," he said again. This time his words were a command. "Tell me."

Phen blinked, sending two silver trails down her face.

"Bandim," she said. "He was the one who killed you. Or at least, it was his goddess. His *darkness*."

Mantos stilled as the words washed over him. At first he couldn't understand them. He and Bandim had never seen eye to eye. They'd been brothers, but never friends. There was no way… Mantos shook his head. What his mother said couldn't be true.

"Bomsoi told me there was sorcery in your death," Phen continued. "That was why she could bring you back, but not your father. And with all of this, with this *magic*, with the talk of the Lunar Awakening and summoning the False One…" Phen gulped a breath, beating back tears. "Bomsoi said it was Bandim who wanted you dead. It was on his orders. That a Moon Rogue cast a spell, and…" Phen broke off. She wrapped her arms around her thin torso. "It's all too much," she breathed. "To think that my two sons are now at war and there's nothing I can do about it."

Reeling, Mantos released his mother and stumbled to his bed. He leaned against the post, chest heaving. It couldn't be true. It just couldn't.

Yet there was a voice in the back of his mind that contradicted that. Of course Bandim would kill him. He hated Mantos. He resented him for what their mother did. He saw Mantos as a threat. He wanted the empire. He wanted to claim what was rightfully his.

Mantos' mind flooded with memories of his violent dreams. Of Bandim, wicked and cruel and jeering. Of himself, being ripped apart in the most horrific agony.

He pressed his talons to his eyes.

Of course Bandim wanted me dead, he thought. *Why would he want me alive?*

Despite this logic, the pain of unanswered questions burned in his mind. "How does Bomsoi know this?" he asked. "And how was she able to bring me back from the dead?"

Phen wilted onto the window seat.

"Queen Valentia says Bomsoi can do things and see things that others can't," she said. "And after seeing her bring you back from the dead, I believe it. I don't know how she knows, but I trust that it's the truth."

Mantos shook his head, still leaning on the bedpost. "That isn't good enough," he said. "You've trusted in a Moon Rogue, just as you did before. Just like Bandim and his worship of the False Goddess Dorai."

Phen, her arms tightly wrapped around herself, looked desperately thin. "Bomsoi's not of the Dark," she said. "I don't know what she is, but I know she isn't evil. What I do know is that we cannot let Bandim destroy this world."

Mantos' lips curled. "What do you mean by that?"

"That's what he'll do if he's emperor of the Masvams and a meddler in dark spirits," Phen said. "Bomsoi said she could bring you back to me, and she did. She said she might be able to save Bandim, too." She took a shuddering breath. "There are many things about this situation I don't understand. What I do understand is that we cannot let your brother lead the world into the Dark. We cannot let him pull us into a bloody war."

Finally straightening and releasing the bedpost, Mantos swallowed. His mother's words cut deep. Peace was what Mantos of House Tiboli lusted after more than anything else. Not war, not combat, not the hunt like his brother and father and grandfather before him. All he wanted was peace. *And in search of this peace*, he thought, *must I send my brother to his death?* The memory of his nightmares returned. Being split in two, cut to ribbons with knives...

And the grinning figure of his brother—his brother, who had killed him.

Mantos, Mantos... Dear brother, I will find you...

Mantos shook his head. Bandim had thought nothing of sending him to his death. Why should he feel any differently? They'd never been close, but this was different. This was evil—perhaps the first step in Bandim's Dark plans. *I owe him nothing*, Mantos thought. Why not give the Althemerians what they wanted?

Braslen's final words returned.

You must lead the empire to new glories. Finish my work and spread the reign of House Tiboli from sea to sea. Continue what my father started, and plant the seeds of glory for your younglings and your younglings' younglings...

Betray a brother, betray an empire, Mantos thought. Betray his father and his grandfather. Betray a way of life that stretched back hundreds of cycles.

Be the Masvam who destroyed the Masvam Empire.

Was it worth it, to seek revenge on Bandim for all he'd done?

A knock at the door heralded a messenger. Mantos turned away. Phen accepted the message at the door. She broke the blue wax seal and unfurled the note.

"It's from the queen," she said. "We are to go to her council."

She crossed the floor to Mantos and held the note out to him, though he didn't take it. He didn't even look up.

"You must do what is right, Mantos," she said.

Mantos finally turned his gaze upwards. He licked his lips and wound his talons together in a tight knot. Eventually he stood. Phen brought a hand up to rest on his armored cheek.

"I hope you make the right choice, no matter what questions are put to you."

Mantos leaned into her touch and nodded.

"So do I, Mother," he whispered. "So do I."

CHAPTER TWENTY-FOUR

Emmy

Dawn rose in a pink wash from the horizon. Emmy perched on a makeshift bench outside the healers' building, where she'd been sitting for hours. The sky had been black and spotted with twinkling constellations: the Rising Prago, the Twins, the Charging Vaemar... Even the elusive Goddess' Throne was visible. The sun swept all that away, bringing light and the low hum of insects.

Several days had passed since Emmy's arrival at the Hutukeshu Encampment, but it felt like a lifetime. Most of the Metakalans who were very old, and those with professions, had moved on. The rest had assimilated into military training, right there in the camp. As a healer, Emmy didn't know if she was lucky or not.

Each day, she worked in a cloud of sickness. She tended the ill—and Zecha's wounded body—and gave what comfort she could, hoping the spread of the Lurking Death would cease. Some of her charges grew well under her care. Others withered and died. As each body was removed, another fell into its shadow. More Metakalans, a handful of Belfoni, and many Selamans, their land destroyed by the Masvams, their hearts bereft. The Althemerians took all manner of folk from the seas—now mostly acquired from the Masvams—but none were free.

"Folk from all places bleed for Althemer," Rel had said. "The queen doesn't care. She needs to keep her borders, but why sacrifice your own when you can sacrifice others?" She laughed, though the sound was hollow. "That's why they call it shipbait. It doesn't matter who you are or where you're from," she added, dipping her head. "Althemer is the great equalizer."

Shipbait? Emmy thought. *Even that isn't strong enough. We're* slaves.

She hunched her shoulders and stared across the compound. An Althemerian female appeared from one of the barracks, clutching a strange brass horn in her hands, ready to wake the troops.

As always, Emmy's mind turned to Charo. She was somewhere in the camp's sprawl, but Emmy hadn't seen horn nor tail of her since their separation on the plinth. Every morning before work began—when she hadn't been working all night, at least—Emmy waited in the growing chill, hoping for a glimpse of her friend. If she closed her eyes, she could almost feel Charo's breath, a steady in and out, in and out.

Yet she saw nothing. No glimpses, no signs.

Nothing.

The Althemerian horn-blower sounded the start of the day, and slowly morning opened. Captured soldiers—soldier-*slaves*, Emmy corrected—emerged from the long wooden barracks. The sun rose, but a chill remained in the air. Emmy scanned each face that appeared in the compound, but none was the face she sought.

A creak cracked behind her. Emmy turned. The healer Rel gently closed the door, then clasped her hands behind her back.

"Good morning, Emmy," she said.

Emmy nodded in return. "Morning greetings."

"I hope you've foregone breakfast," Rel said.

Emmy rose from the bench. Her brow furrowed. "Why?"

Rel's eyeridges rose in part-sympathy, part-apology. "I have to take you for the brand this morning," she said. "It's best to do it on an empty stomach."

Fear rose in Emmy like a dark fog. Her hand went instinctively to her arm as she imagined the sizzle and smoke.

"I've put it off for long enough," Rel said, "but it has to be done."

Emmy said nothing, her hand still on her arm. Rel gestured for her to follow.

They walked through the wakening camp, through the crisp air, as everything came to life. They passed squads of soldier-slaves under the watchful eye of their squad leaders, being marched to receive their morning food. They passed patrolling guards on vaemar, their watchful eyes and intimidating presence ensuring there was no unrest.

Through it all, Emmy scanned the knots of faces, desperate for one glance of Charo. She saw many Metakalans, and a considerable sprinkling of Linvarrans among them, but Charo was still elusive.

"You still look for your friend?" Rel asked as they took a right turn, away from the mess area.

"Yes," Emmy replied, craning her neck to catch one last look.

They walked across the dusty ground, between low-slung wooden structures, and the sound of hammering and ringing grew louder.

"What will you do if she's no longer here?" Rel asked.

Emmy's steps faltered. What would she do? What *could* she do? If Charo had been taken from the camp, off to be a maid or a road-digger, there was no way Emmy could find her. She was stuck in the camp, a slave to illness and injury. *I could escape*, Emmy thought, *with Zecha, once he's better*. The three friends belonged together. They had to find one another again.

Of course, Emmy couldn't say any of that. So instead, she shrugged one shoulder. "I don't know."

Rel's look was one of mild distrust. Emmy looked away.

As they walked, her destination became apparent. Emmy's stomach filled with boulders, and her steps grew slower. The blacksmith's hut loomed just ahead, and the sound of metal on metal grew louder. The day had just begun for the soldiers, but for the blacksmiths it had never ended. Their hammering became the beat of her walk, but it was nowhere near as fast as the beat of her heart.

Rel walked ahead, catching the attention of a thick-armed Linvarran blacksmith who toiled over something—a weapon, Emmy thought. What else would it be? Emmy trailed along behind, half-hearing the conversation between Rel and the male.

As he stopped his work to speak to Rel, the other blacksmiths continued their labor. They stoked fires, heated metal, and toiled in the great heat. Sweat poured from them, even in the cool morning.

When Emmy caught up, the blacksmith was collecting a series of long metal rods with different ends, though she couldn't make out what they were.

"Shoulda been here yesterday or the day before, Medicine-Rel," the blacksmith said as he gathered what he needed. "That's the rules, as you know, an' that's when we did the latest batch. Shouldn't have to do another one now."

Holding up her hands, Rel gave him a mild smile. "I know," she said, "but we're in the grips of another bout of the Lurking Death and there simply hasn't been time."

The blacksmith turned and glared at the two healers with narrowed eyes. A grimace played about his lips. "Lurking Death again, eh? Well, it better not lurk its way here. We got a lot of work to do, too."

The other blacksmiths turned from their work to grumble their agreement.

Rel nodded and lowered her hands. "I understand," she said. "We'll take as little of your time as we can."

The first blacksmith looked from Rel to Emmy and back again. The long poles rattled against one another in his hand. "All right," he said. "Come and sit over here."

He gestured to a chunk of log, huge and round. Emmy hesitated and looked to Rel, who nodded. Emmy crossed to the log, her back stiff and straight, and sat slowly. The blacksmith arranged the poles in a long metal holder. Closer, Emmy could almost see what they were.

The biggest, set in the top of the holder, was a circle. Below were smaller figures, numbers perhaps, and realization bloomed like a bloodstain. The circle showed the Althemerian serpent gods. The numbers showed the date she'd been taken, just like Rel had shown her. Emmy swallowed hard as her head spun.

The blacksmith thrust the holder deep into one of the fires that burned in a stone forge. As it heated, he rummaged on a nearby table. The item he picked up, he thrust into Emmy's hand. It was a metal bit, old and well-used. "Bite down on it when the time comes," he said. "Screams are distracting, and we don't got time for that."

Emmy watched with wide eyes as the blacksmith extracted the red-hot branding iron. Fear rose in her throat, and she gripped the bit tight in her hands.

"In the mouth," the blacksmith said.

Emmy looked to Rel, who nodded.

"It will be over soon."

Emmy looked at the bit, then at the snarling redness of the brand. She placed the bit between her teeth, her chest constricting.

The brand edged towards her, bright and deadly. She couldn't help the whimper that escaped her lips, though she cursed herself for it. *Don't show weakness. Be brave.*

"Lift your sleeve," the blacksmith said.

Emmy pushed her short sleeve up with a trembling hand and squeezed her eyes shut. The heat of the brand came towards her so slowly. Eventually it touched.

The smell of burning flesh hit her before the pain. It was strangely sweet. Then came the bite of the heat. Excruciating pain clamped its jaws around her as she clenched her teeth on the bit, the noise escaping from her mouth like that of a dying animal. The brand pressed into her, marking her as property of the Althemerians. Tears streamed from her eyes and she keened, wounded and terrified.

Then it was over. The blacksmith turned and plunged the branding iron into a deep stone ewer, the water hissing and spitting as the brand cooled. Emmy's mouth ached, her head swam, and her arm was still alight with red-hot pain. The bit fell from her mouth and clattered on the floor. When she opened her eyes, the blacksmith was already back to his previous work, as if nothing had happened. Rel reached for her uninjured arm, still half-sympathetic and half-apologetic.

"Let's go," she said, "and I'll give you something for the pain."

Emmy barely listened, but found herself propelled back through the encampment, past rows of soldier-slaves receiving orders from their leaders. Everything was a blur until they were back in the healers' building, in a canvas-curtained enclave, and Rel's hand was upon her wound.

A coldness as stark as the burning brand shook Emmy from her fugue. She winced as the new pain dove into her arm, but within a moment it was gone. Rel removed her hand and spread a musty-scented unguent over the wound. Emmy blinked several times and shook her head. The coldness. It was real.

In her shock from the brand, boldness took her. She shot out one hand. It clamped around Rel's wrist, and Emmy caught her eyes. They were dark and green and clear, but something lingered within them. Something strange and powerful.

"Who...who are you?" Emmy asked.

Rel gently released Emmy's talons from her wrist and returned to applying the healing paste to the fresh brand. "What a strange question to ask when you already know the answer," she said. "My name is Rel and I'm head of the *tsimi*. Once I held a life-debt to the Althemerians, like you, but now I'm free."

Emmy shook her head. That wasn't what she meant. She knew those things. What she didn't know was what the strange coldness was, and why it blossomed when Rel touched her. She didn't know why the same coldness had flowed through her when she held Zecha, broken and wounded on the boat. She didn't know what the word *Uloni* meant, or why Rel had asked her about an attack when they first met.

"That's not what I meant," she began.

Rel's voice cut across Emmy like a blade. "It's time for work now."

Emmy's shock deepened. Rel stood and walked a few paces away. She clamped the tiny pot of unguent hard in her claws. "Your pain won't return. Now get back to work. We have much to do."

Rel pulled the curtain aside and disappeared from the enclave. Emmy stared as the curtain settled again. Her stomach churned more than it had during the branding.

There was something more to this. The coldness was real. She'd done something on the boat, and now Rel had done something to her. Emmy shuddered at the thought of what it could be. Magic? But magic wasn't real. It was impossible.

Emmy stared at her hands, then at the cooled site of her brand. She snorted and turned her face from the brand. Until now she'd thought a lot of things were impossible. She'd never believed she would get away from Krodge. She'd never believed she would be taken as a slave. And yet, both had happened.

She shook her head. "I need to get out of here."

Emmy looked at her brand again. Beneath the greasy unguent, the two twined serpents stared, their burnt eyes dark.

CHAPTER TWENTY-FIVE

Mantos

The Queen's Palace towered high above the rest of Kubodinnu, rising from the capital city like a gleaming opal spiral. Many windows curved along the walls, glinting in the pale evening sun. On the lower levels, the windows were joined by fine statues of past rulers, hewn into the stone. Each had a hand that reached outward. Some wore expressions of compassion; others were solemn. Some were cold. All wore winding serpents around their necks.

The expression of the current queen fell into the latter category. Queen Valentia surveyed her subjects from the grand windows of council chamber, watching the specks hurrying about their daily business. Her own serpent wound down the length of her arm and back up again.

Mantos clenched his fists under the table. He wanted, more than the moons themselves, to disappear into the swirl, to escape from everything. He didn't want to be in this palace, among strangers. Yes, he had his mother and Fonbir, but it wasn't his land. He had no freedom. But what choice did he have? Mantos suppressed a choked laugh. *It's not like I can go home.*

"Your brother threatens us all," the queen said, still looking through the glass.

Unsurprisingly, she spoke her own tongue. Mantos, as heir, had taken great pains to learn the many tongues of the lands outside the empire. *Not to mention for my letters with Fonbir*, he thought. Closer to the language of Metakala and Selama than Masvam, learning Althemerian had been an unexpected challenge.

"You have had enough time to heal," Queen Valentia continued, turning to look at him. Her serpent slithered upward. "Now it is time to act."

Mantos swallowed. Those gathered at the table shifted in their seats, straightening as the queen spoke. There were the two princesses, Fylica and Valaria. To their left was Fonbir. Mantos and his mother lingered at the far end of the table. Standing aside, cloaked in black, was Bomsoi. Guards in ceremonial robes stood at the door, unwavering.

When Queen Valentia spoke again, Mantos' stomach tightened. This was it. She was about to ask him to open his own veins and spill all his secrets.

"Masvam forces are rutted in our northern forests," the queen said. "They claim lands they have no right to. They murder my subjects." She turned, her eyes lingering in deep shadows. "You're going to help me stop it."

Mantos looked from the queen to Fonbir's compassionate face, then to the twin glares of the princesses. The walls closed in, pressing him back and back. Hundreds of cycles of Tiboli rule in the Masvam Empire weighed upon him, but so did the truth of his brother's betrayal. Faced with a diverging path, sweeping off in two directions, Mantos licked his lips. He tried to speak, but all he mustered was a dry croak.

Princess Fylica tutted and rolled her eyes. "Pathetic."

"Fylica," the queen snapped, "if you do not behave in a manner more suited to the council chamber, I will send you out. Treat everyone with respect, even your enemy. To do less is to become low."

"Yes, Your Highness," the princess replied. She bowed her head, but when her mother looked away, she bared her teeth at Mantos. There was no compassion or learning in the princess' eyes.

Still bereft of words, Mantos sought Fonbir, who ventured a soft smile. The skin around his white eyes crinkled in a way that set Mantos' heart fluttering. *At least I have one friend on Althemer.*

His mother cleared her throat and rose. *Two friends*, he corrected.

"Your Highness," Phen said. Her hands gripped Mantos' shoulders, the pressure a comfort. "My son is not yet well. But, even as mere as I am and as absent as I have been, I was still the Masvam empress for some time. Bandim behaves as his father behaved, and he will do as his father did. He seeks to overwhelm the north of your island. He will establish a foothold and push out from there. If that happens, you will be overrun. I have seen it happen many times."

Princess Valaria sat forward, her expression solemn. When she spoke, her words were commanding: "We cannot allow the Masvams to infringe on our sovereignty."

She was spun from the same thread as her mother, her black armor burnished and obsidian. Most striking of all were her eyes, for they were bright green and ringed with black. Built from iron, she was not to be trifled with. *Though Bandim wanted to do more than trifle with her*, Mantos thought. *Had our father's marriage pact for him gone through, Valaria would have had no choice but to surrender her sovereignty.*

"We must push back," Valaria continued. She jabbed a talon at Mantos. "And you must tell us everything you know. You were the heir apparent, not him. You would have been at the center of your father's plans. There's no guarantee that Bandim will carry out the plans of his father, but it's the only possible intelligence we have. You must tell us everything."

Phen's hands clenched tighter on his shoulders. Mantos suppressed a frown. He knew it all. He knew the plans, the strategies, the weak points. He had lived it, breathed it, *been* it, for so long. He'd killed the Queen of Selama, slit her throat from ear to ear under her flaming banner, all in the name of his father's plans. Mantos dug his claws into the edge of the varnished table. *All in the name of power and glory. All in the name of Tiboli.*

Tiboli. His family name. The name he'd lived with all his twenty-one cycles. The name he was expected to uphold, to protect, to cherish.

But why should he? His brother had killed him. There was no loyalty there. Bandim had acted so quickly that Mantos had no insight into his brother's schemes. He could continue their father's work, or he could begin work of his own. In truth, Mantos didn't know what his brother would do.

A pact with the Althemerians might be the only way to save the countless innocents living under Bandim's rule. Would the folk be allowed to practice their belief in Nunako freely? Or would they now face persecution under the heel of Bandim and his Dark beliefs?

There was no way he could know. Mantos swallowed the lump in his throat. If he betrayed his brother, he might save his folk. But if he betrayed his brother for the Althemerians, he might submit those same folks to subjugation under Althemerian rule. They held life-debts. What was to stop them yoking all the empire under that same law? The Althemerians could save the Masvams from the tyrannical rule of Bandim and place Mantos on the throne, but he would be nothing more than a puppet. Ten cycles was long enough to bring an empire to its knees.

That was, of course, dependent on Bandim being a tyrant. Perhaps he wasn't. Perhaps he would be just and honorable.

Mantos squeezed his eyes shut.

Honorable rulers didn't kill their brothers.

Queen Valentia walked from the window and lowered herself into the seat at the head of the table. The jewels strung between her horns tinkled, but their cheerfulness was out of place in the chamber. She sat back and laced her talons together. Her serpent's tongue flicked out.

"If you don't tell us what you know, the blood of Althemer will be on your hands." Her grey eyes pierced him. She raised her arms, showing her many bracelets. "I have killed and, in the eyes of Ethay and Apago, I am a sinner. But I atone for my sins with good works. I help other nations and their folk. You are also a sinner, Mantos Tiboli. But as the gods teach us, good and selfless deeds wash away sin. Help us, and your soul may be cleansed."

It took all of Mantos' self-control not to laugh. What the Althemerians did was far from offering help to other nations. They were slavers, through and through.

Bomsoi stepped forward and waited. The queen gestured for her to speak. When she did, it was in a voice that commanded all attention.

"It's more than your own salvation, Mantos," she said. "There are strange things happening in the world. I expected as much with the Lunar Awakening, but..." She paused, her eyes flashing. "There is something more."

Mantos watched her as she spoke, looking for any sign of trustworthiness. His mother trusted her, as did Fonbir. She held much sway in the Althemerian court. But who she really was, Mantos didn't know.

"As you know, Your Highness," Bomsoi continued, "I've spent many cycles studying the holy books of many faiths. Not just the Book of the Twin Serpents, as you commanded, but the Gospel of Nunako, and many others. However, none are as dangerous as the Book of Divine Tears. That is the book of the followers of Dorai."

Fylica pressed a kiss to her clenched fist and set it on her heart. A sign to ward off bad spirits, Mantos knew. He'd seen others do the same.

"The followers of the Dark are fools," Princess Valaria said. "Their false god means nothing."

"I'm afraid, Your Highness," Bomsoi said, "it's not as simple as that. The Book speaks of a divine reckoning: *when the moons lie equal and the sun is at its closest, if the True Believer asks for my return, it will be granted.*" Bomsoi paused, as if the words she was to speak pained her. "On the day of the Lunar Equality," she continued slowly, "Bandim Tiboli brought the goddess Dorai back into this world."

Mantos froze. The nightmares. The prophecy. Bandim.

Dear brother, I will find you...

The prophecy was something he'd learned of, through so many cycles of tutelage under his masters. Old Master Abe, behind his desk of piled parchment and books, had spent much time lecturing the Tiboli siblings on its dangers, even before they gendered.

"We know that the goddesses Nunako and Dorai once walked this world among us," old Abe had said. "The evidence is found in many written sources, so we know it to be true."

Bandim had yawned theatrically and rolled their eyes, trying to bring Mantos in on the disrespect. Mantos hadn't reacted, instead keeping eyes and ears on Abe.

"It is also written," the old master continued, "that one day, the goddesses will return to this world, and bring about great destruction."

Bandim had waved a dismissive hand at the master's face and rolled their eyes again.

"Yes, yes, and the world will end," they said. "We've heard this so many times in temple. But it means nothing. Why are you teaching us such folly?"

Abe, gnarled as he was, stretched to his full height and unfurled a long talon towards Bandim.

"Ignorance is your greatest enemy," he said. "And you have much ignorance within you, young princeling. You should look to Mantos as an example. Mantos does not dismiss what is difficult to understand, but instead works towards understanding."

That comment snapped Bandim's temper like straw.

"Mantos, Mantos, Mantos!" In a swift movement, Bandim shoved piles of books and parchment from the master's desk. "Mantos the perfect! Mantos the wonderful! Well, when we gender and I become the male, we'll see who's so perfect then. *I'll* be the prince and you'll have to listen to me when I tell you this is *folly!*"

Bandim had stormed from the room then, a more typical ending to a lesson than Mantos or Abe would ever have liked. Old Abe had stared at the pile of scrolls and tomes on the floor, then looked to Mantos.

"Ignorance is truly your greatest enemy, Mantos."

The true meaning of his words hadn't rung true until now. Mantos closed his eyes. *Bandim is ignorance*, he thought. *I cannot ignore this, for I will be just as ignorant.*

Valentia's voice returned Mantos' attention to the council chamber.

"Bomsoi," the queen said, "does this mean what I think it means?"

The broad female nodded. "I'm afraid it does, Your Majesty."

"*Oatutkubis*," Fonbir whispered. "The Demon Who Rides the Sky."

The moment of silence that followed spoke volumes. The two princesses shared a glance, their faces lined with fear. Phen slumped into her seat, adrift on despair. The queen and Bomsoi were entirely still. Fonbir caught Mantos' gaze, his white eyes willing strength across the table.

Mantos knew the details of Oatutkubis inside and out. It was another of Abe's lessons, saved for when Mantos was the heir apparent. It was his duty, the old male said, to learn the beliefs of allies and enemies alike.

"We believe Dorai is a fallen god," Abe had said, "vanquished from the land by Nunako due to the corruption of her spirit. The Althemerians, and those who share belief in Ethay and Apago, believe that what we call Dorai is no god, but rather is Oatutkubis, a demon from the depths of the underworld. Ethay and Apago banished Oatutkubis long ago, binding him with a thousand chains. But it has always been their belief that one day, Oatutkubis would return, helped by the sun, the moon, and the corruption of hearts."

This prophecy was well-known and widely believed among the followers of Ethay and Apago, in much the same way as the Lunar Awakening and the return of Dorai were considered inevitable by believers in Nunako's Light. Mantos suppressed the shiver that threatened to shake his spine and shook his head. There was one figure who'd never believed, though. The one at the center of all this despair.

"It isn't possible," Mantos said. "He couldn't. Bandim had no faith. He never believed in the prophecy. Why would he bring it about?"

Valentia scoffed. "Is it not true that your brother became enamored with what you call 'the Dark'?" she asked. "To me that suggests he has found faith, as twisted as it might be."

Mantos kept a firm hold on his breathing as that thought sank in.

"I thought—we all thought—the folk who worshipped the Dark were nothing more than misguided fools," he said. "That no one had the power to return Dorai to this world. It was a prophecy that was written, but couldn't come to pass in our lifetime. Could it be possible that Bandim, who had no time for religion, has become so religious?"

"Many things are possible with faith," Bomsoi said. "Bandim Tiboli believes in Dorai and, as you know, is one of two—he believes he is *the* One of Two."

Realization dawned on Mantos. One of Two. They were both One of Two, by the strange occurrence of their eggs being laid together.

"Bandim has returned Dorai—or Oatutkubis—back to this world," Bomsoi went on. "I can feel her presence. It's weak, but she will grow in power. If Bandim can harness that power, we are all in grave danger."

"*If*," Mantos repeated. "That is a word not to be underestimated." He narrowed his eyes and pinned Bomsoi with a glare. "Where is the proof?" he asked. "How do we know? The only evidence we have is what you say, and words written in texts from long, long ago. Who exactly are you, Bomsoi? Why should I believe you?"

Valentia broke in with words like knives.

"Your belief is not my concern," she said, her eyes piercing. "And the Stranger does not need to prove herself to you. She is my most trusted advisor and sees more than any of us can see. You, on the other hand, are the enemy and my prisoner. Whether you believe the Stranger or not, you will do as I command. And I command you to listen to her and obey her wishes."

Before Mantos could retort, Bomsoi stepped forward, the heavy folds of her black cloak cocooning her.

"I need you, Mantos," she said. "The solution to this isn't as simple as taking back your crown. Your brother has delved into powers that will cause great destruction. You were brought into this world together and share a bond, just like the bond that once was between Nunako and Dorai, and exists between Ethay and Apago. You must help me stop him. You are bonded in life and in death."

"And," Fylica snapped, "a sibling knows their sibling's ways better than anyone. If you do not help us, you are as poisonous and evil as he."

That word, again. *Evil*. It echoed, but each time it resounded, it grew louder.

Evil. Evil. *Evil*.

Queen Valentia strode back to the window. She stared into the fading evening for some time, leaving Mantos to stew in silence.

"What would you all have me do?" he asked at length. "I don't know my brother's plans. He killed me so swiftly after our father's death, there's no way I could know what he'll do."

"We would have you do what is right," Valentia said. She continued to stare through the window. Mantos watched her face in the reflection. Eventually she turned to face him. "You will help save my queendom. You will take back the Masvam throne, under our auspices. Your life belongs to me, and you will do as I tell you. But most of all..." She paused, her face hard as stone. "You are going to kill your brother."

Phen choked back a sob. Mantos' throat bobbed as he tried to formulate an answer. *Kill Bandim... Why not?* He'd killed Mantos. And yet, how could he? They were hatched together, raised together. Always, always together. *We share a bond*, Mantos thought. His throat grew tight. *I don't love him, but can I kill him?*

Seizing on the moment of silence, Princess Valaria slammed the flat of her hand on the table.

"Weakness!" she cried. Fonbir shot his sister a vicious stare. But with a temper to match Fylica's, she wouldn't back down. "Your brother will bring this world to its knees—you all will! You Masvams meddle with things you don't understand. You worship false gods and idols, light or dark—it is folly! You think you know best, that you're better than the rest of us." She bared her teeth. "Now look at what you've done. Your brother has brought a demon into this world. Mantos, if you need to kill every last Masvam to bring peace, you should not hesitate. You owe us nothing less!"

"Valaria, *stop*."

The queen's command silenced her. The princess stilled her mouth, but fire was still in her eyes. "I apologize, Your Highness," she said, though she sounded far from reproachful.

Valaria sat, her eyes never leaving Mantos'.

"Much is at stake," Queen Valentia said. Her serpent coiled around her neck. "It's not just your brother's life, or your soul, or my queendom. It's all our lives, our souls, and all the lands of the world. Your brother may bring destruction upon us. You have a duty to stop him." She rose. "You have one day to make your decision. Choose wisely. Promise to deliver me Bandim's head, or I will cleave yours from your neck tomorrow."

She cast a fleeting glance at Phen before she strode to the door. The guards snapped to attention, opening it for her.

Queen Valentia left, flanked by her fiery daughters. Fonbir lingered, half-reaching to Mantos.

"Fonbir, come," Valaria snapped.

The prince's face grew pained. He stepped back, the heavy chain at his waist clinking. Mantos' heart grew cold.

"I'm sorry," Fonbir whispered, slipping away.

The evening dimmed. The sun disappeared below the line of buildings on the horizon. Phen pressed her eyes to stem the flow of tears.

"Oh, Mantos," she said. "We are destroyed. No matter what we do, we cannot win.

If we help the Althemerians, Bandim will die. We betray our own folk, our own empire. If we don't help them and instead allow Bandim to bring this evil into the world, he may kill us all."

As Mantos listened, Valaria's words came back.

Mantos, if you need to kill every last Masvam to bring peace, you should not hesitate. You owe us nothing less!

Gritting his teeth, he shook his head. Words failed him as the impossibility of his choice loomed heavy above him. Bandim had killed him. Why not seek retribution? But, the other side of his mind replied, would that not make them as bad as each other? As evil, as Fylica had claimed?

He looked at his mother, at the way she wrung her claws together and at the despair that flowed from her eyes. Did she cry more for the son who'd tried to end her life, or for the folk she'd once been empress of, who were now in mortal danger?

Or did she cry for her other son, the one who had to make an impossible choice in one day?

Mantos' chest tightened as if the hand of Nunako herself was squeezing his bones. One day. Once, when he was a youngling playing pretend soldiers with Bandim, winding through the palace halls, a day could last an eternity.

Now one day felt infinitesimal. An impossible timescale for an impossible decision.

Kill Bandim and take back the crown, betraying a brother who was, in truth, the rightful heir. Work with the enemy, and live as a puppet emperor on an Althemerian-controlled throne.

The alternative?

Do nothing and die.

Again.

CHAPTER TWENTY-SIX

Emmy

Emmy brushed off her hands and sighed. She sat back on her heels, admiring the blanched fabric dressing she'd wound around her Althemerian patient's injured chest. Days in Hutukeshu Encampment were an endless whir of comings and goings. Between the ill, the injured, and those careless in training, Emmy's hands were never still. She changed bandages, purged wounds, wrapped injuries, mixed healing pastes and potions, all in the confines of her Althemerian prison. However, even in these circumstances there was a glimmer of satisfaction within her. Healing felt right, as if it was what she'd been hatched to do. Despite the tether that tied her to Althemer, Emmy's heart sang with a worthwhile purpose.

Crossing to another patient—a Selaman with a head injury this time—Emmy set to work redressing the wound. The shine was taken off her satisfaction by the branded reminder on her arm. There was no element of choice in her actions. She had to obey. Even so, there were worse ways to serve her time. Rel was kind, and the scowls of Medicine-Yarim and Medicine-Asri were nothing compared to the bite of a sword to her neck. No amount of training could mold Emmy into a warrior. Once more she thought of Charo, whose whereabouts were unknown. Worry weighed like a boulder on Emmy's back. She could play at being a healer all she liked, but it wasn't going to find Charo, and it wasn't going to grant any of them freedom. *You're a fool to feel any satisfaction in this*, she thought. *It's no better than being with Krodge. You need to think about how to heal Zecha, find Charo, and get all three of you out of here.*

Finished attending to the Selaman's head, Emmy set aside the roll of coarse woven bandage. He was the last of her patients for now. As happened when she finished any task, her eyes returned to the one prone form she knew better than the rest.

Zecha still lay on his cot, unconscious but seemingly settled. A healthier pallor had returned to his skin, and under the bandages his stomach wound was knitting neatly. Whatever Rel had done to him had accelerated his healing tenfold, but as yet he still hadn't opened his eyes. Crossing to him, Emmy laid a hand on his shoulder, willing for him to somehow wake and grace her with a glance from his red eyes. Only recognition and an inane comment would settle the ache in her chest.

His eyes remained shut. Emmy sighed. Medicine-Yarim heard her and shot across a glare, but Emmy pointedly ignored her. There was no point wasting time on a waste of time. Removing her hand, Emmy left Zecha's side and moved onto the second part of her rounds.

The work of a healer, slave or not, was far from glamorous. Not only were there wounds to clean and bandage, complete with blood and varying shades and stinks of pus, there was sickness to comfort too. The effluent created by illness was less tolerable than that of wounds, but in a camp where so many folks were kept in close quarters, illness spread like smoke. Although she would rather stitch a thousand wounds in a row than clean up lakes of unmentionable fluids from the sick, Emmy endeavored to treat her charges with compassion. Imagining herself into one of the cots, covered with a rough woven blanket, dignity was what she would prize the most.

Unfortunately, her kindness was not often appreciated. That was why she much preferred unconscious folk—they didn't sling insults with their blood and vomit. Emmy's temper flared at the idea that folk could still despise her and regard her as more of a monster than the Althemerians who captured and branded them. Over and over she bit back her ire. It was nothing she hadn't already endured. Krodge's haggard face flashed in her mind. Emmy shut her eyes as the vision passed. It didn't matter what abuse her ungrateful charges flung at her. She'd heard it, and felt it, all before.

As she wiped the sweaty face of a Lurking Death victim, voices approached from outside. Emmy turned to the door, awaiting the arrival of another wound or illness. She and Medicine-Yarim shared a brief glance, and the latter went to prepare a free cot for their newest arrival.

When the figure entered, Emmy's eyes widened, and she squeaked. "*Charo!*"

Rushing forward and tripping over an errant pile of soiled bandages, Emmy righted herself and grabbed Charo's claws.

Her friend's head snapped up and she blinked with recognition, shaking off some of the confusion she'd entered with. "Emmy?"

"It's me!" Emmy replied.

Charo's mouth stretched with a pained grin. "Why am I surprised you're here? Of course you are."

The reason for her visit was clear. Her temple was badly bruised and bloodied, and her left eye was swelling. To Emmy, it looked like a blow to the head with something blunt—and heavy. She pulled Charo in for a careful hug, squeezing her gently. Relief washed over Emmy in waves.

"Finally," she said, ghosting her fingertips over Charo's wound. "I haven't seen claw nor tail of you since we arrived. I was so worried!"

Bleary-eyed, Charo nodded, blinking against the pain in her head. "I was worried about you too," she replied.

Emmy guided Charo to the bed Medicine-Yarim had prepared. "What happened?"

"Drenna Haldra," Charo replied, wincing as she sat on the canvas cot. "The butcher is no soldier."

Emmy took a closer look at the damage and tutted, before grabbing a mortar and pestle from a nearby trestle table. She plucked the right healing ingredients from her belt pouches and mixed a fragrant paste to relive bruising.

"I'm glad you're safe," Emmy said, sitting on a stool to apply the mixture. "Where have you been?"

Charo winced as the paste hit her wound, but she allowed Emmy to continue.

"I've been assigned to combat training," she said. "We spend a lot of time in the fields outside the camp learning to fight. Or inside the camp, still learning to fight." She ventured a small smile. "They say I'm a fast learner."

The last part was added with a pinch of pride. Emmy shook her head.

"Don't learn too fast," she said. "I don't want to lose you again." Emmy worked the paste across Charo's bruising with gentle claws. "How do they treat you?" she asked.

"Well enough," Charo replied. "There's enough food and, like I said, I seem to learn quickly. That helps a lot. Our instructor Bara—though they call her Stickslice—is fair. For a captor, I suppose," Charo added with a sigh. "For the likes of Drenna, the days must be long and awful. For me, well... I enjoy the drills and the practice. Sometimes I even forget why I'm here. But then I remember..." Her eyes filled with sudden tears. "I remember we're slaves."

Emmy rubbed Charo's shoulder with her clean hand. For a moment, Charo looked desperately young. *She's only fourteen*, Emmy thought. *She is young.*

"I can't believe it," Charo went on, her eyes downcast. "I can't believe I was freed from one set of bonds only to be delivered into another."

"It's not as bad as it could be," Emmy said. "There's food and shelter, and I suppose it's not forever. Who knows? If you're that good, you could earn your freedom sooner than me."

The words were little consolation, and Emmy knew it, but there wasn't much else to say. Charo looked up, her tears replaced with fervency.

"If I did, I'd come back for you," she said. "I'd come back to free you—and Zecha. We're friends. More than friends. You two are the closest thing to family I've ever had."

Emmy tried to smile. *Family*, she thought. *I have no family but Charo and Zecha either.*
An image of Krodge flashed across her mind.
Finished her off, I did.

The words brought a surge of urgency to her chest. She locked eyes with Charo. The sudden need to speak was too great.

"You know, I'm glad Krodge is dead," she said, half-confessing. She tilted her chin up, as if to defy judgement. She grabbed a rag from the trestle table and balled it between her claws. "Krodge was terrible and cruel and deserved to die. I'm glad she's dead. And Bose too."

The sudden turn in conversation made Charo's eyes widen. But she nodded and placed a hand on Emmy's knee.

"I don't think you need to mourn the deaths of those who don't deserve it," she said. "If I found out my old owner was dead, I wouldn't shed any tears over her. I'd kick her ashes to the wind if I had the chance. I had no life with her. At least here there's a chance I'll be freed."

Emmy took in the image of her friend decked in her blue uniform. Wounded as she was, Charo was a far cry from the starved and stabbed waif on Emmy's doorstep. Her fronds were growing fast, reddish-brown, thick and shimmering. Her color was healthy, and her muscles were taut and growing. Even her scars were less noticeable.

Emmy twisted the rag in her hands, wiping excess paste from her claws. "In some ways I feel I should mourn Krodge," she said. "Even though she was dreadful to me, she still took me in when she could have drowned me in a bucket or dashed my head on the back step."

Charo squeezed Emmy's knee. "Ever since you told me the story of how you came to be with Krodge, I did wonder. Why would she take you in but treat you so badly?"

Emmy shrugged, setting the soiled rag aside. She brought a hand up to touch Charo's chin, tilting her head so she could examine her handiwork.

"I don't know," she said. "I've wondered about that all too often. Krodge could have ignored me, but she didn't. Yet she didn't love me." She released Charo's face and sighed. "And now I'll never know her reasons, because she's dead."

Charo grasped Emmy's hand. "She doesn't deserve your thoughts," she said. "You'll never know, just how I'll never know why my parents sold me into slavery—if that's the truth. It's what I was always told."

Charo was right, Emmy thought. Wondering about Krodge's intentions had been pointless when the wretch was alive. Now that she was dead and there was no possibility of learning the truth, it was even more futile.

Charo released Emmy's hand again and touched the side of her head. She winced and stood.

"Thank you," she said, "but I can't hang around. Stickslice told me to come straight back. If I take too long she'll punish me, whether I'm a fast learner or not. Before I go, though," she continued, glancing around at the rows of cots, "I did want to ask, though I'm scared of the answer." She briefly bit her lip. "Have you seen Zecha?"

A smile broke across Emmy's face and she placed a hand in the small of Charo's back, just above the base of her tail. Gently she ushered her across to the cot she frequented the most. Charo grinned, though at the same time her eyes filled again.

"He's alive!" she said, falling to her knees at Zecha's side.

She cupped his face with one hand and hovered the other over his bandaged wound. "I was so afraid he'd be dead," she said. "I can't believe he's okay."

Rel's strange coldness flashed in Emmy's memory but she bit back her words. There wasn't time to talk about what might, or might not, have happened. Instead, she simply smiled.

"The head healer here is excellent," Emmy said. "She's been training me. She can do things that I've never seen anyone do before."

It was the truth. Charo leaned to kiss Zecha's head, her lips lingering on his skin.

"I'm grateful to her," she said. Pulling back, she turned to Emmy. "And to you. I'm sure you're keeping a close watch on him."

"And rehearsing and tweaking the scolding I'm going to give him when he wakes up," Emmy said, holding a hand out to help Charo to her feet.

Charo accepted the hand and rose. Instead of releasing Emmy's claws, she pulled her in for a tight embrace. Emmy stiffened in surprise but accepted the touch, squeezing Charo back.

"We'll get out of here," Charo whispered into Emmy's neck. "I don't know how, but we will. Once Zecha's better, we'll find a way."

The youthful innocence in Charo's words made Emmy feel as old as the sea, but she kept her jaded retort to herself. Escape was unthinkable, though she still yearned for it as much as her younger friend. Instead of brutal truth, Emmy spoke a comforting lie.

"We will," she said. "We will."

They released once another. Emmy kept the smile on her face for Charo's sake as they walked to the door.

"Come back if your pain isn't relieved," Emmy said. She lowered her voice to a whisper. "Come back even if it does, and just say it hasn't. We'll be able to talk more then."

"Will do," Charo said. She edged towards the outside. "Take care of yourself, and Zecha."

"The same to you," Emmy replied.

With that, Charo disappeared. Emmy's heart sank again as the door swung closed, sealing her inside the building again, away from her friend. She turned, and the first thing she saw was Medicine-Yarim's sour scowl. Emmy suppressed a sigh, palmed her face, and went back to work.

CHAPTER TWENTY-SEVEN

Emmy

Emmy stood at the front of the healers' building and shaded her eyes against the dipping sun. There were black figures on the hilltop, silhouetted against the orange sky. She squinted, trying to make sense of the shapes. *I wonder if it's Charo*, she thought. Her tunic clung to her skin and she passed a hand over her forehead, threading her claws through her horn crest. At least now she knew her friend was alive.

She closed her eyes and listened. The forest around the encampment hummed and if she strained her ears, the sound of animals sharpened: hooting, shuffling, and snuffling in the dirt. She hadn't seen trees quite so tall, nor had she encountered plants as fragrant as those on Althemer. As Merish waned and Vhaun waxed, flowers that had been an explosion of color began to dim. They spilled along the treeline, coiling in unkempt tendrils around the fences. The trees, tall and imposing, prepared to shed their canopies.

For Emmy, an appreciation for the outside world was something new. The four walls of the apothecary had been her life. She'd been as much an object as the bottles, plants, and powders. She'd measured and poured and swept and cleaned and...

It was all gone now.

Her perfectly ordered, perfectly painful life had disappeared in a blast of flame. Krodge was dead—and Emmy couldn't bring herself to be entirely unhappy about it.

Days had turned to a week. Zecha was still unconscious. Charo hadn't returned. Once more, Emmy found herself staring across the compound, wishing for at least a glimpse of Charo to prove... What? Emmy shook her head. To prove she was still alive and hadn't been killed in training? That happened more often than Emmy ever expected.

"There you are."

Emmy jumped at the intrusive voice. Rel stepped outside the healer's building. She plucked up Emmy's sleeve to inspect her healing brand, then laid her claws on Emmy's arm. "Come," she said. "I want a word with you."

Emmy nodded, her chest tightening, and followed in Rel's footsteps. What could it be about? An explanation for the coldness? She stopped her laugh before it escaped. Hardly likely.

Insects chirped and bristled. The sun had fallen further. A soldier on the back of a vaemar lit the tall lamps dotted around the camp.

"Catch."

Rel threw something into Emmy's hands. Emmy fumbled, and when she finally secured her grip, she stilled. It was a wooden baton.

"You don't need much help from me regarding medicine," Rel said. She held a wooden weapon of her own. "It would seem whoever trained you before trained you well. However, I can teach you my other skill." She raised an eyeridge. "I can teach you to fight."

"Fight?" Emmy asked. "I thought I was safe from the fighting."

The naivety of her words struck her even as they left her mouth. Emmy's face burned in a flush.

"You're safe from the front of the army," Rel said. She spun with the weapon, moving smoothly from one pose to another. Her muscles flexed under her skin and armor. "However, you're not *safe*. Enemies can sneak in the darkness. They can pick out lonely, unskilled folk and—" She dragged a claw across her throat. "Masvams love to kill *tsimi*. You need to learn to protect yourself."

Emmy stared at the baton, not much more than a stick, and clenched her claws around it. "I don't know how to fight," she said. "Krodge paid a tax so I wouldn't have to join the army."

"No matter," Rel said. "I'll teach you. There's no need for you to become a warrior, but you should know how to protect yourself. Now, hold it—no, with just one hand. It's not a club."

"And a stick isn't a sword," Emmy countered. "What am I going to do with a stick?"

"It isn't a stick," Rel said. "It's an ohza, a wooden baton. But that's of little consequence. Ready yourself!"

Face flushed, Emmy lifted her chin but did as she was told. Rel positioned herself to attack, and Emmy flinched. All that came her way were words.

"Two warriors face off in the forest," Rel said, bouncing a little on her feet. "The first is old, a female skilled with a sword but weakening. The second is young, headstrong, and only has an ohza to defend herself. Who wins?"

Emmy snorted and tried to mimic Rel's stance. "I suppose you're going to tell me the young one with the stick does," she said.

Rel struck out and knocked the ohza from Emmy's grip. Emmy's gasp echoed into the darkening forest.

"No," Rel said, holding her own ohza to Emmy's chin. "The skilled female runs her weapon through the other's middle and kills her."

Emmy blinked. She tilted her head. "Why? Surely the younger is stronger."

Rel clicked her tongue.

"She wins because of her skill," Rel replied. "Youth is nothing compared to knowing what you're doing. But to know what you're doing begins with training. If the younger had a sword and the older still only an ohza, who would win then?"

"I imagine you'll tell me it's still the old female," Emmy said, the ohza still stuck under her chin.

"Yes," Rel said. She withdrew the ohza. "Because it isn't the weapon that wins. It's the skill. And skill starts with the stick, so pick it up."

Emmy retrieved her weapon. Rel took up another fighting stance. "Stand like this, feet apart. Use your tail for balance. Good. Now try to strike me."

Feeling foolish, Emmy made a feeble attempt to land a blow on the older healer. Rel grunted, her arm struck out like a serpent, and she smacked Emmy's ohza away. Emmy withdrew her hands as if she'd been burned.

Rel nodded at the discarded ohza. "Pick it up," she said. "Try again."

Reluctantly, Emmy crossed the packed dirt to retrieve her weapon. When she turned, Rel was bouncing on the balls of her feet again.

"Hit me," she said. "With passion this time."

Clenching the ohza in one hand, Emmy stepped forward and struck out again. There was more force behind her strike but once again, Rel parried and thrust the ohza from her hands.

Rel shook her head and gestured to the ground once more. "Pick it up."

A surge of anger rolled through Emmy and she forced a hard breath through her nostrils. She snatched the ohza from the ground. Rel, seeing her face, smiled.

"That's better," she said. "You're no warrior, Emmy, but you can use what you have to protect yourself."

"What I have?" Emmy asked, the words sharp as daggers. "What do I have?"

"Anger," Rel replied. "You seethe with it. Soldiers are taught to control their anger, but you're no soldier. You can't hope to best someone in battle unless you have the element of surprise. They won't expect you to fight back—less so, to fight back with passion. So come at me again, angry this time."

Emmy gritted her teeth and pressed her talons hard around the ohza. Anger? Oh, yes. Emmy was full of anger. Anger at Krodge and all her cruelty. Her lies.

"Once I'm dead, there'll be no one left to protect you!"

You never protected me, old crone!

She lunged out with force this time, swinging her ohza wildly. This time it took Rel two blows to disarm her. Emmy's breath came in hard gasps and she crumpled her face in a grimace as her weapon clattered away. Rel's grin grew wider, but that only made Emmy's ire stronger.

"Pick it up again!" Rel said. "More anger. More fury!"

Grunting, Emmy wrenched the ohza from the ground once more and squeezed her eyes shut.

She burrowed into her pits of anger. She thought of Krodge and her cruel strikes. She thought of Zecha, lying in a sea of mire, bleeding to death. She even thought of Bose's nasty taunts—and his detached head.

Emmy flew forward with her ohza raised. Rel's face was gone. Instead, she landed blows on the Masvam who'd slipped up the apothecary stairs and killed Krodge.

Then she was striking Pesmam, who so cruelly cut a hole in Zecha's belly.

Then she was fighting a faceless, blacked-out figure with the body of Charo at its feet. Charo's mistress, the one who'd left her for dead.

Emmy struck out wildly. She knew it was really Rel, yet she kept striking. Her hands grew cold as a seething power grew within her. She landed blow upon blow upon blow on all her enemies.

Krodge.

Bose.

Pesmam.

Charo's mistress.

Emmy screeched, her arms flailing, the ohza striking air and Rel in good measure. Anger consumed her, coursed through her body, took away every thought.

Coldness grew and grew within her, filling Emmy with more might than she'd ever felt before. She could do anything. She could *kill*—

Without warning, Emmy was stunned.

She was stilled, enveloped in a freezing wind. Rel's face was thunderous, her arm outstretched. Her eyes were ablaze with blue flame. Emmy's heart hammered, the blueness of Rel's once-green eyes probing deep into the darkness of her heart.

"Who—who *are* you?" Emmy choked.

The wind abated as Rel withdrew her hand. Her power gone, Emmy collapsed, panting and clutching her head. *What happened?* she thought. *What did Rel do? What did I do? And why were her eyes so blue? I don't understand!*

Rel plucked the ohza from the ground, her eyes green once more. She didn't look like someone who'd simply stopped another with the power of...whatever it was. Emmy knelt in the dirt, staring up at her.

"Rel, what was that?"

Staring down at her, Rel narrowed her eyes. Emmy huffed a sharp breath through her nostrils and struggled to her feet.

"Tell me what just happened," she said. Rel remained silent. Emmy's temper snapped. "Tell me! Just...say something!"

Turning away, Rel clutched the two ohza so hard the skin of her knuckles grew white. "That is enough for today."

Enraged, Emmy clamped a hand around Rel's wrist. Fury made her bold in a way she'd never been before. There were too many questions left unanswered and for the first time in her life, Emmy demanded to be heard.

"No!" she said. "It's not enough. You need to tell me what's going on. What did you mean back when we first met when you asked me about an attack and the Uloni? Why do I feel so cold when you touch me? How did you heal my brand with just a touch?" Her throat tightened, but she pressed on. "And how was I able to help Zecha on the boat just by touching him? I can feel the coldness, the power. You know about it and you need to tell me. Now!"

There was silence. Rel's eyes were fixed on Emmy's hand, still clamped on her wrist. As the silence went on, Emmy's fury turned to watery fear. *She's my superior. I can't speak to her like that. She'll have me punished, and—*

"All right," Rel said. Her voice was as quiet as the now-gentle wind. "All right."

"A-all right?" Emmy stumbled on the word.

Gently prying Emmy's fingers from her arm, Rel nodded and patted the back of Emmy's hand.

"Go back inside," Rel said. She handed Emmy the ohza. "Put these in my enclave and get my cloak, a cloak for yourself, and a basket. I'll meet you in front of the building in a few moments."

Questions burning, Emmy wanted to ask why. But the balance of conversation was precarious, as if at one wrong word Rel would snatch away all possibility of telling the truth. So instead of asking, Emmy darted back inside the healers' building and did as she was told.

Medicine-Asri, on duty for the night, shot her a sharp stare when she disappeared into Rel's curtained enclave. Emmy didn't spare him a second glance. Instead she dropped the ohza on Rel's bed, grabbed her cloak from the stand in the corner, and went to leave.

Before she slipped through the curtain again, Emmy stopped. Curiosity overtook her, and she glanced around. Rel's little corner of the building was unornamented. There was a bed, a plain chest that held clothing, and a long, flat box that was locked. The stubs of good wax candles that pooled on a barrel beside the bed spoke of her rank, but little else did; apart, perhaps, from the polished plate that stood behind the candles. It was a fine thing, so shiny that Emmy could see her full reflection in the bronzed surface. It was a sight she hadn't seen in some time.

Turning away, Emmy hugged the cloak to her chest and pushed the curtain aside again. Now wasn't the time for preening and staring in plates. Now was the time for answers.

She tugged the curtain closed once more, ignored Medicine-Asri as she grabbed a cloak for herself and a basket, and hurried outside once more.

Rel was waiting, and had an enormous vaemar at her side.

"This is Sharptooth," she said as she stroked the creature's strong, furred neck. "He's a favorite of mine."

Accepting the offered cloak, Rel attached it around her shoulders by her cloakpins. Emmy did the same. Mounting the vaemar, Rel held out a hand to help Emmy up. "You've ridden vaemar before?"

"Not for a long time," Emmy replied. *Not since Zesi,* she thought, but she didn't want to think much further down that line.

Emmy accepted Rel's help and, with the use of the stirrups, she leapt onto the back of the huge creature, just behind Rel. The vaemar's fur was warm, and his skin undulated with each purring breath. Unable to help herself, Emmy stroked his coat, winding her talons into the softness.

Rel whistled a command and Sharptooth took off at a trot. At the sudden movement, Emmy lurched, and her free arm immediately went to Rel's waist. The healer said nothing as she guided them, astride the vaemar, to the main exit of the camp.

Emmy half-hid as one of the guards approached, clutching the handle of the basket so hard it sliced into her soft palms.

"Where are you going so late, Medicine-Rel?" the guard asked.

Rel tipped her head back to Emmy. "My apprentice and I are going to pick nightshroom," she said.

Realizing her cue, Emmy lifted the empty basket.

The guard stepped back and nodded. Two others moved into place, pulling back the wooden gates.

Emmy swallowed hard as, for the first time since she had been processed, she left the Althemerian camp. Her thousandfold questions kept swirling in her mind, bumping against once another like flotsam in a turbulent sea.

What would Rel tell her? What would happen next?

There were dark questions, too. What if Rel wasn't to be trusted? After all, Emmy barely knew her. What if she was taking her out to dispose of her?

No. Emmy shook her head. She didn't know Rel well, but she'd seen enough of her work as a healer to know she wasn't a killer.

She hoped.

Together astride Sharptooth, they slipped towards the dark forest, under the light of the waning moons.

CHAPTER TWENTY-EIGHT

Emmy

They reached a clearing in the forest not far from the encampment. Emmy's eyes had long adjusted to the gloom. To her surprise, a thick ring of nightshroom glimmered in the middle of the clearing. *I guess we* are *picking them*, she thought.

Rel pulled Sharptooth to the side. The great beast's breath was a soft burr. No sounds of animals or insects crept from the forest. Instead, the clearing was silent.

Motioning for Emmy to slip from the saddle, Rel slid down beside her. She clicked her tongue, and Sharptooth shook himself before padding off and curling into a ball at the edge of the clearing.

Emmy gripped the handle of her basket. She hardly dared to breathe, as if that simple act would disrupt the mystery of this excursion. What was all this? Rel had agreed to tell her what she knew, but here they were, just picking shrooms in the moonlight. Emmy bit her lip as uncertainty churned in her stomach.

Rel walked to the ring of nightshroom and knelt at its side. She bent low to sniff the fungi, then beckoned Emmy over.

"These will do," she said. "Kneel." She gave Emmy a thin smile. "Don't worry. I haven't forgotten what I said."

Reluctantly, Emmy knelt on the grass. It was cool and crinkled beneath her. She watched as Rel plucked the first nightshroom from the ring, then deposited it in her basket.

"Pick," Rel said.

Obedient, Emmy complied. But her mind still whirled with curiosity. What would Rel tell her?

Instead of an answer, she received a question.

"Tell me something, Emmy," Rel said, plucking another shroom. "Why do you say you are a Metakalan?"

Emmy blinked, taking a moment to comprehend the words. Her hand stilled over the basket, a nightshroom ready to drop. "Because I *am* Metakalan," she replied. "I live in Bellim—" Unintended, her voice cracked. She swallowed. "At least, I used to."

Another shroom surrendered to Rel's grasp. "Did the Metakalans treat you badly?" she asked. "For your difference?"

Emmy barked a laugh. The sound was obnoxious in the silent glade, but she wasn't sorry for it. Memories of taunts and fearful glances flashed in her mind.

"Badly?" she asked. "Most folk treated me—and still treat me—like I'm a demon. A Moon Rogue, that's what they say."

Rel chuckled. At the sound of mirth, Emmy's temper flared. The shroom she held disintegrated in her grip. Apologetic, Rel schooled her laughter. "I don't mean to insult you," she said. "It's just that... We have common ground on that front."

Shroom picking abandoned, Emmy's full attention was on Rel. "Who called you that?" she asked. "And why?"

"Oh," Rel said, giving a vague wave, "only...everyone."

Emmy drew her brows low and shook her head. "Everyone?" she asked. "Why?"

Rel grunted. "What do you know about the Belfoni?"

Emmy tilted her head to the side. "Not much," she said. "I've never met one before, apart from you."

Rel sat back on her haunches, she too abandoning the picking.

"In Belfoni, the males rule," she said. "It's like the Masvam Empire. Females stay at home and sew clothing and boil roots and look after the males. That's why you don't see many of them outside of the homeland. Their values are...different." She gestured to herself. "Can you see me sewing clothes and boiling roots?"

Shaking her head, Emmy answered. "No, I don't think I can."

Rel chuckled again.

"I never wanted any of that. I wanted to fight, but in Belfoni only the males fight. No one understood. Even my own parents called me wicked and unnatural. Tainted. Evil, even. They called me *ingufu*, like your word 'Moon Rogue.' No one would give me a chance. So what did I do?" Rel spread her talons, as if revealing a great secret. After a pause, she continued. "Only a youngling, I took nothing but a dagger and I left."

Her eyes rose to the moons, which were little more than slivers, and their light glinted on Rel's face.

Emmy swallowed and nodded.

"I can understand why you did," she said. "Zecha encouraged me to run away, to leave Bellim and Metakala and go find somewhere I could belong." Her tone turned cold. "I never thought such a place existed."

Rel nodded. "Zecha sounds like a good friend," she said. "Now I understand why you worry for him so much."

Emmy's mouth was dry, but her eyes were wet. "He is a good friend," she said, "the best I've ever had."

Rel reached out to pat one of her hands. The cold surged again. "Good friends are like gemstones," she said. "They are rare, and to be cherished."

Blinking against her tears, Emmy brought her sleeve up to her eyes. "What did you do after you left?" she asked, welcoming the diversion from her thoughts about Zecha.

"I did many things," Rel said. "I travelled to many places. I went south to the Great Forests, and then out to the coasts, smelling the salt air of the Easterlies and Westerlies. I went north to the Kingdom of Khin, and lived with the Khinish in their mountains for a time. They're not as unwelcoming as is said of them. But my feet always wanted to move, so I never stayed in one place. I even passed through the Great Northern Range." She paused. Her eyes unfocused, like she was peering into her own memory. "That was where I met the best of all my friends."

Emmy blinked. "Who?"

Rel closed her eyes, and breathed as if she could still smell the clear air of the mountains. She ignored Emmy's question and continued.

"I walked through the Range. I climbed sheer ice faces. I *lived*." She opened her eyes again, and turned to Emmy. "The best thing that happened was the day I met my friend and the Uloni."

Eyeridges pulling, Emmy tilted her head to the side. There was that word again. Uloni. It was strange on the tongue, entirely unfamiliar. "That's what you said to me before," she said. "How had I survived the attack on the Uloni—what does it mean?"

Rel fell silent for a moment and simply looked at Emmy. Emmy shifted. It was as if Rel was peering beyond her flesh, right to her bones.

"Emmy, your parents were Uloni," Rel said, gesturing at her skin and armor. "Your colors are only found in them."

Emmy slumped back, hands pressing into the crisp grass.

"My parents?" she asked. "I never knew my parents. I lived with my mistress, Madame Krodge. I didn't think anyone looked like me. I thought..." She broke off. "I thought I was a freak. Krodge said so, that I was deformed."

"You are no freak, nor are you deformed," Rel said. "You are Uloni."

The word twisted in her mind. *Uloni*. Emmy's heart pumped. A cold sweat broke on her brow.

"There are others like me?" she asked. "I'm not the only one like this?" She sat forward, pressing her claws to her knees. "Tell me about them, Rel," she said. "Please."

Rel plucked another nightshroom from the ring and deposited it into the basket. She did it again and again, the movement methodical.

"When I went to Uloni and met my friend, it was the middle of Vhaun, nearly two cycles ago. Vhaun is cold enough in the lowlands, but in the mountains it's unbearable." She suppressed a shiver. "The higher I climbed, the worse the snow became. As I was driven further and further into the barren wasteland, I thought I was going mad."

She paused, her claws poised to pluck another shroom.

"But what pressed me onward was the rumour of a village full of strange folk. They hid themselves from the outside world, admitting few to their realm. It was said they lived by an ancient religion, and that they loved and tolerated all folk. I so desperately wanted to find someone who would look past my differences and see me for...me."

There was silence as Emmy hung on her every word. What Rel said spoke to her core, and put into words the longing Emmy too possessed.

"What did you find?" Emmy asked, her voice barely above a whisper.

"I found that it was real." Rel's voice fell, as if speaking in the presence of a priestess or even a goddess. "They saw me and allowed me past their gates. And inside was a beauty unrivalled anywhere else. Everything was white and sparkling. They carved such beautiful things from the ice—huge sculptures, perfect orbs that caught the sun's meager light and lit up the whole village. And the folk... The folk looked so *different*. Strange. They looked like..." Rel ducked her head for a moment, as if catching on a careless word. "They looked like *you*."

A shiver rattled down Emmy's spine. She pressed her claws into the crisp grass. "The Uloni," she said. "I'm one of them."

Rel nodded and reached for Emmy's hand. After a moment, Emmy cautiously unfurled her claws, allowing Rel to take them.

"You are," Rel said, "and you are rare. There could only have been twenty-score Uloni, and they were devout. In the center of the village was a temple, painted white, with a roof open at the top. Every Uloni went there daily to praise their god. They worshipped an ancient goddess named Meia, whom they called the Grandmother of the World."

Emmy's brow furrowed again. "Not Nunako?" she asked. "Not Ethay and Apago? Not even Dorai?"

"No," Rel said. "Meia was something else. Something pure and wondrous." A wry grin crossed her face, highlighted by the silver of the moons. "Just like my friend." She sighed, patting Emmy's claws. "I loved that place. There was something special there, something more than I'd ever experienced before. When I went to their temple, it was like my mind's eye was opened to the truth. I..." She faltered. "I never wanted to leave."

"Then why did you?" Emmy asked. "Why didn't you stay?"

For a moment Rel said nothing. Beyond the play of shadows on her face, Emmy could see something more. There was something so closed about her expression it made Emmy's guts tighten. "What happened?" she asked, her voice low.

For another moment Rel wouldn't meet Emmy's eyes. But eventually she met her gaze.

"The prayer bell sounded for morning worship. My friend and I went to the temple.

It was full, as everyone attended every service. We raised our arms to the sky so our prayers could reach Meia. But..." Rel paused, as if overwhelmed by memory. "I smelled smoke. That was odd, for they were careful not to bring flame into the temple. The smell grew stronger and stronger, and then I saw the smoke begin to rise. The temple was aflame."

Emmy's gut twisted with fear as Rel went on.

"We tried to get out, but the doors were barred. Unwelcome outsiders had entered the village. They locked us in and intended to burn us alive." Rel took a shuddering breath. "You could taste the panic. The smoke was so acrid I could hardly breathe. The flames licked over the edge of the roof, ringing us in flames. There was so much screaming... Then the walls collapsed. I was pinned beneath a beam, sure that I was dead. I started to pray. I swore I would do anything if Meia would let me live. There was a terrible shudder when I uttered those words. Then there was silence, just silence, and everything around me fell away."

The pause that followed was heavy.

"And then?" Emmy asked.

Rel looked away. When she looked back, her eyes were dark.

"They were all dead," she said. "All of them. I only survived because my friend saved me. She managed to free us, but we were the only ones. There were bodies everywhere, burned and charred. Every last Uloni was gone. And the outsiders looted everything. All that was left were the smoking corpses of folk I had come to know as friends."

Emmy's throat was dry, and her eyes brimmed with sorrow for a people she had never known. "I'm so sorry for your loss, Rel," she said.

Shaking her head, Rel placed a palm to Emmy's cheek. Once more there was a flash of cold. A sudden wind whipped up.

"All is not lost," Rel said, "because you are here."

Emmy tried to pull back, but couldn't. "I don't understand—" she began.

Rel cut across her, just as she had when she'd closed off conversation several days before. "You were brought to me not just because you were an apothecary, but because of how you look," she said. "You must have been there, a youngling not long hatched. But how did you survive?"

Emmy's whole body froze under Rel's touch.

"I don't know," she said. Her chest tightened, as if the pressure to recall past events choked her. "I don't remember it at all. I didn't know anything about the Uloni—or me—until you, and—" She stopped, her throat closed.

"No matter," Rel said. "Tonight is a night for me to give knowledge, not to receive it." She paused for a moment. When she spoke again, her voice was quiet but unwavering. "There's more to this story. I didn't tell you *why* I was welcomed by the Uloni. I didn't tell you who my friend was."

"You didn't," Emmy said. Her voice trembled, but she carried on. "You didn't tell me why the strange wind blew when your eyes glowed blue, or what the coldness of your touch means. But I want to know, Rel. Tell me. Who is your friend?"

"She's everything," Rel breathed. "She saved me from the fire. She saved me from myself. I pledged my life to her. I'm here because of her—not just that I'm still alive, but that I'm waiting in this Althemerian encampment. She asked me to wait here."

"To wait for what?" Emmy asked.

Rel favored her with a benevolent smile. The crescent moons sparkled in her eyes. "To wait for *you*."

Emmy tried to shake her head, but it was held firmly in place by Rel's hand. "But why?" she asked. "Why me? Why in the camp?"

Rel released Emmy's face and planted both hands on her shoulders.

"My friend knows things and does things I cannot understand," she said, "but I trust her. She saved my life. The Althemerians talk of debts and bonds. For me, it isn't like that. Duty binds me to her, my duty to help her find what she needs. And what she needs is you."

Emmy, her head released, was able to shake it this time. "I still don't understand," she said. "What's so special about me? Other than being...Uloni. It just means I have different colors."

"It's much more than that," Rel said. "You're a full-blood Uloni. You're a rare gem. There is power within you, power that my friend will unlock. That's why you feel the coldness. That's why you were able to save your friend's life when he should have perished on that boat. You're not of this world, Emmy. Uloni are special creatures with a strong connection to the world of the goddesses."

A question burned on Emmy's tongue, even amid the avalanche of information Rel had given her. "If the Uloni were so elusive and didn't like outsiders, why did they let you in?" she asked. "It doesn't make sense."

Rel released Emmy's shoulders and sat back on her haunches. She looked at Emmy and offered a sheepish smile. "I didn't seem strange to my folk just because I wanted different things."

Closing her eyes, Rel schooled her face with the hardest concentration. She crossed her claws and arms in front of her face. There was silence for a moment. Then came the freezing wind.

Rel opened her eyes once more. The more Emmy stared, the more Rel's eyes began to shine. What began as a deep green, almost invisible in the darkness, grew to a fierce and icy glow.

Emmy's mouth fell open as the wind whipped, and Rel morphed and changed. The dark green tinge of her scales drained away, leaving behind a purple wash. It was paler than Emmy's, grayer, yet still as strange. Her pinkish skin blanched to a sickly blue. Emmy's jaw hung loose.

"Rel!" she squeaked. "You're like me!"

Rel gave a small sigh as her fronds turned from green to black, as if her head had been dipped in ink.

"I didn't fit in with my folk because I wasn't one of them," she said. "My father was Belfoni, but my mother was Uloni—that's why I can change my colors. The Uloni are powerful, Emmy. That means *you* are powerful."

Emmy blinked and blinked again. She reached out, hands trembling. When her talons settled on Rel's face, she felt flesh beneath them. It wasn't a phantom.

It was *real*.

"My friend didn't welcome me simply because I was lost," Rel said. "She welcomed me because I was one of her folk. She's a powerful and strange creature who's not entirely of this world. She wanted me to be a Heart, but I couldn't do it."

Rel dropped her gaze. Emmy narrowed her eyes. A heart? What did that mean?

"I couldn't do what my friend needed," Rel continued, "but I knew her needs were great. She said she was running out of time, so I stayed to help her. In return, my friend looked after me and taught me some of what she knew, including how to change my colors. It has been helpful, as I'm sure you can understand."

Emmy nodded, thoughts of hearts disappearing as desire overtook her. "If I could change my colors forever, I would," she said. "I would have changed a long time ago and never gone back, so folk wouldn't hate me just for how I look."

Rel patted Emmy's shoulder once more. "Before long, you'll understand why you are the way you are," she said. "And before long, folk will appreciate you for you."

"But why me?" Emmy pressed. "Why am I this way? Why will folk accept me?"

Rel let her arm fall away. "Because, Emmy," she said, "my friend needs you to be a Heart. You will guide the Hand of the Goddess."

There was that word again. Heart. Emmy furrowed her brow. "You can change your colors," she said. "Why can't you do the rest, whatever the rest might be?"

Rel looked at her hands, willing her skin and armor to change from faded blue and purple to green and pink, then back again.

"As I said, my father was Belfoni. Thus, I'm only a half-blood. I can do some things, such as change my colors. But I can't twist into the depths of the spirits like full-blood Uloni can. Like you can."

Emmy shook her head, her lifelong self-deprecation bubbling to the surface. "I can't do any of that," she said. "I won't be able to. I'm not special. I'm just...me. Nothing."

"Give it time," Rel said. "You'll know much more when you meet my friend."

She plucked up one last shroom and grasped the basket. When she stood, she clicked her tongue. Sharptooth yawned, showing the sharp teeth that gave him his name, before rising and padding back to them.

"We'll return now," Rel said as she secured the basket to Sharptooth's saddle, "and we will prepare."

"For what?" Emmy asked.

She accepted Rel's hand, allowing herself to be pulled onto the vaemar's muscular back. She settled behind Rel again. Rel took Sharptooth's reins and urged him into action.

"We must leave Hutukeshu," Rel said. "Now that I have you, I don't need to stay."

Emmy's neck scales fluttered, and she scowled. "Have me?" she asked. "You don't own me. If anyone does, the Althemerians do."

Rel flicked the reins to bring Sharptooth to a jog. She chuckled.

"My friend will take care of everything," she said. She glanced over her shoulder, her mouth pulled in a half-grin. "I thought you would want to leave the encampment and your servitude."

Still rankled, Emmy shook her head. "Of course I do," she replied. "But I can't just leave. I owe them a life-debt. And in any case, I'm not leaving Charo and Zecha behind."

"Then they'll come with us," Rel said.

She urged Sharptooth into a run, and Emmy squeezed her arms more tightly around Rel's waist. They travelled from the glade in the darkness, the bark and leaves of trees painted silver by the moons' light. Lifelong fear and suspicion squeezed Emmy's throat. She shouted over the thunderous pad of Sharptooth's stride.

"Why should I trust you? This could all be lies!"

The cold wasn't a lie, a voice in her head reminded her. The wind Rel whipped up wasn't a lie. And neither was the fact Rel had morphed and changed before her.

"This could be lies," Rel replied, her voice echoing into the darkness of the forest, "but it isn't. And I'm offering you and your friends release from the Althemerians, not to mention the privilege of finding out who you are, and meeting my friend."

Emmy's chest was as tight as a bow string. Her breathing was shallow with excitement and fear. "You keep calling her 'my friend'," she said, "but she must have a name. What is it?"

Rel looked over her shoulder again. She grinned as she spoke the name. "Bomsoi."

Emmy held onto Rel with a death grip as they rode through the darkness, back to the Hutukeshu encampment. She rolled the night's information around in her head, the thoughts dizzying with their content and speed.

She wasn't a freak. She was an Uloni. Not only that, but there were more like her.

Like Rel.

Like Rel's friend.

Bomsoi.

CHAPTER TWENTY-NINE

Mantos

Once more, Mantos sat in the council chamber. The queen drummed her claws on the lacquered table. Her ever-present serpent stared with its blue eyes. This time the seats around the table were filled with not just the queen's offspring, but with her High Council as well. Mantos knew them all. Nuko Otu, Master of Armies. Chucho Nu, Master of Messages. Dex Darajib, Master of Coin. Juhihas Oturul, Master of Diplomats. *They are many heads together, with little idea of what is to come,* Mantos thought. *And that's why I'm here. They want me to spill our military secrets. What choice do I have?*

The assembled council sat reverently, waiting for the queen to speak. Only Bomsoi, clad in black, stood lingering on the margin. While the council showed Valentia unwavering respect, they sent Mantos scathing glares in equal measure. It was no secret that Mantos was a Masvam, though he suspected they didn't know his significance. *And all the better it stays that way,* he thought, *for if they knew, they'd tear me limb from limb.* This time not even Fonbir's presence was a comfort. The prince sought Mantos' gaze, but Mantos wouldn't return it. If he caught Fonbir's sympathetic gaze, it might undo him.

"We find ourselves in troubling times," Queen Valentia said at length. "Have we had any official communication from the Masvams? Has the Youngling Emperor at least had the decency to give us a formal declaration of war?"

"No, Your Highness," said Chucho Nu. He was a male of middling age, with a heavy chain around his waist and a sheer veil across his face. Mantos knew it had taken much effort and sacrifice for a male to gain such a high rank. "We have heard nothing from him."

Nuko Otu, an older female gnarled by many cycles of battle, who had risen to the rank of Master of Armies, slid her narrow-eyed gaze to Mantos.

"The Masvams' cowardice knows no limits," she said. "They should at least grant us that courtesy."

"They are without any honor," Fylica said.

She and Nuko shot Mantos fierce looks, but he didn't rise to the bait. Valaria regarded him coldly, and it seemed even her serpent looked at him with unveiled disdain. Mantos gripped the edge of the table. *I will not disgrace myself*, he thought, though temptation to loose his tongue through anger and fear was strong. *These Althemerians should show more respect.*

"Then we will give the Youngling Emperor no similar courtesy," Valentia continued. "Our ships are faster, with superior weapons. We know that the Masvams will try to target tactical ports such as Athomur, and try to take over as many as they can. We must fortify our shores and seas."

"Agreed," said Nuko. "With a foothold on our shore, the Masvams can play a longer game. They can ship their troops in and amass an army without fear of having their numbers decimated in open combat."

"Our ships are sinking as many of theirs as they can, or damaging them so much that they must turn back," Princess Valaria said. "We're also taking over their newfound slave-ships."

Mantos sat straighter and blinked. "Slave-ships?" he asked.

Valaria's lips pulled into a smirk. "It would seem the Youngling Emperor is trying to move in on the Valtat's trade as well as our borders," she said. "He's shipping captives from his conquests back to the empire proper."

"That...is a new tactic," Mantos said. There were boulders in the pit of his stomach. He glanced at his mother. Her face blanched, her expression as horrified as he felt. "Masvams have never been in the business of taking slaves."

"No," Queen Valentia said, stroking her serpent's long back, "just in the business of taking away other countries' independence. Hardly a more honorable endeavor."

It would seem that Bandim's style wouldn't be just like Braslen's and Maram's before him. The use of overwhelming force, yes, but never the taking of slaves. *By the goddess*, Mantos thought. *We've never dealt in slaves. We allowed the Valtat through our borders, yes, but we never bought folk and never sold them. It's wrong.*

"What have we in the way of aid?" Queen Valentia asked.

"We know that Mellul is sending us ships," Nuko said, "but we haven't heard from the Linvarrans or the Valtat."

"The latter might be more agreeable to helping us if the Masvams are destroying their ships and their business," the queen replied.

Juhihas Oturul, Master of Messages, shifted and shook her head. Her long fronds were pulled back so severely it was like her face was stretched.

"More agreeable, perhaps, but the slavers are not warriors," she said. "They've survived despite the Masvam threat because they're too far south for conquest. They've had little need to protect their borders, for the lands in the south are more stable."

"They've survived so far," Princess Fylica interjected, "but they won't be safe from the evil forever. The Masvams will come for them."

Her glances at Mantos and Phen were vicious.

Juhihas spoke again. "Agreed."

Valentia nodded and clenched one fist, and turned to Chucho Nu.

"Send a gargon to Oligarchy of Belfon," she said. "We respectfully request they send ships and soldiers west to fortify us. Tell him we'll give the troops whatever they need when they arrive. We'll need to use our grain reserves but as I understand it, we can afford it—at least for now."

She shot Dex Darajib, Master of Coin, a quizzical look. Dex, a female of few words, inclined her head in affirmation but said nothing. Her appearance was striking; white skin, white armor, and red eyes. In many cultures, including Mantos' own, such a hatchling would have been cast out as tainted. On Althemer, however, attitudes were different. Strangeness was celebrated. *Such is why Queen Valentia trusts the Stranger so much*, Mantos thought. He glanced at Bomsoi's purple and blue. *She is indeed strange.*

"We must also send messages to the Va Chressans and the Merr," Queen Valentia continued, turning back to Chucho, "and even the Kingdom of Khin."

"I don't think that will bear fruit," Chucho said, her mouth down-turned. "The Khinish made themselves perfectly clear last time—"

"Last time the Masvams hadn't penetrated our borders," Valentia snapped, pulling herself upright. "The Khinish can no longer sit in their mountains and pretend the Masvams cannot touch them. We thought we were safe, but the rules of the game have been rewritten. I imagine the Khinish will understand that well. If the Masvams are willing to cross the ocean to come for us, they will be willing to cross the Kingdom of Khin's mountains and crush them. I think that Queen Consort Sarkin will understand that, even if the Puppet King Jaka Narr cannot." She kissed her fist and laid it on her heart. "May the gods be kind to him in his madness."

Mantos said nothing, focusing his gaze on his claws. *She's right*, he thought. *Bandim will not stop. The Selamans have fallen, and now the Metakalans. Next, the Merr and the Althemerians. After that the Linvarrans, the Va Chressans, the Belfoni, the Khinish...* He shook his head. *He will stop at nothing.*

"Have you something to say, Masvam?"

Mantos' head snapped up. It was Nuko Otu. She looked at him with her chin held high and her eyeridges drawn together. There was no attempt to hide her hatred. Beside her, Fylica's lips curled into a vicious snarl.

"We understand you are prepared to give us information," Nuko continued. "If you have something to say you will say it, or I will cut out your tongue."

Beside him, Phen shifted in her chair. Mantos shook his head again and shuddered.

"Nuko, cease," Queen Valentia said. Her serpent hissed. "Do not speak such words. It is unbecoming of you."

"Yes, Your Highness," the Master of Armies replied. "You have my apologies."

All eyes were on Mantos. Princess Valaria waved a hand. "Well?" she asked. "What have you to say? Speak or leave."

Mantos glanced at each of them in turn. His heart was in turmoil. Would he betray his folk and his country? Or would his silence in itself be a betrayal, as it would if Bandim was an unfit emperor? Eventually he managed to speak.

"I no longer know the limit of Masvam power, but you cannot be complacent. The emperor is carrying out a plan that has long been in motion, from as far back as the time of his grandfather. Don't underestimate the lengths he'll go to get what he wants."

Nuko snorted and turned in her chair, facing Mantos straight on. "And how do you know this, Masvam?" she asked. "You could be here as a spy, a part of his plans sent to feed us false information and send intelligence back to your kin. You know what they say about Masvams." She pointed a wizened claw at him. "The only good one is a dead one."

There was silence after that. It weighed as heavy as the phantom crown on Mantos' head and the thoughts that plagued him. A stranger in this land, ensconced in a tower, trying to reconcile killing his own folk or being killed himself. *I don't know what to do...* Oh, how he wished for the simplicity of the battlefield and holding a weapon in his hand.

"Speak, Masvam," Valaria growled. "I can only keep my sword in check for so long."

Licking his lips, Mantos spoke. "My military experience was gained in the reign of Emperor Braslen," he said. "He ruled with fist and sword, just like his father before him. Under Braslen came the decimation of Selama, as you know, a vassal that existed alongside the Masvam Empire for hundreds of cycles. Now it's gone, its government persecuted by Maram and finally crushed under the boot of my—" He stopped himself before his dreadful misstep. "—Of Emperor Braslen."

One piece of information shared led to another. He sucked in a deep breath as more truths spilled out.

"The Masvams are coming with the intent to kill as many Althemerians as they can, and to seize the land for themselves. That is always the Masvam goal."

The queen sat forward. Her serpent regarded him with narrow eyes. "So, Masvam," she said. "Have you made your decision? What are these plans? What is it that your folk have been planning all these cycles, skulking behind our backs while smiling at us with painted faces?"

In that moment, Mantos was on the edge of a cliff. Before him, a dark abyss stretched out. Behind him, a battle charge of swords and daggers. *No matter what I do, I will do wrong*, he thought. *If I speak, I am a traitor. If I don't, I become part of my brother's malice.*

He turned as Phen placed a hand on his arm. She tried to smile, but it didn't reach her eyes.

"Tell them," she said. "Tell them so we may save him."

Across the table, Fonbir mouthed words of comfort. *Be brave, Toketa, and do what is right.*

Mantos held his gaze for a moment. Then he looked at his mother. Then he turned to the queen.

And he told all.

CHAPTER THIRTY

Emmy

The world had turned on its head. Everything Emmy did took an age, for her mind was on nothing but Rel's revelations. That strange word: *Uloni*. Rel's friend Bomsoi. The strange ideas. The idea that once, she had a *family*.

Emmy hefted the yoke across her shoulder and began the journey from the healers' building to the well. The two buckets swung and clanked as she walked. Fetching water was usually Medicine-Yarim's chore, for while it was heavy work, it gave a reason to leave the building full of sickness and injury for a time. Emmy could count on one claw the amount of times she'd been allowed to fulfil the chore. She'd barely left the building since being brought there by Rel. Not permitted to leave or move freely in the encampment, Emmy keenly felt the tight grip of capture around her throat.

But this time, glad to be rid of the clumsy oaf Emmy had become, Medicine-Yarim had cast her out by her neck scales. "Feel free to take your time, freak," she'd said.

Emmy had collected the yoke and buckets in a daze, the razor-sharpness of Medicine-Yarim's tone unable to slice her. It was impossible to worry about such triviality when an entire new world had opened in her mind.

Weaving her way through the compound, Emmy stayed clear of the columns of marching soldier-slaves. The sun beat down upon them all, baking the ground. Clouds of dust puffed from the sets of regimented feet, rhythmic as the march itself. Sweat poured down Emmy's face from both heat and exertion, but she kept going. And kept thinking.

It wasn't a surprise that Krodge was not her mother. Emmy had never labored under that illusion. The old crone never wanted to claim the deformed blue and purple monster as anything other than an unwelcome parcel.

Emmy blinked against the sun as she made the final turn towards the well. She had always known she had different parents—*real* parents. In her mind, it was impossible for them to be worse than the heartless stand-in guardian Krodge became. They were poor Metakalans with a huge brood, unable to care for one more mouth, or perhaps a single Althemerian escaping persecution to protect his strange hatchling, only to succumb to tyranny while keeping his offspring from death. Or maybe one or more of the Khinish, too far from home to travel back with a hatchling and keep it alive...

A thousand scenarios had played out in Emmy's head through the cycles. But never once had she imagined her parents were like her.

She reached the well, still sweating as she joined the end of the queue. Midsun was brutal in Decos, especially on a day like today, when no cooling wind blew in from the sea. Emmy kept the yoke across her shoulders as the line crept forward. The wooden frame dug into her shoulders, for the weight of the buckets alone was enough to pain her. She didn't dare put it down. The exertion of hefting it back on bruised shoulders wasn't worth the brief respite from pain.

Despite this, Rel's words took the edge from the yoke's teeth. She was an Uloni. Once she must have lived among them, with her *parents*. Not only did she have folk of her own, but those folks were powerful. She was powerful. It explained the coldness, and...

A thump between Emmy's shoulder blades propelled her forward.

"Get a move on," the male behind grunted. "We're all tired of waiting."

At last it was Emmy's turn at the well. Muttering an apology, she bent to allow the buckets to settle on the ground, then removed the yoke from her shoulders.

Powerful. The word kept echoing back as Emmy lifted the first bucket. That was a word never associated with her before. Freakish, yes. Weak, absolutely. Moon Rogue, used most of all. But never *powerful*. Even when accused of possessing Dark magic—the ability to suck out souls, kill crops, and the endless ream of horrible circumstances she'd been blamed for—she had never been accused of being *powerful*.

The bucket hit the water and slowly sank. Rel had told her of her powerfulness, but for a good purpose. It wasn't to condemn her as a demon, but to laud her. And it was told to her by someone *like* her. Emmy grunted as she turned the well-worn wooden handle to bring the full bucket back up. Seeing Rel change her colors had set fireworks off in Emmy's head: not just because of the impossibility, but because it confirmed Emmy wasn't alone. And it showed that what Rel said was true.

At least, Emmy thought as she swapped the full bucket for its empty partner, it seemed to be true.

Emmy wanted it to be true.

She went through the process of dropping, lifting, and filling the second bucket, then attached them both to her yoke. With that she lumbered past the queue of sweltering faces, back to the healers' building. Her back trembled from the weight of the water, and the yoke dragged on her shoulders. The sun pressed in harder, sending shimmers up from the baked ground.

Rel said she would get her out, away from Althemerian enslavement. Charo and

Zecha, too. That was reason enough to go along with her. Charo was safe for now, but who knew how long it would remain that way? With the Althemerians fighting the Masvams, she could be called out of training and into service at any time. And Zecha...who knew what they'd do with him when he awoke? To stay with the Althemerians would be no life for any of them.

At the very least, they could use Rel to escape. At the most, Rel could change her life. As the healers' building swung into view, Emmy grunted. The decision needed no contemplation.

And if it was a trap? Some elaborate ruse to prove her disloyalty or her tainted nature? The Althemerians would probably kill her, and even that was better than living life as a slave. Listening to Charo's stories of hardship had taught her that.

Emmy set the buckets down outside the main entrance to the wooden building and brought the buckets in by hand, leaving the wide yoke outside. Medicine-Yarim cast her a sidelong glower, as if she'd returned too quickly. Emmy ignored it and emptied the buckets into the water butt in the center of the room. She glanced around, but Rel was nowhere to be found.

Sighing, Emmy glowered at the chaos of stretchers that spread around her like jagged edges. The constant movement of the sick, the injured, and the dead meant it was impossible to maintain order. Old habits were hard to break, and Emmy's fingers twitched as she beat back the urge to straighten the rows. She wasn't in the apothecary now. She didn't need to have everything sit *just so*.

And yet she did.

But before she could start straightening, a weak voice called out.

"I can tell you want to tidy."

Emmy's frown exploded into a smile and she spun around, placing the sound. That voice.

"Zecha!"

She rushed through the mess of cots and fell at her friend's side. "You're awake at last!" she breathed, giving him a careful hug.

Though they were watery and drooping, Zecha's red eyes were finally open. His mouth stretched into a tired smile. "My, my," he said, weak arms returning the embrace, "it's nice to be so loved."

Emmy clucked her tongue, her face flushing with delight. She pulled away, but kept one hand on Zecha's arm.

"I'm so glad you're awake," she said. "I was worried you wouldn't..." Her breath caught, and she swallowed against a lump. "But you're awake now. That's all that matters."

Zecha chuckled at her concern.

"It'll take more than a Masvam to kill me," he said. He peered at his stomach, though the movement pained him. "Is it bad?"

Emmy gave a solemn nod, the slow movement giving her time to think. It should have been much worse. He should have been dead. But he wasn't—because of Rel.

Because she was Uloni, just like Emmy.

It wasn't time to broach any of those thoughts with Zecha. Instead, Emmy squeezed his arm.

"It was a deep wound," she said, "but the Althemerian healer did a good job of cleaning it. Her stitching, however..." Emmy tilted her head to one side and smiled. "Well, it doesn't hold up to mine."

Zecha barked a laugh, though his face drained of color as he suffered for it. "Whose would?" he rasped. As his color returned, he glanced at his stomach. "Can I see it?"

Emmy hesitated, but eventually drew back the covers. It was his body and his choice. Zecha propped himself up on his elbows and stared as she hitched up his shift. When the wound was revealed, he gave a low whistle. "That will leave a nasty scar."

Emmy nodded. "Just be glad you'll have many cycles to be irritated by it."

"It doesn't worry me," Zecha replied as Emmy tugged his shift down again. "I'll say it's a war wound when I show it to my younglings."

War. At that word, Emmy's heart sank. She tucked Zecha in, pressing his shoulders so he would lie back again.

"What's wrong?" he asked, drawing his eyeridges together.

During Emmy's silence, he looked around the tent, as if only realizing where he was. His face pinched as he saw the unusual red heart-in-eye symbol on Emmy's black tunic. He tried to rise, but Emmy kept him down.

"Where are we?" he asked in a low voice.

"We're in an Althemerian encampment," Emmy said. "They were the ones who saved us from the Masvams."

She snorted at her own words. *Saved.* Ha.

"Althemerians?" Zecha asked, his eyes narrowing. "Does that mean..."

Emmy sighed. She rubbed her hand in circles on Zecha's shoulder, trying to find the right words.

"Yes. The Althemerians say we owe them a life-debt," she said. "It's a cycle of unpaid service, or joining their army. If you survive, you're free. If you die, well... I suppose you don't need to worry about it."

"That's barbaric," Zecha whispered. Despair painted his face. "Not even the Masvams hold life-debts anymore."

Emmy patted Zecha's shoulder one final time and shook her head.

"No, but what's more barbaric is that the Masvams were going to take us as forever-slaves. With the Althemerians, at least we're in the shallower of two valleys. There's a chance we'll get out. With the Masvams, I don't think we ever would."

She watched as Zecha mulled the options over. Then a new expression washed over him. His eyes widened, and he tried to sit up once more. "Where's Charo?"

Emmy gently urged him back down again. "She's been taken as a soldier-slave," she said. "I told her to tell them she was my apprentice, and she might have avoided that. But she didn't, so now she's training for battle."

"Is she all right?" Zecha asked.

"She seems to be," Emmy replied. "I haven't seen her much. But when I do, she always asks for you."

Despite the circumstance, Zecha still colored with pleasure. "That's nice of her."

A shadow fell over them. Emmy stood, clasping her hands behind her back as the figure stopped beside them.

It was Rel.

"He wakes at last," the Belfoni said with a chuckle. "I thought you would prove me a bad healer, Zecha."

Zecha's brows crumpled with confusion. Emmy offered an explanation. "This is Rel, the senior healer," she said. "I told her you were my friend from Metakala."

Zecha let out an "ah" of understanding and looked at Rel.

"Thank you for helping me," he said. The skin around his eyes tightened, though he still smiled. "I owe you my life."

Rel chuckled again and shook her head. "You owe me nothing," she said. "The Althemerians, on the other hand, well, they take a different view on things."

"Thank you, Rel," Zecha said. His skin washed out in the dim light of the braziers, waxy with fatigue. "I'd stand to take your arm, but I don't think I can."

"Of course you can't," Rel said. "You need to rest."

As she knelt to examine his wound, his eyes fell closed. His face tightened with something more than pain. "What will happen to me now?" he asked. His voice sounded cycles older than it should have.

"You will remain here until you are fit to leave," Rel said. She shot a sideways glance at Emmy, one corner of her mouth quirking. "After that, we have a little journey to make."

"A journey?" Zecha asked. He rolled his head to the side so he could catch Emmy's line of sight. "What does she mean?"

Emmy opened her mouth, closed it, then opened it again. "There's a lot I need to tell you," she said, "and Charo too."

Rel finished her inspection of her charge's wound, then clapped a hand on Emmy's shoulder as she stood. Familiar cold bloomed.

"Now is not the time," she said. "Medicine-Emmy has work to attend to. But all will be explained, Zecha. You won't remain here long."

Unsatisfied, Zecha tried to rise once more, though his own fatigue pushed him backwards this time. "Emmy, what's going on?"

Biting her bottom lip, Emmy dropped her chin for a moment. "I'll explain everything," she said. "I promise. But not right now."

Rel gently tugged her backwards and propelled her away from Zecha. As Emmy walked, she could feel Zecha's eyes boring into the back of her head. Her heart longed to pour everything out to him, but with their escape from the encampment riding on Rel, she knew it was best to dance to the healer's tune.

Emmy kept her eyes forward as she moved onto her next patient, hoping Zecha would understand.

CHAPTER THIRTY-ONE

Bandim

The Seat of the Empire was unparalleled in its magnificence. Standing high amid the city of Masvam, generations of emperors had stood on the palace balconies, staring across the turbulent sweep of land where the Empire began. Emperor upon emperor had added to the original castle. A circular keep and high curtain wall sprawled into a complex of buildings, towers, further walls, and a huge barbican, complete with a drawbridge over the moat. *This is my palace now*, Bandim thought as he sat on his marble throne. *It's my land, just as it was meant to be.*

As a youngling, he'd pressed his face to the glass of his window in the High Tower and stared at the warren of towers and walls below him. As the cycles passed, his talons twitched. His tongue grew sour. *It was all for Mantos*, he thought. *Everything for him, and nothing for me.* He chuckled, the cold sound echoing through the cavernous throne room. *Now, everything is as it was meant to be.*

There was no need for him to be in the throne room, except to enjoy the feeling of sitting on his throne. There were no grasping courtiers seeking audiences, or members of his council coming to him with matters of law, life, and death. He was alone apart from two guards.

Reclining on the high-backed marble throne, Bandim grasped the arms. For a moment he was still, imbibing the power that coursed with the beat of his heart. So too did he imbibe the feelings of those around him. Ever since the evening with Yameteth and the fire, Bandim had been honing his curious power of reading others' emotions. Not thoughts, for he couldn't hear or read those. But those in close proximity, he could feel the truth of their emotions, deep in their bones.

The presence of his guards was potent. Their thoughts raced, lingering on their younglings and wives, or on their desire to be proved worthy. There were no words, but pictures flashed. Past, present, coveted futures. Bandim could taste their emotions. Love was sweet. Ambition was powerful, harsh and yet desirable. Buried fear was salty, tainting all else.

Bandim wasn't the same now. He was different. He was more. *I am changed*, Bandim thought. *In some ways, I'm not Bandim at all.*

Power surged through him, painting him in ways make-up never could. *I have the spirit of Dorai within me. She gives me her power so that she may live again.* Bandim chortled. *Dorai has returned.*

His laugh, the sound of unadulterated joy in his heart, carried through the throne room, dancing among the handful of lanterns. The carved doors opened, and a figure stepped into the scant light. A ripple of fear passed through his guards.

"Your Grace."

The high voice sounded through the vaulted chamber. Johrann's footsteps echoed in the alcoves. Bandim rose and beckoned her onto the dais. "My dear Heart," he said, reaching for her. "Thank you for coming to me."

Johrann fell into a deep bow, as she always did. She was an anomaly among all those Bandim had encountered since he took Dorai into his heart. He couldn't clearly decipher her emotions. Johrann was closed, as if encased in thicker walls than the palace. It unsettled him, for surely nothing should be impossible for the goddess. However, she was still under his control. He had proved that with her punishment for failure, before his powers awoke. For now, she was back in his favor, where she would remain so long as she was useful.

Bandim let her kiss his hands, then pulled her to her feet. Johrann kept her eyes down. Her dark robes floated like gently shifting fog. Bandim tilted her face upward. "You may look at me."

Johrann met his gaze. "Thank you, Your Grace," she said. "Any time I'm in your presence, I cannot help but supplicate myself to you."

Chuckling, Bandim leaned in. Their embrace lingered. "You are beautiful," he said.

Though he couldn't read her clearly, the mix of sugared joy and turgid pain that flashed from her made his gut clench. It was gone as fast as it arrived. Bandim wrapped his arms around her. "Why is your happiness tainted with despair?"

She tried to look away, but his gaze was commanding.

"No one has called me beautiful before," Johrann said. "I've been called many things. A monster. A fool. Filthy. Dangerous. But never beautiful."

Bandim tasted a sharp vulnerability. He pressed a kiss to her temple and wrapped his arms around her, pressing her head to his chest. When she was in disgrace, her suffering had been sweet. Now she was worthy of his sympathy and compassion, even if it was less sincere than it seemed. Bandim would keep Johrann dancing to his tune, just as she'd made him dance to hers before.

"If anyone disrespects you again, dear Heart," he said, "I'll rip them limb from limb. I will find their town and burn it down. I will kill their kin just so they can taste the pain they inflict. I would kick the very moons from the sky if it would take your suffering away."

Round pearls beaded in Johrann's eyes. "Your Grace is too good to me."

"I am," Bandim said. Then his tone shifted. "Don't ever forget it."

He caught the look of fear in her eyes, but then in an instant everything flickered.

Bandim's vision sputtered like a dying candle. His thoughts flashed quickly, interspersed with deep pockets of nothingness. Images of his youth, of endless boring lessons with ever-perfect Mantos, of playful fights that turned vicious as they grew up, of his brother's yellow eyes, identical to his own, yet filled with nothing but loathing as they looked upon him.

Bandim, Bandim...

His brother's voice, as clear as if Mantos were standing next to him.

Stumbling backward, Bandim fell onto the throne. His chest tightened, and it was as if hot knives were pushed under his ribs.

"Your Grace!" he heard Johrann cry.

The sound was distant, drowned by his brother repeating his name again and again.

Bandim, Bandim...

Hands were upon him. Johrann screeched for a guard to fetch a healer. Mantos' presence rose like a great wave, threatening to consume Bandim's every thought and wish.

Then it was gone.

His eyes snapping open, Bandim pulled himself upright on the throne. His chest heaved as he sucked in desperate breaths, trying to make sense of what had happened.

Why had he lost control of his thoughts? And why had Mantos' presence felt so real?

"Your Grace?"

Johrann's words cleared his mind further. He blinked, trying to adjust to reality again.

"Your Grace, have you returned to us?"

She and the one remaining guard hovered over him with fearful faces. Bandim waved off their concerns, though his heart drummed so hard it caused him pain.

A sudden realization caused greater agony. He could see the concern on the guard's face, but he couldn't *feel* it. Bandim could glean no emotion from him, whereas before it had been as easy to read him as a book. Bandim blinked. *I cannot feel his thoughts.* A coldness passed through him. It was as if Dorai...was gone.

"Your Grace?" Johrann asked. "What ails you?"

"It's nothing," Bandim lied, trying in vain to quiet the panic rising in his throat. "Nothing of consequence."

However, every thought he had was now of consequence. His plans. His actions. His blackest desires. It had seemed so simple just a moment ago. Bandim and Dorai. Dorai and Bandim, together: unstoppable.

But now it seemed so far-off. Unobtainable. It was as though Dorai had forsaken him, leaving him alone, naked, vulnerable.

Bandim tried to bury that fear with words. Strategy. Anything that wasn't the dank feeling of terror that lurked in the pit of his stomach. He reached for the first thought he could find.

"It's one thing to take the land," he said. "It's something else entirely to keep it. There are no guarantees."

Johrann drew back, brows drawn together in confusion at the strangeness of his words. They were a sudden divergence, but as soon as Bandim said them, the thoughts became obsessive, clogging his mind like tar. *Mantos. Is he dead? Is he alive? Why did his presence feel so real? If he's not dead, is he coming for my throne?*

Johrann's words sounded as hollow as a rotten tree. "Your Grace, I promise you will succeed."

Bandim snorted. Then he flinched, memories of sleepless nights jabbing in ragged lines. His brother's face loomed high and clear, no matter how hard Bandim squeezed his eyes shut. *Bandim, Bandim...* The voice echoed on and on.

Bandim's words were sharp with sudden fatigue. "I'll burn anything that doesn't move and kill anything that doesn't obey, if that's what I need to do." He pressed his fingertips to his eyes, willing the memories to flee. Mantos' voice still jangled in his mind. *Bandim, Bandim...* "Taking the land isn't what worries me." His words turned cold. "What worries me is that my brother may not be dead, and if he isn't, he'll seek to take everything from me again."

Johrann laughed like a peal of broken bells. Bandim became very still at the sound. The guard stepped away, descending the steps as if sensing danger.

"Your Grace," Johrann said, "don't fear the machinations of your mind. It's your old life, memories of your old self. Mantos is dead. I delivered him to death myself. He cannot interfere."

"And how do we know he's truly dead?" Bandim's chest compressed, as if anger sought to suffocate him. "I saw his body, I know. But then it disappeared, along with my mother." Seething, he struggled to his feet again. Johrann stepped closer, reaching for him. Bandim batted her talons away. "How do I know he's truly dead? I feel him," he panted. "I see him in my dreams, and when I sleep, I *know* that he's alive somewhere."

Johrann held her hands out, as if to placate a feral animal.

"Someone may have taken his body," she said, "but I took his life. There's no way he can come back from that. I made sure of it. Only my folk have the power to manipulate the spirits and break the spell of death, and there are no other Uloni left. Not one. I purged their village in flames."

Echoes of his dreams kept returning.

Bandim, Bandim... Dear brother, I will find you...

Johrann placed her hands on his arm. He snapped, sudden as unseen rot. "How do you know?" he bellowed. He grabbed her by the fronds, forcing her down the steps. "How—do—you—know?"

He thrust her away and she toppled from the dais, sprawling on the floor in a heap of robes and blood. Her screech bounced against the vaulted ceilings, coming back louder. The guard remained steadfast at his post, keeping his eyes focused on the doors.

As Johrann sobbed, the doors opened, and the second guard returned with a healer in tow. Bandim's ire flared once more. "Get out!" he screeched.

As quickly as they had entered, the two figures disappeared again.

As anger consumed him, the coldness of Bandim's despair abated. His head spun as Dorai's warmth surrounded him once more, like the softest of embraces. He pressed a hand to his head, sucking in deep breaths to cement the Goddess' presence within him.

His eyes found Johrann, and his heart twisted as she clambered to her feet, blood trickling from her nostrils. But the feeling didn't last long. As Dorai returned, the guilt abated too. He had nothing to feel guilty for. He was an emperor and a goddess and could do as he pleased. Though he wasn't sorry, he reached a hand for her. "I didn't mean to hurt you."

Gradually, Johrann climbed the dais, creeping like a beaten animal. However, she accepted his touch. Her voice trembled as she spoke, but her words were full of fearful conviction.

"This is just your old life impinging upon you," she said. "As you become more powerful and as more time passes, you'll care less and less for your life as Bandim. You are Dorai, purer and more powerful than any other. You'll unite us all under your banner."

The return of the Goddess' powers steadied him, and Bandim nodded. "Yes. My campaigns move forward. We're poised to crush the Althemerians, just as we crushed the Metakalans."

There was a twinge in his chest as he thought of the Althemerian royals, Fonbir and Fylica and Valaria, his friends from long ago. Fonbir had been Mantos' close friend, but Valaria was all Bandim ever wanted. As headstrong and vibrant as she was, he couldn't resist her.

Once again, the feeling was fleeting. His thoughts snapped back to the present. To Johrann Maa and her bloodied face. To reality. To his plan to murder all Valaria's folk, and the fact that he'd cause her death as well. *She will die on the battlefield*, Bandim thought. *She will die leading her folk against a force they cannot fight. Against my force. She rejected me. Me! She deserves to die. They all do.*

"This is what the world needs," Johrann said, grasping his face in both hands. "This is the right thing to do. We waited so long for you to return and purge the lies of the

Light. Now you're here, and nothing can stop you." She dared to press a gentle kiss to his lips. He tasted her blood. "Your brother is dead. He cannot hurt you. Your old life is gone. Don't think of it. You will be Dorai. You *are* Dorai. You are the Beloved, the Unparalleled, and if they don't embrace the grace of your presence, the greatest gift you can give them is death." She brought her lips close to his ear. "Even Princess Valaria. Even your *mother*. If they cannot accept your greatness, they do not deserve to live."

His secret thoughts spoken, Bandim felt a strange ease. It wasn't that the words comforted him. Rather, with each syllable Johrann spoke, he felt...less. Less pain. Less confusion.

His mind was clear.

He smirked.

He knew what he had to do.

CHAPTER THIRTY-TWO

Emmy

Late Althemerian Merish days were hot, but the same couldn't be said for the nights. Emmy sat on a fallen bough, worn smooth with sitting, and held her hands to the licking flames. She sat by a small pit-fire that burned near the rear of the healers' building and waited. She watched the dance of orange and red as it rose from the blackened logs, disappearing against the darkness of the clear sky, and waited some more.

A week had passed since Zecha finally woke. Each day he'd grown stronger, and was now well enough to sit and stand without pain. Well, without too much pain, Emmy thought, as her friend lowered himself onto the log beside her.

"Oof," was all he managed to say as he sat.

He shouldn't have been outside with her. In fact, even Emmy shouldn't have been outside. But when faced with the fact that they were somehow, with Rel's help, to escape the Althemerian encampment, small risks didn't seem so risky any longer.

Emmy patted Zecha's shoulder as he made himself comfortable. "You'll heal fully soon enough," she said.

Zecha exhaled a thin breath. He winced as he shifted into what was finally a comfortable position. "I think I'm healing better than expected, considering I thought I was dead."

Emmy tilted her head in agreement. "A fair point."

Zecha was quiet for a moment before he turned to face her. Fire danced in his red eyes, but it spoke of warmth and home, not the destruction that flame often did.

"Tell me again who this Rel healer is, and what she said. I know you've told me what feels like a thousand times already, but I just can't get it straight in my head."

"Oh, Zecha," Emmy sighed. "You'll hear it all again when Charo arrives. Rel said she would explain to her what was happening, and how we're going to get out of here."

Zecha pressed his lips together in a tight line. "I hope she's as trustworthy as you think she is."

Nodding, Emmy smiled as comforting a smile as she could. "She is," she said. "I just know it."

But even the vehemence of her words was tainted by a stain of worry inside. Emmy thought Rel was trustworthy, and she was certainly strange and powerful. But was this real, or was it a game? If it was a game, Emmy couldn't fathom the objective.

The pit-fire popped and cracked. The two friends stared into the flames.

"Is Charo definitely coming?" Zecha asked.

"She said she would be here," Emmy replied. "She's going to feign sickness in her barracks, so she'll hopefully get sent here. If she does, we'll be able to talk. If she doesn't, I suppose she'll have to try again another way." She sighed. "We'll just have to wait."

Emmy shifted and looked at the constellations twinkling in the inky sky. She traced the outline of the Rising Prago, a huge beast with outstretched wings. Its head was the brightest, blinking in the darkness. Its wings spread halfway across the sky, as if it enveloped the whole island in its protection. A prago was a mythical thing, a beast akin to an enormous gargon that dwelled in the mountains. The Metakalans said it slumbered deep in the darkest caves, waiting for the day it could break the chains that bound it and rise once more into the Arc of the Sky.

Something occurred to Emmy that had never crossed her mind before. "Zecha, you know a lot about Metakalan folk tales, don't you?"

"I suppose I do," he replied. "Why?"

Emmy stretched up her hand and traced the outline of the Rising Prago with one claw. "Why was the prago chained in the mountains?"

He looked at her as if she'd asked if water was wet. "Really? You don't know?"

This time it was Emmy who flattened her lips into an irritated line. "I wouldn't have asked if I knew," she replied.

Zecha ignored her ire and sailed into an explanation.

"Each link of the chain was forged when folk denied the prago's existence. The more they denied it, the stronger the chain became. And the stronger the chain became, the less the prago could move freely and prove it was real. So now it's imprisoned somewhere beneath the Great Northern Range, waiting for the day it will be released—or so they say. Who knows if it's real or not real?"

As her eyes traced the prago's starry points, Emmy shook her head. "You know, before Rel told me what she did, I would have said for certain the prago didn't exist. But now? I'm not so sure."

Zecha followed her gaze to the stars, then looked back at her. When she met his eyes, they were soft. "This Rel has made a huge impression on you."

Nodding, Emmy gave a half-smile. "You have no idea."

They sat in silence for a little while, waiting for Charo and Rel to arrive. If she closed her eyes, Emmy could almost fool herself into thinking they were back in Bellim, by the fire in Mr. Charber's back yard. It was a comfort in the maw of danger they stood in. Escape wouldn't be easy.

Eventually their companionable quiet was disrupted by two sets of feet approaching on the parched ground. Emmy and Zecha turned in tandem, faces alight with grins as two figures rounded the corner of the building and stepped into the light.

When their faces were visible, Zecha leapt to his feet. "Charo!"

He bounded towards her, ignoring any pain. Charo ran to him and they embraced, holding one another close. They approached the fireside claw in claw, grinning at one another. In the firelight, they looked as if they were falling under each other's spell.

At least, that was how it had been explained to Emmy. *It's like the other person commands your attention*, Zecha had told her countless times, trying desperately to explain attraction. *It's like looking at someone and feeling like they've been a missing part of you for your entire life.*

Emmy shook her head. She didn't understand the way they looked at each other. She understood friendship, of course, and even now she had a sense of family. But romance? Nothing. That was what she saw between Charo and Zecha, and it was something she didn't feel the need to understand.

Rel grinned as she walked to the pit-fire and gestured to the embracing couple behind her. "You didn't tell me of this," she said.

Emmy chuckled. "In truth, I wasn't sure there was anything to tell. But there it is."

Rel sat beside Emmy as Charo and Zecha babbled, each checking every inch of the other to see if they were really reunited.

"In truth," Rel repeated, "I thought that you and Zecha were something to one another."

Emmy couldn't stop herself. She stuck out her tongue and shook her head. "Never."

At Rel's disbelieving head-tilt, she explained. "It's nothing against Zecha," Emmy continued, keeping her voice low enough that the others couldn't hear. "He *is* something to me, but he's more like a brother. I don't really see anyone the way they see one another. Or at least, the way I think they see one another."

Rel looked at her, expression deadpan. "For certain, that's the way they see one another."

Chuckling, Emmy grinned as Zecha and Charo joined them, sitting on the baked earth across the fire-pit. They sat almost on top of one another, their claws touching.

"You escaped, then," Emmy said.

"I said I thought I was coming down with the Lurking Death, and"—Charo snapped two claws together—"it was as easy as that. I was shoved out of the barracks. I must be a good actor."

"Or they were simply glad to get a moment's peace from you," Zecha chided.

He jabbed her lightly in the ribs, and Charo went to return the gesture, but stopped herself at the look of horror on his face as he shielded himself. "All right, you're safe for now," she said, "but just wait until you heal properly."

Rel regarded them with soft eyes. "I can see why you don't want to leave these two," she said. Her expression hardened as she continued. "But our leaving is what we must discuss."

Zecha nodded, and Charo looked from Rel to Emmy and back again. "Please tell me everything," she said.

And so Rel did. By the time she was finished with the whole tale—of her own background, the Uloni, and the truth about Emmy—both Charo's and Zecha's eyes were wide and glassy.

"That's...a lot to take in," Charo said.

Zecha nodded. "Even on the second hearing, it's a lot," he said. "I can only imagine how you feel, Emmy."

Nodding, Emmy clasped her claws together. "It *is* a lot," she said. "But it does explain some things, like why I look so different. I still have many questions, like how did I end up with Krodge? But," she continued, looking to Rel, "Rel doesn't know all the answers. But she's confident that her friend knows more, and that's who we're going to see."

Charo nodded, although her face was pinched with concern. "How are we going to get out?" she asked. "There are guards all around the perimeter of the encampment. It's not as if we can just walk out."

"Actually," Rel said, the smile returning to her face, "we can."

"How?" Charo pressed. "We're not here by choice. We're here through debt. The Althemerians aren't about to let us leave because we say we need to."

"Of course they aren't," Rel said. She pulled up her shirt sleeve to show her own brand. The date read many cycles before. "I'm free here, and am allowed a pass to go outside the camp for periods of time. That was how Emmy and I left when I showed her my truth. We were able to leave to collect nightshrooms. On that occasion, that's what we did. On this occasion, we won't be coming back."

It was Zecha's turn to voice his concerns. "That might work for you two," he said, "but Charo and I aren't healers. And even if we dressed as such, would the guards Charo mentioned allow four healers to leave at once? Surely it would look suspicious."

Rel nodded and lifted her palms to the pit-fire flames. "It would," she said as she warmed her hands, "but two healers accompanied by two guards wouldn't."

Emmy's mouth formed an "oh" of understanding. "Right," she said. "But why would they allow two soldier-slaves out with us this time when we didn't need them last time?"

"Ah," Rel continued, "a good point. But for once, the conflict among nations will be a benefit rather than a curse. Tensions between the Althemerians and the Masvams rise with every day. There are rumors that the Masvams are planning to invade, and certainly raiding parties have been wreaking havoc all along the coast. It simply wouldn't be safe for two mere healers to travel alone."

Zecha nodded slowly as the plan came together in his mind. "Where will I get a uniform from?"

Rel nodded at Charo.

"Your friend here will strip her uniform tonight, and wear a new gown and hose. I'll tell her superiors that she doesn't have the Death, but rather has a mild sickness. I'll say I've burned her clothing as a precaution, and will request another be supplied before she leaves—including boots. Thus, both Charo and Zecha will have uniforms, and there we have it: two healers with two guards, ready to pick shrooms. It's just that we won't be returning."

Emmy shook her head, exhaling in disbelief. "It seems so simple," she said. "It can't be that easy."

Rel placed a hand on her arm and shook her head.

"It can be, Emmy. Not everything needs to be complicated. And sometimes the best way to escape is to do it in plain sight. No one will look for any of us until it's much too late. I'll procure two vaemar this time, and on their backs, we'll cover enough distance that when our disappearance is discovered, we'll be too far away. That is, if they look for us." She huffed out a breath. "They may simply assume we've been killed. Getting past the guards on the gate is the only difficult part. After that, it's as simple as one vaemar paw after another, until we reach Kubodinnu and my friend."

The little group looked at each other in turn, sharing in the warmth of the fire as well as the comfort of impending freedom. Rel wouldn't betray them. Of this, Emmy was sure. Their escape depended only on getting past the guards.

And not meeting any Masvam raiders, of course, she thought. That was something they couldn't control as easily.

"When will we do this?" Charo asked. Excitement and fire burned in her eyes in equal measure.

"As long as I can get the uniform, we'll leave tomorrow night," Rel replied. "There's no sense in waiting longer, especially if the Masvams are prowling ever closer. Places like this camp are prime targets: coastal, with minimal defenses, as well as being a place for training. If the Masvams destroy this place and kill as many soldier-slaves as they can, they weaken the Althemerians in the face of an invasion."

A shiver ran all the way along Emmy's bones from her neck to the tip of her tail. "The sooner we leave, the better," she said.

At that, Rel clapped her hands on her knees and rose. "That's settled," she said. "Charo, you must come back with me now and feign sickness for the benefit of those around you. Medicine-Yarim is on duty, and will already be wondering where I've gone. I'll bring clothing for you, and you'll leave your uniform here. I'll tell Medicine-Yarim I've burned your uniform in the pit. Emmy, you and Zecha can smuggle the garments back inside."

Emmy shook her head, suppressing a chuckle. "You have a plan for everything, Rel."

The older female gave a sage nod as she walked away.

"I've been waiting here for you for many cycles, Emmy," she said. "I've had much time to come up with my plan. I admit I wasn't expecting you to arrive with companions, but it wasn't difficult to come up with a plan to include them." She stopped and turned. "And I *am* glad to see you have friends, Emmy," she continued. Something glimmered in her eyes. "I know what it's like to be different. I know what it's like to be alone."

Before Emmy could reply, Rel had disappeared through the rear door of the healers' building. Rel did know. Emmy could feel her sincerity. She looked at Charo, then Zecha, and reached to embrace them both. The three friends pushed their heads together, holding one another close. Attraction may have been something Emmy didn't understand, but friendship wasn't.

Reunited, for a moment, there was a pang of happiness between them. Hope crackled with the flames.

They would escape, all three. And they would be together.

CHAPTER THIRTY-THREE

Emmy

Emmy barely slept, knowing what was to follow the next night. The cogs of her mind kept turning the situation round and round, giving her not even a minute of peace. They would escape. They would go to Kubodinnu to meet Bomsoi.

Then what?

Emmy turned in her bed as her thoughts whirled. Rel had said Bomsoi wanted her to do something, that she had some sort of special purpose. A full-blood Uloni. But what was it? Would she even be able to do it? Cycle upon cycle of self-doubt crept upon her like a plague. She wasn't special. She wasn't anything. How could she help?

No.

The word was so clear Emmy bolted upright, clutching her sacking blanket to her chest. "Who's there?"

Her quavering words disappeared into the dimness of her alcove. Her gaze darted to and fro, and she shivered from something more than cold. The word was so clear, she was sure someone was there.

But there was no one. Not even Rel.

Emmy's shiver turned into a shudder. She was hearing things now. Never a good sign. Slowly she lowered herself onto the cot once more and pulled the scratchy blanket to her chin. It was nothing. Just excitement and fear playing tricks on her.

It didn't make sleep come any easier, and by the time her eyelids were heavy and closing, the sun was steadily rising. Emmy pulled herself upright and dug her knuckles into her eyes, trying to push away the weariness. Washing and dressing, she pulled back the curtain of her alcove with a heavy arm, then went about her morning work.

It was difficult not to speak to Zecha and Charo. The temptation to drift over to them and conspire was great, even in her tired state. But Yarim and Asri watched her enough in their distrust. She didn't need to give them further reason to follow her every move. So instead, Emmy tended to her patients and tried to behave as she always did.

Both fortunately and unfortunately, the day would take a turn that would mask anything strange she did.

Rel was called away early in the morning for a meeting with Commander Pama and the others in charge of the camp. Rel had answered the summons with a furrowed brow, for while she was in charge of the healers, she wasn't usually privy to meetings and decisions. When she returned, her furrowed brow had become a dark shadow over her eyes. Within minutes, she had summoned the healers together and ushered them into a curtained alcove. She even called for those sleeping, such as Medicine-Yarim, resting after the night shift.

As Rel spoke, her tone grew weary. "Masvam ships have been seen nearby," she said. "They're sailing for Athomur, the city you arrived through. The Masvams are attacking along the northern coast. They're trying to gain ground so they can storm Kubodinnu."

Medicine-Yarim's bleary fatigue cleared. "What does that mean for us?" she asked, though her tone suggested she knew what was to come.

"It means that some of the battalions here will be marching out," Rel replied. "And where the battalions go, the healers follow. Some of us will remain to continue tending the sick and injured here, but some of us will leave—including myself."

Rel caught Emmy's eye as she spoke the last word.

Blinking, Emmy's heart sank. "Oh," she whispered.

Blackness shadowed Rel's face. "We're to travel with the troops as the healers' contingent," she continued. "I will make my decision on who will stay and who will go today. Those who'll come with me, we leave tomorrow at dawn."

Emmy, Yarim, and Asri fell silent, the reality of the next morning weighing upon them. No one spoke, as if to utter any words would be to condemn them to join the fighting. Emmy pressed her claws into the palms of her hands. She should have known by now that nothing ever worked out the way she wanted it to. She gave Rel a fearful glance, not daring to ask the question that was on her lips. What would happen to their plan now?

Do not fret.

Emmy started at the words, once more so clear—yet no one had opened their mouth. Medicine-Yarim, mistaking her jump for fear, smirked and prodded Emmy's back. "Maybe you should take Medicine-Emmy," she said. "The experience might toughen her up."

"And the experience might clip your arrogance," Rel snapped back.

Medicine-Yarim blanched and retracted her hand immediately. "I did not mean offense, Medicine-Rel."

"But you did," Rel continued, "and that's part of your problem. I will make my decisions based on what I feel is best, not what you think should happen. Now, all of you," she said, gesturing beyond the curtain to the rows of patients, "get back to work."

Slowly, the healers shuffled out, their legs leaden and their hearts even more so. As she went to follow the others, Emmy was pulled back by Rel. Waiting until Yarim and Asri were far enough away, the older healer gave a grim smile.

"Don't worry, Emmy," she said. "We can continue with our plans. In fact, this might be of benefit. I'm going to choose you as one of my companions, but the reasoning is this: you'll need to get armor, and that can only be good for us. We'll still leave this evening. We'll simply be more prepared, and our disappearance will be more believable. With the Masvam threat increasing, we'll be assumed to be dead."

Emmy dropped her voice to a whisper.

"And what if we do come across Masvams, Rel?" she asked. "The closest to a soldier among us is Charo, and she's only had a little training. Zecha's good with a bow, but he doesn't have one, and he's still healing. And I can't fight," she continued, her tone becoming strained with self-deprecation. "What happened back in Bellim proved that. Not to mention our training with the ohza."

Rel grinned in a way that made Emmy's neck scales rise. Didn't she realize how dangerous this was?

"Then," Rel said, "it's even more important that you get armor." She pulled the curtain all the way back, allowing light to spill in from the main room.

"Go and get fitted for armor, Medicine-Emmy," she said sternly, loud enough for anyone nearby to hear. Only Emmy could see the slight upturn at the edge of her lips. "Perhaps Medicine-Yarim is right. A little battle will do you good."

In different places across the room, Zecha and Charo popped up like shrooms. Zecha's eyes narrowed, whereas Charo's widened. Emmy shrugged.

"*I'll tell you later*," she mouthed, although their continued confusion suggested they didn't understand.

As she walked towards the door, Medicine-Yarim paused before she drew her curtain and shot Emmy a vicious glare. Though rage flared inside, Emmy chose not to respond. Instead, she stepped out into the dim morning light.

She wrapped her arms around her waist, though it wasn't cold, and glanced up. Gargons fluttered overhead, carrying messages from one unit to another. On the ground, soldiers carried stacks of supplies, led huge vaemar steeds, or loaded carts. Messengers scurried to and fro in the growing dawn, flitting like shadows. One young messenger was fond of vaulting the barrels being rolled around. Whatever was in them was heavy, for each was pushed by two soldiers. When one broke open, the messenger skidded on its contents, which put an end to his jumping. The tongue-lashing he received was severe.

The barrels were full of sand, though why they were rolling them around, Emmy couldn't fathom. But when one of the females plucked a gleaming weave from the barrel wreck, she understood. They were cleaning chain mail. *That explains why the barrels are coming from the armory.*

The armory was where Emmy was going. It was a wooden structure, full to bursting, the crowd barely kept in check by mounted guards. Soldier-slaves were herded forward like animals to receive their battle garments. Emmy joined the crush, examining the piles the soldiers left with. Mail. Shields. Scrappy leather armor. None of it looked particularly protective.

Jostled with increasing frequency, Emmy's temper flared. Between the shoving and the stink of barely-washed bodies, the desire to cleave an inconsiderate head from someone's shoulders was high, if unlikely. As she was shoved forward and wedged between two burly Metakalans, she gritted her teeth. For once, she wished she'd learned to fight.

Great clangs and crashes sounded from the smithy nearby. The heat was tremendous, even from a distance. The temperature made the stench even more unbearable. As she was jerked to the side again, Emmy wished that Rel was with her. The other soldiers would have given her a comfortable berth if she was flanked by the respected Medicine-Rel.

As the days had passed, Emmy reflected more on Rel and the kindness she had shown. The last thing she'd expected was to find a friend in the Althemerian camp, but that was exactly what Rel was becoming. Not only a friend, but she was also kin of a kind—the only other folk of Uloni blood Emmy had ever found. That and their plan for escape made the ordeal in the armory more bearable. At least they were actually escaping, not walking into the jaws of battle.

The line crept forward. The armorers' craggy faces became clear. They were battle-worn females and bore thick scars on their faces and arms—or arm, in the case of the brutal-looking one whose left appendage had been cut off above the elbow. They all sweated, the air thick with the stench and their swearing.

When she reached the front, Emmy came face-to-face with the one-armed armorer. Her dark eyes looked Emmy up and down, her lips curling. Then she turned, rummaging in racks of blue leather tunics with her one hand. When she turned again, she threw one into Emmy's hands.

"Put it on," the armorer grunted.

Emmy struggled to pull it over her head. The smell of stale leather and old blood invaded her nostrils. The one-armed female jerked the hem down, and Emmy's head popped through the neck hole. The armorer spun her around to get a better look.

"It'll do," she grunted. "It ain't like you'll survive too long for it to matter none."

"I'm a healer," Emmy blurted out. "I won't be fighting."

"Won't you?" the armorer said. She turned and rummaged in a rack, returning with a tattered red sash. She thrust it into Emmy's claws. "That goes over the left shoulder," she said. "Marks you as a healer. And don't think that means you'll be safe," she said with a grunt. "The Masvams love killing healers."

With that, the armorer began to laugh. The sound grated in Emmy's ears as she stumbled out of the armory.

She didn't look back as she crossed the compound. The leather armor was as heavy as a bag of boulders, and the one-armed female's laughter echoed after her.

Nothing seemed real. Blood rushed to Emmy's head faster and faster until it was all that she could hear. *Please let me wake up and be rid of this terrible nightmare. Let me go back to Krodge. Let me go back to what I know.* She knew it couldn't happen. Bellim was nothing more than a distant memory, Krodge a character in a story she had half-forgotten.

When she lumbered back to the safety of the healers' building, she disappeared behind her curtain and fell onto her cot. Dread pooled in her feet, but the sight of Rel through a crack in the material shield bolstered her nerve.

They would escape. They would be safe. They had to.

Emmy swallowed against the lump in her throat and squeezed her claws ever-tighter around her armor.

She had to hope. She had no choice.

CHAPTER THIRTY-FOUR

Emmy

Emmy sat astride her vaemar, waiting in the moonlight. She petted the beast's mane and patted his strong neck through his thick golden fur. The huge feline shifted and whined, pawing the dusty ground. It was as if he could sense the tension within her. The moons loomed high above them, which did nothing for her nerves. Their light bathed the whole encampment in pearlescence, gilding Emmy's fear along with the twined serpents on her blue leather surcoat. Dato was low, hanging just above her head. *We are but small things,* she thought as she rubbed circles on the vaemar's neck.

She turned and looked for her companions, but they hadn't yet emerged. Charo and Zecha were dressing in their armor and mail, and Rel was gathering as much as she could into as small a saddlebag as possible. The more normal they looked, the more easily they'd fool the guards. That meant no huge bags of supplies. Thus, Rel had walked her own vaemar to the rear of the building, for ease of sneaking as much onto it as possible. Only Emmy was ready and waiting, with daggers borrowed from Rel at her waist, trying to settle her mount.

Her mind went back to Krodge's vaemar, Zesi, from many cycles before. Emmy had loved spending time with the gentle and formidable beast, often curling against her soft black belly, escaping from the knives of the outside world. When Zesi died, Emmy was still ungendered. In her youthful innocence, she'd decided she would never love again. Her heart was utterly broken when they sent Zesi away to be burned.

This beast—Skitter, Rel had called him—didn't share Zesi's doe-eyed calm. He tottered on uncertain paws. It was strange for the creature to behave this way, for vaemar were prized for their calm nobility and their steely nerves. Perhaps it was her nervousness that seeped into him, or perhaps he could tell that something was wrong.

"Shh, now, shh," Emmy cooed. She couldn't muster up the love she had for Zesi, but cruelty would do nothing to calm this beast.

"I'm afraid that vaemar is named well," Rel said as she padded to Emmy's side. She rode a muscular, short-coated vaemar, whose fur was dark as the night sky. "His name is Skitter and, as you can tell, he's a nervous sort. But you'll manage. There's a lot to be said for a kind word and a gentle hand."

Emmy nodded. The vaemar whimpered a little more, but as Emmy petted and cooed, he settled.

"The vaemarhands say Skitter cannot be ridden and cannot pull a cart," Rel said. "That was why they were so willing to part with him when I asked for two vaemar instead of one for this journey. They're cruel to him, so he won't obey. But he can read your heart. He knows you are kindly."

Emmy allowed herself a smile as she rubbed Skitter's neck again and bent to whisper into his ear. "Good boy."

When she straightened again, Rel's penetrating gaze was on her. Emmy tilted her head back. "What?" she asked. "What's wrong?"

"Despite that healer's sash, you still look too much a soldier," Rel said. "Here."

She detached a cloakpin. The heart-and-eye glimmered in her palm.

"Put it on," she said as she rearranged her now half-loose cloak. "You need the mark of *tsimi* upon you. The sash is not enough."

Emmy wiped the surface of the little badge with the flat of her thumb before she fixed it to her sash, just over her heart. "Thank you."

Rel too wore the *tsimi* emblem and sash over her soldier's mail shirt and blue tunic. But curiously, her arms were bedecked with hundreds of bracelets, made of many materials Emmy had never seen before. There were leather and cloth ones, and rings of every metal Emmy could name—and more she couldn't. Rel's ears were newly dotted with piercings of stone. There was even a stud under her lip Emmy hadn't seen her wear.

Seeing her intrigue, Rel gave a gentle smile.

"I've seen many battles," she said. "I wasn't always *tsimi*. When I first came here, the Althemerians called me Bonebreaker. I've fought many battles and have saved many lives. I earned each one of these."

She shook her wrists. The bracelets clicked and jangled.

"How do you get them?" Emmy asked.

"It's an Althemerian custom," Rel said. She shook her right arm. "These are for death. These," she shook the left, "are for life. You earn one for every life you take and every life you save. Some folk stack their bracelets up when they have no call to, but it's easy to see through their lies. The truth of the bracelets lies in your honor." She gave a wan smile. "To my shame, on my arms there are more for death than for life, but you'll see that some others leave their left arms barren."

Emmy tentatively reached out to touch the bracelets on Rel's right arm: her kills. "Couldn't you leave your right arm bare if it bothers you?"

Rel shook her head.

"I don't think that would be honorable," she said. "For me, they're not boasts of my kills, but they're reminders that I have taken lives. It's uncomfortable, but I believe that taking a life should never be allowed to be comfortable."

She looked at Emmy for a moment. There was a slow upturn of her lips. She removed two metal bracelets from her left arm and passed them to Emmy. "Have these. One for Charo. You saved her all that time ago in Bellim, so you should show it. The second is for Zecha, as you doubtless saved him on the boat."

"But they're yours," Emmy said.

Rel pressed the bracelets into Emmy's hand. "Yes, so I can do what I like with them," she said. "May your left arm be full and your right empty. I didn't learn that lesson soon enough."

She held up her right arm again. The bracelets clinked and shimmered. She let it drop. As Emmy slipped the metal rings around her left wrist, Rel's grin returned.

Emmy looked at Rel, elegant astride the sable-furred vaemar, her long fronds glistening in the moons' light. Curiosity bred curiosity, and Emmy ventured another question. "Rel?"

"Yes, Emmy?"

"Why are you here? With the Althemerians, I mean. I know you said you were waiting for me, but why *here*?"

"Ah," Rel said, though she didn't look at Emmy. "That's a boring story."

"Will you tell me?" Emmy asked.

Rel shrugged, chuckling.

"I suppose it'll pass the moments before Charo and Zecha arrive," she said. "As I said before, Belfon isn't like Althemer or Metakala or Va Chress, or even the slavers in Valtat. In all those places, the female is the soldier, the ruler. The female is power. In Belfon, things are tipped on their heads. Males have the power—like with the Masvams—and females are permitted little."

"Right," Emmy said.

"Females are expected to abide and obey and stay at foot of the male." Rel's jaw clenched. "But I couldn't stomach that, so I left, and you know the rest of that story."

Emmy nodded. "You said you earned your freedom," she said, "so why are you still here?"

Rel blew out her cheeks and shrugged. The moons painted her green fronds silver.

"I had nowhere to go," she said. "I can't go back to Belfon, even though it's my home. I am *ingufu*. Evil, because I couldn't supplicate myself before the males. I don't belong there. I found a new home with my friend, but now she's gone. She said I had to stay here, and so I did. And here you are, and here I am."

Emmy nodded, regarding Rel with round eyes.

"I know how it feels to have nowhere to go," she said. "I don't want to go back to Metakala. In fact, I don't know where I want to go. Folk treat me like a demon." She chanted, singsong: "'*Moon Rogue, Moon Rogue. Go back to your hole and die*'." That's what they said. Everyone."

Rel exhaled a sharp "ha!" and shook her head.

"Let me tell you about *ingufu*: 'Moon Rogue,' in your words," she said. "The idea of Moon Rogue, someone forgotten by the goddess, is a fable. It's a made-up story to scare little younglings into obeying their parents. They say there are demons in the Dark and the Moon Rogue leads them. These demons spread their wings across the Arc of the Sky to bring eternal night, and all that their shadows fall upon are doomed to eternal punishment, darkness, never-ending pain—*ha!*" Rel made a sweeping gesture across the encampment. "What is this, if not evil? Evil comes from folk, not gods. I don't believe in any kind of Dark. Do you know what the Uloni god Meia does for punishment?"

Emmy sat up in the saddle. The name of her folk sent her heart fluttering. "What?"

Rel shook her head, spreading her free hand to the sky. "Nothing," she said. "Folk bring their own punishment. If you turn from the path of goodness and don't turn back, you turn from god. You push yourself away. And what could be a worse punishment than being far from god?"

Rel's question rang in her mind as Emmy sat back, wondering where Krodge was now—or how close Bose was to his god.

Finished them off, I did.

"Will you tell me more about Meia?" Emmy asked.

Rel inclined her head. The green of her eyes was touched with pewter.

"I will," she said, "but the best one to ask is Bomsoi. She'll tell you all you need to know when we see her."

"Bomsoi," Emmy said.

Rel's eyes crinkled. "Yes, Bomsoi," she said. "I miss her very much. I think you'll like her when you meet."

A creak drew their attention. Both Emmy and Rel turned.

"Ah, they're finally ready," Rel said.

Two soldiers in blue tunics and mail shirts emerged from the healers' building, gleaming in the paleness of the moons' light. It was Charo and Zecha.

Charo's face was too old under her burnished helm. Zecha looked handsome in his uniform. For a moment Emmy was proud. He had always wanted to wear a uniform and fight. But her pride disappeared as quickly as it came. This was no game. With Masvams on the prowl, they could easily be dead within hours.

Her vaemar whimpered again, as if reading her thoughts, and Emmy murmured words of comfort into his tall ears.

"Let's go," Rel said, turning her vaemar towards the guards at the gate. "The sooner we leave this place, the better."

She held out a hand to Charo and pulled her onto the vaemar behind her. Emmy did the same for Zecha, and the four set off in a short arc across the compound. They stopped their vaemar in front of the guards.

"We're going to pick shrooms," Rel said in a tone that asked no permission.

The older of the two guards squinted up at her, shaking her head.

"Is this really the time for that," she asked, "considering the soldiers march in the morning?"

Rel glared, keeping her chin high but her eyes downturned. "This is the perfect time," she said. "And regardless of whether it is or not, I will not justify myself to you or anyone else who knows nothing of healing."

The guard held up her hands and backed away. "Whatever you want."

"Indeed," Rel replied.

She kept her chin held high and her back straight as she urged her vaemar into motion again. Trying to imbibe some of Rel's courage, Emmy tilted up her chin and clicked her tongue to signal movement to Skitter. Her heart pounded so loud in her ears, she was sure the guards would hear it and sense her fear and guilt, but they didn't. And together, the four padded away from the encampment.

As they built up speed, Emmy's heart continued to pound. This time it was with excitement. Only one thought rolled around in her head, keeping time with Skitter's stride.

We're free. We're free. We're free!

CHAPTER THIRTY-FIVE

Bandim

Bandim Tiboli didn't suffer from his nerves. He liked to give the impression he'd never been afraid in his life. Now, as he stood motionless on the pedestal in his chambers, the attendants of his closet wrapping him in silks, the emperor truly believed it.

He had always hated state dress. Layer upon layer of fantastically patterned fabrics were draped over him, all encrusted with jewels and spun metal threads. Only on the occasions when his father had demanded it had Bandim relented and allowed himself to be dressed so. Before, it was frivolousness. Now, it was necessity.

His attendants were quick and, within the hour, they put the final touches to his headdress. It was an ancient circlet of sparkling silver, with red and orange jewels dripping like globules of blood. His horn crest was draped with the finest chains, with horizontal bars running through the loops and letting more gems spill down the sides of his head.

His face was painted, a symbol of his royalty. Only the highest of those in the ruling house were permitted to draw their sigils on their faces. Bandim closed his eyes. Soon the Tiboli lightning strikes would be no more. The palms of his hands warmed with power. *I'm no longer just a Tiboli. I am Dorai.*

Bandim kept his temper long enough for the servants to finish. When they scurried off to the main chamber of his apartments, he stared at himself in the enormous polished looking-plate. Its frame was beautifully carved from the trunk of a giant blackblood tree. It had been a gift from the Selamans to House Tiboli hundreds of cycles before. Bandim ran his ornamented claws, thick with rings, along its smooth surface. He shook his head. His horn jewels tinkled quietly. Selama was gone now.

Soon, they'll all be gone.

There was a quiet knock at the door and the emperor turned, smoothing the front of his robes.

One of his attendants, a lower-order Tiboli, entered and bowed. As he spoke, he kept his head down. "Your Grace, the honored Johrann Maa requests an audience with you before your address."

"Send her in," Bandim said.

The door to the dressing room opened, and Johrann glided in. She smiled from ear to ear, dressed in finery that almost matched Bandim's. Back in favor as his powers grew, she was once again ensconced in his mother's old chambers, wearing his mother's fine jewelry. If she continued to serve him well, he thought, she might even become the empress proper.

"What do you think?" Bandim asked, lifting his arms to show the elaborate drape of his robes.

Johrann supplicated herself. "You look like a god," she said, "as is right."

Bandim shook his head and laughed. He raised Johrann up and embraced her. He could play the kind courtier when necessary, though the branded fingerprints on her neck were a constant reminder that she was never fully safe.

"I had to see you," Johrann said, resting in the curve of his arm. "I can't bear to be parted from you for too long."

"I understand," Bandim said, leaning to kiss her. "Now that the goddess lives within me, I can't imagine being parted from her presence. It must be much the same for you with me."

Fervor bubbled within Johrann and, for the briefest of moments, Bandim could feel her emotions. She brimmed with hope, though there was still a tinge of fear.

"Today, the folk will finally see you for who you really are," Johrann said. "With this proclamation, you will set us off on the path to righteousness and the banishment of blasphemy and false gods." She touched his face, tracing the lightning bolts. "Show them your truth. Show them you are Dorai."

"I will show them the godly way," Bandim said. "I will show them that House Tiboli, the Masvam Empire, and the once-hidden believers in the One True God are not fools to be trifled with."

Johrann's eyes gleamed. "The more the folk believe, the stronger you will become. You'll be able to reach through fire and spread your influence, perhaps even help your troops on the battlefield."

Bandim's mouth spread in a grin, revealing his teeth.

"The more those wretched worshippers of the false goddess see that the followers of the Dark are numerous, the better," he said. "And the more of them who come to the side of Truth, the stronger I will become. Then I will be unstoppable. I will show the Truth of Dorai—the truth of me."

Bandim released Johrann and drew himself to his full height. With one final glance in the mirror, he swept from the chamber, passion for his mission burning bright in his heart.

Servants and officials scurried before him like whirlwinds, all falling into their allotted places. Bandim drew a deep breath as he reached the doors to the balcony. It overlooked the speaker's bowl, which was packed with his subjects, chattering and waiting to hear the emperor's great proclamation. There were worshippers of the false god there, but for each of them, there were two of Bandim's loyal subjects. Gradually, the worshippers of Dorai had emerged from society's cracks, no longer driven underground by the falseness of the Light. There were new believers too, for each passing day of his reign brought more and more to swell the ranks of the followers of Dorai.

Among them, too, were those who feared the noose and the blade. There were those who feared losing their high position in court, gone with a slip of the tongue. There were those who clung to whatever the emperor said was right, believing anything that gilded their lives in safety. Bandim knew this, but had no intention of raking them over coals to extract their truth as thin believers. This was the time for embracing their flimsy hopes and fears, curling them around his claws, shaping the world to his desires.

The executions would come later.

Bandim's heart hammered as if he was racing into battle. Here he was, the emperor, standing near the spot where his brother had been murdered—at Bandim's bidding. But he wasn't afraid. Bandim Tiboli, *Dorai*, was never afraid.

The high-pitched horn blast cut like a blade. The speaker's bowl fell silent as the herald stepped up to speak.

"His Imperial Majesty, Sole Ruler of the Masvam Empire, Protector of the Realm, Conqueror of Heathens, Scorcher of Souls, son of Braslen Tiboli, grandson of Maram Tiboli, Emperor Bandim Tiboli."

Two-thirds of the crowd erupted in an enormous peel of cheering and jubilation. The other third stood with mouths in thin lines, sharing worried gazes. Bandim could feel each one of them, full of sharp fear and burning anger, resentful of the rise of the Dark.

Bandim strode to the balcony lip, his entourage sweeping behind. He imbibed the adoration of his followers and let the false believers simmer. He watched the flicker and snap of Tiboli banners in the wind. Eventually he raised a hand for silence. His loyal subjects immediately obeyed. The others were already silent.

Every ear was tweaked to him. The acoustics in the bowl ensured Bandim's voice would carry to every one of them.

"My loyal friends," he said, his voice clear and strong as steel, "it is with joy that I confirm the great power of the Masvam Empire is once more stretching beyond our borders. Today at last, we will begin our attack on the so-called Queendom of Althemer. Soon it will no longer be a heathen queendom, but rather shall be part of our glorious empire!"

There was a surge of enthusiasm from the crowd, but Bandim quieted them again.

He could feel Nunako's fools stirring, curling their toes in their shoes in their disquiet.

"We have many Althemerian and half-Althemerian folk living in our great empire, just as we have Selamans and half-Selamans, and most recently, our brethren from Metakala. Some of you will be before me now, and all of you will call at least one a neighbor or even a friend. I do not wish to persecute these folks who have long lived in our midst, or indeed, those who have recently come into our fold. The greatness of our empire comes from our breadth of experience and culture.

"However," Bandim continued, strengthening the steel in his tone, "now that I am on the throne, it is time to purge a great evil. It is time that we purify ourselves, and do what is right."

The atmosphere changed, as if the air was singed. Bandim grinned. He raised his hands, allowing his fiery power to pool in his upturned palms. As he spoke, the balls of flame grew.

"From this day forward, every citizen of the Masvam Empire must pledge the new Oath of Fealty. All who pledge this oath forego all practice and supplication to any other false god, and embrace only me, the All-Powerful, All-Wise, and All-Beautiful Bandim-Dorai!"

Believers and nonbelievers alike swelled with fear and sharp astonishment as the fire in his hands grew. For the first time, Bandim could finally reveal his truth to them all. The elation of his followers flamed bright as he continued, "All temples, shrines, talismans, and artefacts dedicated to anything other than me shall be destroyed."

The heretical third glanced over their shoulders at the temple of Nunako in the distance, glorious in white stone and swirling spires, where the beloved Braslen Tiboli was so recently burned. The temple that took generations to build, where their children were blessed on their gendering-days.

"I am your goddess, your lawmaker, your emperor," he said, sending columns of fire upwards from his palms. The crowd pulsed with fear and amazement, every tongue stunned into silence. "Henceforth, any of you who refuse to swear their loyalty to me will be executed. Not only that, but I will have your younglings sold into slavery and your land and property seized! Worship me, or pay a high price for your heresy."

There was no sound among the crowd, except for the snapping of the Tiboli banners in the wind. Bandim softened his excitement and briefly closed his eyes, pulling down a mask of compassion.

"There is no need for anyone to lose their life," he said. He cupped one hand over the other, extinguishing the flames. "It is not my desire as your emperor and goddess to persecute those who have lived as our brothers and sisters for so many cycles. It is not your fault you have been blinded by the False God and the promise of the Light. I wish for us to come together under one banner, to cease the endless to and fro of land and life, all in the shadow of a false promise."

He closed his eyes as he let hunger build.

"The so-called Light, the goddess Nunako—these things are *folly*." He snapped his eyes open. "We will tear down the temples of the heathens. We will root out every notion of false hope and false gods from our lives and embrace my truth and purity— the glory of Dorai! It is not darkness. It is truth, truth, *truth!*"

A sudden cheer swelled from his loyal followers, their greater numbers outweighing the numb silence of the false believers. Bandim jabbed a talon to the sky, sending up a blast of flame.

"From today, I declare war on those who stand against me. The Masvams will be the catalyst for glory, striking hard against the heathens, starting with the Althemerians and their heretical worship of the false gods Ethay and Apago. They will tremble before the might of Dorai!"

To prove his point, Bandim reached out his powers to the many braziers and torches that lined the edges of the speaker's bowl and willed them to ignite. At the same time, every Tiboli banner suddenly changed, hidden sigils unleashed to cover the old. Instead of the Tiboli orange and red and the lightning strike, the flame of Dorai was bright on a field of black. The crowd's fear and fervor burned as hot as Bandim's flames.

"Those who are loyal will be declared true citizens," Bandim continued. "The Dark will grant you land, riches, and the bounty of all kingdoms. You will be saved from the eternal punishment of the Light. You will not burn, but will take your place as righteous stars in my Dark Sky. You will flourish! And those who do not?"

Bandim paused, dimming the many fires he had lit. He waited for a moment to ensure every ear hung on his words. His new banners flickered. Then, with a sweep of his hand, he made the braziers and torches flare once more.

"They will suffer *death!*"

There were screeches from below, and Bandim could taste the salty fear of the heretics. However, they were fewer than his followers. A fervent voice below began to chant and soon, cheers and chanting drowned the despair.

"Long live the Emperor! Long live the Empire!"

"All-Powerful, All-Wise, All-Beautiful!"

More and more voices joined in from around the bowl. His two-thirds of righteous followers filled the air with loyalty. Others joined in, those whose faith was thin, those who sought to protect their younglings at all costs, or those whose throats burned with the promise of a blade.

"Long live Bandim-Dorai!"

Bandim let it wash over him, their allegiance cleansing him. He sent fireballs arcing across the heads of the crowd, coloring their faces and reaching hands. His heart brimmed with elation as they screamed their support for their emperor, their goddess, all among the flapping, victorious sigils of Dorai.

"Go forth from here and tell others what you have seen," Bandim said, braiding twirls of flame above his head. "Tell them my truth and tell them my terms. And never forget," he continued, sending blasts of fire singing through the air, "the time of Dorai is here!"

CHAPTER THIRTY-SIX

Emmy

The further they travelled from the camp, the lighter Emmy's heart became. Despite the potential for danger from Masvams, she grinned. They were free, and there was no going back. All they had to do was travel across the Althemerian countryside to get to the city, and they would be safe.

Emmy nudged Skitter's flanks with her boots to encourage him to ride side by side with the other vaemar. "How far is it to Kubodinnu?"

"The journey will take two nights," Rel replied. "That is, as long as we encounter no obstacles. I say nights because it's safer to travel by moons' light. We're less likely to be stumbled upon and questioned by Althemerian soldiers."

Emmy's heart grew heavier at that. She hadn't considered that danger, only the Masvam threat.

"What will we do if we're discovered?" Charo asked.

Her hands were tightly wound into Rel's cloak, as if afraid of something more than the Masvams.

"We'll hope that Skitter and Jawbone here," Rel replied, patting her vaemar's neck, "are light enough of foot to let us flee. Once we get to Kubodinnu and Bomsoi, we will be safe in her protection—and the protection of the queen."

Behind Emmy, Zecha squeaked. "The queen?"

Rel, undulating on the vaemar's back, nodded. "Yes, the queen of Althemer. Bomsoi is one of her closest aides. Queen Valentia will protect us once she knows we're with my friend." Her face grew grim. "Until then, we must avoid Masvams and Althemerians in equal measure."

Zecha pulled close to Emmy's back, his arms around her waist squeezing tighter. "We're going to meet a queen," he whispered. "Amazing."

As long as we make it there alive, Emmy thought, but she kept that to herself. Instead of replying, she concentrated on keeping Skitter up to Jawbone's pace.

The night stretched on with their journey. The moons rose ever-higher, lighting the darkness. They kept to the edges of forests, eventually crossing into the shadows of high cliffs. At night the roads were almost dead, but the three moons cast enough light to make stealth difficult. Rel guided them down to the coastal path that ran beneath the dark edge of a precipice. It curled around a sharp outcrop, the thin road winding through a narrow gap in a row of jagged rocks. They went one-by-one, Rel leading. But as soon as she rounded the corner, she yanked Jawbone to an abrupt stop. "Whoa!"

Emmy grasped Skitter's reins and pulled him aside, just preventing a collision with Jawbone's rear. The two vaemar grunted and huffed heavy breaths. Emmy urged Skitter through the gap to come to Jawbone's side again. She drew her brows low and looked at Rel and Charo. Even the former's eyes were wide with fear.

"What?" Emmy asked.

Charo raised one arm to point towards the horizon. Emmy followed its direction.

Her stomach went to stone. There were ships silhouetted against the horizon, and they weren't Althemerian.

They were Masvam.

The shapes brought back fiery memories of Bellim and the attack there. Once more, Emmy watched as the tall-masted vessels crept along, dark against the deep blue of the night sky.

"Where are they going?" Zecha asked. His breath was warm on Emmy's neck.

"They can't be going for the capital or Athomur if they're heading in the opposite direction to us," Emmy replied. "We marched south from Athomur."

Rel's face was still as stone, pale as a spirit in the moons' light.

"There's only one place of value in this direction," she said. She never took her eyes from the ships. "That is Hutukeshu Encampment."

Reality spread across Emmy's vision like tendrils of ink in water. If the Masvams were heading for the encampment, Commander Pama and the others certainly didn't know it. The soldiers were getting ready to march, not to protect themselves.

Reality hung heavy upon them, like the stifling air before a Decos storm. Zecha was the first to speak again. "We have to go back."

The truth of those quiet words ached in Emmy's ears. Her own reluctance to do so shamed her. If the ships were this close and Commander Pama had done nothing, it could only mean she truly didn't know. If she didn't know, the encampment was as good as destroyed—and the only ones who could warn her were the four who were running away.

Rel remained very still, her eyes unblinking as they remained fixed on the ships. Behind her, Charo shook her head and closed her eyes. "No, we don't have to go back," she said.

"But Charo," Zecha began.

"No!" Charo's shout echoed into the distance. "The Althemerians kidnapped us, pretending to save us. We don't owe them anything." Her voice hitched, and tears budded in her eyes. "They made me a slave again when I had been freed. No. We don't have to go back. We owe them nothing."

Ever-good Zecha reached out to comfort her, but she batted his hand away. "Charo," he said, "if we don't warn them, who knows how many will be killed?"

"And without the soldier-slaves of the camp," Rel continued, "when they do sail for Athomur, the city will fall. Then the Masvams will march on to Kubodinnu. Once they have the capital, Althemer is lost."

Charo's silver tears spilled. Emmy's stomach churned. Rel was right, but so was Charo.

It was a choice of saving themselves or saving so many others. Emmy had been an almost-slave to Krodge, then taken as a slave by the Masvams. Saved by one Althemerian hand, but enslaved again by the other. She owed them nothing. This was their chance to escape. Surely with the Masvams sailing for the encampment, that would make their path to Kubodinnu clearer.

The thought kept circling in Emmy's head. They owed them nothing.

Yet so much blood will be spilled, she thought. *There will be so much death.*

In her head, Emmy made one choice. But in her heart, she made another.

"Zecha's right," she said softly. The truth of her words pained her. "The Althemerians may be just as bad as the Masvams who took us in Bellim, but at least they spared our lives and there's a chance to be freed." Her brand seemed to burn anew. "I don't want to go back, but we have to, Charo."

Trembling, Charo wouldn't nod agreement. Instead, she looked away, back towards the horizon. In front of her, Rel finally broke her gaze from the ships. Suddenly she looked as old as the sea itself.

"We must go back," she said. "Consider it the way to repay your debt. Then we will go to Kubodinnu with clear consciences."

Charo said nothing and kept her face averted, but the shake of her shoulders told Emmy her tears were flowing freely.

"We'll be okay," Emmy said.

But the words fell flat even to her own ears.

Turning Jawbone around with a nudge to his left flank, Rel urged him back the way they came. As she did, her eyes locked with Emmy's for a moment.

We will survive.

The words were as clear in Emmy's head as if Rel had spoken aloud. But her lips remained shut as she rode onward. As Emmy pulled Skitter around, Zecha tightened his grip around her waist. "We'll be okay," he repeated.

Hearing it from his mouth was no better than hearing it from her own.

Rel kicked Jawbone into a run, and Emmy did the same with Skitter. They pounded back along the sandy cliff path, up towards open ground, and this time thundered along the well-beaten road instead of hiding amongst the trees. Jawbone's sable fur was edged with white, rather than cloaked in shadow.

It was the right thing to do, Emmy knew, as she kept Skitter on Jawbone's strong paws. But that didn't make the reality any lighter on her heart. They were free. Now they were going back.

And whether they would live or die was entirely unknown.

◆ ◆ ◆

The morning was clammy. The wool of Emmy's tunic clung to her skin, pasted beneath the heavy stiffness of her leather surcoat. The daggers Rel had given her hung like boulders from her belt. She stood some distance away from the healers' building, watching the harried preparations for attack. Everything since they'd returned to the camp had been a blur.

Charo had been spirited away back to her barracks, no excuse now for her being away. She was required to be with her fellow soldier-slaves as they prepared for battle, lining the edges of the camp and battling down in defenses Emmy didn't try to understand.

As night turned to morning, dewy mist hung in the air. The sharp tang of salt and seaweed languished, rising from the waterline. As the sun rose, the mist burned away. Now, as Emmy saw the sea again, she wished it would return.

Enormous ships floated in the distance. Their masts rose like thin talons, pointing to the sky in supplication.

The Masvams were ready to strike.

Emmy had escaped the healers' building, thinking anything was better than the suffocating silence of anticipation, of empty stretchers awaiting the injured. Sometimes shadows morphed from the corners of the room, swirling into figures on the cots. Sometimes they were faceless. Sometimes they were Charo and Zecha.

As many of the ill and injured as possible had been deployed back to their barracks. Only those unconscious or unable to move remained, silent in fear or oblivion.

But the sight of the Masvams was worse, and Emmy turned away, weaving between the rows of soldiers and messengers as they assumed their positions and ran messages across the camp. At the sight of her red sash and *tsimi* cloakpin, one heavyset Althemerian lieutenant grabbed her by the collar of her surcoat and thrust her in the direction of the healers' building. "Get to your post!" he snapped.

Head spinning, Emmy stumbled into a run and headed back to the building.

As she approached, her pace slowed. She stared at the weeds growing between the cracks in the parched earth. She looked up, shielding her eyes against the light of the rising sun.

The moons, though gone from sight, hung in her mind like silver baubles.

"Protect us," she whispered. "Please."

Understandably, there was no reply.

Emmy pulled the door open and entered on silent feet. She bit her lip. Burning braziers cast a dim light across the walls. Shadows crept across the stonework.

How likely was it that they would all live? Charo was gone, and Zecha had been co-opted into helping run supplies. Rel was still in the building, but neither that nor the wooden walls would offer much protection, Emmy knew.

Perhaps none of them would survive.

Shipbait, as Commander Pama was fond of saying, was nothing more than arrow fodder. Even if Emmy somehow stayed safe from the battle, Charo and Zecha would surely perish—and Emmy didn't want to think about that.

Medicine-Yarim and Medicine-Asri slunk in corners and alcoves, arms hugging themselves as if to keep the battle at bay. Medicine-Yarim caught Emmy's eye and for once didn't glare. Emmy nodded as she passed, not knowing what to say, and disappeared behind Rel's curtain.

Rel sat on her cot with her head bowed. The long box Emmy had seen before lay across her lap. As Emmy entered, Rel opened the box. Emmy's breath caught at the beauty of what was inside.

It was a sword. Its scabbard was elaborate and beautiful, inlaid with intricate patterns of lacquered wood. It made the daggers slung at Emmy's waist seem no deadlier than blunted kitchen knives.

Emmy sat beside her on the cot, words caught in her throat. Rel reached over and took her hand, squeezing lightly. "You're scared," she said.

Swallowing, Emmy nodded. "Yes."

Rel squeezed her hand again. "I'm not scared," she said. "I've faced death many times. That doesn't concern me." To prove the point, she jangled the bracelets on her right wrist, then patted her sword's scabbard. "No, I'm not scared."

Her weapon's hilt was long and wrapped with soft leather. The pommel was large, a deadly weapon by itself.

"Where did you get that from?" Emmy asked. Perhaps it was a futile question, but in the face of death it seemed like any question was a good one.

Rel took the sword from the box, stood, and in an impossibly swift movement unsheathed the sword. Emmy jerked back as she arced it through the air.

"This is Haelo," Rel said. "She's been my weapon for many cycles—a gift from my friend." She swept the sword forward and twisted around, thrusting its tip towards Emmy. She withdrew it as quickly as she had driven it forward, then held the hilt to Emmy. "Hold her."

Emmy hesitated, but at Rel's bidding, she rose and took the sword in both hands. She staggered under its weight, the tip scraping the ground. She tried to swing, but her arms burned with the effort to wield it. Rel didn't laugh. She slipped behind Emmy to rearrange her grip.

"Haelo is strong," Rel said into her ear. "She knows me, but she doesn't know you. Haelo doesn't like to be held by anyone she doesn't trust. She makes itself too heavy for the untrustworthy to lift."

As soon as Rel's hands were on the hilt, it was as if the weapon was hewn of air. Emmy's jaw dropped as Rel guided her arms. "*How?*"

Rel did laugh this time, and withdrew her hands from the sword. As soon as she did, the blade sank, half-wrenching Emmy's arms from their sockets.

"Haelo becomes heavy because I let it go," Rel said.

"But *how?*" Emmy asked. "How can that be possible?"

Rel retrieved her weapon and returned it to its sheath. She adjusted the belt slung at her waist and attached the scabbard to it. "My friend," she said.

Fear bloomed like a black spot. Emmy grunted and planted a hand on Rel's arm. She gripped hard. "Tell me more about your friend and the Uloni," she said. "If I die, I want to die knowing as much about my folk as I can. I—" Her voice cracked. "I don't want to die feeling alone."

Rel enveloped Emmy in her strong arms. The gesture made Emmy's throat close, and she stiffened, but something made her relax into Rel's embrace.

"You're not alone, Emmy," Rel said. "You've never been alone."

She pulled backwards and held onto Emmy's upper arms. "I wanted your first meeting with my friend to be in the flesh," she said. She gave a low chuckle. "Now is perhaps not the time, but I need you to know you're not alone, Emmy."

Emmy blinked at the sudden light in Rel's eyes. It started low, like a mild haze behind her pupils. She placed her hands upon Emmy's shoulders, and the blue glint spread like unfurling petals.

"I'll show you, Emmy."

Rel blinked, and the whole round of her pupils came up bright and shimmering like twin stars. Her skin and armor morphed to her natural blue and purple. Emmy couldn't look away.

"Rel? What's happening?"

"You're going to see you are not alone."

Her eyes glowing the brightest of blues, Rel touched a claw to Emmy's temple.

The world pulsed and undulated like a storm at sea, and Emmy found herself rolling on waves of bright blue light. She clung to Rel as they hurtled through the brightness, blinded by fear and confusion. Something drew them forward, some kind of power. Rel's heart quickened. Emmy's beat in time with it, as if they were one.

They soared up from the saltwater shore, and the world spilled around them. The moons rose, impossibly bright as they caught the light of the sun. Everything else washed out like a faded pattern. Emmy heard voices, a thousand voices, a million voices, all at once. Talking. Laughing. Crying.

There was only one possibility. This thing that was happening that wasn't meant to be, this unexplainable leap from reality into the rolling blue.

This was magic.

Moon Rogue. The words came as an echo.

Magic.

Moon Rogue.

Emmy couldn't breathe. It didn't feel like the evil others painted her with, like the sharp taint of a curse or a spell woven from darkness and malice. Rel was there, and they were joined at the hand. There was no evil. There was only togetherness and the pulse of their lives, entwined.

Then Rel loosened her grasp.

And Emmy was falling, falling, *falling...*

CHAPTER THIRTY-SEVEN

Mantos

Mantos, Mantos... Dear brother, I will find you...

"No!"

Mantos jerked upright in the bed, his chest heaving. Sweat cooled on his brow. Realization slowly returned. Pain singed as if he had been burned. *Another nightmare*, he thought. *The same cursed nightmare.*

Twilight stretched along the horizon. It had been light when he last looked. He stared at the mound of blankets, at the soft rise and fall of Fonbir's breathing. *He sleeps in peace*, he thought. *I wish I could do that again.*

Mantos perched on the edge of the bed, staring through the window as his breathing settled. When he'd had enough of trying to count the pinprick stars, he turned and began cataloguing every detail of the night, the room, from the soft shift of color from brown to gold to white of the fur bedspread, to the gentle beat of Fonbir's breathing.

They hadn't been together before Mantos returned from the dead. Their love was confined to letters dancing across pages, hidden from prying eyes. Now they *had* been together, it was everything they thought it would be and more. It was something they'd never thought, too. In their adolescent scribblings, even their older princely communications, the sentinels at the door were only to protect them, to allow them to exist in their new world. They were Fonbir's most trusted guards, but they were tasked to keep more than secrets. They had to keep Mantos in. That was never written. It shouldn't have been.

A touch at Mantos' shoulder made him turn.

Fonbir, wrapped in blankets, white eyes hooded with fatigue, gave him a sympathetic smile. "What pains you, Toketa?" he asked. "Did you not sleep?"

It took some time before Mantos answered. "When I sleep, I dream," he said. His words felt like an insult to the silent night. "I don't want to dream and thus, I don't want to sleep. Yet I do, and I'm tortured."

The bedding rustled as Fonbir sat up. His hands went to Mantos' shoulders, working at the knots of tension. "I had a dream," he said. His breath was warm on the nape of Mantos' neck. "I dreamed we were together. Then, when I woke up, I found it wasn't a dream, but reality."

Mantos managed a smile as Fonbir pressed gentle kisses to his shoulders.

"Do we live in dreams?" Mantos asked. "Or do we live in nightmares? Do we live somewhere in between?"

Chuckling, Fonbir wrapped his arm around Mantos' neck and brought their cheeks together. His talons played with the chain around Mantos' throat. "I'm no philosopher," he said. "I haven't read as many books as you have."

Mantos shifted and took Fonbir's face in his hands. "I've read books, but I'm not godly," he said. "You might not have read as many books, but you are good and pure. Your hands aren't tainted as mine are. I have the blood of innocents upon me. You don't."

Placing his hands on Mantos', Fonbir drew his brows low. "Toketa, please tell me what's wrong," he said. "You've never been so maudlin before. I worry."

"I don't feel myself, Nabi," Mantos replied. The pet name was awkward on his tongue. He chuckled. "How long has it been since I said that aloud and not in a letter? My Nabi, sweet and pure."

Fonbir's frown deepened. "Don't change my course with sugared words," he said. "Why do you not feel yourself? Is it the nightmares?"

Exhaling slowly, Mantos shuffled backwards, stretching out along the bed. His tail spilled out, lingering on the rushes. Flashes of memory made him flinch.

"I don't think they're simple nightmares," he said. "Nightmares change. This one is always the same. Every detail is identical."

"You dream of Bandim," Fonbir said. "You dream of your fears surrounding him."

"Yes," Mantos replied. "I do. But these images aren't puppet theatre of the mind. They aren't my fears manifested as symbols, like some would say. They're real, and they've become so much worse since I told your mother all I know. They seem more...real. As if the events aren't dreams but are actual, like I'm pulled from my body and into another world. And the pain, it gets worse every time. It isn't even pain any longer. It's agony."

Memory surged forth.

"I...I..." He rubbed his forehead as a touch of dizziness swirled out of nowhere. He was still disoriented by the dream. "I cannot but think Nunako despises me for surrendering my brother." He blinked and rubbed harder, but the bedroom continued to tip one way and the other. He reached for Fonbir's hand, but couldn't find it. The dizziness transformed into pain, as if his head were cleft in two.

No! I'm not sleeping. I'm awake. I'm awake!

He couldn't think his way out. It was like his eyes were stitched open as he watched, unblinking and unwilling. Once more he was torn apart, ripped at the seams, destroyed by his own brother.

Mantos...Mantos...

Jerking and twisting in vain, all he could do was succumb to the pain. Yet he fought back. "No!"

Mantos woke on the floor, his throat half-closed. Fonbir screamed for the guards. "Get Bomsoi! *Now!*"

"No," Mantos said, though the words were little more than squeaks. "Not... Not her..."

Fonbir returned to his side, brushing fronds from his face. "Shh, shh," he said. "You were overcome by an evil of shaking, but Bomsoi will know what to do. Stay calm, Toketa. Stay calm."

Mantos gripped Fonbir's claws as another tremulous wave rolled over him.

Mantos, Mantos... Dear brother, I will find you...

No, Bandim. No...

He was ripped apart, the dream proceeding as if its teeth were sharper, its mouth hungrier. But two hands dipped into his dream world, hands that were blue and purple, hands that scooped up his pieces, slotted him back together.

Gradually, the pain passed. Reality swirled back, and those hands were replaced by hands that gave gentle caresses. Hands that stroked his forehead. Fonbir's hands. Mantos was in his bed, comforted by the one he loved, cradled on his lap like a hatchling.

But reality came with jagged edges, like shattered eggshell. There were memories of his shaking, and a pair of eyes that watched from the bedside.

I am weak, Mantos thought. *I cannot control my own mind. I cannot live with my guilt. But why do I feel such remorse for speaking out? Why do I feel as though I betrayed my brother, a brother who tried to kill me?*

A voice in his head clarified.

Because you are a traitor.

Mantos shifted under the furs and briefly pressed the heels of his hands to his eyes. He felt as gnarled as an ancient tree, as tied in knots as the most dreadful of tangles. Fonbir cooed and petted, while Bomsoi stayed at a respectful distance. Her armor glittered in the candlelight.

As always, she was dressed in sober robes of black. There was no elegant trim, no jewels, nothing to suggest she was in any way important; yet she was. She'd brought Mantos back from the dead. Now she had dived into his head, a hero of old tales, a savior.

Mantos raised his head, propping himself on one elbow. The shadow of pain made him bold.

"What is your purpose, Bomsoi?" he asked. "My mother tells me you were there not long after I died. She tells me you were the one to save her, and you were the one who took my body. Fonbir tells me he worked with you. He tells me you knew I was going to die. How did you know all this? Why were you in the right place at the right time so many times?"

Bomsoi stepped closer to the bedside. She inclined her head. "I am a stranger in this world, though I have lived in it for many cycles. I am one of you, and yet I am not. I know things."

Weariness threatened to weigh Mantos' head back onto Fonbir's lap. "Why must you talk in riddles?" he asked.

He expected a remark that arced around the truth. But that was not what he received. Instead, he was favored with a knowing look—the sort a mother might give a wayward son.

"I don't think you would believe me if I told you," Bomsoi said. Her eyes gleamed with mystery. "Why waste the words?"

Mantos grunted. Fonbir rubbed small circles on his back.

"I have a right to know," he said. "You meddled with my life. You meddled with my death. And now, at every turn, I see you. I deserve to know what you are so I can understand what you've done to me."

There was an upturn at the corner of Bomsoi's mouth, and something strange that glittered behind her eyes. She gave a shallow nod. "All right," she said. "I will tell you."

Before she could speak another word, her entire body became still as stone. Her eyes shone blue and bright in the darkness.

Mantos' throat tightened.

"Bomsoi?" he asked, bolting upright. At his side, Fonbir stiffened.

There was no response. Mantos' breathing quickened as he watched Bomsoi, immovable as a mountain, staring blankly with those ethereal eyes. It was as though she was encased in ice, or was a statue hewn from silvery rock.

"What in the name of the Dark is this?" Mantos stared at the frozen curve of her mouth. "Look at her eyes! Fonbir, who is she?"

Fonbir licked his lips, fighting for the words. "I don't know, exactly."

Mantos smelled the lie. He grabbed Fonbir's arm. "*Please*, Nabi," he said. "Tell me what you know."

There was a trembling in Fonbir's arm. He licked his lips again.

"Bomsoi is a mystery," he said. At Mantos' derisive snort, he shook his head. "I know that sounds strange, but she is. She's called the Stranger for good reason. She's been an advisor to my mother for many cycles. She's commanded battalions of the queen's army, and it was she who trained Valaria in combat. She trains Fylica now. Before, she worked for the longest time in the encampments with her apprentice. And..." He stumbled, looked away, then looked back. He lifted his free arm and pointed at his eyes. His white eyes. "There's something I've never told you, Mantos," he said. His voice wavered, and he swallowed. His pupils were wide in the stark blankness of the round of his eyes. "There's a reason Bomsoi is trusted by my mother. When I was young, not yet gendered, I caught eyepox. My eyes scabbed over and I lost my sight. Nothing the healers did made it better.

"But Mother had heard stories, from one of the camps, of a healer that performed miracles. Desperate, Mother had her soldiers bring the Stranger to me. She touched my eyes and chanted words I didn't know. Then the scabs lifted and I could see again, though I was marked by her magic—her strangeness. My eyes turned white."

Mantos pulled away, lips tightening in a frown.

"You told me your white eyes came from your father," he said. "Why did you lie, to me of all folk?"

Fonbir's eyes filled, but he blinked the wetness away. "I didn't want you to reject me," he said. "Touched by sorcery, I would carry a taint if anyone knew. I couldn't bear your rejection. Only Mother, Valaria, and I know the truth. Even Fylica thinks Father's eyes were white, because she doesn't remember him."

Reeling, Mantos rose from the bed. He gestured at Bomsoi's gleaming eyes. "What is this creature?"

Fonbir opened his mouth, but he didn't get the chance to speak. Instead, Bomsoi answered.

"I am the Daughter of Gods," she said. "I am the Joiner of Hands."

CHAPTER THIRTY-EIGHT

Emmy

Sweet perfume floated on a gentle breeze. Freezing air licked every inch of her skin, yet she wasn't cold. Emmy opened her eyes, squinting against the streams of light that poured through thick treetops. Blue sky peered through the white canopy, the bare branches shifting like blinking eyes.

She sat up, her hands sinking into the soft bower of snow and curling roots that cradled her. Snowflakes coated her, and her long black fronds swept down her sides, pooling in gentle waves.

The air was silver with euphoria. The sides of the tall grey trees blurred and sharpened in a beating pulse. Soft voices whispered on the wind. Emmy strained to hear their secrets.

She stood, fronds falling around her like a robe. Her feet, now bare, her boots gone, curled into the soft snow underfoot. She tried to run, but her limbs wouldn't obey. She waded through the thick snow, through the trees, still listening to the words on the breeze.

Where are the voices coming from?

Everywhere at once and yet nowhere at all, growing louder with every forward step.

"Rel?" Emmy called. "Where are you?"

She got no response except the voices.

As she walked, a single voice rang louder than the rest. It was different. It was *singing*. The melody was painful, so mournful Emmy felt her heart would shatter.

"Rel? Where are you?"

Echoes of her words were her only response.

"*Who* are you?"

Still nothing.

As the snow thinned, she reached a clearing. The sun's rays skated and bounced off sheer ice cliffs, blinding her. Emmy tried to wrench her head away, but her neck wouldn't obey. She wanted to shield her eyes with her hands, but they wouldn't rise. As she adjusted to the light, the source of the singing became clear.

A female sat among high snow drifts. Her skin was blue, her armor purple. *Uloni!* Emmy thought. *She's one of my kind!*

The Uloni's mouth remained closed, yet she poured forth beautiful music, harmonious and discordant all at once. The words were strange. Emmy shouldn't have understood them, yet she could comprehend. What was this place? Who was she?

She tried to look away, to close her eyes and ears and run, but her senses were sharpened and her feet were rooted in the snow. Against her bidding, she walked forward. Her footsteps made no sound on the crisp snow. Mid-note, the female opened her eyes. The music fell silent.

"You have arrived."

As when she sang, when the female spoke, her mouth didn't open. Her voice echoed deep in Emmy's mind. She stood and walked, her sparkling robe sweeping behind her. Though she was imposing, when she walked, she left no impression on the snow.

Emmy couldn't look away. Her body trembled, and she drank in every detail of the stranger. Her skin was smooth, as if she were still a youngling, but her grey eyes flickered with ancient knowledge, echoes of the past. She was perfection—all except for her first horn, which was cracked.

The great female reached for her, placing her palm on Emmy's face. Her touch was cold, colder than any snow. Emmy tried to speak, but her throat was frozen. Ice travelled through her, stilling her entire body.

"Emena," the Uloni said, locking Emmy's eyes in her gaze. "Emmy."

Emmy tried to pull away, but couldn't.

"I have sought you for many cycles," the Uloni went on. "I'm glad I have finally found you."

She let go of Emmy's face, and Emmy found her body within her control again. She stumbled backwards, clutching her head. "What's going on?" she asked. The words echoed against the smooth ice walls that surrounded them. "This isn't possible."

"I assure you, it is," said the Uloni. "Many things are possible with faith. Emmy, you are here to help rid the world of a terrible mistake."

Emmy shook her head, fear consuming her. No. She wasn't special. She wasn't any good to anyone, just like Krodge had always said.

"I don't understand," she cried. "None of this is real! Rel said... Rel said she would let me see her friend, the one she's been talking about. But this... This can't be real!"

The female chuckled. The sound was deep and warmed Emmy to her core. "Oh, this is real," she said. "I know Rel, and have known her for countless cycles. Rel is my friend and I am hers. I am Bomsoi. And now, Emmy, you are my friend, too."

In her terror, Emmy shook her head so hard she saw stars. "Rel!" she screeched. "What have you done to me?"

Rel wasn't there to respond. Instead, the Uloni—Bomsoi—reached for her.

"What is made cannot be unmade," she said, "but what is made can be destroyed. You are my youngling. You are my blood. And you will help me do what is right."

"How?" Emmy drew her brows low. "None of this makes sense."

Krodge's image flashed across Emmy's mind. She winced, guilt cutting her. She'd never intended to save her. It was Emmy's fault she had burned.

Another image: Bellim, consumed by flames. Leeve and Kain, truly dead. Another: the attack on the Masvam slave ship. Zecha, stabbed...

"What is this?" Emmy asked, pressing her claws to her temples. "Why are these thoughts coming back to me?"

"These are all evils," Bomsoi said. This time, remorse tainted her words. "You have done nothing wrong, but you must help to put right the wrongs of others."

Emmy went to speak, but words failed her. Without warning, the female placed her hands upon Emmy's chest, her eyes shining like blue diamonds.

"You will come to me, and you will be the Heart of Nunako. Live now so that you may live in me."

With those words, Emmy felt a jolt of air slice through her lungs. Her blood froze, cold surging through her body. Her heart exploded with a beat. She stumbled back.

Bomsoi raised her hands to the sky. Emmy wavered. Blood roared in her ears. Her mind darkened as if pitch consumed her. Her consciousness drained away, and the last thing she saw were the three moons, stacked on one another.

And they were *talking*.

◆ ◆ ◆

Emmy woke with a jolt. Rel reached to steady her. The healer's eyes were round with compassion. She still wore her half-Uloni colors.

"Rel, what was that?" Emmy asked through shuddering breaths. She clutched at her chest. "You did something to me. Your eyes, they were blue—just like the Uloni's, like your friend's. And she was there—wherever that was—and I was there, and—what?"

Her breath still coming in rolling waves, Emmy looked around. She was on Rel's cot. Jumping upward, her gaze darted to every corner, looking for the Uloni and her light.

"That was my friend," Rel said. "Bomsoi. I told you she could see things and do things that I cannot understand."

Calming, Emmy exhaled, emptying her chest of all air. Flashes of what had happened kept returning. "It's all real," she said. "The vision, Bomsoi. You. It's all real."

As she spoke, her words hit hard. This wasn't an illusion. Until now, part of her had still clung on to the idea it was all a lie. That Rel was an elaborate trickster. That Bomsoi didn't exist. But now, how could she believe that?

"It is real, Emmy," Rel said. "When the village was burned so many cycles ago, we feared there were no Uloni left. We've searched all over these lands, trying to find someone of pure Uloni blood." She shook her head. "And to think, all it took was a war to find you."

Emmy shook her head. "I'm not at war," she said. "This isn't my fight."

Rel's expression sharpened and she shook her head. One hand went to pat Haelo. "The Metakalans have fallen," she said, "and the Masvams are coming for the Althemerians. Rest assured, young one. You *are* at war and this *is* your fight."

Emmy sat back, rolling the new information around in her head She rubbed her palms over the smoothness of her surcoat, right where Bomsoi had pushed her. "Bomsoi, she said I would live in her. That I would be a heart."

"Not *a* heart, but *the* Heart," Rel said. "The Heart of Nunako."

"But—"

Emmy's protest was stopped by a thundering in the distance. They both stilled.

"Those are drums," Rel said. "The Masvams have come."

"Charo and Zecha—" Emmy began.

Her words were silenced by a high-pitched horn blast.

"Charo has been trained by Althemerians," Rel said. "Soldier-slaves may be arrow fodder, but that doesn't mean they haven't been taught to fight. And Zecha will find his way back here, I'm sure. They will survive, as will we."

She patted Haelo's sheath and stood, then held a hand to Emmy. As Emmy accepted the grasp, Rel's eyes sparkled, blue speckles piercing the grey orbs. Her appearance changed, and she wore her Belfoni mask once more. She held Emmy's hand tight.

"If the unthinkable happens and I don't return," she said, "head to Kubodinnu, the Althemerian capital. Bomsoi is there."

There was a lump like a great stone in Emmy's throat, but she nodded. "Kubodinnu," she repeated.

Rel finally released her and shifted Haelo on her belt.

Understanding dawned at what Rel had just said, and Emmy shook her head. "Wait, you're leaving?" she asked, her voice tight. "Why aren't you staying with the rest of the healers?"

"I told you I was Rel Bonebreaker before I was Hurthealer," Rel said. "I could stay here, but I'm better suited to battle than to waiting."

Fear bubbled anew in Emmy's stomach. "But..."

"If you need me," Rel said, cupping the side of Emmy's face, "call for me. Concentrate hard, and I will hear you."

Emmy brought up a hand to rest atop Rel's. "How?"

Rel gave her a one-sided smile as she withdrew her touch. "Once we know each other," she said, "Uloni can talk in each other's minds." Her smile turned into a mischievous grin. "Don't tell me you haven't heard me."

Flashes of words Emmy had thought were imagined returned to her. "That was *you?*"

"Some of the time, yes," Rel replied.

There was a sharp horn blast in the distance. It broke their companionship. Rel drew back, a hand on Haelo in her sheath. She turned. Her bracelets jangled as she slipped towards the curtain.

She stopped and half-turned. Her expression grew solemn.

"Today will not bring our deaths, Emmy," she said. "Remember: call for me."

Then she was gone.

Emmy lowered herself onto the cot again. Despite her absence, she still felt Rel was with her. The feeling was new. It was...comforting.

Then the memory of her vision returned, of the beautiful Uloni with the cracked first horn.

Closing her eyes, Emmy let the thoughts wash over her. Her mind then went to memories of Charo and Zecha and their Middlemerish celebration. It was a time, though brief, when life was tolerable.

And though she was alone, Emmy didn't feel lonely.

Bomsoi's last words returned, bolstering her courage. Emmy stood as the strange Uloni's voice sounded clear in her mind.

Live now, so that you may live in me.

CHAPTER THIRTY-NINE

Mantos

Without warning, Bomsoi snapped from her trance like a loosed arrow. She brushed her front down, nonchalant as if she'd been caught in a sudden gust of wind. Fonbir gaped. Mantos did the same.

"What in the name of the Dark just happened?" he asked.

"I had business elsewhere, Your Highness," Bomsoi replied, as if what had happened was perfectly normal. "For the longest time, I've searched for those who will rid the world of darkness. At last, just as I have found you, I have found another."

Confusion ran rampant in Mantos' mind. "Who are you really?" he asked. "None of this makes sense."

Bomsoi gave a shallow bow. "I am the Daughter of Gods," she said again. "I am the Joiner of Hands."

Mantos' jaw hung loose as the Stranger grinned at him, as if what she said was as mundane as a comment on the weather. "You're what?" he asked.

Bomsoi bent once more at the waist. She opened her hands, showing her palms. "I am the Daughter of Gods," she repeated. "I am the Joiner of Hands. You asked me who I was, and I have told you."

Mantos pressed his hands to his temples. "You cannot claim to be descended from gods and expect me to believe it," he said. He dropped his hands and tilted his chin up. "You are a Moon Rogue," he said. "You are evil."

"*Mantos!*"

Fonbir's eyes were wide as moons as he stared at Mantos for his impudence. But Mantos didn't back down.

Bomsoi laughed deeply and shook her head.

"Call me what you will," she said, "but I am not evil. Or tainted. Moon Rogues, demons, none of it means anything to me. I don't expect you to believe I am who I say I am. You asked me to tell you what exactly I am, not tell you something you would believe. And now you know."

Mouth still gaping, Mantos whirled on Fonbir. By the paleness of his face, Mantos knew the answer to his question before he asked, but he asked anyway. "Did you know this?" His voice was strained with disbelief.

"I... I did not," Fonbir said. "I knew that Bomsoi was strange and powerful, and that she brought back my sight, but I did not know she was a god."

"I am the daughter of gods," Bomsoi corrected gently. Her smile dimmed. "My descendants are descendants of gods. But I am no god."

"This is nonsense," Mantos said.

Bomsoi clasped her hands in front of her abdomen and shook her head. "It is not nonsense," she said. "It might seem senseless, but it is not *nonsense*." She paused before continuing. "I think it is time we had a long talk, you and I."

"What—?"

But Mantos' words were cut at the quick, and the next thing he knew, he was falling, falling, *falling*...

♦ ♦ ♦

Where am I?

His thoughts echoed from all directions.

Where am I?

Where am I?

Falling and falling into an endless abyss, Mantos whirled through the freezing air. Exposed skin burned with the cold, his fronds whipping up and around as he hurtled through oblivion.

And then he was on the ground again, nestled in a snow drift—yet he was no longer cold.

"Where am I?"

His words didn't return this time. Instead, he received a reply: "You are in my home."

Mantos looked up. It was Bomsoi, resplendent in sparkling robes, one hand outstretched. He allowed her to pull him upright. He stared, drinking in every detail of the icy vista.

There were sheer ice cliffs and towering evergreen trees, all dusted with glimmering snow. The sky was black, pinprick stars blinking and winking in its velvety darkness. The moons rose high above him, murmuring to each other.

"Where am I?" Mantos asked again.

When Bomsoi chuckled, the sound rumbled across the vacuous landscape. It was as though nothing was alive but them.

"You are like all princes," Bomsoi said. "You talk much and listen little. I told you where you are. You are in my home."

Feeling his face flush, Mantos snarled. "Where is your home?" he clarified.

Bomsoi's response was typically vague. "Everywhere," she said. "And nowhere."

Resisting the urge to roll his eyes, Mantos instead closed them. "Why have you brought me here?"

"I need to tell you the truth of this world," Bomsoi replied.

Opening his eyes, Mantos shook his head. He crossed a snowdrift and sat on a bank, his head reeling from the lack of cold. "But why did you bring me here, to *this* place?"

Bomsoi chuckled, the sound like chimes in the wind. "Because here I feel safe," she said. Her laughter abated and she shook her head. "Here I can tell you my story. For it begins in these mountains, where I was hatched and raised."

Mantos turned his palms upright and caught her eyes. "Then tell me," he said. "I have little choice."

Bomsoi chuckled anew, the brightness back in her voice. She glided over, making no imprint in the snow, and settled on top of the drift.

With a sigh, Bomsoi pressed a hand to his cheek. Her eyes glowed blue. When she began to speak, her lips didn't move. Instead, the words sounded inside Mantos' head.

◆ ◆ ◆

Before time existed, the goddess Meia existed. The Goddess Meia, the Grandmother of the World, existed before all things, and all things come from Her.

The Goddess poured forth her love and created the world, and all the stars and moons in the Arc of the Sky. And once She had created the world, She picked the littlest of the claws from both hands, and turned them into two young Goddesses, for whom She would have the greatest love and whom She would call Nunako and Dorai.

Nunako and Dorai split the world, each taking what they wished. While Nunako took the day, she took the moons in the night. And while Dorai took the night, she took the sun in the day. Together they were together, always intertwined.

To Nunako, the Goddess Meia gave the powers of steadfastness and determination, and sent her out to bring into existence the workings of life. To Dorai, She gave the power of lovingness and kindness, and sent her forth to cultivate and care for those to whom Nunako created.

Now Meia created for Nunako and Dorai many worlds and moons, and the two Goddesses created an abundance of life. Nunako brought forth a myriad of plants of the earth and the sea, and Dorai cared for them with loving kindness.

One day, Dorai came to Nunako and told her of a desire to create a new life, a life that could strive to understand their godly nature, with thoughts that could comprehend them and a heart that would worship them.

So, using the bounty of the land they had forged together, Nunako sent forth animals to graze on the grassy fields, to burrow in the mountains and to swim in the boundless seas. But none of these creatures were what Dorai desired. And so Nunako worked hard, and finally created a new life in their divine image.

Thus, the Younglings were born. In the youth of the new life, Nunako and Dorai walked among them. Nunako showed them how to work the earth and the seas and skies, how to tame the animals and till the fields. Dorai taught them to show loving kindness to one another and to the world, so that they would live forever in perfect harmony.

However, as with all things, this was not to last.

Soon the Younglings began to chop down more trees than they needed, to kill more animals than they could eat, and even turned on one another, forgetting the lessons their godly Mothers had taught them. As the Younglings turned their backs on the Goddesses, Nunako and Dorai found they could no longer walk the lands or sail the seas. Both Goddesses turned to one another, not knowing what to do to regain the love of their Younglings. With their power draining away, they took their littlest claws, as once Meia the Grandmother had done, to create a creature to take their place in the world.

But they did not want to risk the new goddess being powerless. A life of both goddess and flesh would surely never be banished from the world. They placed the claws in an egg and left it on the doorstep of a godly male named Aisen Lelg, who had never raised younglings of his own.

And so they waited. And eventually, the savior came to life—the One of Balance.

This new life, part god and part flesh, was to bring the Younglings back into the fold of the Goddesses. But Nunako and Dorai soon discovered that their creation had the strength of a god but the weakness of flesh, and would not do as they asked.

And so, the Goddesses came to hate each other. Enraged, both blaming the other for their failure, Nunako and Dorai turned their backs upon one another. They latched onto the false idols the Younglings carved of stone and wood, the goddesses clawing back what little power they could.

Nunako lived again as the sun goddess, the Lady of Light, bringer of brightness and scourge of evil, holding up a lantern to light the way to eternal paradise.

Dorai became the five-armed goddess of the Dark: three arms on the left and two on the right, the sixth arm torn off to shield believers from the falsehood of Nunako.

Through all of this, Meia could do nothing.

The Goddesses spread their influence, no longer corporeal but appearing in spirits and dreams, commanding the Younglings to build towers and shrines and altars—for the more the Younglings worshipped them, the more powerful they became.

Nunako and Dorai became drunk on their power, demanding more and more. And Meia could only watch and weep.

The One of Balance should have cleared the world of hate, but she did not. She retreated to the mountains and made her own folk, and she did not venture down for many centuries. Not until the Grandmother of the World showed her the thread that was about to unravel.

What has been made cannot be unmade, she told her, but what has been made can be *destroyed.*

♦ ♦ ♦

By the time Bomsoi removed her hand, she was weeping. Unable to stop himself, Mantos placed a hand on her shoulder. For all he'd distrusted her, her grief was palpable, and her story rang true.

"Bomsoi," he began.

"Yes." Tears spilled down her chin. "That is my name. Bomsoi. The One of Balance. But I did not do what I was hatched to do." Her voice took on a razor's edge of rage. "I turned away. I ran. I fled. I could not bear the burden that was placed upon my shoulders, the burden to bring peace to this world. But my cowardice has caused the deaths of so many, of nearly all my folk. And now I must make amends for my weakness. I must do as I was bid and bring balance." She turned her blazing eyes upon him. They were twin blue flames. "And to do that, I need you."

"Me?" Mantos said, withdrawing his hand as if he'd been burned. "Why me?"

"Because your brother meddled with powers he doesn't understand," she said. "He has unleashed the power of Dorai unto himself. He has declared himself the One of Two. It is only a matter of time before his mangled spirit pollutes the goddess. He has taken on the Goddess' power, but he will use it for his own evil gains." Bomsoi clasped her claws together. "But you, Mantos, you are not like him. Even though you were sired together, hatched together, raised together, just like Nunako and Dorai, you are good in your bones. *You* are the One of Two."

Mantos stood and paced away. Then he whirled around, his fronds and tail spinning in his wake. "And what would you have me do? Kill Bandim? Kill my brother, who has become a goddess?"

"He is not a goddess," Bomsoi said, standing again, "but he is corrupt, and has a corrupted Heart. Power will consume him and turn him into a mangled monster, with no hope of redemption. Your brother will unleash an evil on this world that we have never known, and we will not be able to stop it."

Barking a laugh, Mantos shook his head. "Why not? Why can you not stop him? You seem to know a lot about him and his machinations." He jabbed a talon at Bomsoi. "You are the daughter of gods. You are the one to stop him."

"Were it that simple, I would have done so already," Bomsoi said. Each word was laced with sorrow. "Were it that simple, I surely would. But I cannot. I need you. That is why I brought you from the brink of death. I *need* you."

The desperation in her voice echoed into the expanse. Mantos took a pace forward. He tilted his chin in defiance. "What would you have me do?" he asked again.

The pause that followed made his neck scales unfurl.

"I would have you take on the mantle of Nunako," Bomsoi said. "You must become the Hand."

Eyes bulging, Mantos' mouth went dry. "You would have me become a goddess so that I might kill my brother, also a goddess?" he scoffed. "You say my brother is possessed by a mangled spirit. How do you know that would not happen to me?"

Bomsoi padded down the bank towards him. For the first time, he noticed her feet were bare.

"Because the Heart I have for you is strong and brave and pure," she said. "You would not turn from your path."

"You mean like you did?" Mantos snapped, ignoring the strangeness of her words.

Bomsoi winced. "You would not turn from your path," she said. "Not like me."

A thousand thoughts raced through Mantos' mind. "How can you expect me to do as you ask?" he asked. "None of this makes sense. It could all be a trick of the Dark."

Bomsoi stepped forward again and shook her head. "There is no Dark," she said. "There is no Light. There are only choices."

To that, Mantos had an answer. But before he could give it, the half-god, half-flesh creature fell on her knees before him. She supplicated herself with a bent head.

"Please, Mantos of House Tiboli. If you cannot do it for me, do it for your brother. And if you cannot do it for your brother, do it for your beloved mother, who has suffered so much for so long at the hands of poor decisions. And if you cannot do it for her, do it for Fonbir, whom you yearn to spend the rest of your days with."

To that, Mantos had no answer. His throat tightened. His talons clenched. He closed his eyes.

What was he to do?

CHAPTER FORTY

Emmy

As the battle drew closer, Emmy's whole body shook. Medicine-Asri crouched in a corner of the main hall, hugging himself against the vicious jaws of battle. Medicine-Yarim disappeared into her alcove, as if the flimsy curtains would protect her. Those patients that had remained and were able cowered under their cots. Those that were insensible lay still, oblivious to everything.

Most of the cots had been cleared and lay empty, awaiting new casualties. At least, Emmy hoped they'd see new casualties. As macabre as that seemed, it was either that, or the building would be destroyed. Then they would all be dead.

Inside the building there was silence, broken only by the occasional sob. Outside was different. There had been nothing but drums and horns in the distance for some time. But now the first sounds of battle drew closer. Emmy's heart stuttered.

Her friends were out there. Charo was fighting on the front line of a war that was not her own, a freed slave enslaved again.

The enemy edged closer and closer. Emmy gripped the handles of her daggers as the sound of cannon fire boomed ever louder.

She thought of Zecha, wherever he was. He hadn't returned to the healers' building as Rel had said, but instead was still out there following Althemerian command. Hopefully he was somewhere safe.

Emmy's neck scales flexed as the cacophony drew ever closer, bringing her mind from her friends to herself. Drums beat and beat. The air was discordant with the sound of the fallen. Soon they would know the silence of death.

Emmy trembled harder as shadows danced against the walls. She thought of Rel, of her words.

If you need me, call for me. Concentrate hard, and I will hear you.

Rel the Bonebreaker was out there somewhere, a fearsome beast wielding Haelo, felling foes all around, coating her right arm in kills. *Please come back to me, Rel*, Emmy thought. *Too much has happened. There's so much I need to know. And...you're my friend. I need you to come back to me.*

The battle raged too close now. Emmy's mouth was dry. Her heart was in her throat.

The Masvams were upon them, the battle cacophonous in her ears. Screams and screeches grew louder. The sobbing of the healers, protected only by soldiers outside and the walls around them, became ragged with terror.

Rel, and Rel's friend. Bomsoi, Emmy thought, *please protect me. Please protect us all!*

Emmy leapt backward and screeched as the main door splintered, raining wooden shards in all directions.

A Masvam burst through, his breath chest heaving with rage. The first thing he laid eyes upon was Emmy. His face was a dark leer, his eyes black with the fury of battle. He dripped with blood.

The single face struck white-hot terror into Emmy's heart. She knew it was too late. She knew she was gone, even before the Masvam cast his first blow. There was no hope.

"Easy prey!" he screeched.

His call summoned a hoard of fellow soldiers like a dark enchantment. Masvam warriors swallowed up the healers' building,

Before Emmy could run, a sword swung so close to her face she could taste the metal. She leapt backwards, only a frond's breadth separating her life from death. The Masvams bellowed, further overwhelming the building like a bloody wave.

Instinct overtook her. Clenching her daggers, a feral shriek built in Emmy's chest. Determination roared red in her heart.

She swung her weapons in a wide arc and her attackers were forced back. But the victory was momentary. Undeterred, two Masvams lunged forward with their terrifying scimitars. Emmy dropped a dagger and held up a hand, her eyes closed so tightly that moons danced in the darkness. *Stop!* she thought. *Blades, stop!* She envisioned the scimitars stilling, mid-strike. If only such wishes would work.

Now, all she had left was the brief wait before death.

But something happened.

The strange power pulsed through her, the sensation rattling her to her bones. Like when Rel touched her, she was consumed with a stark coldness.

The scimitars stopped dead, motionless in the air, hovering in a cocoon of blueness. The Masvams stared with dumb mouths.

"Moon Rogue," one said. His voice lifted to a shriek. "Moon Rogue, it is!"

That word jolted Emmy from her anger. She stared at the weapons hanging in mid-air, the absence of rage giving way to utter confusion.

"What?" she whispered, breaking her gaze to stare at her hands. She dropped her other dagger. Concentration broken, the scimitars lost their blue and fell to the ground like stones. Emmy's mouth gaped. "How is this *possible*?"

But there was no time to ponder.

"Kill it!"

"Tainted!"

"Moon Rogue, kill it!"

The screeching Masvam swept in, swinging at Emmy's neck with a new blade. Emmy ducked away, shrieking, but wasn't fast enough to dodge a second attack. The aim was off, but the blade caught her arm, slicing her armor.

Emmy whirled away with a shriek, and as she did, her tail collided with a brazier. The hot coals tumbled from their resting place, onto a nearby empty cot. They embraced the rough blankets, which burst into flame.

Within seconds, bright red tongues shot upward. A Masvam, caught by the sudden fire, tried to flee it. He stumbled sideways, knocking another cot into the flames. The fire took it quickly and soon it leapt up the walls, consuming the beams. It licked and bit and spat, belching smoke, burning what seemed impossible to burn.

The Masvams kept fighting through the fire, but more were caught in the blaze. They howled, wrapped in a blanket of flame. Others called to its power.

"Moon Rogue!" a Masvam cried. "Let it burn!"

Emmy's breath came in strangled gasps as she choked and guttered, turning and turning, looking for a way out. The once-familiar building was now a black maze of confusion. She saw nothing. There was only the heat of the blaze. In desperation, she swung wildly with her hands.

I refuse to die today! I refuse to die today! she chanted. *Rel, Bomsoi, whoever you are, help me!*

Death came at her head-on as a Masvam in blood-lust raised his sword above her.

"Moon Rogue!"

Emmy couldn't stop the blade. There was no cold power this time. All she could hear was the rush of blood in her ears, the clang of metal on metal, and the screeches of battle and death all around. Her nostrils filled with the stench of burning building and blood. Heat and smoke and fear choked her.

She waited for the killing stroke.

The Masvam jerked forward. His eyes widened, and his arms stilled before he had the chance to strike. Emmy stumbled away, flames licking all around. When her streaming eyes focused, her heart stopped. The point of a sword jutted through the Masvam's chest. Blood bubbled from his lips and Emmy leapt aside as his body slumped forward. The blade that had come so close to ending her life clattered to the ground. Emmy looked at it and then up again.

Who had saved her?

Charo grinned, standing over the body with a bloodied sword. Zecha, at her side—bedecked with a bow and quiver he got from who knew where—smiled fiercely.

"You're both alive!" Emmy breathed, coughing through the smoke.

Her friends grabbed her uninjured arm, twirling her from the path of another sword. With a skill akin to a hero of old stories, Charo parried the strike and slew another foe, her right arm growing heavier with kills. Zecha swirled and unleashed arrows at impossibly short range, his arm reaching to his quiver so fast Emmy couldn't even see it. His would be another heavy arm.

"Stay close!" Charo commanded.

Her throat tight and her hands empty, Emmy did as she was told. Masvams bore down on them, and even the defenses of Charo and Zecha began to crumble. There were too many attackers and soon they were backed together, a three-petaled flower of green and red and blue, surrounded by glinting blades.

Emmy tried to block the terror of the roaring flames.

Why is this happening? she thought. *Why must life be so cruel? Why must we suffer such torment?*

The same cold power grew again, like vines snaking over her skin. Focusing, she tried to harness whatever the strangeness was. She thought of Rel and her glowing eyes, of her blue coldness. She thought of Rel's friend.

Bomsoi, help me! Emmy pleaded. *I don't know who you are, but I'll do whatever you need. What am I supposed to do? How can I save myself and my friends?*

Blue and jagged spirits swirled around her. Coldness consumed her, tracking her body like frost. The power was breathtaking. Rel's influence shone forth brightly. Emmy could see her in her mind's eye, powering towards them, cutting down Masvams as she passed.

"I am coming, Emmy! I promise, you will not perish!"

The words were so clear in her ears, it was like Rel was with her.

Emmy lifted her hands to the moons. Unadulterated power pulsed through her. Everything shone bright and blue as the noon sky. Succumbing to it, brightness and might pulsed to Emmy's very core.

Dato, I am small, but make me brave, she thought. *Rafa, give your strength to my heart. Akata, give me speed and give me the wisdom to know what is right. By the Goddess, help me!*

Everything stopped.

Every flame stilled, shining blue like shards of ice. Emmy counted her breaths. *One, two, three...* In the stillness, she could feel everything. Charo and Zecha's hearts beat in time with one another, together like stacked moons. Their thoughts echoed, the words unclear but the tones undoubtedly theirs. They dropped their weapons, claws slack.

"What—?"

Emmy crossed her arms over her chest. A jolt of energy burst from within her, the power of the moons flowing through her. It shot up like a lightning strike. The building's roof disintegrated, and power lifted her until she was suspended high in the air, hanging between reality and disbelief.

Around her, Masvams and Althemerians alike screamed.

"Moon Rogue! Moon Rogue! *Evil!*"

She could taste their terror as they fled through shards of fire. The words echoed. *Moon Rogue. Moon Rogue. Evil.*

Emmy's eyes snapped open, and she grinned. *Perhaps I am a Moon Rogue after all.*

The Masvams fled. With their enemies' backs turned, the Althemerians broke from their stupor and pursued their enemies with bloodied blades.

Emmy's victorious grin wavered, however, as a Masvam appeared before her, surrounded by a halo of flame. The vision flickered in and out as if he was a shadow. He was regal, bedecked with horn jewelry. His claws, covered in many rings, reached out for her. Fire cast from his fingertips. When he spoke, his mouth did not move.

"*Who...are...you?*"

His voice was strangled, as if her power constrained him. She didn't know who he was, but she knew he was not of the Light.

Emmy spoke without moving her lips. Gesturing to her frozen flames, she grinned again. A confidence she hadn't known before molded her words.

"I am Emmy," she said, "and I will help to stop you."

Anger consumed the male in the vision. His halo of fire flared, though the vision began to fade. His words echoed as he disappeared.

"*The Dark will prevail!*"

"Not if I can help it," Emmy replied.

Then he was gone.

Suddenly, fatigue fell heavy on Emmy's shoulders. Her power waned. She returned to the ground, her entire body aching with the effort of what she'd done. The words she'd spoken came back to her, and she shook her head. Could that have been her? Simple, strange, nobody Emmy?

Time for introspection was impossible.

Rel appeared at her side, having fought through waves of retreating Masvams. Zecha and Charo were with her too. They didn't run, but lingered back. They were trembling, looking at her with a fear that had never been there before. Emmy's stomach sank.

"What... What is this?" Charo whispered. "Emmy, *what?*"

Emmy shivered. The absence of the strange power left her empty. Alone. The vision of the Masvam haunted her, as did his words.

The Dark will prevail!

"I..." Emmy started, but she couldn't finish.

Rel sheathed Haelo, then planted firm hands on Emmy's shoulders. "What happened?" she asked.

"I don't know," Emmy said. "I asked Bomsoi for help, and..." She broke off, suppressing a sob. "I don't know, Rel!"

Rel pulled her in for a brief hug, then withdrew.

In that moment, Emmy blinked and stared at the carnage around her. Masvams still retreated, disappearing in harried waves. But not all the Althemerians pursued them. Some half-turned, their eyes fixed on Emmy, glinting in the light of the frozen flame.

She knew that look too well. She knew what they would say before any of them moved.

They kissed their fists and tapped them to their chests, a sign to ward off evil. A burly female with a heavy right arm raised her sword in a point, a long extension of her ire. "Moon Rogue!"

Another female, with blood crusting at her temples, spat onto the churned earth. "Evil!" she called. "May Ethay and Apago forgive you for your sin!"

Emmy stepped forward, away from the safe bower of Rel. Indignation rose bright and hot in her throat. She knew her words were futile, but she couldn't hold them in. "I saved your lives!" she said. "How can that be a sin?"

Althemerians encroached, creeping like hunters encroaching on prey. The line of retreating Masvam backs thinned as the Althemerians moved forward. Emmy pointed over their heads. "I've driven the Masvams away," she continued. "I'm not evil!"

Still the Althemerians slunk forward, weapons held at the ready. It would only be a matter of moments before one's fear snapped, and then they would all be upon her.

Rel grabbed Emmy's elbow and pulled her back. She gathered Charo and Zecha to her, cocooning the three friends in her strength.

"It's time for us to leave before they kill us all," she said. "Consider your Althemerian debts repaid. Now, come!"

She pulled them all backward.

"Where are we going?" Zecha asked, his words half-muffled in Rel's grip. But at Charo's sharp look, he said no more.

The air was thick with the stench of smoke and blood. The sounds of the dying pierced the air. They cut to Emmy's core. Her job was to help, to heal, not to run. But the Althemerian soldiers encroached, faster now, all weapons poised to slice Emmy's throat.

Rel propelled Charo and Zecha forward and they fled for their lives, as fast as their legs could run. Rel grabbed Emmy's arm and thrust her forward, wrenching her gaze from the Masvams.

"We must leave," Rel said. "They'll kill you. They'll kill us all!"

The truth broke Emmy's hesitation. It didn't matter that she'd saved them. It was how she'd done it. In their eyes, she was a Moon Rogue. There was no redemption from that.

Nodding, Emmy broke into a sprint, and soon was close on the heels of Zecha and Charo. Rel was just behind her. Just behind Rel was an encroaching mass of righteous Althemerians.

"One day things will change," Rel panted as she ran, "but not today. Now, hold onto me!"

Rel, her Belfoni mask shedding, grabbed Emmy's arm in a vice grip. Immediately, they were enveloped in freezing wind. They rushed forward, Rel gathering Charo and Zecha within her influence. All four lifted from the ground, carried upward on burnished silver wings of wind and cold and power.

The burning camp below them disappeared as they rose into the air. The righteous fury of the Althemerians faded away, replaced by the solace of the sky.

"What's happening?" Charo cried.

But Emmy had no words to explain. She said nothing, instead imbibing the sudden joy of their flight.

Enveloped in Rel's wings, they made their escape.

CHAPTER FORTY-ONE

Bandim

Standing on the grand balcony, right upon the spot where his brother had died with Johrann beside him, Bandim held his hands aloft and concentrated hard. Many parties of his troops sailed for Althemer and he, Dorai, was determined to be at their side. Once he'd mastered the making of a flame, the rest came easily.

His eyes were open, but they saw more than the city surrounding him. His vision leapt from flame to flame, across the sea in lanterns and into the heart of Althemerians' very homes. Anywhere there was fire he could see, though the time spent watching taxed him greatly. His body was too much of the flesh, but it was a sacrifice Dorai had been forced to make to return to the world. Soon, she would reclaim everything Nunako took from her. Nunako, with her claws that built the world. Nunako, so perfect.

Nunako, so *pure*.

Rage rose within Bandim, and he balled his claws into fists. The Goddess' rage was mighty.

All Dorai had wanted was to love the folk. All she had wanted was to be loved in return. But they had turned their backs on her, not listening to her Truth, allowing her to fade away to nothing more than a wisp of smoke on the wind.

Not even the One of Balance could return their love. Bandim's lips pulled into a snarl. What an idea of Nunako's that had been. Something of the goddess and something of the flesh, melded into the worst of both worlds.

Thus, when the One of Two and the True Believer had asked her to return, and their hands and hearts were so fiery, so pure... How could a goddess resist?

Now she was in the body of the Hand. Bandim. Fiery was indeed the word to describe him. But there were qualities she didn't savor in this vessel. Weaknesses that could easily be picked at, like claws at a scab. They needed to be expunged as swiftly as possible.

But these things took time. At least he was learning the ways of the flame.

Bandim's vision jumped from lantern to lantern, across the Sea of Souls to the Althemerian shore. More and more of his troops set their boots on enemy soil. On a whim, he followed their flames south, leaping all the way to somewhere akin to a prison camp. His heart thundering in anticipation, Bandim leapt from fire to fire until a sudden burst of flame drew his full attention.

He followed it inside a building. A hospital, perhaps. Whatever it was, it was aflame.

Fire burst from a fallen brazier, consuming the canvas and rough blankets of a well-worn bunk. Feeling bold, Bandim stoked the flame, pushing it from cot to cot, up and down walls and beams until the whole building was alight. Ecstasy consumed him as he spread scorching destruction around his victorious warriors.

Then it all changed.

Then there was cold. His wondrous flames *froze*.

Disbelief threatened to knock him back to the reality of the balcony but Dorai's strength surged. Bandim's gaze remained in the battle—and he couldn't believe what he saw.

An Uloni, just like Johrann.

But she'd said they were all dead.

Not only was it an Uloni, but it was one wielding enough power to freeze his flames.

Bandim's will almost gave out, but Dorai kept him strong. She bolstered his frailty, pushing him beyond anything he'd achieved so far. Flickering in and out like a dancing shadow, she passed him through the fabric of her magic, surrounding him in flames.

Bandim reached for the Uloni, flames bursting from his fingertips. He spoke, but his lips remained closed. He had eyes only for her. "Who...are...you?"

His voice was strangled, as if her power constrained him. Whoever she was, she wasn't of the Dark. But she was strong enough to make Dorai waver, and that was unacceptable.

The Uloni also spoke without moving her lips, the confidence in her voice terrifying.

"I am Emmy," the Uloni said, "and I will help stop you."

Anger consumed Bandim. His grip on Dorai slipped, and his vision flickered. Try as he might, he could not remain, but he screamed one final time before he lost his hold entirely.

His words echoed as he disappeared.

"The Dark will prevail!"

Flung back onto the balcony, Bandim fell to his knees. Guards rushed to help, their fear surging, but he shoved them away. Agony and weariness consumed him. Bandim stumbled in an arc, heading towards the grand doors into the palace. He forced himself to uncurl his aching back and walk to his chambers. An emperor didn't crawl. Johrann followed on his heels.

As soon as they were in his rooms, Bandim fell to his knees once more. What had happened? How was it possible there was another Uloni? How was it possible she could match him in his power? *How?*

Shaking off Johrann's touch, Bandim crept to his grand dressing table, resplendent with bottles and boxes of the finest perfume and paints. Exhaustion overwhelming him, it took his every effort to pull himself onto the velvet-covered stool.

His trembling claws picked up a handplate. He looked at his reflection. The embers of his frustration smoldered.

He screeched. "How has this happened?"

Enraged, he swept his arm across the table, sending the bottles and boxes flying in a hurricane of fury. The handplate clattered to the stone floor.

His shoulders rising and falling in a ragged rhythm, Bandim turned to Johrann. Her grey eyes, cast away from him, were flat. But he knew they hid fear.

She took a deep breath before she spoke. "I—I did not foresee this."

Keeping his temper at bay, Bandim bent one claw in a gesture for her to come to him. She did as she was told and stopped just in front of him, keeping her hands clasped and her head bowed.

Leaping upward like flame through kindling, Bandim pulled back his hand and struck her full in the face. "Clearly not!" he snarled. "If you had, perhaps this would not have happened!"

Johrann stumbled backward, her hands on her bruised cheek

"What was this strange occurrence?" Bandim demanded, stalking forward. "It's not possible to freeze flame! Only a goddess could do such a thing, and *I* am the only goddess. I am Dorai!"

His throat tightened with every word, as if each one strengthened a stranglehold.

"I did not think it was possible," Johrann began, "but..."

She trailed off and looked away. Bandim's eyes bulged. He thrust his hand out to catch her chin and squeezed.

Eyes widening, Johrann tried to pull away, but Bandim was too strong. His nostrils flared and his neck scales rose.

"What secret are you keeping?" he asked. When Johrann looked away again, he screamed. "Answer me!"

Johrann licked her trembling lips and looked everywhere except at his gaze.

"You are the Hand of Dorai," she said. "You will grow to know your powers. But it is not as simple as taking upon the Goddess' mantle and ruling anew." She sucked in a deep breath, as if steeling herself to reveal a great secret. "There was another reason I advised you to let me kill your brother. It wasn't simply that he was a step to climb over to gain the crown. There's more to it."

Cold unease churned in Bandim's stomach. Johrann took another shuddering breath.

"By bringing Dorai into this world, I opened a conduit from the spirit realm," she said. "The power of the moons was diminished as they spoke to one another, but now that they are free again, their power is renewed. There is a chance that, just as you have taken on Dorai, someone will take on Nunako." She paused, eyes glimmering. "There's only one likely choice for that. Nunako and Dorai were created together, from the claws of Meia. You were not created alone. You are not the only One of Two."

His blood running cold, Bandim's back stiffened. His tail twitched. Rage flared anew. "Mantos."

Johrann tried to nod, but Bandim's grip was too strong.

"Yes. Mantos. I took his life, but perhaps..." She broke off, shaking her head. She twisted her hands together, her shoulders shaking as if something terrible was dawning upon her. "There's no guarantee that he's alive, and even if he is, that he would become the Hand of Nunako. He would need a Heart to do so."

"But you're the last of your kind," Bandim said. "You told me so yourself. There cannot be another Heart. Mantos must be dead. You told me that feeling his presence in my dreams was nothing but my past life infringing on my present." His words tumbled out faster and faster as he went on, and his grip on her face grew tighter until she whimpered. "And, in any case, the only one who can harness the power of the goddess is you. You told me that yourself!"

Those last words were flinty with accusation. Biting her lip, Johrann nodded.

"I did," she said. "But I didn't know there was another Uloni. I never believed there could be, but there have always been rumors. Apocryphal tales. That the One of Balance is still corporeal, that she walks this land, eternally searching for her kind. She... She could know things. She might feel my intentions. If she knew, she could have acted. If she has found another of her kind, she might have a second Heart."

Bandim finally released her. He shook his head, disbelief surging through him.

"It's not possible," he said. "My father searched and searched, and no news of someone of your colors ever returned. He sent troops into the Great Northern Range, and they found no evidence of your folk—the Uloni. He had talons in all corners of the land. He wanted them, wanted to harness their power for his own gains. Had the One of Balance been alive, he would have found her."

"I don't know," Johrann whispered. "I simply don't know."

Stalking forward, Bandim grabbed her shoulders and rammed her against the nearest wall. Her talons scrabbled against the stone, and she keened in terror.

"Not knowing isn't good enough!" Bandim said. His insides churned and swirled, and a pyre built in his belly. "You're supposed to be my advisor. You're supposed to know everything about the spirit world and the goddess. You're supposed to be the last Uloni. You're supposed to be my Heart. *How* could you *not* know?"

The tips of his talons grew hotter and hotter. Johrann whimpered as her skin sizzled. Smoke rose from Bandim's hands as the power of Dorai coursed through him, down to his bones. The smell of burning fabric and flesh consumed him. "You are supposed to know everything!" he cried.

Johrann wailed, the screech ear-piercing, as her shoulders burned. "Please, stop! *Stop!*"

Her sudden pleading shocked him, and Bandim stumbled back. His gaze flicked from the fear in her eyes to the smoking wounds on her body. His talons had scorched even her armor. Her flesh still smoked. Bandim stared at the tips of his fingers. They glowed like embers.

"You will help me find this Uloni," he said. "She's somewhere on Althemer. We need to kill her." He turned away, but half-turned back. "And you should hope that my brother truly is dead. If he isn't, those wounds on your shoulders will be the least of your pains. Now get out!"

With tears streaming from her glimmering eyes, Johrann turned tail and fled. The chamber door slammed behind her, and Bandim was left alone.

Yet truly, he was not alone. He was never alone.

Dorai curled within him like a flame, coiling in rage. If her wretched daughter, the One of Balance, was still roaming the world, she would soon cleave her head from her shoulders. And if the mangled spirit of Nunako managed to crawl from her hole and into the world, it wouldn't matter how strong her Hand or her Heart were.

Dorai was all-powerful.

Dorai could not be stopped.

CHAPTER FORTY-TWO

Emmy

It was still early when Emmy roused. Her bones protested from a night on the unforgiving ground, curled in the roots of a blackblood tree. She felt like she could sleep for days. Stretching, she rubbed her eyes. Her injured arm throbbed as she struggled to her feet.

The little group had put as much ground between themselves and the Hutukeshu—and the angry Althemerians—as they could, eventually coming to rest in a small glade in a deep wood. The army wouldn't be looking for them, for they had more pressing matters to attend to—like a Masvam invasion. Despite this, there was a tightness to Emmy's throat. In spite of everything, she felt she should have stayed behind to help the wounded.

But she hadn't, and there was no going back.

A cool breeze blew through the morning calm. Charo and Zecha curled into one another under the protection of the tree, their limbs entwined and their breath in sync. Rel's eyes were closed, though she sat upright with her back against the rough bark of the tree. Grateful as she was that they survived, Emmy couldn't help but wonder what would happen next. What would Rel have her do? How different would life become—again?

Those questions were too complicated for the dewy morning, and the throbbing pain in her arm took too much of her attention anyway. Pulling up her sleeve, Emmy winced. The slice in her armor was long, and surrounded by a crust of blood. Underneath, her skin was hot and bulging. *I need to clean this before it gets poisoned.*

Emmy rose and walked to the edge of the glade, her boots and bare ankles soaked by dew. It took only a few moments to pluck up what she needed. Wide leaves from a wild sicklestem plant would cover the wound, and the tiniest amount of the same leaf, crushed to release the juice, would help with the pain. A strip of fabric from the bottom of her tunic would serve to bind it. As satisfied with her work as she could be, Emmy grunted and wandered back over to her friends. Before she made it, something caught her attention.

Another tree, huge and gnarled, stood across the glade. Its branches reached into the brightening morning. Above it, a thin covering of cloud drowsed high in the sky, gradually burning as the sun rose.

As she looked at the tree, she imagined how far back its memory would stretch and what stories it could tell her. The time since she'd left Bellim had passed in an instant, yet in some ways, it felt like no time had passed at all. It was so strange, Emmy thought. Everything was strange.

She laid her hands on the tree. It was a twistwart, famed for its unique trunk that grew in a spiral. Emmy knew its many medicinal purposes. She'd used its bark often in her time as Krodge's apprentice. Until now, she'd never seen one planted in the earth.

Her time as Krodge's apprentice. It made it seem like it was cycles ago, but it wasn't. It was barely longer ago than her time in the camp.

The memory of the battle at the encampment echoed in her mind. The surge and burst of power, the tingling of the impossible at the tips of her talons. She had never felt so...alive. So powerful. The events had shattered her existence, and turned her understanding of the world on its head.

Everything had changed. Even Emmy.

She grabbed a low bough and planted her booted feet onto its bark. Arms and legs moving of their own accord, she climbed.

Under the sicklestem leaf, the ache of her wound abated. Before Emmy knew it, she was at the top of the tree, nestled carefully on a curved bough. She sat for some time in the twistwart's embrace, feeling the soft breeze, watching as the orange ball of the sun rose through the morning haze.

The quiet was broken by a rustling from below. The bustling grew louder as Rel hauled herself into the upper boughs with her strong arms. She settled on the branch just below Emmy's and gave her a tired smile.

"We're alive because of you," Rel said. "You should be proud of what you did. You're beginning to realize who you truly are."

Rel still shed the façade of the Belfoni, embracing her blue and purple, but her face was drawn with a weariness Emmy hadn't seen before. Using her powers seemed as much a burden as a blessing.

Emmy slid across her bough, leaving space for Rel if she chose to climb further. The tree creaked under her weight. "Rel," she asked in a low voice, "are you all right?"

With a slow nod, Rel smiled. She pulled herself onto Emmy's branch, sitting close beside her. "Don't worry. I'm fine."

Emmy shook her head, pulling her eyeridges low. "You're not fine," she said. "You look exhausted." Emmy gestured at the slumbering figures of Zecha and Charo, curled together under the protection of a low-slung tree. "We all are. None of us are fine."

Emmy gripped the rough surface of the branch that held her snug and safe in the treetop.

"We'll be better when we to get to Bomsoi," Rel replied. She let out a sudden chuckle. The sound carried into the distance. "She's a strange creature, and for all the time I have known her, I still cannot comprehend her. But we'll be safe with her, so we must go to her."

Emmy looked to the sky. The last sliver of Dato sank below the horizon. Rafa and Akata were nearly gone. The light of the sun sent a yellow wave through the blueness of the sky.

"Yes, we must," Emmy said at length. "I'm not sure if I want to, but I don't think I have a choice."

"You do have a choice," Rel said, shifting on her branch. Her eyes were soft and round. "You've already made it. And as long as I draw breath, I will be by your side to help you."

Emmy resisted the urge to reach across and embrace the other female. And then she stopped resisting, because there was no good reason *not* to embrace Rel. *We've been through so much together,* she thought. *We're friends.*

Rel returned the hug, and wound her fingers through Emmy's thick black fronds. She smelled of worn leather and blood, but it was the most comforting scent Emmy had ever smelled.

"I'm glad I found you," Rel said. "Yet, at the same time, I..."

She tilted her head upwards. Her pupils grew small in the light. Emmy licked her lips and blinked. "What are you thinking?" she asked.

"I am thinking," Rel replied, still staring up at the sky, "that I don't know exactly what I've found you for." She broke her gaze and passed a hand over the side of Emmy's face, slow and comforting. "I know, at least, that it's not for something simple. It's not for something safe. And now that I've found you and I know you, I am afraid for you."

"Afraid?" Emmy asked. "*You?* I didn't think you could feel fear."

With a brief smile, Rel patted Emmy's cheek. "Of course I feel fear," she said, "but I tell myself to fear nothing when I know it will consume me. To be paralyzed by fear is to be vulnerable. But to believe there is nothing to be feared is foolish."

Embracing Rel once more, Emmy nodded into her shoulder. "That makes sense," she said. "How did you become so wise, Rel?"

"Anyone can be wise," came the reply, "if they choose to look beyond the edge of their own experience."

They stayed in the tree for some time, bound together as the sun rose. Emmy drowsed, images of her sixteen cycles floating through her half-sleep. Dreams with Zecha. The sweetness of a friendship with Charo. Fights with Krodge and Bose.

Medicine-Yarim, Medicine-Asri, Drenna Haldra, and all the others she'd known in the encampment. She thought of her old self, angry and outcast, furious at everything, always ready to snap. She'd been helpless. Powerless.

But that life was over. Now she was someone else.

Finished it off, I did.

"Now, come," Rel said, pressing a kiss to the top of Emmy's head. "It's time for us to journey on. We must get to Kubodinnu."

Emmy didn't say anything. A shudder passed through her, as if she'd been dipped in icy water. But it wasn't an unpleasant cold or a feeling of adrift hopelessness.

No. It was a feeling of control.

CHAPTER FORTY-THREE

Mantos

As the day wound on, the sky opened. A deluge of rain like nothing Mantos had ever seen poured down. The silver drops hammered against the courtyard below, drenching any palace servant who dared venture out. From the open window, he stared at the specks that scurried across the square. The fountain spurted uselessly in the storm. The temple chanting was barely audible above the thunderous rain. Mantos didn't care that the wind sent curtains of it into his face. He still watched.

Somewhere in the distance, wind chimes fluttered in the storm. The sound was hollow. It was desperate.

Just like Mantos.

He could think of nothing but the words Bomsoi had said to him. Her voice plagued his mind, insidious in its penetration. He was swept away by memory, back into the strange place of snow and ice that Bomsoi had brought him to.

"I would have you take on the mantle of Nunako," she had said. "You must become the Hand."

Mantos tried to claw out of his memories. He blinked against another barrage of raindrops. The front of his tunic was drenched.

Bomsoi would have him be the Hand of Nunako. The One of Two, the same as his brother, a match in machinations, in order to stop him. Bandim was bent on destruction and desolation, of reclaiming the world and molding it in his own image. To stop him, Mantos knew Bomsoi would have him take Bandim's life before he could strike a dark blow.

Thunder rolled in the distance, and the rain continued to pour.

It was easy for Bomsoi to tell him to become something he wasn't. It was easy for her to suggest he become part-goddess, for that she already was. But she didn't know any better than him. She couldn't know what it meant to be mere flesh and blood. How could she understand?

Though Bomsoi seemed to think she knew him well. "You would not turn from your path," she had said. "Not like me."

Snorting, Mantos leaned out, letting the raindrops pound his face. Their coldness blunted the edge of his pain. How wrong she was, he thought. How utterly wrong.

For of course, Mantos had already strayed from his path.

His Imperial Majesty, Sole Ruler of the Masvam Empire, Protector of the Realm, Conqueror of Heathens, Scorcher of Souls, son of Braslen Tiboli, grandson of Maram Tiboli, Emperor Mantos Tiboli.

The words that were never spoken sounded back at him, said in every voice but his own. Remembering the last words of his father, Mantos shuddered.

You must lead the empire to new glories.

There was no glory now. There was no leadership. There was only the clipped sting of shame that burned his insides. Instead of leading his folk, he'd sold their secrets to a queendom that was his father's enemy.

An unanswered question sounded loud in his mind. This time, the voice was his own.

How can I command an empire if I cannot keep my own house in order?

Mantos snorted. He never needed the answer to that question, never got the chance to command an empire. Perhaps it was for the best. He wouldn't have succeeded, not in the way his father wanted. Not in the way they all expected.

Not *all*, perhaps.

His mother didn't seem to think grabbing every scrap of land was the most important part of ruling an empire. But then, she'd never been empress, not really. She'd barely even lived. His mother didn't make good choices, he thought. That much was clear.

What mother would abandon both her sons to save the life of one? Mantos may have lived, but it was at the expense of Bandim's mind. Chest tightening, Mantos gulped in a breath. The riddle of whether his life was worth that price was unsolvable, like a puzzle missing a piece.

His life was now twice-saved. He could almost feel the freezing prints of death's grasp on his throat. *Twice-saved with nothing to show for it*, he thought. *What a waste.*

He pulled his head from the storm at the sound of a knock. Permission to enter given, the door opened. It was Fonbir, who pulled away his veil and smiled. But his mouth gaped as he took in the sodden mess Mantos had become. "What are you doing?" he asked as he bustled in. "Were you hanging out of the window?"

On another day, Mantos might have chuckled at Fonbir's fond clucking. But today he didn't. Instead, he shrugged. "I was," he said. "I thought the rain might clear my head."

"A soaking will do nothing but make you ill," Fonbir said. "You must change your clothes."

On another day, Mantos might have laughed and pulled Fonbir into an embrace, or spun him across the floor, teasing him with his eyes. But he didn't. Those days were in the letters they'd left behind, dreams that had been trampled by duty and rules and his father's will. *You cannot marry an Althemerian, Mantos,* he'd said. *I will not allow it.* Instead of teasing, Mantos let Fonbir delve into a trunk to fish out a dry shirt.

"Toketa, you must take better care of yourself," Fonbir said, his voice muffled as he dug through the clothing. "You've only just returned to me—to us. It wouldn't do for you to die of sickness now."

Mantos shrugged again and stood, his arms hanging loose at his sides.

When Fonbir straightened and closed the trunk, his lips curled. "Do you need me to remove your tunic for you?"

Mirth danced in his white eyes. Mantos' didn't match. On another day, he would have joined in. On another day, they would have ended up in bed. But this was not another day. *Those times will never return*, Mantos thought. He peeled off his clothing, dried his skin and armor on the proffered cloth, then put on another shirt and tunic that weren't his own.

At the lack of levity, Fonbir sobered. He took up Mantos' hands.

When Mantos spoke, his words were so quiet, the storm almost drowned them. "Do you know what Bomsoi would have me do?"

Nodding, Fonbir tightened his grip. "I do," he said. "She told me."

"And do you know what that means?" Mantos asked. "Do you know what it really means?"

Eyes widening at the question, Fonbir's grip slackened. His lips moved, but he made no sound.

"Exactly," Mantos said. "You don't know. And I don't know. And yet, she wants me to go through with this...*magic*...and become something I'm not. She wants me to destroy my brother. She wants me to help her return balance to the world, the very thing she couldn't do." He snorted and squeezed Fonbir's hands. "If she, a descendant of goddesses, couldn't do it, how does she expect me to achieve it?"

Far-off thunder rolled.

"I don't know," Fonbir whispered.

"She wants me to become the Hand of Nunako," Mantos went on, "so the goddess can inhabit me—so she can take over my life." Chest heaving, he squeezed harder. Fonbir's arms tensed. "But I'm not the right choice. I come from a long line of power-hungry warlords: my father, my grandfather, and now my brother." He shuddered. "How does Bomsoi know I won't become drunk on the power of the goddess? How does she know that I'll be different from my family when I don't know it myself?"

"You aren't like them," Fonbir whispered. He pulled one of his hands from Mantos' grasp and laid it on his cheek. "You've never lusted for power. I trust you'll do the right thing, and I trust Bomsoi. I've known her for many cycles." He waved a hand over his eyes. "And she gave me back my sight. If she says this must be done, it must be done."

Those words, coming from that mouth, felt like a slap. Mantos batted Fonbir's hand away and glared, his temper flaring. "So you'd have me sacrifice myself as well?" he snapped. "You would have me die for the third time?"

Recoiling as though he'd been singed, Fonbir cradled his hands against his chest. His tail stiffened. He narrowed his eyes. "Mantos, that's not what I meant."

"It's exactly what will happen if I go through with Bomsoi's plan," Mantos said. His voice rose with every word, ending in a shout. "I'll lose myself. I might as well be dead. *Again.* And my brother will die, and I'll have no choice and no control!"

Stung, Fonbir bit his bottom lip. He let his arms drop.

"Mantos, I don't have the answers. Bomsoi has said nothing about you dying." He shook his head and reached for Mantos' hand. "All know is that Oatutkubis, the Demon Who Rides the Sky, is upon us. But I have faith. Faith in Ethay and Apago. Faith in Bomsoi. And most important of all, faith in *you*." Fonbir's voice cracked. "You are good and loyal, Mantos. I know you'll do what is right."

Heart growing cold, Mantos stepped back. He snarled. "Then you are a fool."

The words tasted bitter. *Why must you push him away?* he asked. An answer returned as an echo: *Because you're not good enough for him.*

"Mantos, I—" Fonbir began.

"No. Don't." Mantos' words were soft, but they cut like knives, just as he intended. "I think you should leave."

Fonbir's hurt turned to fury. His white eyes narrowed. "As you wish."

Without another word, Fonbir swept from the room, his tail whipping behind him, though he didn't slam the door. He was still a prince, and knew what was expected of him. He closed the door in silence. For Mantos, his absence sounded in place of the slam.

I wish I was more like him, Mantos thought. *I wish I had his grace, his ability to act his rank no matter the circumstance. But I'll never be like that. I can't act my rank at all.*

Alone again, he turned his face to the open window. The rain still poured. The sun couldn't infiltrate the storm. The clouds were dark and churning. Mantos walked to the window as more of Bomsoi's words returned to him.

There is no Dark. There is no Light. There are only choices.

He wasn't sure about the first part, but Mantos was sure about the second. There were many choices in the world. Every day came with decision upon decision. What to eat, what to wear—and, most crucially of all, what to *do*.

As he stalked across the room to the clothing trunk, a new coat of ice enveloped Mantos' heart. He thrust open the lid and wrenched out as many shirts and tunics as he could. He pulled on layer upon layer of clothing that didn't belong to him.

Yes. There were many choices in the world. And Mantos had made his.

With nothing but the clothes on his back, the chain around his neck, the rings on his talons, and the coldness in his heart, he crossed to the open window. He stared down at the empty courtyard. He gritted his teeth. He clambered onto the sill.

Under the cover of the storm, he fled.

Thank you for reading The Moon Rogue , book 1 of Arc of the Sky trilogy.
If you enjoyed the book would you please leave a review?
Simply return to your favorite retailer to do so.

ABOUT THE AUTHOR

L.M.R. CLARKE IS A WRITER from Northern Ireland who writes Young Adult fiction, primarily in the Fantasy genre. She writes with inclusion in mind, especially LGBT+, and explores themes such as sectarianism, racism and other forms of discrimination in her books. She does not believe in shying away from difficult issues in YA. In fact, LMR thinks it's vitally important that young people are given access to difficult topics through fiction in order for them to see the consequences of actions as well as the ability for characters to conquer adversity.

CONNECT WITH THE AUTHOR

Find me on my publisher's website:
https://castrumpress.com/authors/lmr-clarke

BOOKS BY THE AUTHOR

NOVELS

ARC OF THE SKY (3 BOOK SERIES)
The Moon Rogue, book 1
The Sun Emperor, book 2
The World Breaker, book 3

Most books also available in ebook and paperback.
Visit www.castrumpress.com for more.